BOOKS BY JUDE DEVERAUX

The Velvet Promise

Highland Velvet

Velvet Song

Velvet Angel

Sweetbriar

Counterfeit Lady

Lost Lady

River Lady

Twin of Fire

Twin of Ice

The Temptress

The Raider

The Princess

The Awakening

The Maiden

The Taming

The Conquest

A Knight in Shining Armor

Holly

Wishes

The Mountain Laurel

The Duchess

Eternity

Sweet Liar

The Invitation

Remembrance

The Heiress

Legend

An Angel for Emily

The Blessing

High Tide

Temptation

The Summerhouse

The Mulberry Tree

Forever . . .

Wild Orchids

Forever and Always

Always

First Impressions

Carolina Isle

Someone to Love

Secrets

Return to Summerhouse

Lavender Morning

JUDE DEVERAUX

Days of Gold

A NOVEL

Pocket Star Books
New York London Toronto Sydney

Pocket Star Books
A Division of Simon & Schuster, Inc.
1230 Avenue of the Americas
New York, NY 10020

First Pocket Star Books paperback edition August 2010

POCKET STAR BOOKS and colophon are registered trademarks of Simon & Schuster, Inc.

For information about special discounts for bulk purchases, please contact Simon & Schuster Special Sales at 1-866-506-1949 or business@simonandschuster.com.

The Simon & Schuster Speakers Bureau can bring authors to your live event. For more information or to book an event contact the Simon & Schuster Speakers Bureau at 1-866-248-3049 or visit our website at www.simonspeakers.com.

Cover illustration by Alan Ayers

Manufactured in the United States of America

10 9 8 7 6 5 4 3 2 1

ISBN 978-1-4391-0796-6
ISBN 978-1-4391-4979-9 (ebook)

Part One

1

"HAVE YOU SEEN her yet?"

"Nay, I have not," Angus McTern said for what seemed like the hundredth time. He had just come in from the hills, and he was wet, tired, hungry, and cold, but all anyone could talk about was Neville Lawler's fancy English niece, come to the old castle to look down her nose at the poor Scots.

"You should see her," young Tam said as he tried to keep pace with his cousin's long stride. Angus was usually glad to see Tam, but not if all he could talk about was Lawler's niece. "She has hair like gold," the boy said, his voice cracking. He was just coming into manhood, and what the girls said, did, and looked like was everything to him. "She has eyes as blue as a loch, and her clothes! Never did I see such clothes as she has. They're spun by the angels and trimmed by honeybees. She—"

"But then you've never been anywhere to see much to compare her to, now have you, lad?" Angus said—and everyone stopped to look at him in astonishment. They were in the big stone courtyard that had once belonged to the McTern family. Angus and Tam's grandfather had been the laird, but he was a lazy old reprobate who'd gambled and lost everything to a young Englishman, Neville Lawler. Angus had been just nine at the time, living with his widowed mother, and it had been Angus who the clan turned to. In the sixteen years since, he'd done his best to look out for the few remaining McTerns.

But sometimes, like today, it seemed like a losing battle to try to make people remember that they were part of the once-great McTerns. For the last weeks, all they'd wanted to talk about was the Englishwoman. Her hair, her clothes, each word she spoke, the way she said it.

" 'Fraid she won't like you?" old Duncan asked as he looked up at Angus from the scythe he was sharpening. " 'Fraid that great, hairy face of yours will scare her?"

The tension that had been caused by Angus snapping at his young cousin was broken and he gave the boy a rough shove on his shoulder to apologize. It wasn't Tam's fault that he'd never been anywhere or done anything. All he knew were the hills of Scotland, the sheep and the cattle, and the raids where he sometimes had to fight for his life.

"A fancy lady like her would be scared to death of a *real* Scotsman," Angus said, then raised his hands like claws and made a face at his young cousin.

Everyone in the courtyard relaxed and returned

to his or her work. What Angus thought was important to them.

He strode past the old stone keep that had once been his family home and went to the stables. Since Neville Lawler thought more of his horses than he did of humans, they were clean, well kept, and the building was warmer than the house.

Without asking, Angus's uncle, Malcolm McTern, handed Angus a round of rough, thick bread and a mug of ale. "Did we lose many, lad?" he asked as he went back to brushing down one of Lawler's hunting horses.

"Three," Angus said as he sat down on a stool that was against the wall. "I followed them but I couldn't catch them." Saving the sheep and the cattle from the raids took most of Angus's time. As he ate, he leaned back against the stone wall of the stables and for a moment closed his eyes. He hadn't slept in two days and all he wanted to do was wrap his plaid about him and sleep until the sun came up.

When one of the horses kicked the wall, Angus had his dirk out before his eyes were open.

Malcolm gave a snort of laughter. "Never safe, are you, boy?"

"Nor are any of us," he said good-humoredly. As he ate, the warmth crept into him. He was the only one of the clan who still wore the plaid in the old way. It was two long pieces of handwoven cloth, draped about his body, held at the waist with a thick leather belt, and leaving the lower half of his legs bare. His white shirt had big sleeves and was gathered at the neck. The kilt had been outlawed by the English many years before, and those who wore it risked prison time and whippings, but old Lawler turned a blind eye to what Angus did. For all that the man was lazy, and greedy beyond all reckoning, he understood about a man's pride.

"Let him wear the blasted thing," he said when an English visitor said Angus should be beaten.

"Wearing their own clothes makes them think they have their own country. He'll cause you trouble if you don't take him down a notch or two now."

"If I take away his pride, I take away his desire to look after the place," Neville said and smiled at Angus behind the man's back.

If Neville Lawler had nothing else good about him, he knew a lot about self-preservation. He knew that Angus McTern took care of the castle, the grounds, and the people, so Lawler wasn't about to anger the tall young man.

"Go home, lad," Malcolm said. "I'll look after the horses. Get some sleep."

"At my house?" Angus said. "And how can I do that? I lie down there and I have brats crawling all over me. That oldest one ought to have a hand put to his backside. Last time I slept there, he wove sticks into my beard. He said the chickens could use it for a nest."

Malcolm had to cough to cover his laugh. Angus lived with his sister and her husband and their ever-growing family. By rights, it was Angus's house, but he couldn't throw his sister out.

"Go, then," Malcolm said, "and have a rest in my bed. I won't need it for hours yet."

Angus gave him such a look of thanks that Malcolm almost blushed. Since Angus's father had died when he was just a boy, Malcolm had been the closest he'd had to one. Malcolm was the youngest son of the laird who'd lost the lands to the English Lawler, and Angus and Tam were the sons of Malcolm's older brothers. He'd never married, saying he had too much to do in taking care of his deceased brothers' boys to make any of his own.

"Shall I wake you when she goes out for her ride?" Malcolm asked.

"Who?"

"Come now, boy," Malcolm said, "surely you've heard of the niece."

"I've heard about nothing else but her! Last night I almost expected the raiders to turn back and return the cattle they'd stolen just to have word of her. I thought they'd ask me if she wore a blue dress or a pink one."

"You laugh, but that's because you haven't seen her."

Angus gave a jaw-cracking yawn. "Nor do I want to. I'm sure she's a bonnie lass, but what does that matter to me? She'll soon go back south and live in a splendid house in London. I don't know why she wanted to come up here to this great pile of stone anyway. To have a laugh at us?"

"Maybe," Malcolm said, "but she's done nothing but smile at people so far."

"Oh, that's good of her," Angus said as he stood, stretching. "And do her smiles get everyone to do her bidding? 'Yes, my lady. No, my lady,' they all say to her. 'Let me carry your fan for you, my lady.' 'Please let me empty your chamber pot.' "

Malcolm smiled at Angus's impersonation, but he didn't give up. "I feel sorry for the girl. There's a sadness in her eyes that you can't help but see. Morag said the girl has no family left except for old Neville."

"But she has money, does she not? That'll buy her a rich husband who'll give her a passel of brats and she'll be happy enough. No! I want to hear no more of her. I'll see her soon enough—or mayhap I'll be lucky and she'll go back to London before I have to see her angelic . . ." He waved his hand in dismissal. "Too much of the angels for me. I'm going to sleep. If I'm not awake by this time tomorrow, check if I'm dead or not."

Malcolm snorted. Angus would no doubt be up in a few hours and wanting something to do. He wasn't one for lying about.

As Angus went into the room at the end of the stables, he glanced at the riding horse the niece had brought with her from London. It was gray, with great dapples of a darker gray, and now it raised its legs impatiently, wanting to get out and go. He'd been told that the niece took a long ride every day, always accompanied by an escort, a man who rode far behind her. Over and over, Angus had been told what a fine horsewoman the girl was.

Malcolm's bed with its rough sheets and big tartan was a welcome sight, and as Angus lay down, he thought that he'd like to see the girl ride as he'd had to these last two nights. The poor pony was tearing across rocks and shrubs as Angus pursued the raiders stealing the cattle. But the thieves had had too much of a head start, and their mounts were fresh so he'd lost them in the hills.

As he fell asleep, he smiled at the thought of the delicate little English girl holding on for her life.

When he awoke, every nerve in his body was alert. An unusual sound had awakened him, and he didn't know what it was. He'd spent half his life in the stables and he knew every sound, but this one didn't belong. The rustlers wouldn't have dared come this close to the house, would they?

Angus lay still, not moving, not even opening his eyes in case there was someone standing at the open door, and listened hard. It was coming from the stall next to Malcolm's room, the stall the niece's beautiful mare was in. Was this animal that he didn't know doing something? No. He heard breathing, then there was a little intake of breath that made Angus shake his head. Shamus. Whatever the sound was, Shamus was the one making it.

Tiredly, cursing in his mind, Angus hauled himself off the bed, went to the rack of pegs on the wall, and moved one of them aside. Only he and Malcolm knew about the ingenious device his uncle had made so he could look at most of the stables without being seen. "Lazy brats!" he'd said to Angus. "When they think I canna see them, I catch them doing all manner of things that are not work."

Angus looked through the hole and saw Shamus—huge, stupid, mean-spirited Shamus—doing something to the cinch of the girl's saddle, and Angus wanted to groan. Had the man no sense at all? Was he playing one of his cruel tricks on Lawler's niece? While it was true that Shamus was a bully and loved to torment anything smaller than he was, he usually had the sense not to go after anyone who had a protector—as he'd learned as soon as Angus grew to be taller and nearly as strong as the older Shamus was.

But here he was, loosening the girl's saddle. What was his intent? If Angus knew Shamus, it was to embarrass and humiliate her, to make people laugh at her. "That's all we need," Angus said as he closed the peg and leaned his head against the wall. For the most part, Lawler was an easygoing master. But he was unpredictable. A man could accidentally set fire to a wagon and Lawler would laugh it off, but another day a man could break a rein and Lawler would have him flogged. Sometimes it seemed to Angus that he'd spent half his life arguing with Lawler to save the skin of somebody. As for Angus himself, Lawler had never dared touch him.

Angus, still tired—he figured he'd been asleep only a few minutes—looked at the bed and wanted to go back to it. Why was it any of his business if the girl was laughed at? It might be good for everyone if she were seen as human. On the other side of the wall, he heard Shamus lead the mare out of the stall, and he heard that awful little self-satisfied grunt the man made when he anticipated what was going to happen because of his prank.

"None of my business," Angus said to himself and went back to the bed. He closed his eyes and let his body relax. Like all Scotsmen, he prided himself on being able to fall asleep anywhere and at any time. Whereas others had to carry blankets with them, Angus just loosened his belt, rolled himself in his plaid, and went to sleep—which was yet another reason the English had outlawed the garment. "They don't even have to pack their bags when they run," the English said. "They wear their beds on their backs."

"Aye," Angus whispered, and it was a good feeling to cover himself with his own plaid and drift off.

Ten minutes later, he was still awake. If Shamus humiliated, or worse, hurt Lawler's niece, there would be hell to pay—for everyone. Shamus should know this, but he'd never been known for his brains, just his muscle.

Groaning, Angus got off the bed. Would he never have peace? Would there never come a time when he didn't have to take care of every problem on what used to be McTern land? By ancestry, Angus was the laird, but since the land no longer belonged to his family, of what use was the title?

Feeling as though he ached in every joint, he made his way out toward the courtyard.

"You've come to see her, have you?" asked one man after another.

"No, I have not come to see her," Angus said half a dozen times. "I want to see her horse."

"And so do I," a man called.

Angus rolled his eyes and wished he had more hair and more beard to cover his face. If they kept pushing him, he was going to let them know what he thought of their obsession with this English girl. They'd not been treated to Angus's temper for months now, so maybe it was time.

Young Tam was holding the girl's horse, looking as though it was the proudest moment of his life. Holding a girl's horse! Angus thought. Where was all the training he'd given the boy? Where were all the stories he'd heard about the pride of the Scotsmen? All of it forgotten in a moment at the sight of a pretty girl.

"*I* will help her on her horse," Tam said when he saw Angus approach, looking as though he was ready to fight for the right.

"And you may help her," Angus said patiently. "I just want to check the girth. I saw—"

He broke off because an unnatural hush had come over the place. Usually, the area around the decaying old castle was filled with noises of people and animals at work. Steel beat on iron, wood was chiseled and cut, leather buckets hit the stones. There was always a cacophony of sound. Even at night there were so many people in the courtyard that the noise was sometimes too much for Angus. He liked the open places and the quiet of the hills.

He looked up and she was there, standing just a few feet from him, and he drew in his breath. She was more than pretty. She was beautiful in a way that he could never have dreamed a person could be. She was small, the top of her head reaching only to his shoulder, and she was wearing a black dress with a tight bodice, with a little red jacket over it. Her face was oval, with deep blue eyes, a small, straight nose, and a perfect little mouth with lips the color of rasp-berries in the summer. Her skin was as fine as the best cow's cream, and her hair was thick and dark blonde. It was pulled high on her head, but with long ringlets hanging over her shoulders, entwined with red rib-bons tied in a bow at the end. Tipped over the front of her head was a little black hat with a tiny veil that almost reached her eyes.

Angus stared at her, unable to speak. He'd never seen or imagined anything like her.

"Excuse me," she said, and her voice was soft and pretty. "I need to get to my horse."

All he could do was nod and step back to let her pass. As she came closer to him, he could smell her. Was she wearing a scent or was it her own fragrance? For a second he closed his eyes and inhaled. They were right to mention angels and her in the same breath.

Using his shoulder to push Angus aside, Tam clasped his hands and let the girl put her tiny foot in them as she vaulted onto the horse. The minute she was in the saddle, the horse began to lift its front hooves off the ground, but the girl seemed to be used to that and easily got it under control.

"Quiet, Marmy," she said to the mare. "Calm down. We're going. Don't rush me." As she lifted the reins, Tam stepped away, but Angus just stared up at her. "If you don't get out of the way, you're going to get hurt," she said to him, and there was amusement in her voice.

But Angus still stood there, gaping, unable to move.

In the next second, the girth on the horse slipped and with it the saddle. It slid around the horse, sending the girl to the left, toward Angus. She gave a little cry and tried to hold on, but with the saddle falling to one side, there was nothing to hold on to.

Emergencies were something that Angus was used to and was good at. The girl's sound of panic brought him out of his stupor and he reacted instantly. He grabbed the reins and pulled them tight to get the horse under control. Still holding the reins, he tried to catch the girl, but she slid to the other side and fell onto the stones.

By the time she landed, Tam had run forward to help with the prancing horse, moving it forward so that Angus and the girl were no longer separated. He reached down to help her up.

"Don't you touch me!" she said as she got up by herself and dusted at her clothes. She glared at him.

"*You* did this! I don't know who you are, but I know you did it."

Angus wanted to defend himself, but his pride wouldn't let him. What could he say, that he'd seen a clansman sabotaging her saddle and that he, Angus, had tried to save her? Or would he say he should have checked the girth before she mounted but that he'd been so blinded by her beauty he'd completely forgotten about the saddle? He'd rather be flogged than say such things.

"I am the McTern of McTern," he said at last, with his shoulders back and looking down at her.

"Oh, I see," she said, her face pinkened prettily with anger. "My uncle stole your property so now you take it out on me." She looked him up and down, sneering at his wild-looking hair and his full beard, then her eyes traveled down to his kilt. "Is your protest of my uncle why you wear a dress? Tell me if you want to borrow one of mine. They're much cleaner than yours." With that, she turned and went back into the old castle.

For a moment there was no sound in the courtyard. It was as though even the birds had stopped singing, then, in one huge, loud shout, everyone started laughing. Men, women, children, even a couple of goats tied along the wall started a high-pitched laugh.

Angus stood in the middle of it all, and what little of his face could be seen was dark red with embarrassment. Turning, he went back to the stables, and all along the way, he heard the comments that renewed

their howls of laughter. "He didn't want to see her."
"No one could tell him anything." "Did you see the
way he stared at her? You could have cut off his foot
and he wouldn't have felt it." Angus even heard the
women laughing at him. "He's not so uppity now. He
wouldn't dance with me, but she won't dance with
him. Oh, he deserves this, he does."

It was as though in a single minute he'd gone
from being the lord of his kingdom to the jester.

Passing by the stables, he went out through the
gate in the tall wall that surrounded the castle and
headed toward his own cottage. He wanted to explain
himself to someone, to tell his side of what had happened. It was Shamus who had loosened the girth on
her horse and Angus had been about to tighten it, but
the girl had startled him so that he hadn't done it. Yes,
that was a good word. She'd startled him. She'd shown
up wearing her silly little hat and her bright jacket
with the big buttons and he'd been so startled by the
sight of such ridiculousness that he'd been speechless.
And the ribbons in her hair! Had anyone ever seen
anything so foolish? Her clothes were so absurd that
she'd not last ten minutes in the hills. Yes, that's what
he'd say he'd been thinking. He was looking so hard at
the uselessness of her garb that he'd been speechless.

By the time he reached his cottage he was feeling
a bit better. Now he had a story to counteract what
everyone seemed to think had actually happened.

But when he got within a few feet of the door,
his sister came out and she was grinning. She had a

dirty-faced child holding on to her skirt, another one on her hip, and a third one in her belly, and she was smiling broadly.

Behind her, her husband stuck his head out the door. He was still red-faced from how fast he must have run to beat Angus back to the cottage. "Did you do it?" he asked. "Did you loosen her stirrup so she'd fall?"

That was more than Angus could bear. "Never would I hurt a woman," he said, his voice showing his shock. "How could you think such of me?"

His sister said nothing, but she was laughing.

Angus could only stare at the two of them. What had he ever done to make them think he was capable of something this low? He wasn't about to honor his brother-in-law's accusation with an answer. Turning, he started walking away.

He only slowed when he heard his sister call out to him, "Have mercy on me, Angus. My belly slows me down."

He halted and looked back at her. "I have nothing to say to you."

When she caught up with him, she put her hand on his shoulder. "Either we sit and rest or you're going to be delivering this baby by yourself here and now."

That made him sit on a rock, and Kenna sat by him, working to get her breath while stroking her big belly to calm it. "He dinna mean anything bad," she said.

"Your husband or Shamus?"

"So it was Shamus who loosened the girth. I figured so."

"You're the only one. The rest of them think I did it."

"Nay, they do not," she said.

"Your husband—"

"Is sick with jealousy over you," Kenna said. "You know that."

"What does he have to be jealous of me about? He has a home, a family, the best wife there is."

"The home doesn't belong to him and all he seems good at is producing babies. You run everything."

"Yet *I* am the one being laughed at."

"Oh, Angus," she said, leaning against him, "look at you. You've been a man since you were a boy and our father was killed. By twelve you'd taken on everything that our grandfather had gambled away. People have always looked up to you. There isn't a girl within a hundred miles who wouldn't have you, beg for you."

"I doubt that," Angus said, but his voice softened.

"Don't be so small spirited that you begrudge the people a chance to laugh at you. Why canna you laugh with them?"

"They think—"

"That *you* made the girl fall off her horse? Do you truly believe anyone thinks that of you?"

"Your husband . . ." Angus trailed off because he well knew that his brother-in-law didn't really believe he'd loosen the cinch on anyone's horse. If Angus wanted to hurt someone, he'd do it face-to-face.

"Gavin and everyone else either knows or can guess who did that to the poor girl. And as for what she said to you . . ." Kenna smiled. "If she'd said it to someone else, you would have fallen over with laughter. I wish you'd told her that you have a sister who'd like to borrow her clothes."

"Would you like to have a silk dress?" he asked softly. His sister was five years older than he was and the person he loved the most. If the truth were told, there was more than a little jealousy coming from him toward her husband. Since Kenna had married, Angus felt as though he'd been alone.

"Would I like a silk dress? Trade you a bairn for one."

Angus laughed. "If all of them you produce are as bad as your eldest, you'd have to trade six of them for a length of silk."

"He's just like you were at that age."

"I never was!"

"Worse," she said, laughing. "And he's the spitting image of you. Or I think he is, but it's been too long since I've seen your face." Reaching up, she touched his big beard. "Why don't you let me cut that?"

He pulled her hand away and kissed the palm. "It keeps me warm, and that's what I need."

"If you married, you—"

"I beg you not to start on me again," he said with so much agony in his voice that she relented.

"All right," she said as she got up, with Angus pushing on her back to help her. "I'll leave you be if you promise not to take a girl's laughter in anger. She bested you with the only weapon a woman has, her tongue."

"There are other uses for a woman's tongue," Angus said, his eyes twinkling.

Kenna stuck out her big belly. "Do you think I do not know all about the uses of a woman's tongue—and a man's?"

Angus put his hands over his ears. "Do not tell me such! You're my sister."

"All right," she said, smiling. "Keep your belief that your sister is still a virgin, but please do not let anger rule you over this girl."

"I will not," he said. "Now, go back to your husband."

"And what will you do?"

"I'm going to crawl under a rock and sleep for a day or two."

"Good, mayhap the heather will sweeten your temper so that when a girl makes a remark to you, you can reply in kind."

"In kind," he said. "I will remember that. Now go before I have to play midwife to you."

2

Angus managed to avoid seeing the niece for an entire week. He followed the wisdom of his sister and pretended to laugh at himself with all the other people, but when he turned away his smile didn't remain.

At first he'd tried to defend himself, but that only made people laugh harder. It was as though they'd been waiting all their lives to find humor in him and now they were making up for lost time.

However, Angus was glad that no one—except his own brother-in-law, that is—so much as hinted that Angus had been the one to loosen the girth and make the girl fall. No one said so, but they knew who had done it.

Angus didn't catch Shamus alone until three days after the incident. By then Angus had had to answer the same questions a thousand times. "Yes, yes," he said, each time trying hard to smile, "I was quite stunned by the beauty of the girl." "No, I'd never seen anything like her before." "Yes, I'm sure the angels smiled when she was born." "Oh, yes, what she said was quite clever. Never met a girl as clever as she is."

Each time he walked across the courtyard, it was always the same. No one wanted to talk to him about anything but the way he'd stared at the girl—except for his young cousin Tam, who wouldn't speak to Angus at all. Twice Angus tried to get Tam to go hunting with him, but the boy wouldn't. "She depends on me to hold her horse, so now I ride a pony and follow her. I'm one of the few men she trusts. She told me that, and she called me a man." As he said it, he gave Angus a look that told him they were no longer friends.

By the time Angus was able to catch Shamus, he wanted to smash his big face. Angus grabbed him by the collar while he was in one of the horse stalls, slammed him against the wall, and raised his fist. But Shamus wasn't afraid of pain; it was something he'd lived with all his life. When they were children everyone knew to stay hidden when Shamus appeared with a black eye. His father had again beaten the boy. Now, his father was dead and there was no longer any reason for Shamus to do what had been done to him, but old habits don't die easily.

"Go ahead," Shamus said. He wasn't as tall as Angus, but he was older, and bigger. When an oxcart got stuck in the mud, it was Shamus's strength that helped pull it out.

Angus lowered his fist. "Are you mad? To do that to Lawler's niece? She must not have told or her uncle would have had someone lashed. How long has it been since you had the skin on your back torn off?"

Shamus shrugged. "Not too long. A year or two. But I knew he wouldn't do anything. He hates her."

"Who hates her?" Angus asked.

"Lawler hates his niece."

For a moment Angus didn't know what to say. How could a man hate his own niece? For all that he complained about his sister's children, he would die for them, imps that they were. "You're lying."

"If you think so, then you should listen more."

"Should I be like you and sit in the shadows and spy on people?"

"I learn things, like the fact that Lawler can't abide her."

"Then he should send her back to London so she can be with her own kind." Angus spoke of the girl as though she were an alien species.

"Angus!" He heard Malcolm's voice, and when he turned in that direction, Shamus slithered away. For someone as big as he was, he could certainly move quickly when he needed to.

After that, Angus quit letting everyone's constant retelling of that day when he'd been humiliated by a bit of a girl bother him, and he started listening. When all of them lived as they did, under the rule and out of the pocket of one man, it was imperative to know what that man was up to.

They all knew the story—or at least part of it. When Lawler was no more than Angus's age, on one cut of a deck of cards, he'd won from the McTern laird the castle and the acres surrounding it. What no one knew was that since Lawler was the third son of a man with little property, he was not to inherit anything. His father had told him that if he'd go into the clergy, he'd find him a church to preach at. But there was nothing in the world that Lawler wanted to do less than to spread the Gospel.

When Lawler proposed to the drunken old Scotsman that they cut the cards for his castle and lands, Lawler had lied and said he owned an estate in York. Had he lost the cut, Lawler would have had no way to pay the debt. But he hadn't lost.

The next day, Lawler rode north to find the castle he'd won, and although it was a poor estate, it suited him. All he wanted to do was hunt and fish and play cards, so the old keep and grounds were enough for him. He soon found that the McTerns still thought of the place as theirs, so they did the work and the small profits went to Lawler. Now and then one of the Scots would do something he found intolerable and he'd have the man tied to a post and whipped, but he'd never hanged anyone.

And as the years passed and Angus, the young man who would have inherited the property, grew, Lawler left the running of the estate to him, as he seemed to love responsibility and work as much as Lawler hated it.

For days, Angus listened more and stopped letting his anger close his ears to what was going on around him. If Lawler didn't like the girl, why not? No one seemed to know. Morag, who worked inside the castle, said she'd often heard Lawler shouting at the girl, but it was always done behind closed doors, inside the stone walls, and even as hard as she listened, she couldn't make out what they were saying.

"Poor thing, how could he shout at an angel like that?" Morag said, making Angus roll his eyes.

No one missed the fact that every day when the niece went riding, Angus was nowhere to be found. Her mare seemed to know when she was going to show up because it started prancing about in its stall. The moment the mare lifted a forefoot, Angus seemed to dissolve into smoke. He wrapped his plaid about himself and went into the hills to stay away from her.

Of course this caused more laughter, but Angus didn't trust himself to look at her and not lose control. He figured he'd either stand there in a stupor, or he'd— He couldn't think what he'd do if she again made people laugh at him.

On the eighth day after Angus saw her, Malcolm came into the stables very upset. "You have to go after her."

"Who?" Angus asked. He'd been in the hills all night and had just awakened a few minutes ago.

"Her. Lawler's niece. You have to go after her."

"I'd rather face the entire Campbell clan alone than follow her. Besides, she can take care of herself."

"No," Malcolm said, "she's gone off with Shamus."

Angus paused for a moment with a harness in his hands, but then he hung it on a hook in the wall and kept walking. "Why would she do a thing like that? Does she like him?"

"No, you great daft thing. She went riding with him as her guide, her protector. Tam is home sick, puking up his guts, so she looked about the yard and said she'd take Shamus with her. What could anyone do? Tell her that Shamus wasn't to be trusted? He'd beat anyone who said that."

"She's Lawler's niece. Shamus would be afraid to hurt her."

"If that's so, then why did he loosen the cinch and make her fall? She could have broken her neck."

Angus frowned. "She'll be all right. He never hurts anyone more than they can stand."

"You mean he never *kills* anyone. Do you know what he might do to a woman if he got her alone? Angus, he is three times the size of her."

"Tell someone else to go," Angus said. "Duncan or . . . I know, tell my brother-in-law, Gavin, to go. It'll give him something to do besides lay with my sister."

"She'll be angry if she sees anyone else there, and if Shamus sees anyone, he'll clobber him."

"So you want *me* to risk a club on my head, all for a girl who believes the worst of me?"

"Yes," Malcolm said simply. "You can take a pony and disappear in the hills. You can watch and never be seen. No one else can do that. And if you see Shamus doing something he shouldn't, then you can stop him."

"And how do I do that? Ask him to stop? Perhaps I should say please."

Malcolm was a foot shorter than Angus and twice his age, but he looked at him with narrowed eyes. "I have boxed your ears and I can do it again."

The statement was so absurd that it made Angus smile. "All right, but I'll stay far away from her. I don't think Shamus will harm her. And you should send someone to tell Tam to stop drinking whatever Shamus hands him."

"I did that this morning," Malcolm said, his face serious.

Angus lost his smile. He'd meant his words as a jest when he'd hinted that Shamus had poisoned young Tam, but maybe it was true. "I'll take Tarka," Angus said, referring to his favorite pony, one that could cover the rocky terrain easily, and he'd stay off the trail that the girl would most likely take with her elegant city horse.

It wasn't long before Angus found them. She was riding in front, her back straight, looking ahead to the easy, flat trail, seeming not to have a care in the world. Well behind her, Shamus rode one of Lawler's big hunters, looking bored and half asleep. He didn't seem in the least interested in the young woman riding ahead of him.

Angus thought of turning and going back. If she saw him, he didn't like to think what she'd believe.

That he was following her? He stayed well hidden in the rocks, trailing the two of them as though they were cattle thieves, but he saw nothing suspicious. Maybe someone had told Shamus that it was in his own best interest not to do anything the girl could report to her uncle. Maybe they'd all misjudged him when they thought he'd given Tam something to make him ill. Maybe—

Angus's head came up when he saw the girl halt. Turning her horse, she motioned for Shamus to come forward and help her down. The big English sidesaddle she rode was difficult for a woman to climb onto, and it was a long drop to get off of by herself.

Angus thought that if Shamus was going to do something, now was the time. Angus got off his pony and moved down into the rocks to watch them. When he realized that if Shamus did try to do something to the girl, he was too far away to stop him, Angus stealthily made his way through the grass to get closer. He moved on his stomach, the stiff branches and the rocks scraping his bare legs, but it was the way he sometimes stalked a deer, so he knew how to move silently.

"Thank you," he heard her say when Shamus helped her down. "I want to walk."

Acting like a good servant, Shamus nodded, and the girl began to walk, leaving him to hold the reins to her horse. He wasn't sure why, but Angus thought her actions were suspicious. It was almost as though she were sneaking off somewhere and didn't want to be seen. Was she meeting someone? Was that why she was leaving her chaperone with the two horses and going off by herself?

Angus felt sure he'd found out the cause behind her fights with her uncle. Lawler probably knew she was secretly meeting someone, and he was angry about it.

Angus slithered through the bushes on his belly, being as quiet as a snake, not moving too quickly, so he didn't scare up a flock of birds and give her warning that she was being watched. He wanted to see who she was meeting. It couldn't be someone from the McTern clan; he'd know if it was.

But then, since she'd arrived, no one had treated him in quite the same way as they had. Since she had caused them all to laugh at him, no one had come to him to tell of something they were worried about, or to report something they suspected.

He moved slowly, quietly, then as he went over a little ridge, he could just see the top of her ridiculous little hat. She was bending now and he felt sure he saw someone else. There was a flash of something white—a man's shirt? Then he saw her arms move. She was in a love tryst! No wonder Lawler was angry at her.

In the next moment, Angus stood up. He was just a few feet from her and he planned to use surprise to expose her illicit behavior.

His movements were quick. He rose, towering above her, and said, "You are found out!"

What he saw was her sitting on a patch of heather,

a little white sketch pad in her hands, and she was drawing some quail—all of which flew away at the sight and sound of Angus.

"You!" she said, standing up to face him. "You great, ugly, woolly beast of a man, you're spying on me! Shamus!" she shouted. "Help me!"

Angus didn't think, he just turned and ran back to his pony. As he ran, his head filled with the sound of the laughter that was going to come. Never in his life would he live this down! He could live to be a hundred, no, a thousand years old, and this was what would be remembered about him. He'd be known as the man who was sneaking about in the bushes and spying on some English girl as she drew pictures of birds.

Angus jumped on the pony and headed back to the castle as fast as he could. Perhaps it would be better if he went away for a while, a year maybe. He had some money hidden in the stables. He'd get that and—

He was halfway back before he realized that she was on her horse and coming after him. Her big mare would beat his pony in a flat-out race, but he knew secret ways to get back to the keep before she did. As he snaked around on the paths that elk had made, now and then he could see her below him, and he couldn't help but marvel at how fast she was going. She wasn't taking the flat trail back but was going down a road that had been made long ago, and he wondered how she'd found it. Had Tam shown her that way?

His eyes widened in admiration when she and her mare sailed over an old fence, then a minute later leaped across a ditch. Whatever else that was said about her, she could ride!

Angus was so enthralled in watching her that he almost forgot about his own necessity for speed. However, he directed the pony over a stream, across a few gulleys, and got to the castle well before she did. When he was back in a place he'd known all his life, he thought better of running away. He'd fought battles with cattle thieves and had spent his life hunting and living with danger. Why should a girl scare him so that he ran away from his own home?

When she got back, he'd tell her the truth, that Malcolm had asked him to look after her, and that he'd thought she was in trouble when her head disappeared in the bushes. How was he to know that she was sneaking about to draw a bunch of birds? No one had told him that's what she did when she went out. Or had they? Now that he thought about it, he seemed to recall someone mentioning that. But how was he supposed to remember everything he'd been told about her?

She came into the courtyard just minutes after he did and when he saw the state of her mare, he decided to give her a good scolding for working it into such a lather.

When she stopped close to him, he held his ground. She threw her leg over the tall pommel and slid to the ground in front of him. "You're disgusting," she said. "You are—"

She broke off when she saw that Angus was smiling at her. This time he wasn't going to let her beauty make him lose his sense of self. "You are a despicable man!" she shouted. When he kept smiling, she drew back her hard-soled riding boot and kicked his shin. Angus bent with pain and she lifted her riding crop to strike his shoulder, but he moved so the little whip hit him across the neck. He grabbed his neck, and when his hand came away bloody, he lost all conscious thought. Behind her was a big stone horse trough. Without a thought, he picked her up and dropped her into it.

She went under, her little hat slid down over her face, and she came up sputtering.

Angus put his hands on his hips and looked about him. He knew that everyone was there, their eyes glued to what was going on, and he expected them to laugh at the ridiculous sight of her, but no one did. Instead, there wasn't a sound, and no one would look at him. Angus turned his head one way then the other, but no one would meet his eyes, not even Malcolm, who had come out of the stables when he heard the silence.

"Oh, you poor dear," Morag said as she went to the girl and helped her out of the dirty horse trough. "Come inside and we'll get you changed and dry."

Dripping, and already shivering, the girl walked past Angus without looking at him. With her silken clothes wet and her hair down about her shoulders, she looked like a young, frightened child, not the virago he'd come to think of her as.

She paused as she got a step past him. "I won't keep this one to myself. My uncle will hear of this."

Since it was so quiet in the courtyard, everyone heard her, and when Angus looked up this time all eyes were on him. What had he done? Depending on what mood Lawler was in, his punishment of Angus could be severe, anything from flogging to being banished, sent away forever.

Angus realized that his silly game of trying to beat the girl back to the keep, then throwing her into the trough, was going to change his life.

Malcolm came to stand beside him. "You should go, boy. Leave McTern land before she tells him."

"No, I canna do that," Angus said as he straightened his shoulders and walked toward the castle. He could hear the intake of breath all around him. He wasn't going to run. He was going to take whatever punishment was given to him. If the girl who'd been treated so were his . . . What? Sister? If a man had done this to his close kin, he would probably murder him.

Angus mounted the old, wooden stairs to reach the second floor of the castle. In time of war, the wooden steps would be cut away, making it difficult for an enemy to enter. But there hadn't been a full-scale war in the area for a while, so the steps had grown old and rickety.

The castle was really just a big square tower with a smaller square stuck onto the side to hold the spiral stone staircase. There were other staircases inside, but this was the one that went from bottom to top, and on the second floor it opened into the Great Hall, where Lawler spent most of his time with his cronies, men who came and went and did little but eat and drink whatever Lawler—and the Scots—could provide.

When Angus appeared in the Great Hall, the girl, with Morag by her side, was standing in front of her uncle. He was at a square table, two men with him, and they were playing cards. Lawler was an ugly man, with a big red nose, and broken veins all over his face. He had to have a new wardrobe every year because his belly expanded while his legs shrank. Now in his late fifties, his legs were as thin as saplings, while his belly was so big he looked ready to deliver a child.

"What is it?" Lawler asked after a glance up from his cards. Next to him sat William Ballister, an Englishman who was older and uglier than Lawler. They were the best of friends, meaning that Ballister stayed until Lawler got tired of him and told him to leave—which happened about twice a year. On the other side was Phillip Alvoy, who was younger and better-looking, but everyone knew that he had a mean temper. No one ever crossed him or they'd have trouble with Lawler.

"He . . . he . . ." the girl began, but she was shaking so hard from the cold that she had trouble speaking.

"It is my fault," Angus said, stepping forward so

he was between her and her uncle. "I was spying on her and she had every right to do what she did. I alone am at fault."

Lawler put his cards down, as did his two friends, and they looked with interest at Angus and the girl behind him. "Tell me what happened."

"This great beast has been following me all week," the girl said in anger. "Just days ago he loosened my saddle and made me fall onto the stones. I said nothing about it because I didn't want to cause problems. But what he did today was intolerable. He followed me when I rode out, hid in the grass, and jumped out at me while I was sketching. If Shamus hadn't been there to protect me, I don't know what he would have done to me. Then he ran. Like the common sneak he is, he ran from me and I had to hurry back here. And when I got here, I justifiably applied my riding crop to him."

"I see," Neville Lawler said, looking at Angus. "Is that how your neck came to be bleeding?"

"Aye, it is," Angus said stiffly.

"How did you get wet?" Alvoy asked the niece as he sipped a glass of port. The old stone keep might be falling down, but the liquor was always splendid.

"He . . ." She trailed off, shivering too hard to speak.

"I dropped her into a horse trough," Angus said. He was standing with his shoulders back, his legs apart, his hands behind his back. He was ready to take any punishment that was meted out to him.

"You threw her into a horse trough?" Ballister asked, his voice showing his astonishment.

"Aye, I did," Angus said, keeping his eyes level and on Lawler.

In the next second the three men looked at one another and burst into laughter. "Best place for her," Lawler said, nearly choking on his laughter.

"Oh, but I wish I'd seen it," Alvoy said. "Perhaps you could do it again so we could watch."

"Like a play or a pantomime," Ballister said. "A repeat performance."

"What a good idea," Lawler said.

"You're going to do nothing to him?" his niece asked.

"Why should I punish him for doing what should have been done a long time ago?" her uncle asked. "I wish I'd thought of it."

With that, the girl turned and ran from the room, waving Morag away when she tried to follow.

After giving Angus a look that told him he should be ashamed of himself, Morag turned and stamped out of the room. Behind him, the three men were laughing and toasting one another, and congratulating Angus on what he'd done.

Angus could stand no more and left the room, but he paused on the stairs. When she'd fled the room he'd seen tears in her eyes. He'd never before made a woman cry.

When he heard a noise, he glanced up the stairs and thought he saw the edge of her skirt. He knew the keep well enough that he was sure her room was on the fourth floor, but he'd seen her above that. Where was she going? The second he thought the question, he knew the answer. She was going to the roof. But why? She was already so cold she was shivering. A frightening thought came to him, that she was going to the roof to throw herself off. In the next moment he was taking the stairs two at a time.

When he got to the roof, there she was, standing near the edge, a low stone wall the only thing between her and the courtyard a long way below.

When she heard the door, she turned, saw him, and her shoulders slumped. "Did you come up here to gloat, to glory in what you've achieved?"

"No," he said. "I came here to see if you were all right."

"And what do you care? You've been as intolerable to me as my uncle. All the Scots have been so kind, except for you. You—" She waved her hand, as though she couldn't think of anything bad enough to say to him.

"I think you should go downstairs and get on some dry clothes." Slowly, he was moving toward her. If she made a sudden move to jump, he was going to be close enough to catch her.

She didn't move, didn't look at him. "You were probably right to throw me into a horse trough. I wish you'd thrown me off the top of this falling-down pile of rocks. In fact, I should do it myself."

"What could make you want to do something

like that?" Angus asked, truly aghast at what she was saying. "You'll not get into Heaven if you take your own life."

"Wherever I go, it won't be worse than here."

"What could be so bad, lass?" His voice was soft; he didn't want to scare her.

"You know Uncle Neville's friends, those two downstairs, Alvoy and Ballister?"

"Aye, I do."

"Tell me what you think of them."

He was standing just a few feet from her now so he felt he could relax. He could catch her if she tried to jump. As for her question, he wasn't about to answer it honestly. Maybe Shamus was right and Lawler didn't like his niece, but Angus knew he didn't feel that way about his two despicable friends and she might repeat what Angus said.

"Come on," she said. "You can tell me. After what we've been through today, you can be honest with me. Would you like either of those men as your friend? Would you trust either of them?"

"No," he said cautiously, "I can't say that I would, but I'm a Scot. I don't trust any Englishman." He'd hoped to distract her from this line of questioning, but she wasn't deterred.

"Do you think they're smart?"

"That depends on what you call smart. They're both cunning, that's for sure. They tell your uncle what he wants to hear so they get free room and board—and no work."

She nodded, as though she agreed with that. "What about kindness? Pleasant company?"

"I can't say that they are to me, but your uncle likes them well enough." He didn't know if it was the anger that seemed to be surging through her, but she was no longer shivering, even though her clothes were still sopping wet. "It's not for me to give advice, but if I were in your place I'd steer clear of both of those men. I don't think they're who a young girl should spend her time with."

"Now that will be a problem because my uncle says I'm to marry one of them."

Angus looked at her in shock, unable to say anything. Her beauty matched with either of those dreadful men who sponged off of her uncle was not something he wanted to contemplate.

She didn't turn to look at him, just kept staring at the courtyard below. "In four days I'll turn eighteen and my uncle's guardianship will end. He plans for me to marry one of those men at one minute after midnight, then my dowry will belong to my husband, who has made an agreement to give it back to my uncle."

Angus grimaced. It was a very bad situation, but there was nothing he could do about it. "Ah, lass, that is a hard one."

She turned to look up at him, her blue eyes pleading. "Help me escape. Please."

"I can't do that," Angus said as he took a step back from her. "This is my home. These are my people."

"I know that. It's why I've asked *you* for help. People have told me they depend on you. You're the McTern of McTern, aren't you?"

The way she said it made him want to defend himself. "My grandfather was the laird of this clan and some people still remember that. The title of laird may no longer have land, but I carry a responsibility to the McTerns."

"How very romantic," she said as she took a step toward him. "Does that mean that if I were some McTern girl and being forced to marry a man twice my age you'd step in and help?" She was being sarcastic, but when she saw his face she knew the truth. "You *would* help her, wouldn't you?"

"I would feel an obligation, yes, but that hasn't happened in my lifetime. A girl marries who she wants. It's the Scots way."

"It's the English way, too, except that I'm cursed with having a dowry and an uncle who needs money, plus, I have no friends or relatives to help me." She took a breath. "What if I pay you?"

"I couldn't go against your uncle. He owns this place now."

She took another step forward and he took one back. "What if my uncle decided to marry some pretty girl in your tribe?"

"Clan." He couldn't repress a smile.

"All right, your clan. What if my uncle decided he wanted to marry . . . your sister?"

"She's already married and has three bairns."

"Bairns. Babies. She has three children now, but if she didn't and Uncle Neville wanted to marry her, what would you do?"

He didn't say what he thought, which was that Lawler would never *marry* her. He might make her his mistress, but the man had never shown much interest in women. They'd all heard him say that he'd much rather have a good horse than any woman.

She was still staring up at him with those deep blue eyes and waiting for his reply.

"I would have to send her away," he said.

"You would do that for her?"

"I would have to, wouldn't I? Your uncle is a lot of things, but I don't think he'd make a good husband." He was teasing her now, but she wasn't smiling.

"But not me," she said. "So what I've heard is true, that you'd help another woman, but you won't help *me*. Why? Because I'm not a blood relative of yours? Or is it *me* you hate? And why is that? Because I stood up to you? I see the way the girls look at you. Do you refuse to help me because I don't swoon at the sight of you?"

As she spoke she was moving toward him and he was backing up—and he was working hard to keep his amusement from coming to the surface.

"You're laughing at me!" she said. "You enjoyed making me fall, enjoyed humiliating me in front of everyone, didn't you? You know what you are? You're a bully. You're a bully, and I hate you! I really and truly *hate* you!" With that, she once again used her hard-soled boot and kicked him in exactly the same spot where she'd kicked him earlier.

Angus couldn't help it. Maybe it was the relief that he wasn't going to have to hide forever in shame after being caught "spying" on her, or relief that he wasn't going to be punished for tossing her into the cold water. Or maybe it was just giddiness at being so close to this beautiful woman with her wet hair falling deliciously about her neck, but he started laughing. Days of pent-up anger and fear and embarrassment left him, and he leaned against the wall of the roof and started laughing.

"You're disgusting," she said with contempt as she went through the door that led back into the castle. Even when Angus heard the bolt thrown on the inside he kept laughing.

3

E DILEAN TALBOT LEANED against the cold stone wall of her bedroom, looked out the narrow, unglazed window, and stared at the courtyard below. All the people down there seemed so happy—and free. But then, they had families and friends and things to laugh about. She saw a man pick up a little boy and toss him high in the air, and she could hear the child's laughter four stories above.

Turning, she leaned against the wall, then in the next moment she slid down to sit on the old wooden floor. Just three more days, she thought. In just three days she was to be married to some repulsive man. Her uncle's "friends" had made a pact with him that they would make no effort to win her. There was to be no courting, no flowers, no letters, nothing said to her in private. On the day she was to turn eighteen, she'd be asked before the reverend which man she chose, and she was to say which one she would have.

Edilean knew that if she truly believed the marriage was going to happen she really would throw herself off the roof.

Her father, a retired military man, had known he was going to die when his only child was still young and he'd done his best to protect her future. That it hadn't been enough wasn't his fault. He'd spent long hours making what he thought was an ironclad will. Everything he owned was to be sold and converted to gold, and the gold was to be given to his daughter on her eighteenth birthday. He'd written that she was to marry a man *of her own choosing*. He knew that if she married, control of her estate would go to her husband, but he'd trusted his daughter enough to choose a man who wouldn't squander her inheritance. The flaw in his plan was that he'd underestimated his daughter's only living relative, her deceased mother's brother, who was to be her guardian until she was eighteen.

Her father had met the man once or twice, but he didn't really know him. Neville had assured the dying man that he would take care of Edilean after she got out of school and that he'd follow the will to the letter. He'd even signed a document before witnesses swearing to uphold the will. Edilean's father's will further said that in case his daughter died before she was eighteen, the gold would go to charity.

To Neville Lawler's mind, he was carrying out the will exactly as it had been written. On her eighteenth birthday, Edilean would be given a choice between two men, and she would marry one of them there and then.

Neither Edilean nor her father had imagined a

man of such greed and such a lack of morals as Neville Lawler existed.

Now, Edilean knew that she had only one hope, and that was to come from the man she loved: James Harcourt. She'd met James through a school friend of hers. After her father died and their house was sold, when the holidays came, Edilean had to stay with friends. She was well liked both for her humor and because her beauty attracted young men to the houses, so she never lacked for invitations.

But of all the men who made fools of themselves over her, only James Harcourt interested her. He was tall, broad shouldered, blond, and beautiful. His grandfather had made a lot of money in some trade—James was vague about the details—so James was a gentleman through circumstance if not breeding. She'd soon found that he was sensitive about his background, so she asked him few questions.

He was the second cousin of one of her school friends, not a girl she liked especially, but Edilean went to her house rather frequently just in the hope that James would visit.

At first he paid no attention to her. He came to parties and teas, but he sat in silence, playing with the lace at his wrist and rarely looking at the other people there.

This lack of attention was something new to Edilean. For since she was a child, she'd been told she was beautiful, so she was more used to men like that hairy-faced Scotsman who stared at her, dumbfounded, than she was to men who didn't so much as look at her. The truth was, James's inattention intrigued her. It was a relief when he didn't stare at her with great, liquid eyes. In fact, his lack of attention made her start doing things to get him to notice her.

She had a good voice and she could play the pianoforte well, so she played and sang the after-dinner songs. But James yawned and nearly fell asleep.

One day, she suggested that they all go out together and sketch, as she was good at drawing. Later, everyone said hers was by far the best, but James barely looked at it.

She ordered new dresses that she hoped would catch his eye, but even when she asked him if he liked the trim around the low-cut neckline, he only smiled politely.

But one night they were playing whist, and her friend was annoyed that she was losing at every hand. "I'm sure you'll win the next one," Edilean said as she claimed the winnings off the table.

"That's easy for you to say. You can afford to lose all you want."

As the next hand was dealt, James said, "I thought you were staying with my cousin because you have no home."

"That's true," Edilean said, thrilled that James was addressing her directly. "Before my father died, he sold everything and left me the proceeds."

"She means he had it all converted into gold, and Edilean gets it when she turns eighteen."

"Does she now?" James said, but he didn't look up.

After that, James was more attentive. Edilean wasn't stupid; she knew the dowry was what changed his mind, but she was also a realist. To live well, a person needed money, and she had noticed a few frayed edges on James's waistcoats. It looked like whatever money his grandfather had made was now gone.

Whatever the reason that got him to finally look at her, it was worth it. What followed were three weeks of heaven. James came to her friend's London house every day, and he sang and played the pianoforte with Edilean. Their duets became renowned among their friends. He posed for her so she could sketch him, and he heaped lavish praise on her drawings.

Perhaps the dowry had been what made James notice her, but it was their mutual interest in art and music that gradually made them begin to love each other.

The first time he kissed her, she thought she would fall down on the grass right there and let him have his way with her. "Not now," James whispered. "We must wait until you are mine and mine alone."

"Yes," she whispered. She was so in love with him that she would do anything he asked.

When she went back to school for the last half term, she wrote to him every day. He replied, not every day, but often, and his letters were amusing and interesting and full of his love for her. He wrote of how he longed to see her again, how every night before he slept he kissed the miniature portrait of her that she'd given him.

Edilean held James's letters to her breast, sometimes even slept with them, and counted the days until the end of the term when she and James could marry.

During the courtship, Edilean had never given so much as a thought to her uncle Neville. She knew that, legally, he was her guardian, and she'd met him once when she was a child, but since her father died, she'd not had a word from him. She knew little about him except that he lived in a castle in far-off Scotland. "He's a gentleman," her father said, "so all he does is hunt and eat."

To Edilean it sounded very romantic, and she thought that someday she and her husband, James, would visit him.

But then one night one of the teachers came to her room and woke her. "You have to go," she said.

"What do you mean?" Edilean asked, rubbing her eyes. She could see the moon through the window; it was still night.

"Your uncle has come for you and you're to leave with him. Hurry and dress. He says you're to come in what you have on and nothing more. We're to send your clothes to you."

"My uncle?" Edilean asked, her mind befuddled from lack of sleep. "But my uncle lives in Scotland."

"Yes, he does," the teacher said in exasperation. "And he's come from Scotland and he's going to take you back there."

"But school hasn't finished."

"Edilean! Get up! Your uncle is waiting and he has a fierce temper. He was shouting at the headmistress. He wants you to dress and go with him *now*!"

The teacher flung back the covers and Edilean got out of bed, but she didn't understand what was going on. If someone else had come for her, she would have thought that her uncle had died, but he hadn't, and he was her only relative, so what was his rush?

Her teacher helped her to dress in her warmest clothes. "Scotland is cold, so put on your heaviest wool."

"I must get—" Edilean began.

"No! I'll send it all, your books, your clothes, everything. He is waiting."

In spite of her teacher's admonishment, she managed to slip the packet of James's letters into a pocket in the folds of her skirt.

By the time Edilean was dressed, she was filled with anticipation. Her uncle was so impatient to spend time with her that he was taking her to Scotland before the term ended. Edilean regretted not being able to say good-bye to her friends and favorite teachers, but the excitement overcame her sadness.

Scotland! she thought. Edilean had never traveled much in her life. She'd lived in London with her father and she'd attended school in Hampshire, and she'd visited the country houses of a few of her friends. But she'd never been outside the English borders.

Her uncle was sitting in the headmistress's office

eating bread and honey with a pot of tea. When Edilean came in, he looked her up and down in a perfunctory way, then went back to his food. She went to him as though to kiss him, but he pulled away with a face that made her think he'd be horrified by her touch. That was all right with her, as she was a bit put off by the look of him. His face was red, his skin rough, and his little eyes looked like they belonged on a small animal.

While she waited for him to finish eating—he didn't offer her any or even speak to her—two of her teachers worked frantically to pack away as many of Edilean's possessions as possible.

Outside, an old, heavy coach waited for them, and the headmistress told Edilean that they'd been able to pack most of her clothes and they were in the trunk now strapped to the back of the coach. "The books will have to wait," her teacher said as they parted.

Once Edilean was in the coach with her uncle, she asked him why he'd come for her.

He looked at her as though she weren't very smart and told her that it was near her eighteenth birthday. "Why else would I want you?"

Edilean thought of a few sharp retorts to that, but she didn't say anything. She had an idea that it would be better if she made every effort to get along with her uncle and not antagonize him.

It took them nearly a week to get to his stone house. Each night they stopped at some inn for a hot meal and a bed. A couple of the inns were nice, but the others were hideous. The first night, Edilean asked to have a bath brought to her room, and that had caused so much hilarity that she'd never asked again. She made do with what water she could get from any sympathetic-looking maid.

When they reached his house in Scotland, it was late afternoon, and Edilean was tired to her very bones. Her hair was straggling about her face and she was so dirty she itched. She looked out the coach window and saw the tall, narrow old "castle" and wanted to cry. The thing wasn't a castle such as she'd imagined, but a tower made of stones that looked like they wanted to go back to the earth they'd come from.

On the long trip her uncle hadn't addressed a dozen words to her and he'd never once made an inquiry about her comfort. By the time they reached Scotland, she knew that whatever he wanted from her, it wasn't going to be good.

She stepped out of the coach into a stone courtyard, where there were what seemed to be a hundred people staring at her in curiosity. They were all wearing pieces of woolen fabric that had been woven in a pattern of squares and lines. The women had on coarse skirts held in place about their waists with thick leather belts, while the men wore wool trousers and big shirts.

What Edilean liked about them was that a few of them were smiling at her. It wasn't a full smile, but she could see it in their eyes. She knew she must look awful, but they didn't seem to mind. An older man came forward and offered his hand to help her down the coach steps. It seemed as though it had been a year since she'd had such kindness. Turning, she smiled at all of them. "Thank you," she said loudly. "Thank you for your welcome."

Some of the people looked embarrassed by her words, but some of them smiled a bit more.

Her uncle walked toward the old wooden steps leading up to the second floor of the tower, leaving Edilean to make her own way. Right then she knew that this was her only chance to make a good first impression. She'd always been easy in company, and she felt that these people were open to friendliness. Instead of following her uncle inside, she walked about the courtyard and introduced herself as Edilean Talbot. She admired babies and complimented the women on the huge brooches they wore to keep their tartans on their shoulders. She went into the stables and talked to a wonderful man named Malcolm about the horses.

"I think you'll like this one," he said in an accent so heavy that Edilean had trouble understanding him.

She followed him to the end stall and there she saw Marmy, her dappled gray mare. Edilean couldn't help her tears as she nuzzled the horse's nose. Her mare was the one constant in her life. When she was in school, Marmy was boarded nearby, and when she visited anyone, her horse was sent ahead so Edilean would have her own mare to ride.

"She's glad to see you," Malcolm said.

"And I'm glad to see her. We've been together since I was just twelve. She likes her oats."

"Aye, she does."

Edilean spent several minutes talking to the man, having him repeat things she didn't understand, then finally, she went into the tower.

That her uncle'd had her horse brought to Scotland made Edilean think more kindly of him and she wanted to thank him. He was nowhere to be seen, but there was a maid there, a tiny woman named Morag, who took Edilean almost to the top and showed her a cold, bare room that was to be hers. Edilean was shocked at the ugliness of it, but she kept her face from showing her feelings as she turned to Morag and thanked her for her help.

For a couple of days, Edilean hardly left her room. Morag saw that she had food and water and was given the necessities, but Edilean needed rest and to prepare herself for whatever her uncle had planned for her. Her intuition told her it was going to be bad.

When he finally called her to him, it was worse than she thought. He bolted the heavy door behind her so no one could hear them, then he sat down between two men who repulsed her. One was old and ugly; the other was young but had eyes like a mad dog. Her uncle told her that on her birthday, at one minute after midnight, she was to marry one of the men. "You're to *choose* one of them." The way he said the word made it sound as though he thought it was the biggest joke in the world.

"I'm sorry," Edilean said politely, "but I cannot marry either of them, for I'm already engaged."

The three men stared at her as though they'd never heard the word before.

"Engaged to marry," she said, this time louder. It wasn't exactly the truth, since James hadn't asked her yet, but she knew he would.

"That engagement is broken," her uncle said at last. "You're going to marry one of these men. Care to choose now?"

"No!" Edilean said as she backed away from the three of them.

"We'll wait then," her uncle said, then turned away, as though there was to be no more discussion.

"Excuse me, sir!" she said. "I am *not* going to marry either of these—" She looked them up and down with all the contempt she felt, and lowered her voice. "My father's will says I may marry a man of my own choosing and I certainly don't choose either of these . . . men."

"You will do what I say," her uncle said, and raised his hand in dismissal.

"I will not!" Edilean shouted at him. She'd spent most of her life in boarding schools, and she was fed up with people telling her when and how she was to do things.

"You will," Neville Lawler said, "and if you try to get out of it, I'll make your life such a misery that you'll wish you'd never been born. And if you tell any of these nosy Scots about this, I'll make you sorry. Now get out of my sight!"

The two men beside him looked at Edilean in triumph. The younger one gave her a look up and down that told her what he wanted from her.

Turning, she fled the room.

After that day, war between her and her uncle was declared. Edilean wrote a letter to James and told him the horrific circumstances that had befallen her. But her uncle took the letter from Morag, whom Edilean had given it to to post, and that night read it back to her with great drama in front of the two men, Ballister and Alvoy; then he threw it into the fire.

"You'd better reconcile yourself to your fate," her uncle said. "You're here now and you'll stay here. The gold your father left is being sent to me two days before your birthday. It will never leave here. As for you, *you* will do whatever your husband wants you to do." This made the three men laugh heartily.

Edilean spent the rest of the day in her room and realized that it was up to her to save herself.

When Morag brought Edilean her dinner on a tray, she made sure the softhearted woman saw her weeping. "Oh, miss, what ails you?"

"I've had a quarrel with the man I love," Edilean said. "I wrote him an apology but my uncle says he doesn't deserve such concern. My uncle tore my letter up." Edilean was watching Morag and saw the color flush her neck. So! It looked like Morag felt some guilt at having the letter that had been entrusted to her taken away.

"You write him again and I'll be sure it gets to London," Morag said.

"You won't let my uncle see it?"

"Trust me. I won't come between lovers. I was young once."

"And I'll bet you had lots of beaux."

Morag smiled. "In those days the laird liked me, but he married someone else."

"The laird?"

"The chief."

"Oh, I see," Edilean said, but she was too busy composing her letter to James in her head to listen. One thing that she'd seen when her uncle read her first letter aloud was that it was too dramatic, too full of danger and warnings. Her next letter would be calmer, just stating the facts, and telling James everything she knew, including what her uncle said about the gold being brought to Scotland.

She sealed the letter and gave it to Morag, praying that the woman wouldn't betray her and give it to her uncle. When Edilean heard nothing from her uncle about the letter, she hoped it had gone through.

Besides appealing to James for help, Edilean decided to try to make her uncle see reason. For days, Edilean argued with him, and she soon learned how far she could push him before he got so exasperated that he raised his hand to her. He never hit her, but that was only because she learned to duck and run quickly.

Outside the tower, or "keep" as she learned it was called, the Scottish people were extremely nice to her. Every day she went riding. On the first day, she tried to escape, planning to ride all the way to London by herself, but her uncle came after her. For all that he was fat and rarely moved, he was a great horseman. He sat atop his big hunter as though he'd been born on it, and he grabbed her reins and halted her. "You try that again and I'll have your mare shot," he said, and she knew he meant it.

For weeks, she behaved herself and waited. She had arguments with her uncle, and since he was always careful that the doors were closed, Edilean got the idea that he knew that if she asked the Scots for help they might give it.

A boy, Tam, about fifteen, was assigned to help her on and off her horse every day, and after her escape attempt, he rode a pony behind her. But Edilean knew he couldn't help her. He was too young, too inexperienced.

But sometimes she saw another Scotsman in the background, and he looked strong enough that he might be able to help. She didn't know what she was going to need, but, somehow, she was going to have to escape, and she meant to take her father's gold with her.

The man's name was Shamus, and she saw the way others got out of his way when he walked by. If she was going to get away from her uncle, she would need someone like him.

As the days passed, she stopped fighting with her uncle and began, instead, to ask him questions. What she wanted to know was when the gold was coming in and how it was going to be transported. He wasn't fooled by her questions and told her to get away from him.

More days passed and there was still no word from James. Had she mistaken him? Did he not want her and her dowry? Was he shrugging his broad shoulders and letting her go?

She seemed to be at the depths of her depression when a man she'd never seen before, a man as tall and as big as James, but with thick black hair that he didn't tie back, and a beard that looked as though it had never been cut in his life, loosened the cinch on her horse and sent her flying onto the stones. Wasn't her life bad enough without some man playing hurtful tricks on her? She looked at the shortness of his outrageous garment—something she'd never seen before—and spat some cutting remarks at him. She was glad that when she walked away everyone started laughing at him.

Later, she was angry about what the man had done, but she didn't tell her uncle about him. She liked the Scots and didn't want to betray them. Because there was one bad apple didn't mean that the others were rotten. Besides, everyone she spoke to told her who the man was and that he would never hurt her. They wouldn't say who had cut her cinch, just that it wasn't the bearded man.

For days Edilean's life stayed in the routine she'd

developed. But every day she grew more nervous and more frightened as she waited for some word from James. Had he received her letter? Maybe he was in France now and the letter was waiting for him in London. Maybe when he received it, she would already be married.

When it got down to four days before her birthday and there was still no letter, Edilean was so jumpy that she nearly screamed at every sound. Morag asked her what was wrong, but Edilean couldn't tell her.

When she went out for her ride, her escort was the man Shamus, and she was glad of it. Maybe she could talk to him and tell him . . . She didn't know what she could tell him. She was sure he could get her away from there, but then what? She had no relatives to go to, and her friends were still in school, too young to help.

As she sat in the bushes and sketched, as she did every day, she was nearly scared to death by the hairy-faced man jumping out at her. When he shouted, "You are found out!" Edilean wondered why she didn't die from shock right then and there. She thought he meant that her uncle had found out that she'd written a letter to James.

After the man jumped up and yelled at her, he ran away as though he were five years old. She'd called for Shamus and he came running, but he only saw the man disappearing into the bushes.

"He's the man who made me fall off my horse," she said.

"Oh, aye, that he is. A true terror with the women. I wouldn't get too near him if I were you. He's not right in the head, if you know what I mean."

"Where's he going now?"

"Back to the keep to tell everyone how scared you looked when he jumped out at you. He wants to make them laugh at you."

"Oh, he does, does he?" She started running for her horse, Shamus right behind her. He easily lifted her onto the saddle, and she took off, using trails that she'd persuaded Tam to show her. He'd been told to keep to the road, but Edilean had smiled and coaxed him into showing her the more secret ways.

When she got back to the keep, the man was already there, and she was pleased to see that no one was laughing at having heard how she'd jumped when he'd leaped from the bushes. She slid off her horse and it was as though weeks of frustration and rage came out and she unleashed them on him. She was so angry she could think of few words to say, but she kicked him hard in the shin, then hit him with the whip. She'd meant to hit his arm, which was covered by a thick shirt, but he'd bent and the whip hit his neck, cutting him.

She was on the verge of feeling sorry for having done it when he picked her up and dropped her into a horse trough. Yet again, the only consolation she had was that the people seemed to be on *her* side. Dear Morag helped her up the stairs and Edilean went straight to her uncle to tell him what the man had done to her.

She didn't know what she expected from her uncle, but for him to laugh at her and side with the hairy man wearing what Edilean considered women's clothing was not it. She left the room, trying not to let the laughing men see her tears.

But the man who was making her life worse than it already was followed her to the roof. She didn't know what it was about him, maybe because it was so close to her birthday, and because the man was the chief of the McTerns, but in spite of Shamus's warning, she blurted out the truth about everything and asked him to help her escape.

To her horror, the man started laughing at her.

She ran from him, slammed the door behind her and bolted it, locking him on the roof. She was so angry that if she could have, she would have thrown him off the roof and watched him splatter on the stones below.

The next morning she awoke with the words "three days" in her mind. It was just three days until her birthday and the end of her life as she knew it.

And now, as she sat on the floor, wanting her life to be over, the door opened and Morag entered. "It's here," she said as she handed Edilean not just a letter from James but a package.

"Does anyone know?"

"No one. The letter was given to me and only I saw it. You go on and read it now. Mayhap it will cheer you."

"Yes," Edilean said, but she didn't open the package until Morag left the room. Inside was a little bottle with a stopper in it and a red wax seal.

"Darling," James wrote. "I'm sorry I've taken so long to get back to you, but I've put a plan in motion. It has taken me a long while to find out what I needed to know, but I did it. You shall repay me for this with kisses."

Edilean held the letter to her breast for a moment and closed her eyes. He *did* love her!

"You must do exactly as I tell you," he wrote. "You must follow my instructions exactly or the plan won't work. You can't vary it by even an hour, as everything is timed precisely. Do you understand me?"

Even though she was alone in the room, Edilean nodded, then read on.

4

"HER BIRTHDAY IS tomorrow."

"What?" Malcolm asked his nephew as he scooped out a load of oats.

"Her birthday. It's tomorrow."

"Oh, aye. Her. You know, do you not, that she has a name?"

"I heard it, but I don't remember it." Angus had been out all night, searching out cattle and checking that none had been stolen. But as he roamed the hills, he kept counting down the hours until Lawler's niece would have to marry one of those demons Lawler called friends. When it came to the moment, which one would she choose? Old Ballister or the young, bad-tempered Alvoy? That night, Angus had tossed about in his plaid as he'd imagined her alone with one of them.

She'd asked Angus for help—but he'd laughed at her. That thought had haunted him for the last two days. Now, in the afternoon, sitting in the stable and watching Malcolm work, he still couldn't get his mind around what he'd done.

"What's eating you, lad?" Malcolm asked.

Angus told him. He sat on the stool, fatigue pulling him down, and he told Malcolm all of it.

When he finished, Malcolm looked at him. "What are we going to do to save her?"

"We are going to do *nothing*!" Angus said. "We have to think of the whole. We have to think of the babies and feeding them. If we thwart Lawler—if we rebel—*we* will be punished, not her."

"Have ye got that out of your system now?"

"Aye, I have," Angus said, and as he looked at Malcolm, the tiredness began to leave him. He felt energy moving through his body. "What I thought is that they can't marry without the kirk."

"Do you mean to burn it down?" Malcolm asked, eyes wide in horror.

"Nay," Angus said. "I just thought we'd take the pastor for a night out."

"He must know that Lawler wants him here tonight."

"I thought . . . Mind you, it's just an idea that passed through my head, but I thought that we might get Shamus to help us make the pastor forget his appointment. If we showed up at the vicarage with a little or mayhap a lot of Lawler's port, perhaps the old man would forget he's to be at the kirk tonight."

"Why Shamus? When did you start to trust *him*?"

"In my eyes this is a sin sure to get me sent to hell. If I have to go, then I want someone with me who *deserves* to go."

"Excellent idea," Malcolm said, trying to look serious, but the corners of his lips were twitching in merriment. "But if we stop the marriage tonight, what do we do about tomorrow? And the day after?"

"I don't know," Angus said. "I think we'll have to secret her away and somehow hide her. Then we'll . . . Why are these problems put onto *me*?"

"Because you always come up with a solution for them," Malcolm said. "Do you want me to go with you to see Shamus?"

"Nay. I want you to steal a barrel of port."

"That will take but a moment," Malcolm said. "Go on, go to Shamus. You'll have to use the coins you have hidden in the third stall to bribe him."

Angus didn't pause to ask how his uncle knew about those. There was no time to lose.

"What do you mean that you canna go?" Angus asked Shamus as he was eating. They were in the small, dirt-floored old cottage where Shamus lived with his tiny mother and three younger brothers. His four older brothers had left as soon as they were tall enough to stand up to their abusive father. To this day some people still wondered how Shamus's father had fallen off a cliff in broad daylight. Whatever the cause, no one had been sorry to see him go.

"I have to drive a heavy wagon to Glasgow tonight," Shamus said.

"Since when are *you* a driver?"

"Since the little miss asked me to do it."

Angus sat down at the table across from him. "What are you talking about?"

"Lawler's niece asked me to drive a wagon to Glasgow. What more is there to say?"

"The niece? Not Lawler?"

"He knows nothing about it. I had to meet the wagon two miles from here, and one of my brothers is watching it now. I'll go when I finish my meal."

"What's in the wagon?" Angus asked.

"Six heavy trunks. They're bronze statues from Greece and she has someone in Glasgow waiting to sell them for her. I'm to bring back the money and give it to her."

"You? She trusted *you* to bring money back to her?"

"She likes me," Shamus said, grinning. "She says I'm the only man in Scotland who has enough courage to help her. She calls me a man of honor." Shamus was laughing at this very idea.

"How much did she pay you?"

"None of your business," he said.

Angus thought he saw the girl's plan. Somehow, she'd got hold of valuable items and was going to sell them. Maybe, if she got enough money, she could buy her way out of having to marry someone she didn't like. All in all, Angus thought it was a good plan, except that she'd tried to use Shamus. She'd never see a cent of the money. He'd stay in Glasgow, or board a ship, and no one would ever see him again.

Angus had to quickly put together an alternate plan. "I'll go with you," he said. "There's danger on the road. You'll need someone with you."

"My brother is going with me."

"Then I'll alert Lawler to be ready for the money."

Shamus gave Angus a vile look. He could see that he wasn't going to get away with his original scheme. Only if everything was done in secrecy could he sell the goods and keep the money. If Angus told, Lawler would send fifty men after him before he'd gone ten miles.

"You take the wagon," Shamus said, his face contorted in rage. "You go and sell the old things, then bring the money back here. I'm sure the young miss will be grateful to you." His tone made it sound as though there was something dirty going on between Angus and the niece.

The last thing Angus wanted to do was to drive a wagon all the way to Glasgow, but he didn't know anyone he could trust. He followed Shamus outside the little house, ducking through the short doorway, then went behind the house and saw the wagon.

As he stared, he could hardly speak. It wasn't a normal wagon, but a very heavy one, seeming to have been reinforced so it could hold a great weight. More extraordinary were the horses attached to it. They were two magnificent Clydesdales, gorgeous animals, with their heavy hooves and thick manes.

As Angus stood there staring in astonishment, he realized why Shamus was so angry. Whoever had arranged this had spent an enormous amount on the rig. The statues must be worth a fortune.

Shamus handed him a piece of paper. "She wrote it. It tells the name, address, and time on it. James Harcourt. Red Lion Inn. Glasgow by midnight tomorrow."

As Angus put the paper in his sporran, he thought that it was going to be difficult to get to Glasgow by that time. "What's in the back?"

Shamus threw back the tarpaulin to reveal six heavy, ironbound trunks that had been bolted to the bottom of the big wagon.

"And there's a coffin," Shamus said with a smirk.

"A coffin?"

"The little miss told me it was a mummy from Egypt."

"A . . . ?" Angus said, a shiver of revulsion running through him. He got himself under control. "Did you look inside it?"

Shamus shrugged. "I wanted to, but the miss said it had a curse on it, so it was better not to look. I took her word for it."

"As well you should have," Angus said, throwing the tarp back down and fastening it. He was going to be traveling the roads in the middle of the night with a mummy on board. All for a woman who said she hated him! Angus looked at Shamus and for a moment he felt guilty at thwarting his plans to get away. "Keep the money she gave you to do this," he said kindly, "and Malcolm will give you more if you do what he tells you to." Angus climbed up on the wagon seat. "Tell Malcolm I'll be back as soon as I can with some money and we'll get her out of this."

"Who?"

"The young miss," Angus said, his voice exasperated. "Shamus, for once in your life, do what's right. Go now, and tell Malcolm I'll be back soon." He picked up the reins. "Do you know where the young miss is now?"

"Morag said she's been locked in her room for days."

Angus glanced toward the keep, the top barely seen over the trees. With one more look behind him, he started for Glasgow.

He wasn't a mile down the road when young Tam came riding up, and Angus's heart leaped. Maybe the boy would go with him.

"Malcolm told me what you're doing, and he sent this." He tossed Angus a package. "Clothes and food. They won't want to see you in the city wearing that."

"Would you like to go with me?" Angus asked. "With these beautiful horses?"

"Nay, I can't. I must stay with her. We can't let her be forced into marriage to one of those lecherous old men. She should marry a McTern and put the land back in its proper name."

Angus smiled. "Maybe she could marry you." As the only child of the second son of the old laird, Tam was next in line to take on the responsibility of the McTerns.

"With you gone, that's my idea," he said, smiling at his cousin for the first time in days. "I'll see you when you get back." Turning his horse, he lifted his hand in farewell, and Angus sighed. He dreaded the long trip alone.

5

Angus had been on the road a mere three hours and already he was bored and tired. Because of "her" he hadn't had much sleep in the last few days and now, because of "her" he wasn't getting any more. Every time he dozed off, the well-trained horses stopped moving. Twice, Angus woke with a jolt and saw that the beautiful horses were munching on the grass at the side of the road. At this rate, he'd never get to Glasgow. If it had been up to him, he would have pulled into the forest and slept for a few hours, but he couldn't. He had a deadline to meet. For "her."

It seemed that it had hardly turned dark when Angus heard galloping horses and a shot fired into the air. He reached for the loaded pistol he had under the seat, but a voice to his right said, "I wouldn't do that if I were you."

The horse behind him had been a distraction. Damn! Angus thought; he'd been lax. Between anger and fatigue, he hadn't been vigilant. Why hadn't he found someone to go with him?

He pulled on the reins to the big horses and they slowed to a halt.

There were three brigands, each with his face masked, pistols held out and aimed at Angus's head.

"What foolishness is this?" the man who seemed to be the leader asked. "They send one man on a rig like this? Just one of those horses is worth your life." He put his pistol in the holster on his horse and scrutinized Angus in his outlawed kilt. "You look like a man from one of the old clans. I like a man who stands up against the English. Get down and I'll let you live."

It was one thing to try to help a girl he didn't know, but quite another to give up his life for her. "None of this belongs to me," Angus said in an affable voice as he got down from the wagon, "so I lose nothing."

One of the men moved forward and touched the neck of one of the big Clydesdales. "I've never seen such beautiful horses. Who's your master?"

"No man is my master!" Angus said quickly, making the first man laugh.

"Rightly said for a Scotsman. What do you have in there?" He nodded toward the back.

"Things for a museum," Angus said, backing away from them. For all that they sounded friendly and were saying they weren't going to harm him, he didn't trust anyone holding a pistol aimed at his head. The first man had put his weapon away, but the other two still had theirs out. In the back, half hidden in the dark, was a fourth man who hadn't so much as blinked. His pistol was held at arm's length and he kept it aimed at Angus.

"I'd like to see that," the first man said as he got down off his horse. Since the man was just a few feet from Angus, he thought about leaping on him and grabbing his weapon, but the thief in back kept too steady of an aim.

Angus untied the corner of the cover and showed the trunks.

"They look heavy," the robber said.

"Bronze statues from Greece," Angus said.

"Worth anything?"

"Not to me," Angus answered.

The thief looked to the man in back, and he motioned with his pistol that he wanted to see all the contents of the wagon.

Angus untied the rest of the tarpaulin and threw it back. When they saw the coffin, the robber stepped away and the man in back's horse pranced a bit.

"What the hell is that?"

"A mummy," Angus said.

"Bless me," the man in front said as he moved his horse forward to take a look at the wooden box.

At that moment, a sound came from inside the coffin, and it was all Angus could do not to take off running into the forest, but in the next second he realized Shamus had done it. No doubt he'd put a cat in the coffin to scare Angus.

"It's just a mummy," Angus said. "It's been dead for a thousand years. Nothing to be afraid of." When their eyes were fastened on the coffin, Angus saw his time to make a move. He leaped at the man standing near him, grabbed his pistol, and put it to his head.

But it didn't matter that he did, because in the same second, the lid on the coffin moved to one side and a woman with sickly white skin and clothes sat up. The moonlight hit her in a creepy, eerie way that made all of them, including Angus, stand absolutely still.

In the next second, the men wasted no time in running away. The man Angus had at gunpoint ignored him as he leaped onto his horse and took off into the dark of the forest, the other two close behind him.

Angus stood where he was, seeming to be paralyzed to the spot. He recognized Lawler's niece, but was she dead and rising?

"You'd think they could have cleaned it out," Edilean said as she wiped at the white sawdust on her face. She was blinking hard, as even her eyelashes were covered in the fine dust of the newly made coffin.

Angus was standing still and staring at her. "Holy hell! It's you."

"And it's *you*," she said angrily. "What have you done with Shamus?"

Angus looked up at the moon for a moment. At last he was beginning to understand what was going on. "It's after midnight. Who's locked in your room at the keep?"

"No one," she said, rubbing at her face and

clothes, then coughing at the dust. "Morag knows I'm not there, but she covered for me. Unlike you, other people don't stand by and do nothing when another person's life is threatened."

"I hardly think marriage is death."

She stood up in the coffin, unsteadily, and grabbed the back of the wagon seat. "If you were a prince and forced to marry an ugly princess you'd not be so calm about it."

"Me, a prince?" He was still standing in one place and looking up at her.

"Could we just *go*? If it's after midnight, then my uncle will come for me soon."

Angus was trying to think about what to do. "I'll get you back to him as soon as I can, and we'll sort this marriage out."

"I'm not going to return to him."

"Yes, you are," Angus said as he climbed onto the wagon seat. "I'll talk to him. We'll *all* talk to him. He'll find some handsome lad for you to marry, and—"

"Handsome!" She was standing in the back of the wagon, and he was on the seat, so their faces were nearly level. "Do you think *that* is my worry? Do you think all this is about whether or not I have a beautiful husband? No, it's about those!" She pointed to the trunks.

"Some old statues?"

"No. They're not historical objects. Those trunks are full of gold and they're my dowry. I told you that the man who marries me gets the gold. But my uncle has made an arrangement with Ballister and Alvoy that if I marry one of them, my uncle will keep the gold and give my husband and me only ten percent of it. I'm not only fleeing a hideous marriage but poverty as well."

The full realization of what Angus had become a part of was coming to him. It would look as though he'd kidnapped Lawler's niece and stolen six trunks full of gold. Hanging would be too light a punishment for him. This crime was so great they'd have to invent a new way to kill him.

"Why are you looking sick?"

"They will hang me," he whispered.

"For what? Stupidity?"

"Kidnapping and stealing!" he said loudly as he put his face close to hers.

"Oh. Yes, I see. If it helps any, Shamus didn't know either that I was in the wagon or that he carried gold."

Angus wiped his hand over his face. "And what would have happened when he found out?"

"He wasn't supposed to." She reached into her pocket and pulled out a little bottle. "James sent me a bottle of laudanum, and it was to keep me asleep the whole way. James was to wake me with a kiss," she said, smiling dreamily.

Turning, Angus looked over the horses' heads to the road. Was there a way to right this? "And this James is . . . ?"

"The man I love. James Harcourt. I wrote him

of my predicament and he took care of everything. He found when the gold was to be shipped to my uncle, took it, and put it on this wagon. He also put the coffin in the back for me. All I had to do was get someone—Morag—to let me out of my room and get someone else—Shamus—to meet the wagon and drive it back to James."

"So where is he?"

"My uncle?"

"No! This man you say you love. Where is he?"

"Waiting for me in Glasgow."

"Then he himself took *no* risks. He gave a drug to a woman he loves, let her travel in a coffin at the mercy of a man like Shamus, not to mention highwaymen, and he—"

"What's wrong with Shamus?"

"I would need a week to tell you," He looked about at the dark forest. "We have to go. Now."

"To my uncle?"

"Do you think he'd believe the truth, that I knew nothing about this?"

"Shamus could tell him—"

"The Shamus you seem to think is so good is—" He threw up his hands. "We have to go and I need to think."

"I don't have to get back in the coffin, do I?"

"I ought to put you in it and nail it shut." Instead, he had to practically lift her over the back of the seat to sit beside him. A minute later, they were moving. Angus was grinding his teeth as he thought of the situation he was now in and how to get out of it. How could he ever again go *home*?

"I don't know why you're so angry at me," she said. "All you have to do is drive to Glasgow and let me off. James will take care of everything after that."

"Then what? I go back to my own clan? To my own family? Do you think your uncle is too stupid to know *I* took his rich niece, that *I* stole his gold?"

"This isn't the way it was supposed to happen. Shamus—"

"Do not mention his name again. If he'd taken the wagon all the way to Glasgow—which I doubt—whatever money he got he would have kept and he would never have returned to Clan McTern. One by one his brothers have left, so he would have too."

"And if I had woken up early in the coffin?" Her voice was a whisper, as what he was telling her was beginning to sink in.

"Let's just say that by the time you got to this John—"

"James."

"Harmon—"

"Harcourt."

"To this man who doesn't risk his own skin to get both a bride *and* a wagon full of gold, you wouldn't be something he wanted."

"Oh." She moved closer to Angus and looked around her with frightened eyes. "Shamus is actually bad?"

"Very, very bad."

She moved even closer.

"The worst I've ever seen."

Edilean slipped her arm through his, and pressed her body close to his.

Under his beard, Angus couldn't help smiling. "Shamus would probably have held you somewhere for days and tortured you. Tickled your bare feet with a goose feather."

She looked up at him in puzzlement, then grimaced. "You're teasing me."

"Yes, fool that I am. Now be quiet and let me think."

Angus was sure that when the girl was found to be missing, Malcolm would get Shamus and figure out what had been done. Malcolm would even figure out about the coffin—and he would make sure he misled Lawler long enough for Angus to get to Glasgow.

At these thoughts Angus relaxed a bit and he could feel the girl, still close by him, slumping so much he wondered if she'd fallen asleep. Laudanum was a powerful drug. Take too much and a person never woke up.

As he drove, Angus began to realize the enormity of the situation. He could never go home again. Never again would he see any of the people he'd known all his life. He wouldn't see his sister's children grow up. Wouldn't see young Tam grow into manhood.

He couldn't help it as a tear came to his eye and it dropped on the girl, making her stir. "Ssssh, lass, go back to sleep." Had she been any other girl he would have put his arm around her and held her while she slept, but not her.

But she didn't go back to sleep. "Were you telling the truth when you said you can't go back? Or were you just angry at me?"

"I canna return. It's one thing to stand before your uncle and admit you threw his niece into a horse trough, but another to admit to . . . to this."

"I'm sorry I hit you on the neck with my whip. I meant to hit your shoulder, but you bent and . . ."

"The whip hit my neck," he finished for her. "It healed."

"How can you tell under all that hair?"

"Some girls like my hair."

"I never cared for facial hair on a man." She was quiet for a moment. "What will you do? Where will you live?"

"I'll be all right. Don't worry about me."

"I'm sorry I got you into this. It's all my fault, Mr. McTern. I know! Why don't you go to the New World with James and me?"

"Is that what you have planned?"

"Yes. He has the tickets, and we have the best cabin on the ship, the *Mary Elizabeth*. James did so very much work. After I wrote him of my predicament and the treachery of my uncle, he planned everything."

"So he'll take care of you as soon as I leave you there?"

"Oh, yes. He's meeting me at the inn with men to

load the trunks onto the ship. Then the next day we sail at four P.M. and James says we'll be wed by eight. We're going to get married on board the ship." When he said nothing, she added, "By the captain."

"Aye, I understand."

She was quiet for a while. "Do you leave a sweetheart behind?" She looked at him in shock. "Do you leave a *wife* behind?"

"No, no wife, no bairns, but there will be at least a dozen women who will be heartbroken."

She knew he was making light of the situation, but it was a serious matter. By trying to save her, he'd inadvertently given up his entire world. "What will you do?" she asked again, not knowing what else to say.

"You're not to worry about me. I can take care of myself."

"Do you think my uncle will send men to hunt you?"

"Aye, I'm afraid he will."

"Then, Mr. McTern, you *must* go to America with us. People are free there. Or more free than they are here, anyway."

"What would I do in a new country?"

"What will you do in this one?"

"I don't know, lass, but that's a big decision. To leave my homeland? I don't know if I can do that. But it is kind of you to worry so about me."

For a moment, with the moonlight on her beautiful face, he found himself leaning toward her.

But she moved away and said quickly, "James will take care of you."

Angus's shoulders stiffened at her comment. Her words hurt more than that little whip on his neck had. She'd reminded him of the class difference between them. She could play the lady and talk of "helping" him, but when he got too close, she pulled away, and spoke of how a higher-class man would "take care of" him.

Unaware of his thoughts, Edilean sat in silence for a moment, looking at the dark around them. There was a lantern on the wagon, and they could see the road, but the darkness surrounded them.

Angus didn't know what he was going to do with his life, what his future would be. The only thing he was certain of was that he'd never put himself in a position where "James" would have to take care of him.

6

EDILEAN KNEW SHE was talking too much, but she was trying to cover her nervousness. She felt bad that her problems had changed this man's life. The reason she'd asked Shamus to drive her to the port near Glasgow was because she'd sensed that he was like her and an outcast. But this man wasn't.

After her first encounter with him, people had gone out of their way to tell her that it wasn't possible that Angus McTern had loosened her saddle. "He takes care of us all," she was told.

In the week between when she'd struck him and when he'd dropped her into the horse trough, she'd heard nothing but good about him. Wherever she went, someone told her about Angus. Often, she wasn't told directly. She'd visit Marmy in the stables and people would suddenly appear outside the stall and they'd put on a "conversation" about Angus.

According to them, he was the epitome of every

virtue known to mankind. After four days of these staged talks she'd wanted to shout, "Do you expect me to *marry* him? Is that what you're after?"

During the last of that week, as Edilean went over every point in her life, she thought that she shouldn't have been so awful to the man. She should have worked harder to make him like her. If she had, then maybe he would have helped her when she'd asked him to. She even thought that maybe she could have offered the current laird to her uncle as an alternate husband. If Angus McTern was half as honorable as she'd been told, he might have been persuaded to relinquish the gold to her uncle.

But then what? she thought. Was she to go live with him in one of those two-room stone cottages and make a baby every year?

Now, she could feel the warmth of him at her side. It was cold, and she wished she could move closer to him, but things had changed when he'd leaned toward her and she'd acted as though she found him repulsive. But she didn't. It was the way she'd survived years of aggression from too-friendly men.

She brushed at her hair with her hands. "Am I still covered in sawdust?"

"A bit, but I'm sure he'll like you."

She rubbed her hands to warm them, glancing up at him, but he said nothing. "Maybe by this time tomorrow I'll be married."

He hadn't been fooled by her attempt to cover her nervousness. "You'll do fine, lass."

"Do you think my uncle will be searching for us soon?"

"In a day or two," Angus said softly. "Malcolm will figure out what's going on and he'll give us some time."

"By then I'll be gone," she said.

Angus saw her scratching at the sawdust on her neck and decided to let up on her. He halted the horses, and immediately she was scared. But he nodded at her and said he just needed a bit of . . . privacy. He took a big bag from under the wagon seat, tossed it to the ground, got down, and lifted his arms up to her. "Like to stretch your legs?"

She nodded and put her hands on his shoulders as his big hands encircled her waist and lifted her down. For a second, they stood together. They were strangers but they were both facing whole new lives. It created a bond between them—a bond that she knew would end when they got to the city.

She didn't go far from the wagon to take care of her private needs, but he still beat her back. He'd changed clothes, removing the tartan and exchanging it for trousers, a shirt, and a big jacket. He'd gone from looking like the hero of a romantic novel to looking like a man who worked on the docks.

She smiled at him, but she knew he could feel the difference. Yet again, she felt that he thought she was lacking in some way.

"Shall we take you to your future husband?" he asked as he lifted her onto the wagon.

They drove all that night and through the next day. When they reached the city, Angus skirted the center the best he could as he went toward the dock and the Red Lion Inn, which were both south of the hustle and bustle that he hated so much.

Edilean yawned. She'd slept half the way, her small body leaning against Angus. Twice, he'd fallen asleep, but she'd woken him up. One time, she said, "I could drive the team."

"You?" he'd asked with so much humor that he'd roused from his sleepiness.

"Why do you persist in telling me that I can do nothing?"

"You have sawdust on your nose," he said.

"Oh!" Edilean exclaimed, rubbing it hard. When she looked at Angus, she narrowed her eyes. "You're making fun of me."

"It keeps me awake," he said. "Does Harcourt tease you?"

"No," Edilean said. "He loves me so much that he never teases me."

"Doesn't he make you laugh?"

"He sings with me and we go riding together. And we sit in summerhouses and read together. Sometimes he reads poetry to me. Do you like poetry, Mr. Mc-Tern?"

"Very much," he said. "Sometimes I read a poem or two before I go to sleep. It helps me get calm."

She looked at him hard. "Are you making fun of me again?"

"Yes," he said, smiling at her. "But I mean no harm, lass. The truth is that I'm usually too busy trying to keep thieves from stealing your uncle's cattle to have time to sit and sing with a girl."

"But you have dances. Morag told me about them, and one of the women said you were a good dancer."

"But not for the dances that you know," he said.

After a while, Edilean quit trying to hold a conversation with him. It always seemed to end in her not knowing enough about . . . Well, about life, to be able to talk to him. She'd tried different subjects, but he only ended up teasing her and making her feel useless and incompetent.

She didn't say so, but she vowed that she was going to do the best she could to make up for causing him to lose everything in his life. She'd asked him why he'd changed her plan of using Shamus, and when he told her about his idea of getting the pastor drunk, she felt even more guilty. In the end, he had tried to save her, and all he was getting for what he'd done was banishment.

A couple of times Edilean stole looks at him, thinking how she knew her uncle much better than he did. She'd seen the way her uncle pretended to be something he wasn't when the men were around, and she knew he would never show his true self if any of the Scots were near. They wouldn't work so hard for him if they saw the way he raised his hand to strike a woman they'd all come to like.

Edilean knew that Angus—Mr. McTern—seemed to believe that he had some time before her uncle came after them, but he hadn't seen the man's greed as she had. Somehow, she had to persuade this Scotsman to go to America with her and James. The plan she was coming up with was to get James to open one of the trunks and give Angus a large helping of the gold. That way, Angus would be able to buy himself some land in America; he could build a house for him and the family he'd start.

"What's that look for?" he asked.

It was midday and she was hungry and tired, but excited too. It wouldn't be long now before she saw James. "Where will you stay when we get there?"

"I'm going to lie down in the straw in the stables and sleep for three days."

"You can't do that. You'll miss the ship."

"Oh, aye. The *Mary Elizabeth*. Is it a big ship, then? Does it have room to spare for a poor Scotsman?"

She ignored his teasing tone. "I'll make sure you have a place on the ship even if the captain has to share his cabin."

"Spoken like a woman who has had everything all her life."

Edilean gave him a hard look, but he didn't see it. That was hours ago, and they were in the city now and there were other wagons. He'd halted now and then so she could buy them food, and he took care of the horses' needs, but mostly he plodded on.

The day turned into night and they were all, including the horses, very tired.

Just when she was ready to say that she could go on no longer, she saw the sign for the inn. "We are here!"

"Yes," Angus said tiredly. "We're here at last." He drove the exhausted team into the open doors of the stable, and immediately a man came out from the shadows. He was exquisitely dressed and had a face that Angus thought would look better on a girl.

"Edilean!" the man said sternly, "I'd almost given you up. I've been standing in this filthy barn for hours, waiting for you. Couldn't you have at least tried to hurry?"

Angus stared at the man, and even if he hadn't spoken, he knew he would have disliked him on sight. To Angus's mind the man was Ballister and Alvoy, only a few years earlier.

"I knew you'd be in a hurry to see me!" Edilean said, and launched herself into his arms. He caught her, but just barely.

"You're filthy! What is that all over you?"

"Sawdust. That coffin you sent for me was full of it. James, darling, aren't you glad to see me?"

"Of course I am," he said, but he pulled away when she tried to kiss him. "Look at what you've done to me. I'm as dirty as you are. Here! You!" he shouted to two burly men standing at the back of the wagon. "Be careful of those. I don't want the bottoms falling out." He moved away from her to direct the men in the unloading of the trunks full of gold.

Angus was still sitting on the wagon seat, too tired to get down. Two young men had come from the back and were unhitching the horses. "Be sure you feed them well."

"Mr. Thomas raised them from colts," one of the men said. "He won't like to see them used this hard."

"Nothing I could do about it," Angus muttered as he got down. He looked about at the stalls, hoping to see a clean one so he could sleep in it.

"Did you see him?" Edilean asked as she went to Angus, her beautiful face alight.

"Aye, I saw him," he said, not able to keep from smiling at her. "He's as bonnie as you are. They should put his face in a storybook."

"Oh you! You're always teasing me. I want you to stay here while I get some money from James. I want to give you something for your time and trouble."

"I will make my own way," he said stiffly. "It was my choice to do this, and you paid Shamus for the task. You shouldn't have to pay twice."

"But you can't end up here with no money. You have to at least have a place to stay tonight."

"Are you asking me to share your room?"

"No!" Edilean said, her eyes wide, then she shook her head at him. "What would it take to make you too tired to laugh at me?"

"That will never happen. Now you should go to

your young man. Perhaps this time tomorrow you'll be married to him and you'll be a happy bride."

"Yes," she said, but she didn't move away from him. "Will you be all right?"

"Yes, of course." He kept looking down at her, and tired as he was, what that man said when he first saw her kept running through his head. Now the man was overseeing the unloading of the gold while his bride-to-be was left alone. Maybe Harcourt didn't realize how much she wanted to see him, or how much she'd been through to get to him.

"All right, then," she said. "I guess this is the last time I'll ever see you."

"By tomorrow you won't even remember my ugly, hairy face."

"I don't think that's true," she said softly. "I will never forget your face. I think I might remember it for the rest of my life."

He wanted to touch her, wanted to put his hand to her soft face, but he didn't. "Go, lassie," he said. "Go to your husband." It took some doing on his part, but he turned and walked out of the stables and into the night.

His bravery lasted until he was at the front of the inn, when he saw a handbill with a woodcut of his picture on it. It had been nailed to the side of a fence and offered a five-thousand-pound reward for him. Angus tore the paper off the fence and stared at it. How had they done this so fast? And where had the likeness of his face come from?

He looked down the dark streets, fearful that someone would recognize him, but no one was looking at him. He was just another man in from the country, wandering the streets and looking for a way to spend his money.

Angus went back into the stables to give himself time to think about what to do. He'd been so sure that Malcolm would keep Lawler away from him, that Angus hadn't even been anxious during the trip. So why hadn't they found him?

He knew that the answer was that someone had told Lawler a lot of lies. If the truth had been told, Angus would have been caught a day ago.

He stood inside a stall, leaning against the wall, with the handbill crumpled in his hand. He could read the numbers on it enough to know how much Lawler was offering for his capture, but he didn't know what else it said about him.

"James," he heard Edilean say, "I don't want to stay in my room all day tomorrow. I want to be with you."

"Well, you can't!" Harcourt snapped.

Turning, Angus could see them through the openings between the boards. Edilean looked radiant, thrilled even, to at last be with the man she loved, but Harcourt didn't look glad to see her. He certainly didn't look like a man who was about to be married to a beautiful, intelligent, and very rich young woman should.

Harcourt took her hands away from his face. "I

have things I have to do to get ready for our journey," he said, his voice kinder. "And you have to take a bath and get some sleep."

"I've slept too much," she said. "I slept most of the way here."

"Edilean," he said, sounding like a father talking to a disobedient child, "I have things to do for *us*. I've been working since I got your letter. I wish you'd not waited so late to tell me what was happening. I've needed every moment to prepare for going to another country. Here." He handed her another bottle of the laudanum. "Take this and you'll sleep all day. I'll come and get you tomorrow at midday and we'll go to the ship. After that I'll keep you awake for days." He kissed her, but only quickly. "Now, will you obey me?" he asked.

"Yes, but I don't want to," she said, sounding sulky. "I wish I could spend every minute with you. Did you get my dressmaker in London to make me a wardrobe? I could bring nothing with me."

"I got what I could," he said, "but there wasn't time to get much. When we're in America we'll buy what you need."

"But this is Glasgow. I could shop here."

"Edilean!" he said angrily. "Will our entire lives be like this? Will you disobey everything I say?"

"No," she said, her head down. "It's just that I'm frightened. James . . ." When she saw the anger on his face, she drew back. "All right. I am rather tired. I'll sleep tonight and I'll see you tomorrow."

"That's a good girl," Harcourt said. "I'll get someone to take you to the inn. This one isn't safe, and that driver of yours knows where it is. I don't trust the look of him."

"Angus McTern?" she asked. "But he's the reason we're together. If he hadn't—"

"Yes, dear, I'm sure he's the finest of his class. Now, listen. I've hired a room for you on the top floor of the Green Dragon, and—"

"But I want to be near you."

"I *am* staying there," he said impatiently, then calmed himself. "You'll have quiet up there and I'll see you tomorrow."

"All right," she said, turning away.

"Don't I get a kiss from my bride?" Harcourt asked as soon as her back was turned.

"Oh, yes, James," Edilean said as she threw her arms around his neck and put her lips on his. But he soon pushed her away and began dusting himself off.

"If I don't leave now I'll never be able to go. I'll see you tomorrow, and Edilean . . ." His eyes softened. "I look forward to our wedding night."

Smiling, looking as though she had stars in her eyes, Edilean turned away and went to a maid standing in the doorway and followed her out of the stables.

Angus stood where he was, his head leaning back against the wooden slats of the stall, and closed his eyes for a moment. Something wasn't right. He could feel it in his bones that something was wrong. Maybe it was the way the man treated the girl, but, too, there was something not right in what he'd said. Angus couldn't put his finger on it, but he didn't like James Harcourt, and certainly didn't trust him.

When Harcourt left the stables, Angus followed him.

7

ANGUS HAD HAD a lifetime of disappearing into the bushes in daylight, so sneaking about the darkened town was easy for him. Twice he saw handbills with a drawing of his face, and both times he pulled them down and stuffed them inside his shirt.

Harcourt didn't go far. Just two streets away, he went into a pub, and Angus saw through the window that he went to a table to join three men who welcomed him with loud cheers. And why not? Angus thought. Tomorrow the man was leaving for another country and he was getting married. Perhaps the reason he was so anxious to get away from his bride was because he wanted one last night with his friends. Angus could understand that, and for a moment he considered turning away. Maybe he'd go to Edinburgh. Maybe he'd go far into the Highlands and live. He doubted that the men up there would ask too many questions about where he came from.

But Angus couldn't make himself leave. There

was something about that girl and the way she trusted people that made him feel he had to take care of her. "Just until she's on the ship," he told himself as he went into the pub.

He knew he was taking a chance by showing himself, but no one looked at him. He had a couple of coins with him so he ordered a beer and took it to a table near where the four men were sitting. For a moment Angus was tense, concerned that Harcourt would recognize him, but he didn't look at the dirty, bearded man who sat at the next table.

"I make a toast to my new wife," Harcourt said. "She may not be a beauty, but as an earl's daughter, she does have a title."

Angus put his tankard down and couldn't help but stare at the man. No beauty? Edilean was no beauty? And what title did she have? But then titles had never been part of his world, so maybe she had one but he hadn't heard of it.

"So her father is rich, heh?" one of the men asked.

"No dowry," Harcourt said, "and no beauty, but our children will have that title."

"But, James, with your looks you could have held out for more. You should have got a wife who comes with a wagon load of gold."

At that, Harcourt laughed so hard he nearly choked. "That's just what I did. I got trunks full of gold, but I just didn't take the soldier's daughter who owned them."

Angus was staring openly, trying to figure out what the man was saying.

"Here's to my lady wife," Harcourt said, "may she sleep well tonight, for at dawn we board ship and sail to the New World."

Dawn? Angus well remembered that Harcourt said he'd pick up Edilean at midday, but his ship would be long gone by then.

Angus drained his mug of beer, then quietly left the pub. What he had to do was to warn Edilean. He had to— He made himself stop thinking along those lines. What could he do to make her believe him? He imagined breaking into her room and telling her that the man she thought she was to marry was . . . What? Angus wasn't even sure of the answer. Maybe he'd misheard Harcourt.

I am staying there. The words seemed to echo in Angus's head. Harcourt had said he was sending Edilean to the same inn where he was staying. Surely, if the man already had a wife, he wouldn't put Edilean in the same inn. But then, he'd given Edilean that damned laudanum, so maybe he expected her to obey him and sleep all day. Besides, if he was leaving at dawn, when she did wake up he'd be gone—with her gold on board.

Angus started running back the way he came, staying in the shadows so he wouldn't be seen, but going toward the Red Lion. If Edilean was to walk to it, the Green Dragon couldn't be far away.

He saw the painted sign with the picture of the

dragon from some distance away. It was the middle of the night. How was he going to find out which room belonged to Harcourt's wife?

He went to the back of the inn and stood in the shadows as he tried to think how to find out, when the door opened and out came the maid who'd escorted Edilean out of the stables.

He quickly stepped in front of her, and for a moment she looked frightened, but then her face changed. "I saw you," she said, a little smile on her face. "I saw you hiding with the horses and spying on those two."

"And I saw you," Angus said, giving her a look up and down. "Harcourt sent me to make sure you got the rooms right, and that you didn't mix up the women."

"Can't mix up those two, now can I? Don't look much alike, do they?"

"You put the little one on the top floor?"

"I did," she said and took a step closer to him.

"And the other one?"

"Ground floor, like he said. She ate half a haunch of beef for supper, and I was glad I didn't have to carry it up the stairs." She gave him a hard look. "Have I seen you somewhere before?"

"Not me, lass," he said as he moved into the darkness where she couldn't see him. She called out for him to come back, but he stayed where he was until she gave a little snort and walked away. He knew he'd made an enemy, but worse, he knew that sooner or

later she'd remember that she'd seen him on the handbills that seemed to be all over town.

Angus walked around the inn, looking in the
windows, trying to figure out which one was a bedroom. Since there were only two windows with curtains drawn across them, he figured they were a good
bet. He tried the first window and it wouldn't open,
but the second one did.

He crept into the room and waited while his eyes
adjusted to the darkness. He could hear someone in the
bed lightly snoring. It would be my luck to have walked
into the wrong bedroom, he thought, and imagined a
man who slept with a loaded pistol under his pillow.

But he was used to the dark, and after a while he
could see clearly enough to move about. As he got
closer to the bed, he thought he could make out the
outline of a woman. There was flint and tinder on the
bedside and, taking a chance, he lit the candle. When
he looked at the person in the bed, he gave a gasp. It
was a woman all right, and she was as ugly as a witch
in a children's fairy story. She had a big, hooked nose
that curved over thin lips and a chin that stuck out
in a point. Her head was covered by a big cap with a
ruffle around the edges.

And her small, dark eyes were open.

"Pardon me, ma'am," he said. "I must have the
wrong room."

One second he was standing there looking at
her, and the next he was in bed on top of her as she'd
grabbed him and pulled him down. She was a big

woman, not fat but muscular, with strong arms, and he could feel her huge body under his.

"You're a treat," she said as she tried to kiss him. "And I think you have the right room."

"Ma'am," he said as he pushed away from her, but he only succeeded in landing on the other side of the bed. Instantly, she rolled on top of him.

"The door's bolted, so you came in through the window. What did you come for? To rob me? To have your way with me?"

"Well, no, I, uh . . ." She was sitting on him, her big thighs clutching his hips. She had on a white nightgown that was so low cut he could see most of her prodigious bosom. She wasn't young, maybe midthirties, and she was very strong.

"So? What did you come for if not for me? For that puny husband of mine?"

"Yes," Angus said as he grabbed her wrists and held them so they couldn't reach his head. It was hard to think when a woman who weighed as much as she did was sitting on him. Using all the strength he could muster, he rolled out from under her. When he was again standing and she looked like she was about to leap on him, he put up his hand. "Nay, have mercy, ma'am."

Sighing, she lay back down on the bed. "What is it? James owes you money and you want to get it before we sail?"

"Aye," Angus said brightly. "That's it. So it's true that he leaves tomorrow? He owes me ten pounds."

"He doesn't have it," she said as she rolled onto her side to face him. "Why don't you humiliate him by spending the night with his wife?"

"As tempting an offer as that is . . ." Angus said, trying to smile but still protecting himself. "So he did marry? You're the earl's daughter?"

"I am that," she said, turning onto her back. "And I look just like my father."

"Oh, well, he must have been proud of that," Angus said, trying to be polite.

"I'm thirty-six and just got married. What do you think?"

"But now you have a husband," he said and began inching his way around the bed. On the bedside table was one of those little bottles that James Harcourt was so fond of giving to the women in his life. Laudanum. "If you are an earl's daughter, then I should go to your father to pay my debt."

"He has less money than James does."

"So . . ." Angus said. He was at the foot of the bed now and about to turn the corner to reach the table. "You married for love."

The woman laughed at that as she turned toward him. "He married me for the title that will pass to our children. Bastard! He only pretended to love me." She was looking at Angus by the light of a single candle. "Under all that hair you're a fine-looking man, aren't you?" As she said it, her eyes widened and Angus knew that she'd seen the handbills and recognized him.

"I think perhaps you *will* spend the night with me or I shall start screaming. You wouldn't like that now, would you?"

"Depends on why you're screaming," he said as he moved closer to her.

"Not from my husband," she said, her eyes alight. "I don't know how we'll have brats when he hasn't much down there, if you know what I mean."

"I know," Angus said as his hand slipped around the bottle of laudanum. As he put his knee on the side of the bed, he halted. "How do I know you're the bride of James Harcourt?"

"You can look in that chest over there. All the documents are in there."

"Well, then," he said slowly. "Mayhap I will take the repayment out on Harcourt's wife after all. But do you have anything to drink? You look like a woman who's going to make a man thirsty."

"There's a bottle of wine on the table."

"Ah, yes, I see it," Angus said as he blew out the candle.

Thirty minutes later, he was outside her door, and in his hand was a leather portfolio full of papers that he'd found in the trunk. On the other side of the door he could hear the woman snoring. In the end, he'd had to put most of the bottle of laudanum in her wine to make her sleep. In the wrestle before she slept—of her pulling at him and Angus pushing her away—his clothes had been torn and were now askew on his body, but he'd found what he was sure were papers that proved her connection to Harcourt.

"She's not worth this," he said as he thought of Edilean and tried to straighten what was left of his shirt as he hid the portfolio inside, then he went out the front door of the inn. The next thing he had to do was catch Harcourt and keep him off that ship.

8

ANGUS HURRIED TO the pub and saw that Harcourt and his cronies were still drinking, still laughing. As he looked at him, Angus marveled that a man could live with himself with what Harcourt was planning to do. He'd married one woman to get her title and he was taking the money of another woman so he'd never have to support himself.

And of what use was that title going to be when he got to America? Angus had heard that those people didn't believe in aristocracy.

Angus was too tired to think about any of it. Right now he had anger pumping through him, which was keeping him awake, but when this was done, when the girl sailed away on her ship, he meant to hide somewhere and sleep for a week.

When Harcourt came out of the pub he was with the other men, but they soon separated.

"Going to your bride, James?" one called in a teasing voice.

"Will you make the first babe tonight?"

"I might have to hire one of these Scots to do that task for me," he said, his voice slurring as he spoke.

For a moment Angus felt sorry for the woman he'd married. She was big and ugly, and very strong, but she wanted love just like the rest of the world.

When the men left Harcourt, Angus slipped up behind him.

"What do you want?" Harcourt yelled in fear.

"Quiet! I'm the driver, remember?"

"Oh, you. Yes, I remember you. What do you want? I believe you were paid for your trouble, so go away."

"She wants you."

Harcourt shivered. "She always does. Morning, noon, and night, she wants more."

"More than you have?" Angus said under his breath.

"What?"

"Do you want more than you have?" he asked louder.

"What are you blathering on about, man? Out with it!"

"Edilean Talbot wants to see you," Angus said.

"Tell her I'll see her tomorrow," Harcourt said and started into the inn.

He isn't so drunk that he forgets his lies, Angus thought. "No, sir." He nearly choked on the "sir." "She wants to see you *now*."

"Oh, I see," Harcourt said, and he had a look on his face that Angus wanted to knock off with his fist.

"Now. Tonight. Yes, I can see that. My last hooray, so to speak. The last time—" He looked at Angus in speculation. "And she sent you to tell me this?"

"She did."

"And I guess she paid you to do it?"

"Not a cent." Angus again wanted to hit the man.

"I think I *will* go to her. You stay here." He gave Angus a look up and down, then straightened his clothes and went inside.

Angus slipped in behind him, and when Harcourt reached the top floor, Angus was hiding at the end of the hall.

Harcourt used his nails to scratch at the door. "Edilean?" he whispered, glancing at the other doors down the hallway. "Edilean? It's me, James."

If she's taken that drug she'll never hear him, Angus thought, and tried to come up with another plan to get to her.

But he'd underestimated Edilean. She opened the door a crack and looked out. "James? Is that you?"

"Yes, darling," he said as he tried not to slur his words. "I couldn't stay away from you. I want to see you one last— I mean before I sleep. May I come in?"

"Of course," she said. "You're very nearly my husband." She opened the door wide, and Harcourt, after a stumble, went into her room.

Before she could get the door closed, Angus slipped inside. In one swift motion, he grabbed a candlestick off the table by the wall, and whacked Harcourt hard on the head with it. He went down in an instant.

When Edilean opened her mouth to scream, Angus looked at her and said, "Don't."

She closed her mouth but went on her knees to James. "What have you done? Are you insane? Get me that cloth! He's bleeding."

"He's all right," Angus said as he sat down on a chair. "This night has been hell."

Edilean got a cloth from the basin on the table, and sat on the floor to wipe the blood from James's head. "Did you do this out of jealousy? Is it that you cannot stand to see me marry another man? *Any* man? Even one who loves me? Or is this about the gold? James, darling James, please wake up."

Angus shook his head at the ridiculous things she was saying and pulled the portfolio from inside his shirt. "Look in there. I think that should explain my actions well enough."

"What is this?" She picked it up and opened the buckle, and went through the papers inside. "It's our passage to America. Everything that James and I need to get on the ship is in here. Even the captain's name. And here's our marriage certificate. It's . . ." She looked at him. "I don't understand. This isn't my name on the certificate and it says James was married last week."

"Harcourt's wife's name is on there because he married her."

"No," Edilean said impatiently. "That's not possible. *I* am to be his wife."

Angus put his head back against the chair. Maybe

he'd go to sleep right there and then. "He already has a wife."

Edilean got up off the floor to stand before him. "Angus McTern, so help me, if you go to sleep now, I'll hit *you* with the candlestick."

"Please do," he mumbled. "Then I could sleep for sure."

She pulled back her foot and kicked his shin, just as she'd done twice before. But she forgot that she had on her nightgown, and her feet were bare.

The next moment she was hobbling about the room in tears of pain. "I think my toes are broken. Your shin is as hard as stone." She sat down on the end of the bed to examine her foot.

Angus couldn't help smiling. She looked sweet in her white nightgown, holding her foot and looking at it. He pushed himself out of the chair, sat down beside her, lifted her foot, and pulled each of her toes. "None of them is broken."

She looked at him, his eyes red from weariness, holding her small foot in his big hand, and said, "Could you please tell me what is going on? Why did you hit James and who is the woman on the marriage certificate?"

He put her foot down, but stayed seated beside her. In her nightclothes she looked, if possible, even more beautiful. "I didn't trust him so I followed him, and I heard him talking about his wife who is the daughter of an earl."

"But my father wasn't an earl."

"I know," Angus said. "That's the point."

Edilean was at last beginning to understand. She looked at James lying on the floor, still unconscious. "My friend, his cousin, told me that James was holding out for a woman with a title."

"But he agreed to marry you for the money," Angus said softly, looking at her hair in the candlelight. He raised his hand to touch it but dropped it when she turned back to him.

"I heard James tell the men to put the gold on the ship. Was he planning to sail off with his *wife* and *my* gold?"

"He was," Angus said softly.

"But he can't do that," she said. "That gold belongs to me, not to him."

"It's called thievery and it's been done for a while now."

"Will you please stop treating me as though I'm a silly child? What am I supposed to do now?"

"I think you should go to America on your own. Your dowry is already on the ship, and the passage is booked."

"Alone? I'm to go to a new country by myself?"

He looked at her beautiful face and thought how every fast-talking, dishonest cad in the country would go after her, and she'd fall for the first pair of blue eyes she saw. "Just be careful about the men who will flock around you," Angus said.

"What does that mean? You make me sound like a pile of oats."

"Rich oats."

Edilean leaned back on her arm to look at him. "Why are your clothes torn, and what's that mark on your cheek?"

"I, uh . . ." Angus began, trying to come up with a lie.

"You got those papers from his wife, didn't you?"

"I did."

Edilean got off the bed and put her hands on her hips. "What enchantment does this woman have that she's taken the man I love and . . . and *you*?"

"Me?" he asked, astonished, but then his eyes began to twinkle. "It's not so much her virtues as it is . . . well, lass . . ." He made a movement with his hands to show a huge bosom.

"That's it?" Edilean said. "You and James fell for a woman with great—"

When she realized Angus was again teasing her, she shook her head in disgust, then looked at James on the floor. "I can't go to America alone. I can't do it. I've never done anything alone before." She looked back at him. "You'll have to go to the ship's captain and tell him that I want my gold back."

"And who should I tell him says that? Mrs. Harcourt? That gold on the ship is under *his* name, not yours. If you or I tried to take it off, they'd shoot us."

"But how will I live here without money? I can't very well go back to my uncle's house, now can I?"

"No, you canna. You have to do what I tell you

and that's to get on that ship by yourself. Tell them you're Mrs. Harcourt and that you're a widow."

"But what if the captain knows her or James?"

"Wear a veil. And add some padding to make yourself look bigger. Better yet, tell the captain that you're leaving because Harcourt got married."

"I don't understand," she said, then her eyes widened. "Oh, no, you don't. I'm not getting on that ship as James's . . . as his mistress."

"It's only for a few weeks. When you get to America you can be whoever you want to be. Change your name. You'll have the gold and you'll be well set up."

"Then what do I do? Marry one of those men in the New World? Savages is what my uncle says they are."

"Then why did you want to go in the first place?" Angus half yelled. He was still sitting on the end of the bed and all he had to do was fall back into its softness and close his eyes.

Reluctantly, he made himself get off the bed. "I think—" he began, but stopped because out of his shirt had fallen one of the handbills he'd torn off a wall.

Edilean picked it up and looked at it. "This is the picture I drew of you from memory. I think it's a good likeness, don't you?" When he just stood there staring at her, she looked back at the handbill and realized what it was. "This is serious," she whispered. "You have to get out of here. You *have* to leave Scotland."

"I can go to Edinburgh or to the Highlands. I can—"

"No you can't," she said as she stood close in front of him, her eyes big. "You don't know my uncle as I do."

"I've known him a great deal longer than you have."

"This isn't a matter of time, this is a matter of knowing him *well*," she almost shouted. "You can't stay here. My uncle will hunt you down."

"I'll be all right, lass," he said, smiling and wanting to touch her so badly that it was like a pain in his chest.

Behind them, James groaned and Angus reached for the candlestick.

9

"DON'T YOU DARE!" she said, then went to the bedside table, got the bottle of laudanum, and poured it into a glass of water. "Hold him up while I get this down him."

Angus did what she said. "So you didn't drink this as he told you to?"

"No. I don't like that concoction. It makes me dizzy. Here, James, darling, drink the wine. That's a good boy."

"You've forgiven him?" Angus asked incredulously.

"Ha!" Edilean pinched James's arm hard. "That will cause him a bruise tomorrow."

"Oh, aye, it will," Angus said.

"If you start laughing at me again I'll not help you get away."

"You help me?" he asked.

"Yes," she said as she stood up. James's arm had been across her but she let it fall to the floor. "Hope his wrist breaks," she muttered. "While you've been lolling about in the chair and lusting over my foot, I've been making a plan."

"Lolling?" he said as he put James's head on the floor. "Lusting? You are *not* talking as a lady should."

"In the last few months I've had too many horrible things happen to me to be ladylike. If I were a lady I'd not let you stay in my room while I'm in my night wear."

"That you wouldn't, but I like that thing you have on."

"You liked his wife too and if you step closer to me I'll scream."

"That's the second time tonight a woman's said that to me."

At that, Edilean turned her back on him and folded her arms across her chest.

"All right," Angus said, but he couldn't keep the laughter out of his voice. "I apologize. Please forgive me. Now what is it that you have to say? What is this plan of yours?"

Turning, Edilean looked at James, then at Angus. "I know what we're going to do."

"*We* are not going to do anything. *You* are going to get on that ship and sail to America, then you're going to—"

"You're going to be my husband."

"What?"

"We'll say that you're James's brother. If the captain has met James, we'll just say that there was a misunderstanding and that his brother Angus is the one who is going across the ocean."

"Me be your husband?" Angus said. "Have you lost your mind? How can I be your husband? Look at me."

"You'll wear James's clothes. If he put my gold on the ship, he's probably put his clothes on board too. You'll wear what he has on now, then later you'll have his wardrobe." She walked around him. "We have to clean you up. A bath, a shave; we'll wash that hair of yours."

"A bath? Are you mad, woman? I'll catch my death."

"You're going to die a worse death if my uncle finds you."

"I don't like this."

"You think I do? The man I loved . . ." She kicked at James's foot, but he just smiled and curled up on the floor. He looked quite happy. She looked back at Angus. "You're right. We don't want people to see you. My likeness of you is much too good. We'll need help for a bath, so we'll have to forgo it."

Angus's look let her know he thought her idea was preposterous. "How am I to shave? I brought no razor with me."

"Obviously, you wouldn't know how to use it if you had one."

Angus backed toward the door. "Somehow, I'm going to return to my own people. They need me."

"Balderdash!" Edilean said. "They'll be quite fine without you."

Angus backed away from her, but he put his

hand up to his beard. Considering that half of Scotland was looking for a man with a full beard and wild hair, it might not be a bad idea if he shaved.

As for the clothes, he looked at James curled on the floor and was sure that his waistcoat was silk. What would a man like Angus be doing wearing silk?

"Well," she said, "I'm waiting. What do you have to say for yourself? Are you a coward or do you have the courage to go to a country where you know no one?"

"I canna do that," he said, "but perhaps to shave and look different from the picture you drew of me would be good. Tell me, lass, what possessed you to draw a likeness of me? Did you plan to put it under your pillow so you'd dream of me?"

"I don't have time to deal with your vanity. You have to make a decision now. And, no, I won't help you shave and cut your hair if you aren't going to America with me."

"You're going to shave me?" he asked, his eyes teasing. "Perhaps I should take a bath after all. I'd like your help with that."

"You are trying my patience. You're allowed no more jokes; you have to decide. If you don't, you're going out that door and I'll never see you again."

"Not even one?" he asked. "Every Scotsman needs—"

Edilean went to the door, threw it open, and stood there, waiting for him to leave.

Angus didn't move. He knew he should. If he had

any sense he would leave the room and never look back, but there was a big part of him that knew this was an opportunity that he'd have only once in his life. No matter what he did now, he knew he couldn't go back home. He couldn't go to his sister, and he'd never again toss her children aloft. He'd never again see his uncle Malcolm or any of the rest of the McTern clan.

"Well?" Edilean asked. "Are you going or staying?"

"I guess I'll stay," he said softly.

"You'll go to America with me?"

"Aye, lass, I will."

Edilean turned her back to him as she closed the door and tried to compose her face so he'd not see her joy. She knew she couldn't stay in England or Scotland, but the thought of going to a new country by herself was almost more than she could bear. When she turned back to him, she had her emotions under control. She looked at him in speculation as she thought how she was going to transform him into looking as though James's fine clothes weren't alien to him. But Edilean had nothing with her. She'd worn her nightgown under her dress, and she had a tortoiseshell comb that she'd put into her pocket, but she had no scissors or razor.

As she looked at him she saw his eyes beginning to close. Heaven help her but he was falling asleep standing on his feet! "How did you get the papers from James's"—she nearly choked on the word—"from his wife?"

"Laudanum," he mumbled. "Harcourt passes it out to all his women. He must grow the poppies in his back garden."

"If James could afford a garden, I wouldn't be in this mess," Edilean said. "Are you telling me that she's still asleep?"

"I hope so."

She put her hand on the small of his back and pushed him toward the door. "I want you to go back into her room and get what I can use. I need scissors and a comb and a good, sturdy brush, as well as shaving gear."

"How am *I* to find these things?" he asked, waking up a bit. "I don't know lady's things."

"If you ever cut your hair, you'd know that men also use a comb. And a razor." As she looked at him she knew that he'd never get all the things they'd need. "How did you get into the bedroom?"

"Through the window. But I went out the door. If she's still asleep, the door is unlocked."

"Then I'll go with you. Here, help me get James's jacket off."

"You want to undress the man?"

"Please don't start your prudery on me. I'm going to put the jacket on over my nightdress and we're going down to raid that woman's room."

"You should put on your clothes," he said rather stiffly.

"I don't have time to lace myself into a corset, and I'd never fit into my dress if I don't put it on. Hurry up! It's only a few hours 'til dawn, then we must get on the ship."

Angus shook his head a few times to clear it of sleep, then helped her get the jacket off of James. Edilean gave him another pinch on his arm when he had only the shirt on. "Dishonorable man!" she said.

"You fell out of love with him soon enough," he said.

"He married someone else and stole my dowry. Those are two things a woman cannot abide."

"I'll remember that the next time a woman loves me."

"You should," she said as she slipped her arms into the heavy coat, and ran her hands down the sleeves. Whatever else was said about James, he had taste. "Are you ready?"

He was smiling at her. She looked good in her long white gown with the man's jacket over it. The coat was dark red, with a lining of burgundy silk, and the colors suited her. He picked up the candle and went out the door, Edilean behind him.

She had no shoes on, and the minute her feet touched the dirty hall floor, she let out a cry, but Angus gave her a hard look and she quit complaining. They went down three flights of stairs in order to reach the ground floor, and Angus went to the door at the far end. He put his fingers to his lips, motioning her to be quiet as he slowly opened the door. He listened for a moment, heard Harcourt's wife's slight snore, then waved at Edilean that it was all right to go inside.

When they were inside and the door closed behind them, the first thing she did was walk to the bed to see the woman. Angus couldn't help himself, but he stopped her. He knew there was no reason for her not to take a peek at James's wife, but he didn't want her to. He knew she'd laugh and be relieved that James was now stuck with an ugly wife, but Angus didn't want Edilean to see the truth.

He caught her arm and motioned her to the trunk in the corner of the room. It was small, with a dome-shaped lid, and he had an idea that all their possessions that weren't already on the ship were in it and it was ready to be taken when they left in the morning.

When Angus nodded toward the trunk, she went to it and opened it. On the top was a leather case containing shaving gear, and under it looked to be folded-up dresses. When Edilean reached for one of them, Angus shook his head that there wasn't time to go through the garments. He well knew that she had only the clothes she'd been wearing when she ran away, but he also knew the dresses in the trunk would be much too big for her.

Reluctantly, Edilean left the dress where it was and took a small sewing kit that was tucked into a tray on the side. It would have scissors in it.

When Angus started out the door, he thought Edilean was right behind him, but when he looked back, she was at the bed, moving the blanket back to get a look at the sleeping woman. Angus caught her hand just as she was about to see the woman's face.

He held her hand until they were outside the door in the hallway.

"I just wanted to see her!" she said in a loud whisper. "What's so wrong with that? Both you and James have raved about her beauty and how you want to spend your lives with her, so it was only natural that I'd want to have a look at her."

"Spend my life with her?" Angus whispered as they started up the stairs. "Are you truly mad? Were you bitten by a rabid dog?"

"Yes, one named James Harcourt," Edilean muttered angrily.

Angus paused on the stairs, held the candle aloft, and said, "I do believe, lass, that you made a joke."

"So I did. Maybe it's a disease and I'm catching it from you," she said as she went up the stairs past him, but she was smiling.

Once they were back in the room, Edilean took off the coat, told Angus to sit down, then walked around him, looking at his head and trying to figure out how to go about it.

"This is more than you can do," he said. "I think we should forget this and I should head out to the Highlands tonight."

She put her hand on his chest to push him back in the chair. "The best thing would be to shave your head and get a wig."

Angus put his hand up to his head in protest.

"But we don't have time for that. First, I must

comb it, then I'll cut it. Once it's tied back, I'll start on your face. This is going to take hours."

Angus wasn't sure if he'd like someone fiddling with his hair, but the moment she touched him, he relaxed.

"Go on, go to sleep," she said. "I don't need you to make fun of me while I do this job."

"Go to sleep with a woman with scissors so near my face? I couldn't trust you so," he said, half teasing, half serious. But in the next minute his head nodded forward, and he began to doze.

Edilean was glad he'd gone to sleep because she could at last relax. It took a lot of energy to pretend to be strong and know what she should do with her life—and what another person should do. In one night she'd gone from being in love with James Harcourt—she glanced at him, still on the floor—to being alone in the world. All she seemed to have now was this man, who'd made it clear many times that he thought she was useless in the world, someone he had to look after night and day.

When Angus's head tipped forward on his chest, she got the pitcher of water, filled a glass, and began to slowly comb the thousands of knots out of Angus's long, thick hair. She hadn't told him, but she'd never been this close to a man before. Oh, she'd had a few moments with men who stole kisses when no one was looking, James included, but she'd certainly never been in a room alone with a man and touching his hair.

It took over an hour to get the tangles out.

Twice she'd had to use the scissors and snip away a knot that she couldn't loosen. And several times, he'd nearly awakened when she pulled too hard. But she'd been able to at last get the comb through it, then she trimmed it so it was just shoulder length. She snatched the black silk ribbon off James and put it on Angus's hair.

When she finished, she stepped to the front of him to have a look. She could see his forehead now and saw how well shaped it was. She ran her fingers over his cheek, then drew back when he stirred in his sleep and almost woke.

Next, she had to tackle that hideous beard of his. She was sure that he'd wake up as she began to use the scissors on it, but he didn't. Yet somehow she knew that if she were to do something like, say, cock a gun, he'd wake in a second. It made her feel good that he trusted her so much that he allowed her to use scissors near his face.

It took a while to cut the whiskers down to a length where she could shave them. She had amassed a great pile of hair by then and she gathered it up and tossed it out the window. As she did, she looked at the sky. Morning was coming and with it the sun. It wouldn't be long before they would be on the ship.

When Edilean turned back, she drew in her breath. Angus was still asleep, his head against the back of the chair. His hair was no longer standing out around his head but was tied back neatly at the nape of his neck. His beard didn't spread out until it covered even his neck but was now just a thick stubble of black whiskers.

She blinked a few times, looking at him hard. She wasn't sure, but she thought maybe he was handsome. No, not just handsome, but beautiful. Perhaps even better-looking than James, but dark, with black hair and dark lashes.

She'd often seen her father shave when she was a girl, and she hoped she remembered how to do it. She had no hot water, so she'd have to make do with cold water and James's scented lather.

She put the cold lather on his face and he didn't so much as stir, but when she held the long straight razor to him, he grabbed her wrist, his eyes open and staring. "If I'm to cut your throat, you must release me," she said calmly.

"Aye," he murmured, "murder me in my sleep. I nearly forgot the plan." He dropped her wrist and went back to sleep.

She marveled at how he could sleep—and joke—through all this, but he did. He was perfectly still as she shaved him, removing every trace of the hair on his face and neck. When she finished, she stood back and looked at him in disbelief. Angus had heavy black brows, thick lashes, a perfectly formed nose and lips. . . . She didn't think she'd ever seen such beautiful lips on a man. They were full and soft, and as sculpted as those on a statue. Beside him, James was ordinary-looking.

He must be aware of this, she thought. No one could look as he did and not be aware of it. Had he grown that enormous beard to hide his face?

"Mr. McTern," she said softly, "it's time to get up now. You have to get dressed. We'll get on the ship soon."

He didn't move.

"Angus!" she said sharply. "Wake up!"

Slowly, he opened his eyes, and looked at her with a smile. When he turned his head he felt the lightness, and ran his hand over his bare face. "What have you done to me?"

"What should have been done long ago," she said. "You have to stop sleeping now and get ready to go. We have to get James's clothes off of him and I have to get dressed. I apologize but you're going to have to help me with the strings to my corset."

"To your . . . ?"

When she looked at him she could see that his face had pinkened. "My goodness, McTern of McTern, are you blushing?"

"Nay," he said, but he turned away as he stood up. "You'll have to show me how to . . . to do what you need to have done."

"I will," she said, hiding her smile.

She got the clothes she'd worn the day before out of the wardrobe and laid them out on the bed, watching Angus as she did so. She would have thought he'd want to see himself in a mirror. It must have been a long time since he'd seen himself without that beard, but as far as she could tell, he showed no evidence that he was even curious.

She watched as he bent and grabbed James under the arms, then hauled him onto the bed. For a moment Angus just stood there, looking at the man lying on the bed, happily asleep.

"I don't like this," Angus said. "To steal a man's clothes like this is not right."

Edilean rolled her eyes, and went to James and loosened his cravat. "Then I'll undress him."

"You'll not," Angus said, sounding shocked by the idea. "I'll tend to him. You go and do what you need to."

Edilean glanced out the window. The pink of dawn was approaching. "I think we should go down to the wife's room as soon as we're dressed. I'm sure James will have someone coming to rouse him to get him to the ship on time. He likes to stay up late and hates to wake up in the morning."

"Good idea," Angus said.

He was on the other side of the bed, and the hangings kept her from seeing what he was doing, but she could hear the movement of cloth as he took off his own clothes and put on James's. An unusual feeling was running through Edilean. Just a few feet from her was a man in his undergarments. And not just any man, but one who had been kind to her. Well, not always, but in the end he'd taken care of her. If it hadn't been for him, she'd now be asleep in the inn and James and his wife would soon sail off with her dowry.

"I need help with the laces," she said softly. She'd put the corset on over her nightgown, but the laces were in the back. "Should I come 'round there?"

Angus took the few steps to get to the foot of the bed and Edilean could only stare at him. He had on James's tight tan breeches and his big-sleeved shirt and nothing else. A lifetime of being outside, of riding horses and climbing, had given him thighs that were heavy with muscle.

Angus was smiling at her in a way that let her know he knew what she thought of him.

She wasn't about to tell him that he looked so good he took her breath away. She turned her back to him, presenting the laces for him to fasten. "When we get to the ship it will be better if you don't speak," she said.

"Not a word?" he asked as he grabbed the sturdy laces and pulled the stiff corset together.

"Your accent and the way you say things will give you away. No, it's better that you let me do all the talking."

Angus gave a jerk on the corset laces that nearly broke her ribs.

"Do you mean to cut me in half?"

"I thought you'd want a waist as small as that of other women. I do apologize. I'll loosen the strings."

Edilean grit her teeth. "You can tighten them more than that."

"Ah, a medium waist is what you want."

"I—" she began, but knew this was her own fault.

She held on to the bedpost as he pulled. "All right! You look good. And you can talk all you want. What do I care? Do a dance on crossed swords for all it matters to me."

When he tied the strings at the bottom, she looked at him and his eyes had that look of teasing that she was beginning to know well. "You're a dreadful man, you know that?"

He went back to the other side of the bed, picked up the waistcoat, and put it on while Edilean stepped into her dress. Yesterday she'd done her best to clean it of the sawdust, but she could still see that it wasn't at its best. She hoped that there was a wardrobe full of clothes on board the ship. She knew she'd have to take the dresses in, at least in the bustline, but she could do it.

When she was dressed and her hair smoothed back, she went to Angus. He was leaning against the bedpost, his eyes closed, and his vest buttoned crookedly.

"Come on now, wake up," she said as she unfastened his vest, and buttoned it straight.

"I had a dream about you," he said softly, looking at her in the candlelight and the pink dawn that was coming through the window.

"Was it a good dream?" she asked as she held up James's coat for him to put on.

"The best. You and I were together in a field. I could see it all clearly. It wasn't Scotland, but a place that I'd never seen before."

"Maybe it was America."

"Aye," he said gently, and reached out to touch her hair. They stood there for a moment looking into each other's eyes and she swayed toward him. "When we get to America I'll give you some of my gold and you can—" She broke off at the look he gave her.

"Ever even mention such a thing to me again, lass, and I'll have no more to do with ye."

She could tell by the anger in his eyes how much he meant his words. She started to apologize, but in the next moment a ray of sunlight came into the room and her opportunity was gone.

"We must go!" Angus said.

He grabbed James's boots in one hand, and her hand with his other, while she snatched the bundle of shaving and sewing gear.

They ran down the stairs, Edilean trailing behind him, never letting go of his hand. When they got to the room, they had just shut the door behind them and were standing there breathless when the landlord pounded on the door. "Your carriage is here!" he shouted, seeming not to be concerned that he might wake his other guests.

Angus left the room, Edilean behind him, but when she saw the coachman standing in the doorway, she ran back into the room, closed the bed curtains, then told the coachman to get the trunk in the corner, and not to wake her sleeping sister. Edilean made sure Angus didn't hear her do this, as she knew he wouldn't like it. She was taking the woman's clothes. But Edilean didn't know what had been put on the ship. She didn't want to spend the several weeks of the voyage in only one gown.

Outside the inn a beautiful hired carriage with four prancing horses was waiting for them. "James spares no expense for himself, does he?" Edilean said in sarcasm.

"Do you think we might get something to eat before we go?" Angus asked as he tried to move his arms in the tight jacket.

"Do you ever think of anything besides food and sleep?" Edilean snapped at him.

"Aye, I do," Angus said slowly, "but not when I'm with a woman who's as ill tempered as you are. Did I tie your laces too tight?"

She leaned back against the seat and closed her eyes for a moment. "I'm just nervous, is all. I know my uncle knows who James is from the letter he stole from me and he—"

"Did you tell Harcourt this?"

"Yes," Edilean said. "When I wrote James the second time I told him everything, but my uncle could have made some inquiries to find out about James having booked passage on the ship. He could—"

She didn't say any more because the coach suddenly came to a stop and she heard men shouting.

"Say nothing," Angus said. "I will deal with this."

"You? But—" She broke off at a look from him.

The door to the carriage was thrown open and two rough-looking men peered inside. Angus didn't move, just stayed leaning back against the seat, seeming to pluck a bit of lint off his cuff.

"Have you seen this man?" one of the men said as he held up the picture of Angus.

"I should think not," Angus said, barely glancing at the handbill. "I would have shouted for help if I'd seen such a ruffian."

On the seat across from him, Edilean's mouth dropped open in surprise. Angus's normally thick Scottish burr was gone, and he sounded as though he'd been raised in the salons of London.

"Would you be so good as to shut the door, my good man?" Angus said as he held up a lace-trimmed handkerchief to his nose. "The dust is not good for me."

The man, with two teeth missing on the upper front, looked at Edilean, then down at something in his hand. "Here, she looks like the lady that's run away from her uncle. He's givin' a reward for her return."

"Are you saying that my wife looks like someone's niece? And he has money? I say, old man, where does he live? We shall visit him and tell him this is his lost niece. Do you think he would believe us?"

"Bleedin' fob," the man said in disgust as he slammed the carriage door. "Go on with ya."

Angus shoved the handkerchief back in his pocket and looked at Edilean, who was staring at him with wide eyes. "You have something to say?"

"No. Nothing," she said, blinking quickly. "But where did you learn that?"

"From listening. It's nay so hard to do." His heavy accent was back. "Would you like for me to talk like Harcourt all the time?"

"No," she said quickly, "I wouldn't."

Smiling, he turned away to look out the window, and a moment later, he said, "I can see the ship. We're almost there."

10

EDILEAN WAS VERY nervous and she kept glancing at Angus as they made their way up the gangplank to the ship.

"Calm down," Angus said. "You're shaking so much I fear you'll fall into the bay."

"What if the captain knows James and says that we've kidnapped him?"

"How is he going to know that?" Angus asked in astonishment, then smiled. "Would you like for me to do the talking?" As he said it, he held out his arm and she slipped hers through it.

She knew he was getting her back for her saying that she should do all the talking, but she was too nervous to respond.

"Ah, Mr. and Mrs. Harcourt," Captain Inges said as soon as they stepped aboard. "At last we meet." He held out his hand to shake theirs and reminded them of his name. He was an older man, quite tall, and with a pleasant smile—and he couldn't take his eyes off Edilean. "I had no idea that you were so charming. I had heard . . . differently."

Angus put his hand over hers on his arm and smiled lovingly at her. "My dear, has that rascally brother of yours been telling tales about you again?" He looked at the captain. "Were you told that she was tall, heavy, and not the best to look at?"

The captain smiled in understanding. "Yes, I believe I was the recipient of such a jest, but I'm happy to see that it was just that. You must want to get settled, so I'll have the first mate show you to your cabin. I hope you'll dine with me this evening, and perhaps you would like breakfast in your quarters."

"Yes," Edilean said quickly, still holding on to Angus's arm. "My husband is very hungry and we would like something right away."

"Then this way, please."

But before they took a step, the captain frowned as one of his officers whispered something to him. Captain Inges looked back at Angus and Edilean. "I fear that I have some bad news. As you know, we are not usually a passenger ship, but sometimes, as in your case, I do take a few people with me. However, on this voyage, I've had the great misfortune to be assigned nine female prisoners to take to America."

Turning, Edilean looked down at the dock and saw several women in leg irons looking up at them. She moved closer to Angus.

"I apologize," Captain Inges said, "and I would understand if you'd prefer to postpone your voyage."

"No!" Angus and Edilean said in unison.

"We'll be all right," Angus said. "We're not so squeamish as to let a few prisoners bother us, are we, dearest?"

When Edilean said nothing, he saw she was watching the women as they started coming up the gangplank. Most of the women were dirty and looked exhausted and forlorn, but the third one in line was looking about her with an insolent smile, as though she thought everything going on was a joke. She was a tall woman, inches taller than Edilean, and she was plump and had a pretty, pink-cheeked face.

When the woman saw Angus, her eyes bulged for a moment, then she lowered her lashes in a coquettish way.

Edilean moved closer to him and held on to his arm tighter. Angus smiled down at her, thinking she was afraid of the prisoners. He stepped back to let them pass, keeping his face straight when a couple of the women made remarks about him.

"Cor, but ain't he a beauty?" one of them said.

When at last the prisoners and their two guards were past and the women had been led down into the ship, the captain apologized again. "I am so sorry for this. We will, of course, do our best to keep them separate from you."

"What have they done?" Edilean asked, looking at the last woman to go down the ladder.

"Anything short of murder. Thievery mostly. They weren't bad enough to hang, just to banish to America. They'll never be allowed back into England."

"And that's punishment for them?" Edilean asked.

"The judges think so, but personally I like the new country, especially Virginia."

Edilean's eyes widened. "You'll have to tell us every word about it," she said as she looked up at Angus. "Won't he, darling?" He was staring at where the women had gone down and frowning.

"Then I can look forward to seeing you this evening for dinner?"

"We would love to, wouldn't we?" Again, Edilean glanced at Angus, but he was still frowning. She pulled sharply on his arm.

"Oh, aye," he said, and seemed to come back to where he was.

"Captain Inges has asked us to dine with him. We would like that, wouldn't we?"

"Oh, aye," he said. "That would be—" He seemed to realize that he'd lapsed back into his accent so he corrected himself. "We would like that," he said in the accent of James Harcourt.

"Then I'll let Mr. Jones show you to your cabin."

Edilean and Angus followed the young man down the ladder at one end of the ship to belowdecks. When he opened a door, Edilean smiled. The entire end of their room was window.

"How lovely," she said to the young officer.

"This is usually the captain's cabin, but he's given it to you for this journey. You must have done something he liked."

"I'll need a hammock in here," Angus said abruptly.

"A hammock?" the young officer asked.

"Aye . . . Yes. That is what the men sleep in, don't they?" There was one narrow wooden bed at the end of the room. "That's too short for me," Angus said.

"But the captain had it made for him and he's—" the young man began.

"My husband is being kind," Edilean said. "It's because of me. I am, well . . . with child, and he fears for my health so he needs his own bed."

"Ah, I see," the young man said, smiling. "I'll see what I can do. And here is your breakfast. Enjoy the fruit, as it won't last long."

A sailor brought in a platter of bread and boiled eggs and cherries, plus big mugs of ale, and set it on the round table by the glassed-in window.

When they were alone, both Angus and Edilean went to the table and nearly attacked the food. "With child," Angus said. "That was fast."

"Not as fast as you and those women prisoners," she said as she peeled an egg. "What possessed you to stare at them like that?"

"I was thinking how close that was to being me. If things had turned out differently, *I* could have been in that hold."

"But not with those women," Edilean said.

"No, not with those women." He was smiling at her. "So what will we do on this trip? It'll take three weeks, maybe even six if the weather is bad. How will you occupy yourself?"

"Reading, I suppose. I wonder if the captain has any books he could lend us? Mayhap you could read to me."

He arched an eyebrow as he took the peeled egg she handed him.

"And what is that look for?"

"When would I have gone to school to learn reading and writing?"

Edilean paused with a cherry in her mouth, her hand on the stem. She chewed a bit, and removed the pit. "Then I will be your teacher."

"I do not need you to be my teacher," he said, his face contorted into a scowl.

"Isn't it interesting how your humor completely leaves you when *you* are not in charge? Why does the idea that I—worthless, good-for-nothing me—could teach great, glorious you something infuriate you?"

Angus bent his head closer to his plate, but she could see that the scowl was gone. "Glorious, am I?"

"In your own eyes, you seem to be," she said. "Wait! You can't take the last of that fruit!"

"Do you think not?" he said as he grabbed a handful of cherries and turned away from her.

"You pig!" She ran around the little table to reach for them.

Angus held them aloft and she grabbed his wrist—just as he transferred them to his other hand.

"You selfish . . . Scotsman!" she said, reaching for the cherries.

He was laughing. "Is that the worst you can think

to call me? Did you learn nothing in that rich school you went to?"

"Not anything that I'd tell a *man*," she said, then made a lunge at him that landed them chest to chest as she reached up to his hand to get the cherries.

His face was less than an inch from hers and she could smell the lather she'd used to shave him. And there was another smell about him, that of Man.

"Are you asking for more than you can handle?" he asked softly, then he moved a bit as though he meant to kiss her.

Edilean turned her head, as though she were going to accept his kiss, but then she grabbed the cherries and sprinted away from him. "These are sweeter," she said as she put a cherry in her mouth.

"How do you know what a fruit that you haven't tried is like?"

"Great imagination." She finished the cherries. "Mmmm, so delicious."

Angus started to go after her, but he stopped himself. Instead, he sat there looking at her with serious eyes.

"I'm so happy to be away from all of it that I feel that I could . . . I could almost fly." For a moment she put her arms out and danced about the small room. "I'm not married to any of those awful men and I'm going to a whole new country." Stopping, she looked at him and saw that he was frowning.

"Nay," he said, "this canna be."

She sat down on the chair across from him. "What can't be?"

"This," he said softly. "This teasing, this . . . this playing and grappling, and touching."

"You don't like it?" she asked, smiling at him through her lashes.

"I like it too much."

"Well, then, what could be the problem?"

"Stop it!"

"Stop what?" she asked, looking at him.

"I am not one of your dandies who you can flirt and tease to your heart's content. For all that you have me dressed as a popinjay, I'm still Angus McTern, a man who's spent more time outdoors than I have inside a house. And I've never spent any time in the fancy houses that you've lived in."

"So now I'm a snob?" she said. "Shall we add that to the list of things you've found wrong with me? According to you, I can do nothing, have no talents that are of any use to anyone, and now you tell me you think I'm a snob."

"Please don't pretend to misunderstand me," he said, leaning toward her, his face serious. "It was your idea that I travel with you as your husband, and I agreed because there was no time to do anything else."

"And you needed to get out of Scotland," she said.

"Aye, I needed to get out of Scotland, but if I'd gone on a ship by myself I would have traveled in the bowels with the sailors, not here, in this." He motioned to the beautiful windows in the room.

With a sigh, Edilean leaned back in the chair. "What is it that you're trying to say to me?"

"That I don't come from your world, and that I don't know these games you people play. I don't—"

"What does that mean? 'You people.' How am I different from you?"

He took his time in answering her. "I'll stay with you in this room on one condition, and that's that you don't continue playing the temptress."

"The what?" she asked, already offended by what he was saying.

"A temptress, a woman who entices a man into doing what he shouldn't do. An Eve with her apple held out to him, tempting him into sin."

"Why you . . ." she began, and crossed her arms over her chest. "I do apologize for trying to make you sin. Tell me, Mr. McTern, what can I do to keep you sin-free and pure?"

"It is *you* I am trying to keep pure," he said in a low voice. "You're a beautiful young woman and just looking at you is enough to drive a man mad with desire. I don't know how I'm going to stand being in this room with you day after day and not . . . not disrobe you. I'm saying that if I'm to stay so close to you, you must treat me as . . . as your brother. And I must try to think of you as my sister, although that will be nearly impossible. Am I making myself clear?"

"I, uh . . ." Edilean began but could think of nothing else to say. Flirting was something she was good at, something that was much done at the houses of the girlfriends where she stayed. In fact, at school she'd often given lessons to her less fortunate classmates on how to flirt. She couldn't be angry at him for saying what she knew to be true. She *had* been flirting. And, besides, it was impossible to be angry at a man who was telling her that he thought she was so beautiful he was having trouble controlling himself.

"If you don't do this, I'll go below and sleep in a hammock. Do you understand?"

"Yes," she said. If he'd been any of the other men she'd met in her life, she would have batted her lashes at him and asked if this order meant there were not even to be any kisses. But when she looked at Angus's handsome face, she didn't dare. It occurred to her that she was now dealing with a man, while they had been boys.

"I'll make it as easy for you as I can," she said. "I'll behave myself. No laughter, no teasing, no wrestling. Is that what you want me to say?"

"I want you to say . . ." He looked at her across the table. He felt bad that his words had taken her from wanting to fly because of such sublime happiness to now being so serious. "I'm sorry for my Scots gruffness, lass, but I'm a man and I canna bear being so close to you."

"I understand," she said as she looked down at her hands on her lap, then back up at him. "But what if you and I fell in love?"

For a moment, Angus looked shocked, then he smiled at her in a patronizing way. "You didn't love me when I was wearing what you called a woman's dress. And not long ago you were saying that you hated me. Do you know what a time I had getting off that roof after you locked me there?"

"No," she said. "I was too busy trying to keep from freezing in my wet clothes from where you'd thrown me in the horse trough."

"That's not a deed I'm proud of," he said. "But, lass, you must listen to what I'm saying. You look at me now in these fine clothes, with my hair tied back and my face shaved, and you laugh and flirt with me and you talk about love. If you love anything, it's the clothes, certainly not the man. Under this silk, I'm still just a poor Scotsman and I'd embarrass you in front of your fine friends."

"I think you're my—"

"Your savior," Angus said. "You think I'm the man who rescued you from a fate worse than death. Aye, I know all that, lass, but never forget that I did no such thing. All I was going to do was get the minister drunk and maybe save you from one night. It was an accident that I got on that wagon and found you in that coffin."

"Nasty, dirty thing," Edilean muttered. "I think it was half full of sawdust and when I got in it the dust billowed up around me and nearly smothered me. But by then I'd already taken that awful laudanum James had given me, so I could barely stay awake long enough to pull the lid over me."

"The fright you gave us when you sat up in that

coffin!" Angus said. "I swear my heart stopped."

"You knew who I was, so you knew I wasn't dead."

"I thought maybe your uncle'd murdered you to get your dowry."

"So you thought I was a ghost?"

"I did until you started complaining about the dirt and telling me that I'd again done something you didn't like."

"I did, didn't I?" Edilean said. "I think it was the dust up my nose that woke me, and I heard shouting and my head ached. Then when I woke up and saw you there and not Shamus, I—"

"You could not have chosen anyone worse to help you. If you had combed all of Glasgow *and* Edinburgh, you could not have found anyone less heroic than Shamus."

"But you saved me—reluctantly, mind you—but you did save me, and now you tell me I must be careful not to touch you."

He could tell by her tone that she was laughing at him. "I'm saying that for my sanity, you must not tempt me more than I can bear."

"I will do my best," she said, smiling, "although I think the real reason you were staring at those women this morning was because of that pretty one with the fat chest."

"The—?" He was smiling. "Oh, aye, I do like a fat chest. More to strap into one of those whalebone things you wear." He glanced at her chest, which though not "fat" was certainly full enough.

"Now who is flirting and teasing?"

"Ah, but *you* are not tempted by me," Angus said. "That is a great difference." There was a knock on the door and he got up to answer it.

As he walked across the room, all six feet plus of him, she looked at the way the fabric clung to his heavily muscled thighs. She was not tempted by him? Was he insane?

"The captain had me bring these to you," the officer said. "He thought you might need them."

Behind him four seamen carried two heavy trunks.

"Put them in that corner," Edilean said from behind Angus. "And thank you for bringing them."

The seamen looked at Edilean as though they'd never seen a woman before, and backed out of the room with their caps in their hands.

"I guess if you were a sailor you'd be like those men," she said as she went to the trunks.

"If I were them and a beautiful woman was on the ship, I'd do what I could to get her to notice me."

"But not now and not me?" Edilean asked, curious.

Angus gave her a look of great sadness. "Alas, I have come to know you. Knowledge of the lies and betrayals, of the injustice done to you, hinders my advances."

Edilean couldn't help laughing. "As if you care! Shall we see what James has stolen for us?" As she said it, they felt the ship move, and for a moment she lost her balance and almost fell, but Angus caught her arm.

"Do you get seasick?" he asked.

"I don't know. I've only been on little boats on lakes that were as still as glass. What about you?"

"I don't know either," he said.

Smiling at each other, they turned their attention to the trunks and unfastened the latches. The one she opened had been in the room of James's wife.

Edilean gasped when she saw that in the bottom were folded what looked to be many dresses, each one more beautiful than the other.

Angus watched as she pulled one dress after another from the trunk and admired it, exclaiming over embroidered silks in beautiful colors of apricot and golden yellow. "These are divine," she said. "Truly beautiful. I've never seen dresses more exquisite than these. They're—"

She stopped when she saw some papers in the trunk, and as she read them, her face turned angry.

"What is it?"

"Look at this!" She thrust the papers at him.

"I can read the numbers, but I don't know what it says," he said stiffly.

"I can tell you what it says. That blasted—may he rot in hell!—James Harcourt charged all his wife's dresses to *me*. The name on these bills is *mine*."

Angus gave her a one-sided smile. "He thought he'd be gone so you'd have to pay for dresses that you never got, but now he'll be charged for dresses he doesn't have."

For a moment Edilean stared at him, then she started laughing. "That is good! My dressmaker in London said she is so sick of people not paying that she's hired men with clubs to go after them. I can assure you that *I* paid her in a very timely manner."

Angus threw back the lid to the second trunk, and when he looked inside he saw James's clothes. Digging down through them, he pulled a piece of paper from the bottom and handed it to her.

Edilean grinned. "Also charged to my account. James's name but mine under it as cosigner for his debt."

They laughed again, and she turned back to the trunk to see what else was in it. "Oh, my," she said when she got to the bottom. "Look at this." She opened a large, thin, dark blue box and held it out to him. "It's a parure."

"A paw-roo?" he asked, saying the word with the French pronunciation she gave it. "What's that?" He took the box from her and looked at the contents. Inside, neatly arranged on satin, was a matching set of diamond jewelry. There was a necklace with two strands, the bottom one making scallops on the edge, and three bracelets. The earrings had hanging diamonds, and a large brooch had a gem that was as big as his thumb.

"What is it?" he asked. "Other than jewelry, but is it something special?"

"James's new wife was an earl's daughter, wasn't she? It's my guess that this was her mother's and hers before her, and I'd be willing to bet that James knew nothing about it. If he had, I think he would have pawned it. Let me see it," she said, taking it from him, then she removed an earring and used her nails to unlatch a tiny hook. "See? They can be worn as drops or as a cluster." She put the earring back in its place. "I would imagine that all the pieces are like that. The brooch can probably be worn as it is or as two clips or as one smaller piece, and the necklace can probably be changed from one strand to two. Jewelers are such clever people." She handed the box back to him.

"What do I do with it? You can wear these to dinner tonight."

She was looking in the trunk. "I'd rather shave my head than wear any of those."

Angus carefully put the box on the floor beside her.

"You must keep them," she said.

"Me? What would I do with them?"

She gave him a look of astonishment. "Don't you know that wearing diamond earrings is the latest fashion for men in London? I'm sure the captain will have on his tonight."

Angus blinked a couple of times, then smiled. "Oh, lass, you almost had me that time. These things are for a woman and you should wear them."

Edilean sat back on the floor. "But I won't wear them. They belong to another woman and I won't have them on me."

He picked up the jewel case and started to put it

back into her trunk. "Then we'll send them back to her."

"They don't belong to her *that* much!" Edilean said. "For all I know, she and James were working together. I want you to take those jewels. If you won't take gold from me, then take those. Do what you want with them. Sell them and buy some land, some cows, pigs, whatever you want."

"Or give them to my wife?" he asked softly.

"It's my observation that your taste in women runs to ones who are too fat to get them around their necks," Edilean said, giving him a false smile.

He laughed. "I don't think—"

"Don't you *dare* tell me you can't keep them! You've done a lot and risked a great deal. You can't be so proud as to make yourself end up in a new country without a penny to your name. What will you do? Sell yourself as a bound man? It would be seven years before you're free. But then, perhaps your employer will be kind and not beat you too often, and maybe he'll give you a pound or two when you leave his employment."

"You have a sharp tongue on you."

"It's been sharpened by men who look at me and see only gold."

Angus didn't say anything for a moment but looked at her with soft eyes. Her hair was falling down about her face and he couldn't resist pushing it back behind her ear. "I see gold but not what you find in a bank. This is worth more than gold."

"*Dignitas praeter aurum*," Edilean said, translating what he'd said into Latin. For a moment they looked at each other in silence, then Edilean remembered all that he'd said to her just minutes ago about keeping her distance. She broke eye contact, looked at the dress on her lap, and held it up between them. "This woman is as big as you are. How will I ever make the dresses fit me?"

Angus put his hand on hers and made her lower the dress. "Thank you," he said. "I'll take the jewelry. It is more than generous of you to give me this."

To hide her blushes, she leaned over so her face was inside the trunk. "You gave up a great deal more for me than just a pile of ugly old jewelry."

"So that's it, is it? The lot of them are out of fashion?"

"Horribly so. My grandmother—if I had one—wouldn't wear those things." The lightness was back between them, and she was relieved. As she pulled the last gown out of the trunk, she said, "What will you do when you get to America?"

"I haven't had time to think about it." He stood up, stretching, towering over her. "I guess I'd like to buy a piece of land." He glanced at the jewel case on the floor by his feet. "I've thought that I might ask my sister to come to America to be with me."

"And Tam," Edilean said.

"Tam?" Angus asked. "The boy who was in love with you?"

"All the Scots were in love with me," she said. "Except you."

Angus smiled. "I think they were. Even my uncle Malcolm adored you."

She raised her hand to him, and as he helped pull her up, for a second they looked into each other's eyes.

"What do you say that we go to the top and see the wind in the sails?"

"I would love that."

"But I must keep you safe," he said, smiling at her. In the next second, he picked up the jewel set and looked about the room. He saw some cabinet doors under the big window, opened one, and put the case inside, standing it on its side so that it couldn't be seen at first glance.

"And why is my safety so important?" she asked when he joined her at the door.

"To protect my wee bairn," he said, as he offered her his arm and opened the door. They laughed together as they left the room.

11

As Captain Inges watched the young couple walk about the deck, he sighed. He and his wife had been like that once. He saw the way the tall Harcourt hovered over the beautiful young woman, his eyes only on her, listening to every word she said. As for her, she looked at him as though he'd hung the moon.

"Nice couple."

The captain turned to his first mate, Mr. Jones, and nodded. This was their third voyage together and he liked the young man. "Yes, they are. Reminds me of my wife and me when we were that age."

"I would like to find a woman who looked at me like that," Mr. Jones said.

"That, or would you like a woman who looks like her?"

"Both," Mr. Jones said, smiling. "Do you think they've been married long?"

"My guess is that it's been hours, but maybe it's been years. Who knows?"

He and Mr. Jones stood by the rail and watched

the young couple as they walked about the deck, looking at the sea that was rushing past them. The wind was good and they were moving quickly. At this rate they'd be in Boston in just three weeks.

When Mrs. Harcourt stood on tiptoes to look over the side of the ship, both the captain and Mr. Jones held their breaths. She looked so small and she was leaning over quite far. She must have worried Mr. Harcourt too because he put his hands on her waist and held her so she wouldn't fall. When she turned and said something to him, he shook his head no. She spoke again and he shook his head more vigorously. When she frowned at him, Mr. Harcourt's shoulders slumped for a moment, but then he lifted her up so she could see farther over the side. She held her arms straight out for a moment and let the wind hit her in the face.

When Mr. Harcourt put her down on deck again, the captain and Mr. Jones let out their pent-up breaths.

"She does get her way, doesn't she?" Mr. Jones said.

"I think perhaps that young man would do anything in the world for her. Walk into fire, throw himself in front of a cannon. Whatever she needed, he might do it."

"So would I," Mr. Jones said. "If I had a wife who looked like her I'd—"

"Mr. Jones," Captain Inges said, "I'm not talking about looks, I'm talking about love."

"Yes, sir," Mr. Jones said. "Excuse me, sir."

The captain left the deck and went below.

❦

"My wife told me that she can sing but I've never heard her," Angus said to the captain as they sat at the dining table with him and Mr. Jones.

"Haven't heard your own wife sing?" Mr. Jones asked in astonishment, and looked at the captain.

"We married quickly," Angus said.

"Yes," Edilean said. "Our first meeting was memorable and our second was explosive. We've rarely been apart since then."

Angus put his napkin to his lips to cover his smile at her words, and his eyes twinkled. In spite of his misgivings and apprehensions—none of which he'd told Edilean—he'd done well at the captain's dinner. There were just the four of them, the kindly captain, young Mr. Jones, and Edilean and Angus. He had been concerned about holding up his end of the conversation and being able to keep up the English accent he was using. Sometimes he forgot himself and lapsed back into his natural Scottish burr.

But he needn't have worried, for Edilean kept the talk going. As he watched her, he saw that she was adept at drawing people out. It had been his experience that pretty girls came to think that they didn't have to do anything but sit still and be seen. And due to some extensive traveling he'd done in his youth, he'd seen several lady hostesses.

He watched her as she got Mr. Jones talking

about himself, then pulled the captain into the conversation. Angus was sure that by the end of the meal both men knew more about each other than they had before they sat down.

And Edilean didn't forget him. She could hardly go three sentences without saying "my husband." "My husband knows about horses." "My husband has spent a great deal of time in Scotland." "My husband is quite good at that."

Angus couldn't help it, but every time she said "my husband" he found himself smiling.

By the end of the meal—which was excellent— she started talking about the plans she and her husband had. "We want to buy some land and build a house," she said.

"Then you're going to the right country. The soil is rich and fertile," the captain said. "Leave a plow in the earth for two weeks and it will sprout leaves."

"That's what we want to hear, isn't it?" she asked Angus.

He blinked at her. "My . . ." He hesitated over the word. "My wife is the gardener, not me. I don't know a weed from a stalk of wheat." Did they grow wheat in America? he wondered.

"True," Edilean said. "My father died when I was young, so I was at the mercy of my school friends when I was growing up. If they didn't invite me to their houses for the holidays I had to stay at the school with whichever teacher was made to stay behind with me. I lasted through one of those holidays and I can tell you that after that I learned how to make friends."

Mr. Jones and the captain laughed at her story, but Angus stared. Maybe what had happened to her was the reason why, even though she was so beautiful, she knew how to make an effort to be liked.

"You must have had many invitations," the captain said. "I can't imagine that you were left behind very often."

"Not after that first lonely time. No one has a worse temper than a young teacher who's had to cancel her own holiday to stay with the only girl in school who has nowhere to go. But after I learned to be a friend, I got to visit some of the best houses in England. I loved the gardens and used to sketch them in the hope that someday I'd have my own land to design."

"And will you give it to her?" the captain asked Angus.

"Yes," he said quickly. "I plan to give her her own town to create." He smiled as he said it, but when he bent his head, the smile left him. What did he have to give Edilean? If she hadn't given him jewels, he wouldn't even be able to buy himself some land.

"And your house?" the captain asked.

"I shall design that also," she said. "I know exactly what I want. Tell me, Captain, have you seen much of America?"

Angus noted that she never let the conversation stay on herself for too long before she started asking others for information about themselves—and her interest made them feel comfortable. Angus listened as the captain told about his own life and how he and his wife used to sail together.

"But after the children came, she stayed home with them. Next year I expect her to be back with me."

"How wonderful for you!" Edilean exclaimed. "You must miss her so very much."

"I do. And seeing you two together has made me miss her even more."

Edilean put her hand on Angus's and held it for a moment. "My husband and I want to spend all our time together too. Isn't that right, dear?"

That's when Angus interrupted by saying he'd been told that Edilean could sing.

"Now you've done it," Mr. Jones said. "Captain Inges loves to play his mandolin and he laments the fact that I can't tell one note from another."

"What music do you like?" she asked the captain, and her eyes seemed to say that she'd never heard anything more interesting than that he could play a mandolin.

"I'm afraid I'm not much of a musician," he said. "I just pick and strum to entertain myself."

"He's being modest," Mr. Jones said. "Sometimes he plays with the men and we dance on board."

"And now you have the women to dance with," Edilean said, and the three men looked at her blankly. "The women downstairs."

"Oh." Mr. Jones looked at his plate.

The captain straightened his shoulders. "This is the first time I've had prisoners on board. I'm not quite sure what to do with them."

"Let them have some fresh air," Angus said instantly. "They can't stay below for the entire voyage."

"When they recover," Captain Inges said. "Now all but two of them are under the weather."

"Seasickness," Mr. Jones said.

"You seem to be a good sailor," the captain said to Edilean. "No sickness? Either of you?"

"We're too happy to have escaped to be sick," Edilean said, then when they looked at her in question, she said, "I mean we're happy to have escaped our well-meaning friends and relatives who never hesitated to call at our house in London to wish us well on our marriage."

"Ah," Captain Inges said, "am I right in guessing that this is your bridal tour?"

"Yes," Edilean said. "A belated one." Again she reached for Angus's hand.

"Perhaps, Mrs. Harcourt, I could persuade you to sing for us," the captain said. "And I will try my hand at the mandolin."

"I would love to," she said, pushing back her chair as the steward came in and began to clear the table. "What would you like? Psalms? A bit of opera? Or perhaps a folk song from the English countryside?"

"What about a Scottish ballad?" Angus asked. "Something that we might all know."

"I'm not sure I know any Scottish songs," Edilean said, looking at him in curiosity before turning back to Captain Inges. "My husband has an uncle who lives in Scotland, and he used to spend his summers with him in a romantic old keep set on a hill, so my husband knows a lot about Scottish ways."

"I thought I detected a bit of a burr in your voice," Captain Inges said. "You're lucky that you aren't in Scotland now, as there is a murderer on the loose. Perhaps you saw the flyers with his picture when you were in Glasgow."

"We did," Edilean said. "He looked quite dangerous, although I did see something of kindness in his eyes. Or perhaps it was just the expertise of the artist that put it there."

Angus gave her a look as though to say he didn't know whether to laugh or grimace.

"I thought the drawing looked rather ordinary," Mr. Jones said. "I think it was a bit out of proportion, but, worse, he made the blackguard look almost handsome. It's my true belief that what we are shows on our faces. A man that bad could not be anything but as ugly as sin."

"I agree," Angus said, smiling broadly.

It was obvious that the captain had planned to play after dinner, as his mandolin was nearby, and he opened the case to lovingly remove the beautiful instrument. "Now, what shall you sing?"

Before Edilean could speak, Angus said, "Do you know the tune to 'Greensleeves'?"

"Yes, of course," he said, pleased.

He began playing quite skillfully, and the music of the old melody filled the small room. Edilean knew the ancient ballad, reputed to have been written by King Henry VIII, but just as she opened her mouth for her first note, Angus surprised her by starting to sing. His voice was rich and deep and beautiful. Edilean sat still and listened to him.

He sang what was probably an ancient song about a young lord whose father sent him away to school in the care of a servant. As soon as they were out of sight, the servant showed his true nature by sending the young lord out into the world penniless and in dirty, torn clothing, while the servant took his place and met a beautiful princess.

When Angus got to this part, he looked at Edilean; he was singing to her. The princess's father wanted her to marry the man who said he was a lord, but she begged him to wait. In the meantime, she fell in love with a stable lad—who was the real lord.

At this, Angus took Edilean's hands in his and held them. He told how the boy had sworn not to tell his true story or the servant would kill his family, so the clever girl persuaded him to tell his horse.

Edilean laughed. A prince in the clothes of a workman and a fine horse had played a part in their lives.

After the princess heard the story, she wrote the young man's father, and he came with an army and told the truth about who was the rightful prince. At the end, the servant was executed, and the young lord married the beautiful princess.

When Angus stopped, the captain played a bit of a flourish, and they all laughed and applauded.

"I do say but that was good!" Mr. Jones said. "A story and a song in one. Perhaps we could have another one."

Angus started to speak, but Edilean gave a yawn that she ostentatiously covered with her hand. "I'm afraid not," he said as he offered Edilean his arm. "It looks like my wife has had enough for one day. If you will excuse us."

Once they were outside she kept her hold on his arm. "That was wonderful. Truly beautiful. Your voice is so good you could have a career on the stage."

"Maybe that would be better than chasing after stolen cattle," he said.

"Or better than farming?" she asked.

When they got back to their own cabin, they saw that a hammock had been hung up and the trunks had been repacked. Edilean watched as Angus checked that the box of jewels was still where he'd hidden it, and smiled when he saw it was still there.

Minutes later, she asked him to untie her corset laces, and he groaned. "You've made rules that I cannot touch you, but I have not said the same to you," she said.

"Take that back or I'll let you sleep in that cage all night."

Smiling mischievously, she said, "Then I'll have

to go to that adorable Mr. Jones and ask for his help."

"You are a truly wicked woman," Angus said as he quickly untied her laces, then went to the far side of the room.

Edilean undressed slowly as she thought about the evening and how it felt to belong to someone. Since her father died, she'd always been someone's guest. She'd always had to "sing for her supper" as she thought of it. She'd had to walk when she didn't want to, talk when she wanted to be quiet. She'd been a guest, never the owner of the house—and the worst had been in her own uncle's house. There, she'd been a prisoner.

But now it was nice to think that she had her own husband and they were going to a new world and would build their own house. Even if it wasn't quite the truth, she liked to think of it.

Minutes later she was in bed and lay in the shadows, watching Angus struggling with the hammock. He rolled from one side to the other and seemed about to fall out.

"I want to hear you say my name," she said.

"What?"

"You heard me," she said. "You've never said my name to me and I've sometimes wondered if you even know it."

He took a moment before he spoke. "Edilean," he said softly. "Edilean . . . Harcourt."

"I guess it is. If the captain has seen the handbills

of you he may have heard of the missing Miss Talbot. And you are Angus Harcourt."

"That I am—for now anyway. Maybe when I get to Virginia I'll name my place McTern Manor."

"So you want to go to Virginia?" she asked, her voice quiet. She could hear the ocean outside, and inside she could hear Angus breathing. "I'm not sure, but I think Virginia is a long way from where we're landing in Boston."

"I like the sound of this Virginia."

"So do I," Edilean said sleepily. She'd had no sleep the night before when she'd cut Angus's hair and shaved him, and today she'd met people and had many new experiences. When she fell asleep, it was so deep that she didn't hear Angus when he fell out of the hammock and hit the floor hard. Nor did she awaken when he pulled the quilt over her and stood looking at her for a long while.

He used the blankets from the hammock to make a pallet on the floor on the far side of the cabin and settled down to sleep. As he dozed off he remembered that he'd said he'd like to give her an entire town to design. "Edilean, Virginia," he whispered just before he slept, and he liked the sound of it.

12

"No, no, no!" Angus said as he stood up from the chair and backed away from her. "I'm so sick of this I'm going mad. You hear me? Mad! Insane!"

Edilean looked at him in consternation. It had been raining hard for four days now, so they'd stayed inside the cabin and she'd started teaching Angus how to read. The process would have been easier if he'd bothered to apply himself, but he kept looking out the window at the sea. One time she asked him what he was thinking and he told her he was remembering Scotland and his family.

When he'd said that, Edilean moved away to sit on the bunk and let him have his own thoughts. She was glad that she was leaving no one behind who she really cared about. She had a few friends from school she'd like to exchange letters with, but there was no one she would really miss.

Too often, she thought of James and wondered how he liked his life with his new wife. She was glad that since he was now married, he'd never again have a chance to fool some schoolgirl into thinking he was in love with her.

But she didn't miss *him*, the man. In fact, as she got to know Angus, she realized that she'd never known James. In the few days she'd been with Angus she'd learned what he liked to eat—meat—and what he hated—seafood or anything that looked what he called "suspicious." She knew how easily he was embarrassed, and how his sense of humor was always just under the surface. When he got frustrated at trying to learn his letters, she'd seen that if she could make a joke, he'd get his good humor back.

She'd thought about what he'd told her about not flirting with him and acting as though they were brother and sister, and she'd done the best she could. It hadn't been easy. Leaning over him hour after hour as she corrected his work had been difficult. Sometimes she inhaled the fragrance of his hair and closed her eyes, the physical pleasure of the scent of him nearly overwhelming her.

In the days they'd spent together, they'd developed habits that now seemed second nature to them. She got out his clothes each morning while he shaved—he'd refused to let her do that task for him— and she tied his cravat, as he could never seem to do it correctly. And he helped her with her corset morning and night—and was already so used to it that he often yawned while pulling and tying.

For Edilean, the days had been wonderful. They were as close as she'd come to having a home and family since her father died. But now Angus was saying that he'd hated those days.

"Why are you trying to make me into him?" he asked, glaring at her.

"Into who?" She stepped back from him.

"Harcourt. You're trying to make me into that peacock you were so in love with."

"I'm doing no such thing," she said. "I've never tried to make you into James."

"Oh? And what is this?" he asked as he took off the beautiful blue silk jacket he was wearing and flung it on the chair. "And this?" He untied his cravat and tossed the snowy white tie on top of the jacket.

"Are you planning to remove any more of your clothing?" she asked as coolly as she could manage. "If you are, I want to make myself comfortable so I have a clear view."

"You canna make light of this," he said, not smiling at her joke. "I'm Angus McTern, not your dancing boy who trails after you."

Edilean sat down on the chair and looked up at him. "So now you've decided that all this is my fault?" she asked softly.

"And who else's fault is it? If you hadn't come to my home I'd be there now. I'd be in the heather this very minute and tonight I'd see my nephews and Malcolm, and I'd—" He took a breath and lowered his voice. "Instead, I'm here on this ocean, going to a foreign land, with no friends or family. And you're trying to make me into something that I'll never be. What is it that you want? To create a man you can show off to your highborn friends?" He was getting angry again. "Shall I be your trained monkey that you dress up and display? You'll say, 'Look what I did! I made an illiterate ruffian into a gentleman.' Will your snooty friends applaud you?"

Edilean was so taken aback by his words that she could hardly speak. "What friends do I have in this new country?" she asked. "I was teaching you to read because I thought you wanted to learn. Forgive me."

"Why do I need to read? What good will it do me? I'll buy some land and work the soil. No more hills and heather for me. Yet you're trying to—" He broke off and in the next moment he left the cabin, slamming the door behind him and leaving her alone in the room.

"I will not cry," she said. "I will not cry." But she did. She flung herself down on the bed and cried hard. She hadn't felt so bad since her uncle dragged her from school and later told her that the only thing he wanted from her was money.

She knew that Angus was right. When she thought of what he looked like when she first met him and what he looked like now—all because of her—she wanted to beg his forgiveness. She hadn't consciously tried to make him into the man she thought James was, but she'd done it. Angus was what she'd wanted in James. Angus was as beautiful as James, and nearly as well spoken when he put on his English accent. He could even sing, and he was certainly well liked by everyone. One day when the rain had stopped for half an hour, they'd gone up on deck and when a rope got stuck, Angus had helped the sailors pull it loose. Since then, he'd been a favorite of the men as well as the officers on the ship. At night, both Mr. Jones and Captain Inges asked him to sing one of his Scottish ballads. They liked them better than when Edilean sang an aria from an opera.

"But I've not changed," she said, sitting up on the bed and wiping her eyes. She was exactly the same as when she'd met Angus. And she had to face it that she was someone he didn't like. He never had liked her, and it seemed that he never would. He didn't like the world she'd been raised in, and he thought that she was a useless person—which he'd told her one way or the other many times.

She glanced out the big windows and saw that the rain had let up. Captain Inges said they'd sail out of it soon, and he'd been right. Edilean smoothed her dress—the only one she'd been able to cut down from the huge gowns that were in the trunk—and decided to go up on deck. Maybe if she apologized to Angus, he'd forgive her. She didn't like for him to be angry at her.

❦

As soon as Angus stormed out of the cabin, he regretted every word he'd said. Being near Edilean day after day was too much for him. Her kindness, her constant desire to please, the way she looked after him and noted what he did and did not like, was more than he could bear.

Why couldn't she be the snooty, arrogant snob he'd first thought she was? Why couldn't she order him about as the underling she must think of him as? He remembered how justified he'd felt when he'd thrown her into the horse trough. But Angus knew that he'd judged her based solely on what he thought she was like. He'd not listened to anyone when they'd said Lawler's niece was sweet and kind. He remembered making fun of that idea to Malcolm.

At the thought of that name, Angus went up the ladder to the upper deck. He needed to get some air to keep himself from going insane. Just weeks ago his life had been laid out before him. He knew what his duties were and where he fit in the world. But now all he knew was confusion about what his future was going to be. And his very soul seemed to be torn by a very young, very beautiful girl who was making him forget all that he knew about himself. She was a woman he could never, never have—but wanted oh so very much.

For the first time, six of the women prisoners were on deck. He was glad to see that their leg irons had been removed, but three of them still looked sick. It seemed that most of the sailors had come onto the deck and were doing tasks that didn't need to be done while they gave the women surreptitious glances.

Usually the scene would have amused him, but not now. Angus walked to the far side of the ship and looked over the rail.

"Have a fight with the little miss?" asked a woman's voice, and he turned to see the pretty one who'd stared at him when she'd come aboard. "I'm Tabitha."

"Angus Mc—" He hesitated. "Harcourt," he said.

"Nice to meet you, Angus Mc . . . Harcourt," she said, her eyes teasing.

When he said nothing else, she leaned back against the rail on her elbows and looked at the other women. "We've had a hard time of it, what with most of them puking up their guts for days."

"And you didn't?" Angus asked, still looking out at the sea.

"Naw. The sea don't bother me at all." She turned back to him. "So did you have a fight?"

Angus gave her a look that said his personal life was none of her business, but his expression made her laugh.

"I used to work for a woman like her. Such fine manners. Had to have everything just so, but I couldn't please her no matter how hard I tried."

"So you stole from her?" Angus asked idly. He didn't really care what she'd done. His mind was on his argument with Edilean. Or was it a true argument when he'd yelled and she'd said nothing in defense of herself?

"No," Tabitha said quietly. "Her husband stole from me the only thing I had that was mine alone."

At first he didn't know what she meant, but then he realized she was talking about her virginity.

"His wife kicked me out when she saw I was carrying her husband's child. No references, no money.

I had just the clothes on my back and the child in my belly. I stole a loaf of bread to survive and I was caught. By that time, I was too tired to run and prison looked good."

She was taking his attention away from his own problems, and he liked hearing her Scottish accent. He glanced at her flat stomach.

"Stillborn," she said. "Poor little fellow wanted nothing to do with this world, and I don't blame him. The judge let me off easy with just this banishment to America. It wasn't like I left a country that had been good to me. So why did you leave?"

"To build a new life," he said without thinking. "My wife and I want to buy land and . . ." He trailed off, unable to add to the lie.

Tabitha smiled at him with a knowing little smirk. She'd seen the way he looked when he'd stepped on deck minutes before. Only a person close to you could make you that unhappy. "So what did you fight about?"

"My wife and I—" he began, but stopped. He was so sick of lying! "I want more; she wants less. What else do men and women fight about?"

She laughed so loud that everyone on deck looked at them.

"And what will you do in America?" Angus asked, changing the subject.

"I hear that a hundred people will be at the dock waiting to meet us. We'll have to go to the courthouse to register, but after that we're on our own. We can take job offers from those people on the dock. Or . . ." She gave him a suggestive look. "Or marriage proposals. I may marry one of those American men. I hear they're a rough bunch, but maybe I can find myself a strong, sturdy man and we can make a life together." She turned back toward him and lowered her voice. "What I want is my own home. That's something I've never had. I cried for weeks after the baby was born dead. For all that it cost me everything I had, I loved the wee thing."

"Why are you telling me all this?" Angus asked.

"No reason, but I'm good at judging character, and there's something not right about you." She looked him up and down. "Clothes, wife . . . something doesn't match. I saw it that first day. That you'll talk to someone like me says a lot. I think maybe you and I are more alike than it looks from those clothes of yours." She glanced down at him, at his big legs in the tight trousers and the shirt that clung to his chest in the wind. "I don't think you're like her."

One of the sailors had come on deck with a squeeze-box and had begun playing a reel.

"Come on!" Tabitha said. "Dance with me."

"I don't think I—" Angus began, but then he shrugged. Why not? He walked to the middle of the deck. A sailor added a flute to the music, and the next thing he knew, he was dancing with one woman after another. All but one of the women were from Scotland and they knew all the dances that so reminded him of home.

One of the sailors joined them and soon they were whirling about the deck in a frenzy of action. Angus was so glad to have some exercise that he grabbed a woman about the waist and lifted her high in the air. There was another woman, older, and she was quite wide below the waist.

"You won't be able to lift me," she shouted over the music and clapping of the people watching.

Angus grabbed her and lifted her as though she were a girl. "Marry me! Marry me!" the woman shouted, making everyone laugh.

Angus's shirt was open to his waist and he was drenched with sweat, but he kept on dancing so fast and furiously that he didn't notice when Edilean came on deck. She stayed in the shadows, out of the limelight, watching Angus dancing with the women and enjoying himself.

But Tabitha saw her and moved past the crowd to stand near her.

Edilean looked at the woman and had to resist the urge to move her skirt aside so it wouldn't touch her. She knew, just by looking at her, what kind of woman she was: She was the type men liked but women hated.

"If I had a man like that in my bed, I'd never leave it," Tabitha said in a suggestive way.

"Perhaps never getting out of bed is why you don't have a man like him," Edilean said over her shoulder.

The woman laughed so loud that Angus turned

to her, and when he saw Edilean, the smile left his face.

When Tabitha saw Angus's expression, she laughed harder. As she left to go back to the group, she swished her long skirt and turned back to Edilean. "Be careful another woman don't take him from you. And my name's Tabitha," she said, then turned and ran back to the dance. When Angus grabbed her about the waist, her eyes were on Edilean.

Edilean looked away and went back down to their cabin.

Hours later Angus returned to the cabin. Edilean was there with one of the dresses across her lap, and she was sewing. "Feel better?" she asked.

"Much," he answered, smiling. He was sweaty and his shirt was open so his muscular chest was showing and his black hair was in slick curls about his face.

Edilean had to look away or the beauty of him would weaken her resolve. "Good," she said as she put down her needle. "I have something to ask of you. As you've repeatedly told me, you owe me nothing while I owe you everything, but I ask that during this voyage you not humiliate me."

"I didn't mean to—"

"I know," she said. "That one prisoner's quite pretty and she likes you. You have every right to pursue her."

"I wasn't 'pursuing' her," he said. "I was dancing with *all* the women."

"Yes, of course you were. Again, I apologize for what I've done to your life. You were right when you said that if you'd never met me you would still be at home and blindingly happy."

He wiped his sweaty face with a towel from the bowl and pitcher at the far end of the room. "Lass," he said, "when a man's angry he says things he doesn't wholly mean. Sitting here day after day with nothing to do but struggle with words in a book nearly drives me to madness."

"Yes, you made that clear." She picked up the dress again. "As I said, I apologize for what I did to your life. I know I have forever destroyed your chance for happiness."

"Nay, lass, you haven't."

Edilean threw down the dress on the table. "Would you please stop talking to me as though I'm a child! You may see me that way, but I can assure you that other men don't. I'm trying to apologize to you. I wish with all my heart that I'd thought to tell the captain that you and I were brother and sister, but I didn't. So now we're stuck together until the end of this long, dreadful voyage. I made a mistake when I thought to repay you for all you've done for me by teaching you to read. Fool that I am, I assumed you wanted to be something different than what you are. I was wrong. You consider yourself perfect as you are and want no change."

"I don't think that's quite true," Angus said. "Perhaps learning to read would be good for me. In fact . . ." With a smile, he went to the book she'd been using for a text. She'd found stationery, quills and ink, plus a few novels in the bottom of the smaller trunk, and she'd been using them to show him how to form his letters. He knew numbers and could add and subtract in his head, but he wasn't used to writing them down. "I think I'm ready for another lesson now," Angus said. "The exercise did me much good."

Edilean gave him a little smile. "I'm so glad it did."

He took the seat across from her and picked up his quill, dipped it in the ink, and wrote his name. It took him several minutes, but he did it. "There. What do you think of that?"

Edilean didn't look up from her sewing. "Mr. McTern, I am no longer going to be your teacher or your dresser. You can do whatever you want and I won't interfere."

"I see," Angus said as he put the paper down. "It's that woman, Tabitha, isn't it? But you shouldn't be so hard on her. She's had a bad time in life. She told me her story, and it's truly awful. She's been treated unfairly by both people and the law."

"Poor thing," Edilean said coldly.

"I think you should have some Christian charity toward her. She's not had the gentle life you've had."

"My life gentle? Yes, Mr. McTern, you're right. My life has been so easy. My mother died at my birth and I was raised by my father. But as he was an officer in the army, I saw him so rarely that I spent my life in boarding schools. One time my father came to visit me and he didn't know which one of the girls was his daughter. He died when I was twelve and I was suddenly without home or family. In school I had to pretend to like girls I despised just so I'd have a place to spend Christmas. Then, when I was seventeen, I was taken from school by an uncle who cared only for the gold my father left me. Since then, I've done everything to save myself from having a future as bad as my past."

"I didn't mean—" Angus began, but she put her hand up.

"Unfortunately, *you* have been involved in my life in these last weeks, but that was never my intention. The first time I asked *you* for help, you not only turned me down but you also laughed at me, so I knew to ask nothing more of you."

"I apologize for that. I didn't mean—"

"Didn't mean?" she asked, her voice rising. "You've caused me a great deal of misery that you didn't mean to do, haven't you, Mr. McTern?"

"I have," he said, his jaw stiff as he stared at her.

"But, ultimately, you did save me. Because of your diligence I didn't sleep all day then find out James had sailed off with my dowry. There's not enough in the world that I could do for you or give you that could thank you for that. That I have any future is the result of your care and concern for me."

"Lass, I—"

"I have a name!" she half shouted.

Angus sat up straighter. "Would it be Miss Talbot or Mrs. Harcourt?"

"Mrs.," she said, then gave a sigh as her anger left her. "I really am sorry for all this. You're right that I've been bossing you around. What was it you said? That I was treating you like a trained monkey? That I was trying to make you into what I hoped James was?"

Angus took a while to answer. "Yes," he said at last, "I said those things in a moment when I was so homesick I couldna think of anything else. But it was just a matter of bad temper and it meant nothing."

"It meant everything to me," she said. "Every word you said was true. Mr. McTern, I will make a vow to you that I will never again interfere in your life. You can wear what you want, talk any way you want to, dance with whomever you want. All I ask is that you do not humiliate me on this voyage. Everyone thinks we're married, so I beg that you not . . . not carry your lust for the prisoners to the point where people look at me with pity. So far in my life, I've avoided that particular embarrassment, and I'd like to continue to do so. Do we have an agreement?"

Angus was sitting ramrod straight in his chair, blinking at her. He felt bad for having yelled at her that morning. But he wondered why she wasn't like other women who fought back in a way that ended with Angus putting his arms around her and comforting her. Right now he wanted to go to her and hold her, tease her until she was smiling again, but the way she was looking at him made him unable to even make a joke.

"Do we have an agreement?" she repeated.

Before Angus could reply, there was a knock on the door.

Edilean got up to answer it, but she paused at the closed door. "May I please have your answer?"

"Aye, I agree to not embarrass you," he said.

She opened the door, and one of the women prisoners was standing there. It was the heavy woman Angus had flung about in the dance just an hour before. "This is Margaret," Edilean said, "but then I think you've met."

"Aye, we have," Margaret said, grinning and showing missing teeth. "I think he agreed to marry me." Quickly, she turned to Edilean. "Beggin' your pardon, miss."

"That's fine," Edilean said. "My . . . I mean, Mr. Harcourt is his own man. He does what he wants when he wants and I don't interfere in his life. Would you excuse me for a minute?" She left the cabin.

"Bloody hell," Margaret said as she sat down at the table across from Angus. "What did you do to her? Was it the way you were makin' eyes at Tabitha?"

Angus stared at the woman. He knew it wasn't right for him to feel this way, but he didn't like her familiarity with him. Nor did he like the way she'd just plopped down on the chair as though she owned the place. As he felt this, he told himself he was being ridiculous. He and the woman were equals, and he wasn't a snob. He was . . . "Why are you here?" he asked.

"She didn't tell you? She asked the captain if one of us women could sew. She's promised me money if I'll fix her dresses for her." She looked at him. "I woulda thought a woman would tell her husband about somethin' like that. Askin' a criminal into her nice cabin and all." She looked about the room. "This is as nice as a house. You could live here. Where we are stinks worse than some jails I been in."

Angus couldn't help it as his temper rose. Yes, Edilean *should* have talked to him about hiring some woman who'd done heaven only knew what to get herself banished from her homeland. It was not a wise thing to do. If the cabin weren't so full of valuables he'd go after Edilean and tell her what he thought of her hiring this woman.

"Margaret," he said finally, "my wife isn't feeling her best right now. Perhaps you should come back later. We'll call you." As he said it, he went to the door and opened it, but Edilean entered the room.

She went to the trunk to get out the dresses that needed to be almost totally remade.

"Cold enough in here to freeze snow," Margaret said, her eyes on Angus.

"Excuse me?" Edilean said while giving the woman a look that told her to keep her opinions to herself.

"Beggin' your pardon, ma'am," Margaret said

with a little curtsy. "Now what was it you wanted me to do?"

⬡

Edilean sat at the table, looking out the windows at the ocean. It had been a week since she'd told Angus what she thought of his behavior, and now everything was different. There wasn't a day when she didn't mentally kick herself for her stupid, childish thoughts she'd had before that day. It was true that she'd tried to make him into something he wasn't, but for the last week she'd made it up to him by not interfering in his life. In fact, she'd done her best not to say much at all to him. Their dinners with the captain and Mr. Jones had changed, so they weren't the happy events they had been. The first night after their argument, Angus said, "Sorry, but my wife isn't feeling well," and they'd left the dining room soon after the meal. Edilean had spent most of the week inside the cabin reading any book she could find. Angus spent his time on the deck. If he was with the women prisoners, she didn't want to know about it.

When the door opened, Edilean looked back at her book and ignored Angus. No more did she lay out his clothes for him, and he'd learned to tie his own cravat. She'd even arranged for Margaret to come to her cabin twice a day to help her with her corset.

"I'll need a job in the new country and you need a maid," Margaret said the second day, heavily hinting that Edilean should hire her.

Edilean had given the woman a cool smile and

said she'd think about it. But the truth was that she'd never hire a woman who'd done whatever Margaret had to get herself transported.

Now, Angus said, "Lass! You should get out of here more."

"I have work to do before we arrive in America, so I need to get it done."

"And what work would that be?"

"A house," she said without thought. "I think I'll have a house built to my specifications."

"And what would they be?"

Edilean didn't answer him because she hadn't been thinking about a house or her future. In fact, when she thought of the new country and being utterly alone, she nearly froze in fear. Never in her life had she had any independence, and now to go from having no freedom to being entirely on her own scared her.

"What's that look for?"

"Nothing," she said. "Did you enjoy your dancing today?"

"Did you enjoy your sulking?"

She didn't answer him, as it seemed that every word she said started a fight with him.

Angus picked up the quill pen, dipped it into a pot of ink, and paused over a sheet of paper. "About a year ago your uncle sent me to London to run an errand for him." He made a few lines on the paper, then looked up at her. "Now that I think about it, I believe the errand was about you. I had to meet a man outside a bank and he gave me a letter to take back to your uncle Neville. At the time I wondered why he didn't just post the letter, but now I think it was about the gold, and it told Lawler something he wasn't supposed to know."

As Angus talked, he was making quick marks on the paper. Edilean wanted to see what he was doing but the pile of books she'd borrowed from the captain was blocking her view.

"Anyway," Angus said, "as I was riding, I saw a house that had been built only the year before. It was rather plain and very simple, but I thought it was the most beautiful house I'd ever seen."

He pushed the paper toward her, and she saw that he'd sketched a truly lovely house. As he'd said, it was a rather plain house with five windows on the second floor, four windows and a door on the ground floor.

"It's beautiful," she said, not able to suppress her praise. "And your sketch is excellent. How would you arrange the interior?"

"I have no idea. It's not as though they invited me in for tea. If I'd been wearing this getup and talking like James, they would have, but not as I was then."

Edilean's face still showed her surprise at his drawing. He had an eye for proportion, and for all that he held a quill as though it were a foreign object, the rendering was very good. Edilean ducked her head to hide her smile, but he saw it.

"Was that a smile?"

"No!" she said sharply.

"You've been angry at me for a whole week! Can you not find it in your heart to forgive a man who took his homesickness out on you?"

"You blame me for all your misfortunes."

"That's because you're the cause of them." When she looked away, he said, "But now that I've talked to some people about this America, I think I might like it."

"How could you when you left your family back in Scotland?"

"About that, lass, perhaps my life there was not as good as I said it was."

"According to you it was pure heaven."

"Did I tell you that my father left me a cottage?"

"No," she said. "In fact, you've told me very little about yourself—except that you were the happiest man on earth and I destroyed it all for you."

"Perhaps that was a wee bit of an exaggeration."

For a moment she thought about picking up her book and moving away from him, but she'd missed him in this last week of coolness. "So you owned a cottage?"

"It was a pretty little place with a thatched roof and deep windows. My mother grew roses on one side and I'd wake up to the smell of them."

"You've never mentioned your mother," Edilean said. "Or for that matter, your father."

"Died long ago," Angus said in a tone that told he'd say no more. "It was just my sister and me left and she . . ." Pausing, he shook his head. "She fell in love with a man who is very lazy, and takes great joy in belittling other people, me in particular."

"Worse than Shamus?"

"Different. If you held a penny in your hand and Shamus wanted it, he'd break your arm to get it. But my brother-in-law, Gavin, would say how greedy you were and that if he had a penny he'd give it to the church. Of course you'd have to give it away. Either way, you'd end up penniless."

"How drunk did you get at the wedding?"

Her question startled Angus and made him laugh. "Oh, lass, but I've missed your humor. But you're right. I drank so much I had a sore head for a week. My sister and her new husband were to move in with Gavin's mother, but Kenna—that's my sister—stood it only six months. Gavin's mother was just like him, and she used Kenna as a maid."

"So they moved in with you?"

"Aye, they did," Angus said. "And three months later, she had her first bairn."

"Three months? Doesn't it usually take longer than that? Or is Scotland better in that too?"

"They started early. It seems there's one thing Gavin isn't lazy at. My sister's had three babes in two years of marriage."

Edilean couldn't keep from smiling. It had been a long, boring week, with Angus and she speaking so little.

"About this week," he said softly. "It's not been easy for me."

"Nor for me," she said.

"But this time has given me a chance to think," he said. "What could have happened to me there in Scotland? I was where I was going to be. But thanks to you, I have a possibility of a new life."

"It took you a week to think of that?"

"Three days," he said, grinning. "Since then I've been talking to everyone who's been to America and asking questions. I think a man could make something of himself in this new land."

"And what would that be?" she asked.

She saw by Angus's face that he was about to make some smart retort to her question, but he seemed to change his mind.

"My own home," he said at last. "My own horses. My own . . . all of it. Everything owned by me. No more spending my days wet and cold and looking for another man's missing sheep."

"But I thought you loved the climate of Scotland. And you hate wearing James's clothes, but that's what a landowner wears."

"Maybe I could grow used to shaving every day," he said, his eyes twinkling.

She looked back at his sketch. "If this were my house, I know just how I'd make the interior."

"And how would that be?"

She picked up the quill to do the sketching but put it back down. "Few rooms. Tall ceilings. I've heard that Virginia has a warm climate, so you'd need height for the hot air to rise. And a big central hallway on both floors so you can open the doors and let the air come through."

"So you like what you've heard of this Virginia?" Angus picked up the quill and began to sketch the floor plan she'd described.

"Captain Inges told me it was a beautiful place. He said that when he retires he plans to live there, and he said the Boston winters are brutal." She was watching him intently as he drew, and she was glad that he'd decided to quit railing at her that she'd destroyed his life. It was too heavy a burden of guilt to carry.

"What will you do when we get there?" she asked softly.

He was intent on his drawing. "I think I'll go to this Williamsburg Mr. Jones told me about. It seems to be the center of all that's about to happen."

"What does that mean?" she asked quickly. "What's about to happen?"

"Americans are talking about becoming independent from England."

"That's absurd. How can they become independent? How can they do without a king?"

"Bloody well, I'd think."

"How can you say that? A king is someone who's born to rule. It's a God-given right. The king—"

"Do you mean to start another fight between us?"

"No," she said softly.

"Lass . . . I mean, Mrs. Harcourt, I've had a great deal of time to think this week and I see how different you and I are. Do you think there's even one subject we agree on?"

"No, I guess not." She wanted to tell him how afraid she was of being alone in the new country, but she could tell that he had no fear. He was a young man on his way to an adventure, and thanks to her gift of the jewels he'd have a lot of money. For a moment she thought of saying she wanted the diamonds back. If he had no money maybe he wouldn't run off and leave her alone on the docks as soon as the ship dropped anchor.

"And what is that long face for?" he asked.

"You're looking forward to arriving in America, aren't you?"

He looked at her for a moment before returning to the paper. "Have you considered that Harcourt will have made arrangements for him and his wife in America?"

"No," she said slowly. "I haven't." The thought lifted her spirits a bit. "You mean maybe he's arranged accommodations?" The idea of a place to go to made her feel better. She'd never lived in a hotel before and didn't want to, and she dreaded having to.

"I think that everything he did was a long time in the planning. Did you know that he booked passage on this ship seven months ago?"

"But how could he? He didn't know what my uncle was going to do."

"Are you sure? Lawler was closemouthed, but those two men who nearly lived with him weren't. I think Harcourt planned everything for around your eighteenth birthday. I doubt if he eloped with the earl's daughter, so he must have been courting her while telling you he was going to be with you. My guess is that Harcourt meant to go through a false marriage ceremony with you. Then, when he had your gold . . ." Angus shrugged.

Edilean sat there blinking at him, thinking about what he'd said. She didn't want to think about James's betrayal, but having a home was a different matter. "So you think that maybe in America there's a house or at least somewhere for me to live? Not that I can go there, but . . ."

"Why not? It'll be a month before Harcourt can get a letter here, and everyone will know you as Mrs. James Harcourt."

"And you as my husband," Edilean shot back.

Angus smiled. "I will quietly disappear the minute we're there, so you'll be free to be whoever you want to be. A widow perhaps."

"And what do I do when James shows up?"

"Show him the marriage certificate saying he's married to the earl's daughter, not to you. If there is a house, I doubt if it's been paid for, since he was waiting for your gold."

"But—" Edilean began, then broke off. "I think you have the mind of a criminal."

"Thank you," he said as he handed her what he'd been drawing. "Is this what you meant?" He showed her a floor plan that was perfectly proportioned.

Downstairs was a wide hallway with a big stairway in it. The hall was flanked by four rooms, each looking large and airy. The second floor was nearly the same, but on one side the two rooms weren't equal size, with one half again as large as the other.

"The big room is for your books," he said. "You can put shelves floor to ceiling on three sides and fill them with books."

That he'd thought of her while drawing almost made tears come to her eyes. "Where did you learn to draw like this?"

He shrugged. "Not all the men who've visited your uncle have been like the two you met. When I was a boy, younger even than Tam, a rich young man came to stay, and he wanted to draw the old castles of Scotland. He paid me to travel with him up into the Highlands while he drew. I watched and I learned."

When Edilean said nothing, he glanced at her. "Why are you looking at me like that?"

"It's just that you always surprise me."

"Because I'm not the ignorant Scot you think I am?"

She didn't smile. "I've thought a lot of things about you, but never that you were . . . 'ignorant.'"

Angus frowned as he began sketching on another piece of paper. "Have you done what you said you would and fallen in love with me?"

"When did I ever say such a thing?"

"In those first days when you looked at me with eyes full of adoration."

"Of what? I can assure you that I have never 'adored' you."

"After I saved you from Harcourt—"

"After I saved you from the gallows."

"Caused by your hiding in a coffin," he said.

She couldn't help smiling. "I will always remember your face. It was whiter than mine, and I was covered with sawdust."

"But you were still the most beautiful—" He cut himself off and put down the quill. "I need to go out," he said abruptly, and in a few steps he was out the door, leaving Edilean gaping.

"Now what have I done?" she asked aloud as she picked up his drawing. "He should train as an architect," she whispered and immediately had an idea of the two of them living together in the house he'd drawn. He'd work in the big room upstairs, surrounded by rolled-up sheets of drawings. And he'd ask her opinion about every building. "You know that you're better at interiors than I am," he'd say. And, "What color do you think I should paint these walls?"

Edilean could see herself in a blue silk dress, her hair in curls about her neck—and a baby in her arms and one standing, his little hands on her skirt. The vision was so clear that she could see the faces of the children. The older one was a boy and he looked like Angus, and the baby was a girl who looked like her.

Getting up, she went to the windows and looked out, trying to rid herself of the vision, but it stayed with her. Maybe it was his drawing of the house that was making it all so clear to her, but it was as though she were looking into a crystal ball and seeing the future.

But that was ridiculous! Angus McTern had made it clear that he wanted nothing to do with her once they were in America. She was on her own.

Turning, she picked up one of the books the captain had lent her and set her mind to reading it.

❦

Angus stood by the ship's rail, looking over the side. Part of him wanted the ship to slow down and another part wanted it to hurry up so he could get the good-byes over with. The captain said that if the weather held, they'd be landing at Boston harbor in about a week.

And that would be the end, he thought. That would be the last time he'd ever see Edilean. "Edilean," he whispered, with only the sea to hear him.

The last days of her coolness had been difficult for him, but he'd been glad for her anger. He knew that if they'd kept on in the way they had been, he would have gone insane with wanting her. Wanting not just to touch her but also to make her smile, to laugh, to come back at him with one of her little rejoinders that made him want to pull her into his arms and kiss her.

But he couldn't do that. Oh, he knew that she was beginning to think she was in love with him, but that had happened before with other girls. What was different was how he felt about her. No other woman had come close to making him feel as she did, as though he could do anything. It wouldn't surprise him if she told him she believed he could fly. And when she looked at him with such wonder in her beautiful eyes, Angus thought maybe he could develop wings and soar away.

No, he couldn't do that, he thought. She was just a girl, barely past eighteen, while he was, at twenty-five, not old, but compared with her, he felt as though he'd lived a thousand years. He'd never told her, but her uncle had sent him on many errands, some of them a great deal less noble than protecting some sissy Englishman as he drew pictures of old castles.

Angus knew Edilean thought she'd had a difficult life because she'd not had a mother and father to tuck her in at night, but he knew she'd been sheltered and taken care of. Her father's money had been there, even if he hadn't been there in person. So she spent a week or two with some girl she didn't like. What horror was that?

She'd not seen her father die before her eyes, as Angus had. She'd not seen her mother waste away from too much work and the loneliness of her life. And Edilean hadn't been told since the day she was born that she was responsible for the health and well-being of an entire clan of people. More than once, Malcolm had taken him by the shoulders and said, "The fate of Clan McTern rests with you, lad. It's all up to you. You must undo what your grandfather—my father—did."

All his life, Angus had heard in detail what a nasty piece of work his grandfather had been. He'd raided other people's sheep during the night, had stolen from everyone within a hundred miles. He'd been caught often and several times had escaped death by mere minutes. When he was thirty a young woman, a lover, had rescued him from the gallows. Three days later his wife gave birth to Angus's father. But his wife forgave him for whatever he did. It was said that all the women forgave him for anything.

Maybe his wife forgave him, but his three sons didn't. The eldest one lived to adulthood, but he was killed when his son, Angus, was only five. The second son had tried to follow his father, to be as "tough" as he was, but he couldn't. He died in a nighttime raid and a month later his young wife gave birth to Tam. Only Malcolm survived his father's treachery.

Angus's father had done his best to hold the clan together, but too much hatred had been created over the years. During a raid on McTern sheep, Angus's father was stabbed in the stomach by a man hiding in the bushes. He'd lived long enough to get home, but died soon after, with his wife and young son beside him. His last words had been to his little son, telling him he had to take care of the McTerns. "Don't do to them what my father does." He'd held the hands of his wife and son. "I'm glad I won't see the old bastard as I know he'll go to Hell." He'd smiled at the words, then closed his eyes and died.

It was said that on the night Angus's grandfather gambled away everything on one cut of the cards, the moon was full and the wolves came out to howl in protest. No one knew what happened to the old man after that. He'd laughed off every bad deed he'd done, every tear—and every death—he'd caused, but losing his family's past as well as their future was too much even for him. Three weeks later, he was found sitting in a chair in a pub in Edinburgh, dead.

Angus's mother died a few years after that, leaving Angus and his sister alone.

"And why that sad look?"

Turning, he saw Tabitha standing close to him, her dark eyes giving him suggestive looks. Had he met her a year ago, he would have liked the way she looked at him.

"You have another fight with the missus?"

When he gave her a look that said he was going to tell her nothing, she laughed.

"I'm going to find out the truth between you two," she said.

"There is no hidden truth," Angus said. "We are what you see."

Tabitha gave a little laugh to let him know she didn't believe him. "Will you set up a house together in America?"

"Yes, of course," he said, gritting his teeth. The woman really was an annoying creature. He'd seen her three times since the first day and she was always prying into his life—and nearly always right. She saw what others did not. "If you're so perceptive, how did you get caught by a man?"

"Love," she said quickly. "You can't help what love does to you, now can you?"

He didn't bother to answer but turned back to look at the sea. Behind them a man yelled that the women were to go back down below.

"They're afraid we'll corrupt the men," Tabitha said.

"And haven't you?"

"Any corruption I've done has been mutual," she said as she went to where the other women were gathering and grumbling about having to go down again.

Angus looked back at the sea and thought about how Edilean was so jealous of Tabitha. At even a hint of the woman, Edilean's eyes flashed fire and she looked like she wanted to attack someone.

Love, Angus thought. Tabitha said she'd had an affair with her employer because of love, and Angus knew that Edilean was beginning to think she was in love with him. But she wasn't. She was just scared of being alone in a new country. And alone she had to be. Or at least separated from him, from Angus Mc-Tern.

It was tempting—oh, so very, very tempting—to make a few advances toward her, to "accidentally" touch her hand, to look at her in a way that would let her know what was in his mind. He knew that if he did, it would take only minutes before she fell against him, before she gave herself to him.

But then what? he thought. He had to close his

eyes as he imagined delicious weeks, perhaps even months, of lovemaking. They'd have quiet dinners that they'd never finish because they'd be on each other's bodies.

But somewhere in there he knew that their true selves would begin to show. Edilean had spent her life in school, while Angus couldn't read. Edilean loved silk dresses and afternoon tea; Angus liked to roll in a tartan and sleep on the ground.

There was no common ground between them. Now, on the ship, with Angus wearing another man's clothes, and using a false accent, it was almost as though they were equals. He saw the way her beautiful face lit up when she saw he could do something besides run through the heather.

But that wasn't him. He couldn't spend his life trying to be someone else. It wouldn't take long before people saw through him. Even Tabitha, a woman who'd lived in the dregs of society, had seen through him. She knew he was an imposter.

Angus had a vision of some handsome young man who had a degree from a university making Edilean laugh about some French poet. And that night she would look at Angus with contempt.

What if they married? He could see her telling their children not to ask their father. "He knows nothing," she'd say. Or no, she'd be too polite to say it, but they'd know. He'd be in the midst of a family that laughed together over poetry and stories written in Greek, and Angus would be left out of it.

Even now he could imagine his anger at being so treated. What would he do? Have an affair with a woman like Tabitha? While his wife and children were at home in their pure, innocent beds, would he be like his grandfather and spend his nights out with loose women? Would he need them to feel like a man?

Angus ran his hand over his face to clear away his ugly thoughts. All he knew for sure was that he could not continue to be with Edilean after the voyage ended. He knew that when they docked she'd no doubt look at him with her "save me" eyes. They'd be near to tears, and she'd be so beautiful that he'd be ready to grab a sword and lead an army into war for her. But he had to resist her!

If he knew anything in life, it was that if he stayed with her, married or not, they'd come to hate each other. She would hate him, or worse, come to despise him, because underneath the elegant clothes he was no gentleman. And he'd hate her because he couldn't make himself into what she wanted him to be.

He took a few breaths and tried to strengthen his resolve. No matter how she looked at him, no matter what her eyes said—he doubted that her pride would let her say the words—he wouldn't give in to her. For all that she loved to think she was a grown woman, she wasn't.

When they got to America he'd stay long enough to make sure she was set up in a society of her own, then he'd leave. For all that she said good things about

Virginia, he couldn't see her living anywhere but in a city, and from what he'd heard, Boston was as bristling as London.

Angus pushed himself away from the railing. If he ever needed strength in his life, now was the time.

13

O N THE DAY they were to reach Boston, Edilean awoke feeling calm. She hadn't slept for the three nights before as she lay awake, worrying about what was coming, but last night had been different. It was as though her fate was sealed, there was nothing she could do about it, so she resigned herself.

But she couldn't say the same thing about Angus. As far as she could tell he was a nervous wreck. Yesterday as she'd been packing, he'd hovered over her, asking if she had everything, was she sure she wasn't leaving something behind?

"Captain Inges said he would be in Boston for weeks, so if I do leave a hairpin behind I can return to the ship and get it," she said patiently. "Why don't you sit down and draw something? Or go up on deck and dance with those women?"

"Are you sending me to Tabitha? Or maybe you'd like for me to go down into the hold to see her?"

"If you're trying to make me jealous, you aren't even coming close. Once we get to America, you're a free man. You can go after Tabitha and buy her for all I care."

"Buy her? Oh, her bondage papers. Yes, I could do that," he said, still looking about the cabin and pacing now and then. "And maybe I will marry her. She'd make a good wife." When Edilean said nothing to that, Angus kept on. "She's already proven that she's fertile." As he spoke, he looked at Edilean as she knelt by the trunk, putting away the clothes that Margaret had remade for her.

"Has she?" Edilean asked without much interest. "How nice for you. Did the father keep the baby?"

"It was stillborn."

"If it ever existed."

"What does that mean?"

Edilean got up to get a book off the table where they'd eaten breakfast together every morning of the entire voyage. Angus was right behind her. "You sound like you don't believe that Tabitha had a baby."

She put the book in the trunk. "I'm sure she's done what it takes to create a baby."

"As you have not," Angus said, looking at her.

She turned, her hands on her hips, and glared at him. "Why don't you go on deck and bother someone else with your questions? You could ask each of the women if she's had a hard time in life, then you could tell yourself that compared to them, my life has been easy because I have money."

"I never said— I never meant— You don't think that I—"

"Go!" she said as she put her hands on the small of his back and pushed him toward the door of the cabin. "Get out of here. I have work to do, and I can't do it with you in here trying to start a fight."

"I was doing no such thing," he said as he went through the door.

When he was gone, Edilean leaned against the door, closed her eyes for a moment, and smiled. She enjoyed his nervousness, because it was the same way she felt. The prospect of a whole new country was daunting. But more than the idea of a country, the thought of her future scared her. She'd reconciled herself to the fact that she and Angus would separate when they arrived, but that was easier for him than for her. Angus had shown that he could be anyone he wanted to be. He could put on the clothes of a workman and get himself a wife who would spend her days scouring floors, then at night pop out a pair of ten-pound twins. Or he could put on James's clothes and get a woman who read Cicero in the original Greek. Whatever he wanted, he could have.

But Edilean knew that her choices weren't going to be so easy. By her manner and dress, she'd be able to have only one type of man, meaning someone like James. But Angus had made her not want a man like James. Whereas once she'd thought of James as elegance personified, now when she thought of him he seemed rather useless.

But she knew she wasn't to have a choice in what she was to do with her life. Because of the trunks of gold in the hold of the ship—which Angus had checked on four times—her life had been decided for her. She was where she was now not by choice but because of gold.

When Angus returned to the cabin a couple of hours later, he was sweaty and in a much better mood.

"Dancing again?"

"Rope climbing and betting," he said. "I won."

Smiling, she wished she could have seen him. No doubt the sailors thought that Angus was, well . . . as unlike James as it was possible to be. "The sailors must have been surprised at what you could do."

"Aye, they were," he said as he sat down at the table and picked up the quill and began to draw. Since he'd made the sketches of the house, he hadn't stopped drawing. Out of curiosity, she'd asked him to draw something besides buildings, and she'd even posed for him to do her portrait, but he couldn't. He'd turned out something little better than a child would. "I think I'll stay with my buildings," he'd said, and she'd agreed.

I can't think about this, she told herself. If she thought about leaving and never seeing Angus again, she knew she'd start crying and never stop.

Now, as she woke and, as she always did, glanced over at Angus, she felt more calm than she had in days. It had taken him a week, but he'd finally learned how to sleep in the hammock without falling out of it. When she looked, he was staring at her, and his eyes were so red that he looked as though he hadn't slept all night.

"Are you all right, lass?" he asked softly.

"I'm fine," she said and meant it. Surprisingly, she was all right. In fact, she was feeling a bit of excitement running through her as she thought about what was to happen today. They were to disembark in a brand-new country.

It was Angus who was the nervous one. "What if there's not a house ready for you?" he'd asked yesterday. "What if Harcourt didn't make provision for you?"

"You're the one who said he would have made arrangements for himself, so I'll just use them as long as I can. Please stop fretting so."

"I have never 'fretted' in my life," Angus said, looking affronted, and she had to hide her smile.

Hours later, when the ship had at last dropped anchor and they were in the harbor of Boston, Edilean was sure she'd never seen so much hustle and bustle in her life. She'd spent a lot of her life in London, but this place was different. It was louder, dirtier, and bigger. She could see people and wagons and animals far down the streets. But for all the noise and dirt, there was an excitement that she'd never felt in ancient London.

"It's wonderful," she said to Angus, who was standing close beside her.

"It smells bad." He took her arm in his and held it tightly.

"No more than London," she said.

"That's what I said. It stinks."

She laughed, then pulled away from his arm. "Come on, we have to oversee that the trunks are brought up. I want to count them to make sure that no one runs off with one of them."

"Too heavy," Angus said grumpily, but he followed her away from the rail.

Minutes later they were back in their cabin and Edilean was having a last look around. "I think we got everything. I don't think we left anything." She started for the door, but Angus caught her arm and pulled her close to him.

"Lass," he said, looking down at her. "If you ever need anything, anything at all, I'll come to you. You know that, don't you?"

She put her small hands on his chest and looked up into his eyes. "Yes, I know that, and if *you* need anything, I'll help you."

"Me? What could I need?" he asked, his voice full of amusement.

"If you marry Tabitha you'll need a lot of everything. Be sure she doesn't steal you blind."

"I don't think that'll happen," he said, smiling, his arms loosely about her waist.

"Let me go," she said and pushed against him. "The captain will want to say good-bye to us, and I need to see if anyone is waiting for me. Do you think it will be a man?"

"A man?"

"Yes," she said, smoothing her skirt. "A man. You've heard of them, haven't you? If I'm to stay in this country I think I'm going to need a husband. I don't like living alone."

"A man," Angus said.

"Will you stop repeating that? What did you think I was going to do when I got here? Sit in my parlor doing my embroidery and pining away for you as you romp with Tabitha or someone of her ilk?"

"I think I should see any man you want to marry," he said, his jaw set in a firm line.

"But you don't need to do that," Edilean said. "You've spent these weeks teaching me what is valuable in a man. I won't fall for a pretty face again, and I won't fall for a man who just wants my money. I'm going to hold out for a man who likes me, one who doesn't see me as a nuisance of a child as you do."

"You have been a sweet companion," he said, looking at her as though trying to memorize her face.

"And you have been . . ." She hesitated. "When you weren't making a fool of yourself over Tabitha's bosom, you've also been a good companion."

"A fool of myself?" he asked, repeating her words under his breath as though he couldn't believe them.

"Shall we go?" she said, looking at the door, waiting for him to open it.

"Yes," Angus said as he held the door for her.

As soon as her back was to him, Edilean let out her pent-up breath. She congratulated herself on carrying that off as well as she had. It hadn't been easy to pretend to be unaffected by their parting. For all that she felt excitement at the prospect of a new life, the

idea of leaving Angus was about to split her in two.
If she let herself go she would have thrown her arms
about his neck and begged him to stay with her. But
she knew that he'd tell her something about their not
being of the same class or the same education or some
other nonsense, then he'd put on his "hero face" and
do whatever he thought was noble and good—and
leave her. Since there was no hope at all that she'd
be able to make him change his rock-hard, stubborn
mind, she wasn't going to let him have the satisfaction
of knowing how she felt about him.

"Mrs. Harcourt," Captain Inges said as soon as
they were on deck. "It has been a pleasure. I hope we
meet again."

"Yes," she said. "Maybe we'll see each other here
in town or in Virginia. Maybe—" She broke off because the captain had turned to look at the dock.

"There it is!" he said. "I was beginning to wonder
if the letter your husband sent me was correct or not."

"Letter?" she asked.

"When he booked the passage. Surely, he told
you."

"Yes, of course," Edilean said, "but I guess I forgot."

"A woman in your condition can be forgiven
lapses in memory," he said, sounding like an adoring
grandfather.

Edilean had almost forgotten that she'd told Mr.
Jones she was with child. All that seemed so long ago.
Right now Angus was belowdecks supervising the re-

moval of the trunks of gold and whatever else James had arranged to be shipped to the new country to use for his comfort and enjoyment. "What exactly was in the letter that you're referring to?" she asked.

"The green carriage. There it is." He looked down at her and saw her lack of comprehension. Quickly, he glanced about, obviously looking for Angus. "I do hope I haven't ruined a surprise. Your husband's sister is to meet you here, and I was told to look for a dark green carriage with the crest of an earl on it. I can't make out what it says on the side of that carriage, but I think it looks like the one, don't you? But then, I'm sure you'll recognize your sister-in-law."

"No," Edilean said. "I've never met her."

"Oh, dear, I really have spoiled the surprise. I do apologize."

Edilean could only stare in fascination at the carriage. What did she do now? The gangplank hadn't been put into place, so she couldn't run. James's sister? She hadn't known he had a sister. A sister would know everything about her brother's wife and about the gold and maybe, somehow, she was going to know that Edilean had drugged her brother and left him on a hotel floor. And, worse, she might somehow know that Angus was wanted for kidnapping.

Edilean felt a strong hand on her shoulder and knew without looking up that Angus was there, and he knew what was going on.

"Be calm," he whispered. "We'll fix this. We'll get out of it."

She looked up at him. "I think you should go," she said. "I think you should take the jewels and get out of here. I've done nothing wrong. I just took what belonged to me, but you stand accused of kidnapping, and I don't think the court will believe me when I say that I went with you willingly. Go!"

Angus didn't move but stood beside her, his hand on her shoulder as he stared at the green carriage. It was so rich-looking that he wouldn't be surprised if he were told it was the best one in all of Boston. He'd seen carriages like it before, and he was sure it had been made in England.

"I'm not leaving you," Angus said at last, his fingers tightening on her shoulder when the carriage door opened.

Out stepped a woman who was tall and thin, and from the gray in her hair, she looked to be much older than James Harcourt. She shielded her eyes from the sun with her hand as she looked up at the ship, scanning the faces of the people standing at the side. Instinctively, Angus and Edilean stepped back out of her view.

"You can't go with me," Edilean said, her hands on his chest. "You can't let her see you. If she calls the authorities you could be put in jail."

Angus knew the truth of her words, and he also knew that if he had any sense at all, he'd take what he could carry in his hands and leave. But even knowing what could happen wouldn't make him leave Edilean unprotected.

"It may not be as bad as you think," he said, "so I'll stay with you until you know for sure what's happening."

"You wouldn't like to hire a wagon and take me and my gold with you to Virginia, would you?" she asked, only half in jest.

"Nay," he said softly and raised her hand to kiss the palm. "But know that I will miss you most dreadfully."

"Angus . . ." she began, but he wouldn't let her finish the sentence.

"We'll walk down the gangplank together, but not touching. You can tell her that I'm a fellow passenger who looked after you during the voyage."

"And what do I say when she sees that her brother isn't with me?"

"Tell her he was delayed. If she knows him at all, she'll know that he probably ran off with his drinking friends and wanted nothing to do with you."

"He might have let *me* leave alone but not with the trunks of gold."

Angus smiled. "You're right in that, but maybe she doesn't know that. My sister thinks that whatever I do is good, so maybe this woman feels the same way about her brother."

"But you do tend to do good," she said, "so that means your sister knows you as you are."

Angus shook his head at her. "I will miss you every day. I will especially miss the way you look at me. Now, go! You must get to her before she meets the captain. See if you can tell one of your stories and make her think that all this was James's idea."

She held on to Angus's arm, not wanting to leave him. He thought she was kidding about the wagon and running off to Virginia, but she hadn't been.

"Come on," Angus said. "You can do this. Remember that you hid in a coffin. That was worse than this is now."

"I was drugged," she said, then her eyes brightened. "Do you have any more of that laudanum left? I could take some now and you could tell her that I died on the voyage over. You know, like in *Romeo and Juliet*. But wait! You probably don't know that story. Why don't we go back to the cabin and I'll tell you the whole thing?"

While she'd been talking, he was leading her to the gangplank. When they got into view of the carriage below, he took his hands off of her. "Straighten your back," he said under his breath. "Margaret is not as good as I am at tying your corset strings. You should have let me continue to do that."

"Margaret leaves enough room for me to breathe, and you were enjoying it all too much for my taste."

Chuckling, Angus gave her one last push to go down the gangplank. He was just a few steps behind her but trying to look as though he barely knew her.

The woman was standing at the bottom, looking up at her, watching every step Edilean took—and she was frowning.

"You're not the earl's daughter," the woman said

when Edilean was in front of her. She was a handsome woman, midforties, much taller than Edilean, almost as tall as Angus, who was hovering nearby, looking with interest at the crates that were being unloaded. "You look more like the other one."

"I think I am," Edilean said, then drew in her breath. She'd spent most of her life with females and out of necessity she'd learned to size them up quickly. "I'm the pretty one with the gold."

Edilean heard a soft groan of horror from Angus, who had his back to her.

The tall woman gave a little smile. "So how did you get your gold out of my brother's sticky hands?"

"There are always men willing to rescue pretty girls with trunks full of gold."

"Such as this one who's hovering around you now? Here! You. Yes, you," she said when Angus turned to look at her. "You can go now. I'm not going to hurt her."

"She's—" Angus began but the woman cut him off.

"She's here and I'm going to take care of her." She looked back at Edilean. "Did you bring the gold?"

"Yes."

"Good! I have a wagon to transport it to a bank vault. Everything is arranged." She walked ahead to the carriage, then stood still as a uniformed footman held the door open for her. "Come along, I don't have all day. There are people waiting."

"I think there's been a mistake," Edilean said, and

went to the woman so she wouldn't have to shout. "I'm not married to your brother," she said quietly. "He married someone else. She—"

"Yes," the woman said impatiently. "I know what he planned. He married one woman for her title but seduced another one for her dowry. His plan was to steal the dowry and keep the title. Did I miss anything?"

"No," Edilean said. "But it didn't go that way. James did marry the earl's daughter, but I found out what was going on—actually, I was told. I didn't find out anything by myself. I trusted your brother completely."

"You shouldn't have done that," the woman said. "James has never done an honest thing in his life. The first words out of his mouth as a babe were lies."

"Oh, I see," Edilean said.

The woman was still looking at her with impatience. "Is there more?"

"No," Edilean said. "It's just that there is no reason for you and me to . . . Well, to know each other."

The woman turned to look at Edilean. "I want to know any woman who can outdo my philandering, lying brother. And as for you, I would imagine that you ran off in a hurry, so do you have somewhere to stay in Boston?"

"No," Edilean said. She was beginning to like this woman and her forthright manner.

"I have a house here. It's not paid for, of course, because my brother had something to do with it, but

I think you can remedy that. You can put yourself and that man who keeps hovering about you up in a hotel, but if you do that you will be besieged by men who you won't know from Adam. You could find yourself once again swept off your feet by a handsome face." As she said it, she looked directly at Angus, as though he were a man who was in pursuit of all that Edilean had.

Edilean just stared at the woman, not sure what she should say. In her life she'd always had weeks to make a decision. One Christmas she'd had three invitations and she'd taken four weeks to make up her mind. But since the night her uncle took her from school, it seemed that every decision she'd made had been done with the speed of lightning.

The woman was scowling at Edilean, waiting for her to decide to get into the carriage or not. When the younger woman didn't move, the older one gave a sigh. "I'm Harriet Harcourt. I am forty-two years old, a spinster largely because my family scared away every suitor I ever had. I have no income and no hope of one. I participated in this latest scheme of his because it was either that or live with my cousin who hates me and would have worked me to death. James sent me to America months ago to get a house ready for him and whichever bride he showed up with. The house has been secured with only the tiny bit of money he gave me, and if I do not pay the rest within a week, I'll be thrown out into the streets."

She looked at Edilean. "Does that answer your questions about me?"

"I think so." Edilean hesitated. Angus still had his back to her and she was waiting for him to say something, but she wasn't sure what. She had a hope that he might turn, pull her into his arms, and say that he couldn't live without her and to please go to Virginia with him. Instead, he turned slightly toward her and gave a curt nod. He was giving her permission to go with the woman. And he nodded toward the trunks of gold in a way that let her know he'd make sure they were taken to a bank.

Minutes later, Edilean was in the carriage, sitting on its beautiful dark red leather seats, and looking across at Miss Harcourt.

"Do you know if James will come to Boston soon?" Edilean asked.

"How can he? He has no money nor does his wife." She gave a bit of a smile. "Wouldn't it be tragic if he had to go out and get a *job*?"

Edilean saw the fine lines around the woman's eyes begin to crinkle and in the next moment they were laughing together. In spite of all that James Harcourt had done to both of the women, he was the one who'd lost, not them.

They stopped in front of a tall, narrow building that was close to several others and set on a pretty, tree-lined street.

When Edilean paused on the steps into the house and looked about her, Harriet said, "What is it?"

"Nothing. I just . . ." She trailed off. She could have sworn she'd seen Angus, but of course she hadn't.

By now he was probably trying to sell the jewels so he could run off to Virginia and put many miles between him and the woman who'd caused all his life's problems.

"Well, then, come inside and we'll go over business."

"Business?" Edilean asked.

"Yes, certainly. What you're going to pay me for being your housekeeper and looking after you and this house that you're going to buy."

"I see," Edilean said and glanced up at all four stories of it. She held up her skirt as they went inside. The house was sparsely decorated and what was there was in the most somber taste imaginable.

"As you can see," Harriet said, "I didn't buy much furniture. I didn't have the money and I had no idea what an earl's daughter would want. I hope you don't want gilt mirrors and gold frames on the chairs."

"No," Edilean said. "I rather like Chippendale. I've seen a lot of his work in other people's houses, and I like it."

"Then I hope you can draw what you want so we can have it made here. Now, about finding you a husband. I haven't had much time to think on it, but I know a few men who might do very well as possible suitors."

"Husband," Edilean said, as though she'd never heard the word before.

"Yes. That's what you want, isn't it? That's what you were after with my brother, wasn't it?"

"I thought I was in love with him," Edilean said as they walked into the parlor. There were two high-backed chairs upholstered in a heavy red fabric and a tiny tea table, but nothing else in the room.

"Yes, of course. My brother's face is easy to love. It's when you get to know him that he becomes intolerable. Are you hungry? We could have tea in this room."

"Tea would be lovely," Edilean said as she sat down on a chair and looked about the room. The windows were bare and she could see the people walking by outside. Several passersby looked in at them in curiosity.

When Harriet left the room, Edilean collapsed against the back of the chair. Curtains, tea, Harriet, male suitors, James's face, it all seemed to whirl around and around in her head until she thought she might faint.

When Harriet returned with a tray full of tea and little cookies that she had herself baked, Edilean was leaning against the chair and sound asleep. Harriet put the tray on the table, took the chair across from her, looked at the young woman, and nibbled on a cookie.

The truth was that Harriet was very glad that her odious brother hadn't shown up with an earl's daughter. In fact, she was glad that her brother hadn't shown up at all. She'd already decided that tonight she'd write him a letter saying that she'd met the ship he was supposed to be on but he hadn't been there with the gold as he'd said he would be. As a result, Harriet'd had to get out of the house she'd rented and was now living with a nasty old woman as a paid companion. Better yet, maybe she'd say she was working as a housekeeper for a widower with six children. She'd say most anything that she thought would keep James from coming to America and ruining what could turn out to be a very good job.

When Edilean moved in her sleep, Harriet smiled. She was such a pretty girl, and with her wide eyes she looked as though everything in life was a wonder to her. Harriet tiptoed into the little sitting room off the kitchen, picked up a cotton quilt, and took it back to spread over Edilean. Poor dear, she was probably tired to death.

For a moment Harriet stood over her, then reached out and tucked a strand of Edilean's hair behind her ear. If she'd had a daughter she would want her to look exactly like this young girl.

"We'll do fine," she whispered. "We'll make a life for ourselves as best we can." Smiling, she went into the kitchen to see about dinner. Maybe now that they had some money they'd be able to hire a cook.

14

EDILEAN WAS ASLEEP in the new bed she'd bought from the cabinetmaker, under the new sheets she'd bought straight off a ship as it came in from France. On the table were dishes and a lamp from estate sales. The huge chest of drawers had come from an auction of a man who was going back to England. To get the bed hangings, she'd had to drive three hours across roads that were hardly roads at all to the farm of the woman who'd embroidered them.

When Edilean heard the noise at the window, she paid no attention to it, just fluttered her lashes, and went back to sleep. Even when the lamp was lit, she still didn't wake. But when the hand went over her mouth, she woke up in alarm and tried to scream.

"It's just me, lass."

She felt the big, warm hand over her mouth, and when she felt Angus's body next to hers on the bed, she flung her arms around him, and the tears began as she clutched on to him, her head against his chest. She could hear his heart pounding. "I thought you'd gone away to Virginia and that I'd never, ever see you again. It's been months and months since I saw you, and—"

"Sssh, lass," he said, stroking her hair. "It's only been six weeks. Has your life been that bad to make you think it was so long?"

"Yes," she said. "I mean, no, it hasn't been bad, but I was used to seeing you every day." She was clutching onto him with all her might, but he hadn't put his arms around her. One hand was on the bed and the other was at her hair.

She moved her head away to look at him. He hadn't shaved in days and his eyes looked worried. "What's wrong?"

"Nothing," he said as he moved to sit up on the foot of the bed. "I came here to see how you are. How is this woman treating you?"

"Harriet?"

"Aye, that's her name. The old spinster."

"Don't call her that! She's a good woman. She's been very kind to me, and we spend a lot of time together."

"So you like her?"

"Very much." When Edilean reached out her hands to him, he took them in his and looked at them in the pale light of the room. "Something is wrong. Why are you here? Why aren't you in Virginia?"

"I liked it here, that's all," he said, still holding her hands and looking at them. "I'd almost forgotten that hands as small and soft as yours exist."

He was wearing James's clothes without the jacket, but she could see that something was different. "I want to know what's wrong."

"Nothing," he said loudly, then glanced at the door. "Where is she?"

"Don't worry. Harriet sleeps like a dead person. She wouldn't hear us even if we started making love."

Angus dropped her hands. "You say that as though you know what it means."

"I've had enough suggestion of it that I should know," she said with a grimace.

"And what does that mean?"

"What do you think it means but that every man in this country wants to marry me, that's what. I've had old men, young men, short, fat, never wed, widowed, you name it, they've all come to visit me and try their hand at winning me."

Angus leaned back against the bedpost, his long legs across the bed. "And which one of them do you want?"

"None," she said, but when she saw his smile, she changed her mind about telling the truth. "There have been a few who've enticed me. Some of them are quite elegant gentlemen."

"But you've said yes to none of them?"

"What are you up to? Did *you* come here to ask me to marry you?"

Smiling, he got off the bed and walked about the room. "I never left Boston, and I've heard about you. You're causing quite a stir with the men in this town.

A rich young beauty with a fine house. Yes, you're set-
ting this town on its ear."

"What do you mean you haven't left Boston?"

He sat down in the chair beside the bed. "I didn't
come to talk about me. I want to know about you.
What have you been doing? How do you get along
with Harcourt's sister?"

"I already told you that she's a good woman." She
was looking at him hard, studying him. Something
was very wrong but she couldn't figure out what it was.
"Have you lost weight? You look on the thin side."

"I've had no woman to make sure I eat," he said,
smiling. She was in her nightclothes and he'd never
seen anything more beautiful in his life.

"Angus," she whispered, then pulled the corner of
the bedclothes back a bit in invitation.

"You're a she-devil," he said. "Now stop tempting
me. I plan to leave this city tomorrow and I wanted
to say good-bye, and I wanted to hear from you that
you're all right."

"Yes, I'm . . ." She closed her mouth and looked at
her hands for a moment before meeting his eyes. "No!
I'm not going to lie. I'm bored to the point of insanity!
Oh, Angus, these men . . . They're all so very *boring*.
Sometimes I think I'm going out of my mind with the
sheer tedium of them. They either try to impress me
with their great education or they talk to me about
their crops."

"They can read, then?" he asked, smiling.

"So much so that I sometimes wish they couldn't.

They think to court me with poems or serenades. They think that if they read to me in Latin that I'll look at them with love."

"And you don't?"

"Not hardly," she said, waving her hand in dismissal. "Please tell me what you've been doing. I've missed you so much."

"Have you?" he said. "I've—" He didn't want to tell her how he'd thought of her every day. He'd been unable to pry himself away from the city where she was. Every time he tried to make himself leave for Virginia, he couldn't do it. There was rarely a night when he didn't stand in the street and look up at her window. He knew when she blew out the lamp and knew the nights when she stayed out late.

"How's Tabitha?" Edilean asked, the name like a curse in her mouth.

"Fine. We're to be married tomorrow before we leave for Virginia."

Edilean's eyes opened so wide her skin almost cracked.

"Oh, lass, I've missed you too! I've not seen Tabitha since we got off the ship. We said farewell"— he didn't say how "fond" Tabitha made it—"then she slipped away. For all I know, she may have married someone else by now."

"Whatever she did, you can bet that it wasn't good."

"What made you hate her so? Because I danced with her?"

"She has no morals."

"That's a bit harsh, isn't it?"

"I couldn't care less about her. Are you really leaving for Virginia tomorrow?"

"Aye, I am. I have a wagon loaded and ready and a couple of good horses."

"And what will you do when you get there?"

"Buy land. Build a house."

"In Williamsburg?" she asked.

"I can't bear a city, you know that. This Boston is too loud for me, and there are too many people. I like a place where I know everyone."

"Like in Scotland," she said softly.

He shrugged. "It's what I know. And what about you? What do you want? Besides a man who doesn't bore you, that is?"

"I don't know." She threw back the covers, got out of bed, and reached for a dressing gown on the chest by the foot of the bed. But she didn't pick it up. No, she'd rather walk around in just her nightclothes in front of him. "When I was in England I knew exactly what I wanted to do with my life, but here it's different. I don't know what it is, maybe it's all the sunshine, or—"

"The sweltering heat," he said. "I can hardly bear to wear clothes it's so hot."

"I hear that it'll get hotter," she said and took a step toward him. He was sitting in the chair and she was standing, with just her nightgown on, with not a stitch beneath it. "And it's hotter in Virginia than it is here."

"I imagine I'll get used to it."

She moved closer to him.

"What are you playing at?" He frowned at her. "I don't think I should have come."

"Angus . . ." she began. "I want to go with—"

"Don't say it," he said as he abruptly stood up. "Don't ask of me what I canna give."

"Please," she said. "When I'm with you I feel alive and full of energy, as though I could plan things and accomplish them. Here in this house I feel my life is the same as it would have been in England."

"And wasn't it enough for you then?"

"Perfectly, but then I knew no better. I had no idea that there was more out there." He had his back to the window and she took a step toward him.

"You don't know what you're saying. You lived in those boarding schools with other girls. You've not seen how it is with a man and woman when they live together."

"I'd like to hear all about it," she said. "You could tell me. Or *show* me."

He put his hands on her shoulders and held her away from him. "Lass, please believe me when I tell you that what you think you want canna be. You want me to be something that I'm not."

She shook his hands off her shoulders, and turned away from him. "So we're back to that, are we? You've led a life of hardship while I've been pampered all my life."

"More or less," he said.

"Are you laughing at me again?"

"I usually do, don't I?"

She smiled. "Yes, you do. And you make me laugh at myself." She sat down hard on the edge of the bed. "Oh, Angus, what am I going to *do* with my life?"

"Marry some nice man and have a hundred babies," he said, even though a lump formed in his throat as he said it. They wouldn't be *his* babies. She was sitting on the side of the bed, and all he'd have to do was gently push her backward. He ran his hand over his face. "I shouldn't have come here tonight."

"Shall I send you an invitation to my wedding?" she asked and there was anger in her voice.

"No," he said softly. "I don't think I could stand that."

She looked up at him and saw the longing in his eyes. In one motion she went to him, stood on tiptoe, and put her arms around his neck. "Hold me. Just once, hold me as though you don't think of me as a childish nuisance. Pretend I'm Tabitha and hold me as you would her."

He ran his hands over her hair, which was hanging down her back in fat waves. It gleamed in the lamplight. "This is the gold you own that I like," he said, his voice barely a whisper. He picked up a tendril of her hair and held it to his nose, then to his lips. "Those men are fools if they don't make you laugh, if they don't throw you across a horse and run away with you."

"Will *you* do that with me?" she asked, looking up at him, her eyes on his lips.

"I canna," he said, his accent heavy.

"Why?" she demanded even as she moved her hips close to him. "Sometimes it seems that every man in this city wants me, but none of them interest me, and you know why?"

"No," he said as he put his cheek against her hair. "Why are you not in love with one of those fancy young bucks I've seen go in and out of this house?"

"Because I compare them all to you and find them wanting."

"Me?" he asked, smiling down at her as his hand stroked her hair, then her cheek. "They're men who've been raised as you have, who know what you do. What don't they have that I do?"

"What would one of *them* do if he found a woman in a coffin in the back of his wagon?"

Angus laughed in a way that she could feel as she pressed her breasts against his chest. "For one thing, they wouldn't be driving a wagon themselves. They'd pay someone else to do it."

"My point exactly," she said. "Angus, you don't understand that I love you."

"Don't say that." He dropped his hand from her hair. "You don't mean that."

"I do mean it. And don't tell me I don't know what love is. People are born knowing what love is. Even the people who've never had it know when it's missing from their lives."

"You're young and you—"

"So are you. To hear you talk, you'd think you were an old man, but you're young, with your whole life before you. I want to go with you. I want to share your life. I want to—"

He pulled her arms from around his neck and his face lost its humor. "You don't know what you're saying. You're in love with what you think I am. In your mind I'm a . . . a . . ."

"A romantic Scotsman?" she said, her arms at her sides, her fists clenched. She'd just told him she loved him, but he was telling her she didn't. "Do you think I see you as something out of a novel, a man with no faults?"

"I think—"

She didn't let him finish his sentence. "I know what you're like. I know you better than you think I do. You're stubborn beyond all imagining. Even now when you have the offer of the love of a woman who is rich and not bad to look at, you're so damned stubborn that you won't take her up on her offer.

"And you have an awful temper," she continued. "You take out your anger at other things on me. You like to tease, but when you're teased in return, that magnificent pride of yours makes your whole body turn into marble. You freeze, with your backbone rigid, and your face shows me that I have dared to make light of the McTern of McTern."

"If you find so much fault with me, I canna see what you'd want with a man like me."

"There!" she said. "Look at you. You climb up a wall to sneak into my bedroom, lounge about on my bed until I'm mad with desire for you, but when I tell you I love you, you tell me I'm too much of a child to know what love is. And now *you* are getting angry at *me*! You're not only an uneducated man, you're a stupid one too. Go on, get out of here! Jump out the window. Run off to Virginia and—"

She broke off because he pulled her into his arms and put his mouth to hers. Edilean would have said that she was knowledgeable in kissing, as it had been a favorite pastime of hers when she'd visited the country houses of her schoolmates, but those schoolgirl kisses were not like the one Angus gave her.

His kiss wasn't gentle, and it wasn't light. It was filled with all the longing and pent-up desire that he'd felt from the moment he'd first seen her. Since the courtyard in Scotland, when she'd made a fool of him in front of everyone, he'd wanted her. During their weeks of being in the same room together on the ship, she'd driven him mad with desire. A glimpse of her hand as it pushed a golden strand of hair behind her ear would make him want her so much that he'd had to leave the cabin and go on deck.

At first he kissed her with his mouth closed, but when she pressed her body fully against his and went limp so that her whole weight was in his arms, he opened his mouth. When his tongue touched hers, she gave a little moan that sent the blood coursing through his body.

When her legs gave way under her, he lifted her and carried her the few steps to the bed. He'd seen her in bed many times, and always, he'd wanted to lie beside her, to hold her, to touch her. There were nights when he lay in his hammock and just looked at her, watching her sleep. He knew every little sound she made—and loved all of them.

His kiss deepened and her body became more pliant as he stretched out beside her. Her leg went over his hips, and his hand went under her gown and up her bare leg, her thigh, then over her round little bottom.

"Edilean," he whispered as he kissed her neck, her cheeks, all the places on her beautiful face that he'd so longed to touch.

"Yes," she said. "Do with me what you will."

Angus groaned at her words. He'd never known that you could want a person as much as he wanted her. As her gown went up, she moved her body even closer to his.

"Make love to me," she whispered. "Please. I've desired you for so very long."

"As I have you," he whispered, kissing her bare shoulder as the nightdress slipped to one side. One hand was buried in her soft, fragrant hair and the other was under her gown on her smooth, perfect skin.

She was kissing his face and he groaned with the joy of it. Her breath was so warm, so sweet.

He kissed her lips again, and as her hands wandered over his body, his voice caught in his throat.

"Make love to me tonight," she said again. "And tomorrow we'll be married and leave for Virginia."

"Mmmm" was all he could say as her lips moved down over his chest, and her soft hands made their way under his shirt. His head was back and he couldn't think clearly, but somehow, a word made its way to his brain.

"Married?" he whispered.

"Yes, married." She brought her mouth back up to his neck.

"No," he said, and gave her a push. When he looked at her, he groaned again. Edilean in a parlor drinking tea was a beautiful sight, but this woman with her hair spread about her bare shoulders and her eyes half closed with desire and passion was more than he'd ever dreamed about.

But he could not let this go on. He couldn't bear to see that love turn to hatred. He couldn't bear to give her what she thought she wanted, then later see her look at him with contempt and disgust. No, he'd rather go away with this image of her in his mind and live with it for the rest of his life than to ever see her look at him with hatred.

"I canna," he said. "You're not for me and I'll not defile you."

In just a few seconds, he'd pushed away from her and then he was gone, out the second-story window, and down the way he'd come in.

It took Edilean minutes to come out of the pool of ecstasy she'd been in to realize that the man she loved was gone. She'd offered him not only her body, but her love and her life as well. And he had left her! He'd refused all that she'd offered him.

Before she could fully realize what had happened, the door to her bedroom opened and there was Harriet, her hair covered in a nightcap, a dressing gown over her white cotton nightdress, and she was holding a candle.

"He's gone," Harriet said, looking at Edilean lying on the bed, her eyes still showing her desire, but there was something else coming into them as she was fully realizing that Angus had again left her.

"He's gone," Harriet repeated as she put the candle down, sat on the bed beside Edilean, and pulled her nightgown down over her hip.

"He left me," Edilean whispered, her eyes wide in disbelief. "I told him I loved him and he ran away."

"I know," Harriet said.

"You don't know; you can't know."

"I do," Harriet said. "When I was your age I was in love with a young man, but after he talked to my father and found out I had no fortune, he left me too. I know what it is to love and lose."

"But I have money," Edilean said in wonder. "He left me because . . ." She looked up at Harriet. "I don't know why he left me. I don't know why he doesn't love me as I do him." As she said these words, the tears began to come.

Harriet opened her arms, Edilean went to her, and she began to cry in earnest.

"I love him," she said. "I love him but he didn't believe me. He thinks I don't know him but I do. I know him well."

Harriet would never tell Edilean, but she'd heard every word of what had happened. She hadn't been able to sleep, and from her room on the second floor of the house, she'd heard someone outside. She got up to go to Edilean and warn her, but then she'd heard their first words, and she knew who it was. It was the man from the ship. She'd asked Edilean about him, but she'd just waved her hand and said he was someone she'd met. He wasn't important. Harriet hadn't been fooled. She knew Edilean was in love with the young man. And as the days passed and Edilean found all the men she met to be "boring," Harriet knew for sure that Edilean was in love with someone else—and she guessed it was the man from the ship.

Tonight, Harriet had unabashedly stayed outside Edilean's bedroom and listened. It all took her back to the one time in her life when she'd been in love like that. The difference was that her beau had tried time and again to make love to her, but Harriet had told him they must wait until the wedding night. After her father's talk sent the young man packing, Harriet wished she'd spent nights of passion with him. She wished she'd conceived a child and been sent to Devon or even Cornwall to raise the child on her own. But back then she didn't realize she'd not get a second chance at love.

When Edilean and her young man seemed to be on the verge of making love, Harriet had walked away, smiling, happy to see the young woman she'd come to care about find happiness.

But just minutes later Harriet heard a noise on the roof. When she looked out her window, she saw a shadowy figure disappearing down the street and she realized that Edilean's young man hadn't stayed with her. It had taken Harriet minutes to recover enough from her shock before she could go to Edilean and comfort her.

Now, she held Edilean like the daughter she'd never had and let her cry on her shoulder. "There, now," she said. "It may not seem like it, but you will survive this."

"No, I won't. I don't understand. He seems to love me but then he doesn't."

Harriet had an idea that the young man loved Edilean as much as or more than she loved him, but he was that rare breed of man: one of honor. When Harriet was standing outside the door, she'd heard enough to know what his problem was and she agreed with him. For all that Edilean liked to think she was just like everyone else, she wasn't. She'd been pampered all her life. She had no idea what it was like to want something, even a new dress, and not have it. If she were to marry Angus now, Harriet felt sure that she'd come to dislike him.

"Sssh," Harriet said soothingly. "I'm going to get you some sherry, then I want you to sleep."

"I can't sleep," Edilean said. "I don't want to sleep."

"I know," Harriet said. "But you need to. Things will look better in the morning."

"No, they won't. I know I'll never recover from this."

Harriet took Edilean's hands in her own and looked her in the eyes. "No, you won't recover from this, but in your lifetime you're going to go through several events that you'll not recover from, will barely be able to survive. It's how life on this earth is. Only in Heaven do we get true peace. Now lie down there and be still, and I'm going to get you some sherry, maybe a whole bottle of it. Do you understand me?"

"Yes," Edilean said as she lay back on the pillows and pulled the cover up to her neck.

15

"PLEASE, I BEG of you, on bended knee, I beg you to stop moping," Harriet said two mornings later as she looked at Edilean sitting at the table, an untouched breakfast in front of her.

"I am not moping," she said, but then after a glance at Harriet, she sighed. "All right, perhaps I am a bit. But, really, it's more that I'm . . . sad, maybe. Rejection hurts."

"He didn't reject you," Harriet said for what had to be the hundredth time. She'd made Edilean tell her every word of what happened so she could talk to her and not let Edilean know she'd been listening outside the door. "He has very good reasons for what he did." Harriet didn't tell her that she thought Angus was right.

But no matter what was said to her, Edilean was still in pain. For days, she'd gone over and over what had happened. Maybe Angus was right and she'd been spoiled all her life. Maybe she'd had it too easy with men. She knew they liked her. They liked the look of her, the way she smiled at them, and, yes, they liked that she came with a dowry that could support them comfortably all their lives.

But when she'd finally made up her mind about a man, he'd rejected her. "And that makes two," she whispered.

"What, dear?"

"Two men. I've chosen two men and they've both rejected me."

"Edilean, no one has rejected you," Harriet said. "If you want to hear rejection, let me tell you about *my* life."

Edilean looked at Harriet. She was going through the morning's post, perusing the many invitations in it. If anyone in Boston gave a party, they were sure to invite the beautiful Miss Edilean Harcourt. As she looked at Harriet's tall, lean figure, at the gray in her hair, and when she thought about how Harriet had been shuffled from one relative to another in her life, Edilean shuddered. Would she end up like her? Alone, unwanted by any man? Or would Edilean have to settle for a man she didn't like as well as she did Angus?

She got up from the table and went upstairs to her bedroom. Two men, she kept thinking. First James had betrayed her in a spectacular way, and if it hadn't been for Angus— She didn't like to think what her life would be like now if James had succeeded in his diabolical plan. She would have had to go back to her uncle and live on his charity for the rest of her life. After all, if men she fell in love with didn't want her when she had a dowry of gold, who was going to want her when she had nothing?

She looked at her bed, now freshly made up and looking so calm, but she remembered the way she'd thrown herself at Angus. Harriet had told her how her former fiancé had done everything to get her in bed with him, but she'd refused.

"But not me!" Edilean said out loud. "Not me. I offered myself to two men, but neither of them wanted me."

She didn't know exactly what happened, but one moment she was standing in the doorway and the next she was attacking the room. There was a little desk with a penknife on it, and she opened the blade and began to stab at the bed. She tore off sheets, blankets, then the mattress, attacking it all with the sharp little knife. She swept her hand across her dressing table and sent bottles crashing, then over-turned the table. She was pushing over the big chest of drawers when a man grabbed her about the waist and picked her up. She hit at him and clawed, but he didn't let her go.

Vaguely, she heard Harriet's voice over what sounded like screaming, then someone was thrusting a cup at her lips and telling her to drink. Edilean fought the hands that were holding her down, but someone put strong fingers to her jaw and forced her mouth open. She tried to keep her teeth together, but the hand tightened and the liquid was poured down her throat. She was choking and coughing, but they

kept pouring. Someone was holding down her feet
and someone else was holding her arms out from
her body.

After a while she began to feel dizzy, and the
anger and rage began to recede into a cloud of calm-
ness, and she slept.

Edilean awoke slowly and she wasn't sure where she
was. When she tried to sit up, her body ached and she
winced with pain.

Immediately, a lamp was turned up and Harriet
was hovering over her. "How do you feel?"

"Awful," Edilean said as she looked about. "Why
am I in your room?"

"You've been asleep for a couple of days and it was
easier for me to watch over you in here."

Edilean lay back against the pillows. "Why did I
sleep?"

"I drugged you."

"You—?" She sat up abruptly, but then it was as
though all the blood rushed to her head and it felt
like it might explode. She fell back against the pillows
with a groan. "What happened?"

"What do you remember?"

Edilean turned and looked at her with eyes as
hard as steel. "I don't know what I remember. I want
to be told the truth. What happened?"

Harriet sat down on the chair by the bed. "Do
you remember Angus coming to your room?"

It took Edilean a moment, but then she remembered every second of that night, every word, every touch. Most of all, she remembered the way she'd begged him to marry her and take her with him. But he'd turned her down. Spurned her. Tossed her away, as though she were worthless.

"Yes," she said at last. "I remember all of that. But why am I . . . ?" She looked at Harriet. "I tore up my room."

"Yes," Harriet said. "You cut the bed to ribbons with your penknife and you broke all the furniture except for the big chest. You even cut up your pretty dresses."

"Good," Edilean said. "They were never mine anyway. Who brought me in here?"

"Cuddy."

Edilean looked at her in question.

"Cuthbert, the second footman. I'm afraid I'm going to have to let him go. He enjoyed holding you to the bed much too much."

"Don't discharge him, give him a pay increase," Edilean said. "It's nice that some man on earth *wants* to touch me. I guess you gave me laudanum. Your brother was a master at passing it out."

For a moment Harriet didn't say anything as she looked at Edilean. "Please don't let this make you bitter."

"And what should it make me? Happy that I got away from a man who doesn't want me? I could have married him and spent the rest of my life trying to prove to him that I was more than just a useless piece of fluff. You know what he told me? That he should marry someone like Tabitha."

"And who is Tabitha?"

"A thief on the ship, one of the women prisoners. She told Angus a long story about how she'd been unjustly punished because she fell in love with her employer. She even said she'd given birth to his stillborn child. Oh! And having the baby was why she stole in the first place. According to Tabitha, the Holy Mother wasn't as good as she is." Edilean looked at Harriet. "You know what the truth was?"

"What?" Harriet asked, frowning, her worry about Edilean's anger showing.

"Margaret told me Tabitha was one of the best pickpockets in London."

"Margaret?"

Edilean waved her hand. "Another one of the prisoners. She did some sewing for me. Margaret told me that Tabitha had grown up on a farm, but she ran off because she wanted the excitement of the city, and that's where she learned how to pick pockets."

Edilean raised her fists in the air. "But Angus believed every word that lying woman said! She told him a sob story about her life and he swallowed it. He was like a fish taking the bait and waiting to be reeled in. Yet he never believed anything *I* said. I told him I'd had a difficult life and he said I'd always had the cushion of my father's money to fall back on."

Harriet put her hands on her lap and didn't look at Edilean for fear she'd see the agreement on her face.

Maybe Angus was wrong to believe a thief—if he actually did—but he wasn't wrong in his assessment of Edilean. She took the way Harriet ran the household and looked after her in stride, never once questioning that these things should be done for her.

Edilean again tried to sit up on the bed but collapsed against it, as she was still dizzy.

"You still have the laudanum in your system," Harriet said as she went to her. "I think you should sleep some more. Tomorrow will be soon enough to—"

"Start a new life?" Edilean asked, one eyebrow raised. "Another one? A new life when my father died, a new life with my uncle, a new life with James, and now I'm in a new life in a new country. What am I to do this time? Choose one of those namby-pamby men you introduce me to and marry him?"

Suddenly, Harriet had had all she could take. "If you don't want a namby-pamby man, then you should stop being such a delicate lady." With that, she left the room, closing the door loudly behind her.

"What does that mean?" Edilean called out after her. "I'm not delicate, I'm—" She started to get up, but her head hurt so much that she lay back down. She stayed in bed but she didn't sleep. Later, she heard Harriet closing up the house before she climbed the stairs and went across the hall into Edilean's bedroom and closed the door. She didn't say good night.

"Why does everyone think I'm worthless?" she whispered in the dark. Angus said she was a woman who waited for a man to rescue her and that they always showed up. While it was true that James had rescued her from her uncle, and Angus had saved her from James, there had been times in her life when she'd done things on her own. She'd . . .

Think as hard as she could, she couldn't remember a single time when she'd been her own rescuer. Just as Angus had said, she sat in one place and waited for a man to come and fix whatever was wrong in her life.

Since she'd been asleep for days, she didn't want to waste more of her life unaware of what was going on. It was still night when she got up and went downstairs to Harriet's big secretary desk in the parlor.

First, she needed to take care of Angus. When she thought of the night he'd climbed into her bedroom—if she could put her mind away from the touching and the kissing and the way she'd humiliated herself—she remembered that she'd sensed there was something wrong with him. For one thing, he'd lost weight. For another, his clothes were worn around the sleeves. The diamonds had been enough for him to buy new clothes, but he hadn't. Why? Was he too cheap to shell out the money? For all that she knew him, she really didn't know how he handled money.

She spent hours thinking while drawing a pen-and-ink sketch of a face she knew as well as her own.

When the sun came up, Edilean went upstairs to dress. She quietly knocked on her bedroom door, and

Harriet answered. She was already dressed for the day.

"Are you still angry at me?" Edilean asked.

"I don't like the destruction of property, and I truly *hate* feeling sorry for one's self."

"Not me," Edilean said. "In fact, I've thoroughly mastered self-pity."

Harriet couldn't help but smile.

"But I'm going to stop it," Edilean said. "As of today, I'm no longer going to sit in one place and wait for some man to come rescue me."

"And what does that mean?"

"I have no idea in the least," Edilean said brightly. "But I do know that I don't want to end up old and alone. Oh!"

"It's all right, it wasn't what I wanted either."

Edilean's face turned red at her faux pas, but she smiled. "When I get what I need to do done, I'm going to find you a husband."

"Oh, that's a good one," Harriet said. "And how will you do that? Conjure him from a bottle?"

"If I have to, I'll buy him."

Harriet blinked at her for a moment. "With a farm?" she asked softly. "Not a large one, but something nice with big trees. A widower with children would be all I want in life."

Edilean stared at Harriet, unable to say anything. They hadn't been together for long, but during that time she'd never once thought that maybe Harriet would like something more in her life than taking care of Edilean and listening to her bellyache all day about how boring her suitors were. "Widower with a farm and children," she said. "I'll do it if I have to buy all of Boston."

"Your belief that you can do anything and that you deserve everything is what I like best about you— and what drives me mad." Harriet picked up a stack of clean linen and left the room, but she was smiling.

Edilean looked about her bedroom and saw the aftermath of the destruction she'd done. The little tables had been taken away to be repaired—or thrown into the fire, she didn't know which. The bed had huge gashes in it where she'd attacked the wood with the knife, and there were more cuts in the big chest of drawers.

When she looked inside, she saw that there were only two dresses. It looked like she'd ruined the rest of them.

She put on one of her remaining gowns and made a mental note to go to the local dressmaker. But first, she had some other things that had to be taken care of.

An hour later, she called the footman, Cuddy, into the parlor. She sat while he stood. He was a man of medium height and medium looks, a person you'd never remember ten minutes after you met him— which is why she wanted him for the job.

"Feelin' better now?" he asked in an insolent way, but she was already used to the way of the Americans. They didn't believe they were anyone's servants, and they let their employers know it.

"I'm feeling fine," Edilean said, "and I have a job for you to do."

"Anything I can do to help," he said with a bit of a smile.

"For one thing, you can take that look off your face," Edilean said. "If you want to remain here, then I suggest that you act like you want the job."

"Yes, Miss," he said, straightening up.

"I want you to find this man." She handed him the picture of Angus, which had taken her hours to draw. It was a good likeness of the way he looked now, without his beard and wild hair.

"What's his name?"

"I don't know what name he's using."

The man's eyes widened. "Is he the one that attacked you?"

"Attacked me? Who told you such a thing?"

"Miss Harriet said that——"

"Forget that," Edilean said. "No one attacked me. A man——" She took a breath. "I threw a very childish temper tantrum because I didn't get my way, and that's an end to it. I think this man is in trouble and I want you to find out what you can about him."

"He's here in Boston?"

"I think so. At least he has been for the last six weeks. He may have left for Virginia, but I don't think so. I want you to find out where he's been for these past weeks and what he's been doing. Do you think you can do this?"

"Is he wanted for a crime?"

"No!" Edilean said. "At least not in this country. Here." She handed him a little leather bag full of coins. "I'll want an accounting of how you spend that. If you find him in three days, I'll give you the same amount for yourself."

"Yes, Miss," Cuddy said, then left the room, the picture in his coat pocket.

At lunch, Harriet asked Edilean why she was so nervous.

"No reason," Edilean said. "I just thought I heard a noise, that's all."

"Probably another man come to see you. I wish you wouldn't be so nice to them. It makes them think they have a chance with you."

"I did like one of them, that young man Thomas Jefferson. He was quite good-looking."

"Then you should *marry* him!" Harriet said. "Take what you can get when it's offered. Don't wait."

"The man didn't ask me to marry him, he just visited with those other young men. But he's as tall as Angus and nearly as handsome, but he lacks—" She stopped when Harriet sat down across from her to stare at her.

"Please don't do what I did and compare all men to one of them. After the man I loved jilted me, no one else would suit me. There was one man I didn't like because of the sound he made when he sneezed."

"I won't do that," Edilean said. "I promise that if this man Thomas Jefferson asks me to marry him, I'll do so. Now do you feel better?"

"No," Harriet said, getting up. "I don't know you well enough yet, but I think maybe you're up to something. Did I see that dreadful young man Cuddy coming out of the parlor this morning?"

"I think I'll take a walk and buy the newspapers," Edilean said, then left the room quickly.

It took Cuddy only two days to find Angus, and he rightly guessed that the information was being kept a secret from Harriet, so he stepped out of an alley when Edilean was in town alone.

"Good heavens!" she said. "You nearly scared me to death."

"I thought maybe you wanted to keep this quiet."

"I do," she said. They were between two tall buildings, and Edilean was using her open parasol to hide from passersby. "What have you found out? Did he leave for Virginia?"

"No. He's still here. He runs a tavern and a carriage stop about ten miles south of here. He don't own the place, but he does all the work. He's well liked by the people who go through there, and he stands for no nonsense. It's clean too."

Edilean looked at Cuddy but she didn't see him. "Angus is running a tavern?"

"His name is Harcourt, same as yours. Is he your brother?"

"No, he most emphatically is *not* my brother!" she said. "What did you see? Who did you talk to?"

"Maybe I shouldn't say this, but he was easy to find. I asked a coach driver and he knew him so I rode out there and there he was. Your drawin' is a good likeness. I had a drink and a meal and watched what was goin' on, then I went into the yard and talked to the stablemen. They all like him."

"That's well and good, but why was he there?"

"They said the owner was a lazy man and he'd hired Angus to work in the stables, but he was so good at everything that the owner just turned the whole place over to him."

"I understand that he's good at his job. What I don't see is *why* Angus is working there." She was talking more to herself than to him, and when she looked up, she saw that the man couldn't understand what she was asking. Didn't everyone work for a living?

Cuddy handed her a paper with the name of the tavern on it and a little map of how to get there. She thanked him, and later, at the house, she gave him the second bag of coins that she'd promised him.

But all day, the question of why Angus had taken a job in a tavern haunted her. Why hadn't he sold the diamonds and bought the land he wanted?

That afternoon, Harriet asked what was wrong with her. "You're very distracted, as though you're thinking hard about something."

"It's nothing," Edilean said. They were in the tiny garden behind the house, and Harriet was pulling the weeds from around the asparagus. She'd not let them eat all the asparagus, saying that some of it had to be left to grow into beautiful, tall, feathery ferns.

Edilean had said, "I think they would look good with roses."

"Then get us some roses," Harriet replied, but at the time, Edilean had been too busy being miserable because Angus had left her to think about anything else. So today, Edilean was planting roses while Harriet worked on the weeds.

"Nothing's wrong."

"Hmph!" Harriet said. "What are you up to?"

"Nothing," Edilean answered sweetly as she stood up. "So few people in these cities have gardens that they might *buy* our roses."

"What a ridiculous idea," Harriet said quickly. "Let them grow their own. I want to know what's in your mind. You can't go from destroying an entire room in a wild rage to being so peaceful all in a few days without there being something devious going on in your mind."

"Not devious, but maybe good." Edilean stepped back to look at the roses she'd planted. It was late in the season for them, but a neighbor had given her cuttings that were well rooted. Edilean knew that the plants had been given to her because the neighbor was curious, wanting to know the who, why, where, etc. of her life, but Edilean had just smiled, thanked her for the roses, and told her nothing.

"I don't know what's in my mind," she said, looking at Harriet. "It's as though I have an idea in my head and it's just about to emerge, but it hasn't yet."

"Let me know when it does so I can remove the furniture."

Edilean gave a little laugh. "I think that was a one-time event in my life. I don't plan to do that again."

"Good!" Harriet said, and sat down on the wooden bench by the low wall that surrounded the garden, and took off her gloves. "Did I tell you what I did after I was jilted? Other than cry bucketsful, that is."

"No, you didn't." Edilean sat down by her. "Tell me every word."

Over the next few days, Edilean was tempted to tell Harriet the story of the diamonds and Angus, and ask her opinion of what was going on. But Edilean couldn't tell Harriet about the diamonds because, legally, they belonged to James's wife, which meant that they were closer to belonging to Harriet than to Edilean or Angus. No, it was better that Edilean figure out things herself.

After much contemplation, she came up with some reasons why Angus was working at a tavern. One, he wanted to be near Edilean, so he'd taken a job nearby. But that made no sense. With the money from the sale of the diamonds, he could have bought a place outside of Boston. He didn't have to spend his days cleaning someone else's stables.

The second thought was that he no longer had the diamonds. She wondered whether, if the jewels had been stolen, he would tell her about it. No. They could drive nails into him and he'd tell no one. His insufferable pride would never let him tell anyone anything.

There was the third thought—that he'd changed

his mind about selling the diamonds and they were now locked away in a safe somewhere. But Edilean dismissed that idea. She well remembered that Angus had said he wanted his own home. If she knew him at all—and she did, no matter what he said—then he'd buy himself a place and work to death to make money from it, probably while vowing to repay Edilean.

The more she thought, the more she was sure that some catastrophe had caused Angus to lose the diamonds.

"And I know just where they went," she said under her breath.

"What was that, dear?" Harriet asked.

"Nothing. I was just thinking out loud."

"You seem to be doing a lot of that lately," Harriet said. "Not the out loud part, but the thinking." She was frowning because Edilean was refusing to tell her what was in her mind.

That evening Harriet went out to buy some fish from the men just coming in on their boats, and Edilean again called Cuddy to her. "I want you to find this woman," she said and handed him a drawing of Tabitha. There was a face and beside it was a full-length picture of Tabitha in her clothes, with her heavy top and bottom.

"Oh, yes, Miss," Cuddy said. "I'll like finding this one."

"You get too near her and she'll steal your purse. She has fingers like an eel sliding through jelly. Remember that and stay six feet from her."

Cuddy nodded solemnly and put the picture inside his jacket.

"You should go now and look. I think she probably works better at night."

"Will she be with the man at the tavern?"

"No," Edilean said. "At least I don't think so. Angus might not be able to see through her, but she'd know he'd catch on sooner or later. Go, now, and let me know what you find."

"Yes, Miss," he said, and hurried out of the room.

16

IT TOOK CUDDY over two weeks to find Tabitha. During that time Edilean had to deal with Harriet wanting to discharge him. "And why shouldn't I get rid of him? He's not here to do the work."

Edilean would have done most anything to keep Harriet from finding out what she was doing. Besides the set of jewelry she wanted to hide, there was the fact that Edilean had told Harriet she was going to put Angus behind her. "I'll do the work. What does a footman do?"

"Muck out after the horses, for one thing," Harriet said, her hand on her hip and giving Edilean a look that said it would snow in July before Edilean did such a thing.

But Harriet hadn't taken into account all the years Edilean had spent at other people's houses—and all she'd done to get away from people. She borrowed one of Harriet's workday dresses, hiked it up under a heavy belt, and went into the stables.

Four hours later, there was a pile of horse manure in the stone courtyard and fresh straw in the stalls.

Afterward, she was tired, but it felt good to have done something besides sit in the parlor and listen to young men try to impress her. Harriet had been so shocked she'd been unable to speak. Edilean considered causing speechlessness in Harriet a triumph.

When Cuddy at last returned, he looked the worse for wear. His clothes were torn, and his face was dirty. "Pardon me, Miss," he said as he sat down heavily on a chair in the kitchen.

Edilean sent the cook away. "What did you find out?"

"She was bought by a man at the docks."

"Yes, a bondwoman," Edilean said. "It's for seven years, isn't it?"

"That's what she agreed to, but the man said she stole him blind the first night, then ran away. I liked to not have found her. If it weren't that I know some people who are of, shall we say, a less than better class, I wouldn't have found her."

Edilean knew he was elaborating so she'd pay him more, but she didn't have time for that. "Did you find her? Did you *see* her?"

"I did," the man said. "Do you mind if I have a bit to eat and drink?"

Impatiently, Edilean went into the larder, got some cheese and bread, and put them on the table. She saw that there were also some bottles of homemade beer on the floor, and she picked one up. "I don't know who in this house drinks beer, but you can have one."

"Miss Harriet," he said as he sliced off cheese. "She makes it and gives some to us men. She's a good brewer."

Edilean stared at him for a moment. It was her own house, paid for by her, but it looked as though things went on in it that she knew nothing about. She sat down on a chair across from him, even though she knew that sitting in the kitchen with a footman was something that her friends back in England wouldn't have done on penalty of death.

"Where is she?" Edilean asked again.

"Living rough in the woods with a band of other prisoners. I think they mean to move south and buy a place to live, but they'll stay here for a while."

"And how did you learn all of this?"

"I stayed with them for a night."

"Did you?" Edilean asked, her eyes lowered as she poured Cuddy some more beer. "And you saw Tabitha?"

"Thank you," he said, taking a deep swallow of the beer. "I did. That picture you drew of her looks just like her. If you were a man, you could take to the road doing portraits."

"I'll keep that in mind. Did Tabitha have on any jewelry?"

"Not that I remember." His head came up. "Wait! One morning I saw a sparkly bracelet, and when she saw me looking at it, she pulled her sleeve down over it. It was just a bit of glass."

"More like coal," Edilean said under her breath. "When you finish that, I want you to come into the parlor and describe everything you saw, from the look of their camp to what Tabitha and the others were wearing."

Cuddy looked as though he might be sick. "I didn't look at what she was wearin'."

"Did she have on a dress like mine?" Edilean was wearing a gown of apricot-colored silk, embroidered across the bodice with tendrils of lavender sweet peas.

"Not likely." He was laughing at his own joke.

"So then, you *did* notice what Tabitha was wearing."

"I guess I did," Cuddy said, impressed with his own intelligence.

"I'll be waiting, but hurry up because Harriet will be back soon."

"Oh, right, Miss, I'll be there in two shakes."

❧

Edilean had to use all her cunning to keep the secret of what she was doing from Harriet. Since Edilean had "lost her mind," as Harriet put it, and destroyed her room, Harriet kept constant vigil over her. It was as though she thought Edilean was going to go insane at any moment. And all her humming and smiling and keeping busy didn't fool Harriet a bit. She looked at Edilean suspiciously.

In the end, Edilean had to pay an exorbitant

amount to a maid who worked two houses down for a dress that would fit. It was a plain gown with a home-spun skirt and a white cotton top. The first time she tried it on she'd been alone in her room and Harriet had almost barged in with the clean linen. Edilean'd had to make up a quick lie about what she was doing behind a bolted door.

On the night when Edilean planned to go out and find Tabitha, she was tempted to put laudanum in Harriet's tea, but she didn't. While it was true that she planned to sneak out, she told herself that if she wanted to, she could walk out the front door and not tell Harriet where she was going or why. But Edilean knew that Harriet's "hmph!" could be worse than being yelled at.

Instead, Edilean arranged with Cuddy to put a ladder up against the house, and she climbed down it just after midnight.

"Are you sure you want to do this, Miss?" Cuddy asked. "Those people are dangerous."

"You have the pistol?"

"Loaded and ready," he said, "but that don't mean I like this. If I told the bailiffs where they were, they'd go out there and round them up."

"And what do you think would happen to the goods they've stolen? Do you think that the robbers who escape would leave it there?"

Cuddy looked at her in shock. "Is that what you want? What they've stolen?"

"I want one item," she said. "And it doesn't be-long to me."

Cuddy looked at her as though he was putting two and two together, what with having found Angus Harcourt and her asking why he was working for someone else, and now talk about the bound girl who'd stolen something that belonged to someone else.

But Cuddy didn't say anything. He just raised the lantern and led the way to the carriage house, where two saddled horses were waiting. "Are you sure you know how to ride, Miss?" he asked. "That one you're on can be feisty. Maybe I should take him."

"I'll do my best to hang on," Edilean said without a hint of humor in her voice. "Do you think you can find this place in the dark?"

"Easy," Cuddy said as he climbed into the saddle. "You just follow me, Miss, and I'll try to go slow so you can keep up."

"That's kind of you," Edilean said as she got into the saddle.

"Now, Miss, if you'll just move over a bit so I can turn around and head out, we'll get goin'."

Edilean took the reins in both hands, made a few clicking noises, and backed her horse straight out the door. But once the animal was out in the cool night air, it decided to rear up on its hind legs. "Stop that!" she said, and brought the horse back to earth. "If you keep on like that I'll cut your oats ration." Turning, she looked back at Cuddy, who was just coming outside.

His eyes were wide. "I ain't never seen no girl ride like that."

"It's nice to know that someone somewhere thinks I can do *something*," she said as she pulled to one side so he could lead the way out of the courtyard and into the road.

She'd planned the journey for a full moon so they'd be able to see the road and where the cutoff was that led to Tabitha and her gang of thieves. Maybe Cuddy had been right and she should have gone to the authorities, but Edilean felt that this was something she had to do for herself. And she knew that if she'd even hinted to Harriet what she was thinking about doing, she would have said Edilean was jealous. Harriet would have said that Edilean was angry because Angus had turned her down for some poor, downtrodden girl who would never have what Edilean did. And Edilean wouldn't be able to defend herself because she couldn't tell Harriet about the jewels.

As she rode behind Cuddy, her mind strayed back to her own horse, Marmy, whom she'd had to leave behind in England. She thought that maybe, when she was settled, she could somehow get her mare back.

But even her sad thoughts couldn't keep her restless spirit still. She said she'd ride ahead and meet him. She couldn't let the horse run flat out, as there were too many holes in the road, but she could let the animal show itself a bit, let it dance about—and let Edilean get some exercise as she used her thighs to guide the animal. The horse wasn't as well trained as Marmy, but it wanted to run.

The night ride reminded Edilean of Scotland and her hell-bent ride back to the old keep. She'd been determined to get back before Angus did so he couldn't tell his side of what happened before she told hers.

When she stopped, she leaned forward and patted the horse's neck. It seemed that from the moment Angus McTern had stared at her, looking as though he'd never before seen a woman, her life had revolved around him.

When she'd gone so far that she knew Cuddy would have trouble keeping up with her, she turned and waited. She didn't want the horse to get too sweaty on the cool night.

"Lordy, Miss," Cuddy said when he caught up with her. "Where'd you learn to ride like that?"

"In England many women are known for their horsemanship. Do you know where we turn?"

"About half a mile from here, but we can't take the horses. They'll hear us."

"I didn't plan to," Edilean said. "I plan to sneak in and put this to Tabitha's throat." She pulled a long, thin-bladed knife out of a leather holder at her waist, hidden under her jacket.

"But that isn't the plan you told me. You can't—" Cuddy began, but cut himself off. All he could do was look at her with wide eyes. "You're going to get yourself killed," he said.

"Maybe," Edilean answered. "But I owe someone something and I'd like to pay it back." She looked at him. "What I really plan to do is create a diversion, a loud one that will distract everyone in the camp. And while they're looking at something other than Tabitha's tent, I want you to go inside and get the jewels."

"Jewels?"

"Necklace, earrings, all of it. They may be in a box, but they may be in a bag. Whatever they're in, I want you to get them, then get out."

"And what do you plan to do to distract them?" he asked suspiciously.

"I have some things in mind. Just follow my lead and I'll try to keep people from seeing you. Are you clear on this? Any questions?"

"No, Miss," he said, still wide-eyed, and thinking that maybe she'd planted a barrel of gunpowder somewhere and it would be set off. That would send everyone running.

It wasn't long afterward that Cuddy rode beside her and whispered, "Here. This is where we go in. Miss, I was thinkin' about it and I don't think you oughta do this. It's dangerous. You only know one of the women, and she's a thief. There are men in there and there's no tellin' what they've done. I think they'd as soon slit your throat as let you take anything away from them."

"Then I'll have to risk it," Edilean said. "I told you that I owe someone and I mean to repay the debt."

"Is it worth your life?" Cuddy asked, and his tone wasn't respectful.

"It is," she said, looking hard at him.

"Well, then, I guess we better go."

"No, Cuddy, you stay back. I'm going to go in there alone, and when you hear a commotion, you're to come, and you know what you're to do."

"Wouldn't be much of a man if I followed your plan exactly, now would I?"

She smiled at him. "If you see me draw my knife, get out of the way. I may do some of my own throat slitting."

"I'll do that," he said as he smiled back at her.

They tied their horses firmly to trees, and began the long walk into the forest. The moonlight was bright, but the overhead branches blocked off much of the light.

Edilean, walking behind Cuddy, had difficulty keeping up with him. His stride was much longer than hers and she was trying not to trip on fallen branches and stones.

"There!" Cuddy said at last.

Through the trees she could barely see what seemed to be a fire, but it was a small one.

"It looks like they're all asleep," Cuddy whispered, "but they probably have a lookout posted somewhere. Miss, I really think we should go back. This isn't for us to do."

Edilean just shook her head no, and silently motioned for him to follow her. They were very quiet and got within sight of the camp within minutes, with no alert being sounded. Near the fire were half a dozen or so tents that consisted mostly of blankets draped over a rope, but they'd keep the rain off. Inside each one, Edilean could see the dark forms of what had to be people.

"Which one is hers?" she whispered to Cuddy.

He pointed to the one on the far end.

"Stay here and I'll go to it," Edilean whispered, but Cuddy shook his head no.

She nodded back in return, letting him know that he couldn't keep her from doing this.

Reluctantly, Cuddy obeyed her—or seemed to. Ten seconds after she disappeared into the forest, he went after her.

Edilean silently made her way through the woods to the tent that Cuddy had pointed out. Her plan was to sneak inside, put her knife to Tabitha's throat, and tell her it was either her life or the diamonds.

Edilean put the hilt of the knife in her mouth, and went to her hands and knees to crawl into the tent. Her heart was racing and her breath was coming fast, but she had no doubt whatever that this was what she had to do.

She lifted one side of the blanket tent and looked inside. There Tabitha was, lying on her back, one arm outstretched, and looking as innocent as she told people she was. Just two more feet and she'd be there. When she was at Tabitha's head, Edilean sat back on her legs, lifted the knife and—

The next second, she was grabbed from behind by the waist and swung out of the tent and into the cold air. For a moment she thought it was Cuddy who'd grabbed her, but she saw it was a man she'd never seen before. He had black whiskers and his breath was foul.

"Let me go!" She fought against him.

"You expectin' him to come save you?" the man asked, his big arm tightening around her waist.

She looked to one side and saw Cuddy lying on the ground in a heap. He didn't seem to be breathing.

"You've killed him!"

"Naw, he's all right."

Edilean saw Cuddy move, but she couldn't tell how badly he was injured.

"What the hell are *you* doin' here?" Tabitha asked as she crawled out of the tent and saw the man holding a squirming, fighting Edilean.

"Came to kill you," the man said, his voice highly amused. "Woulda too, if I hadn't caught her."

Tabitha looked genuinely surprised. "You wanted to kill me? Why?"

"You have something of mine," Edilean said.

"Angus ain't here."

"I'm not—" Edilean gave a double backward hit with her sharp elbows to the man, and he released her.

"I oughta—"

"Go away," Tabitha said to the man, dismissing him as though he weren't of any worth. She looked back at Edilean. "I didn't take your man."

"He's a bit big even for you to slip into your pocket," Edilean said, and she heard someone suppress a giggle. She didn't look around her, but she could hear sounds of people moving about as they got up to watch the drama.

Tabitha picked up Edilean's knife off the ground and looked at it in shock. "Why would you come out here to do this? My life ain't bad enough for you?"

"Bad life?" Edilean said in anger. "You told Angus a lie about why you'd been transported and you ran away from the man who paid your bond. It seems to me that *you* have caused the bad, not them."

Tabitha glared at Edilean, her eyes flashing in the moonlight, then she pulled down the side of her blouse to reveal her shoulder. Even in the moonlight Edilean could see the red scars. "He branded me! Put his initials on my shoulder with a red-hot branding iron. He did it because I told him that I'd work for him but not sleep with him. Yes, I'm a thief but I'm not a whore."

Edilean refused to be swayed by the thick, raw mark on Tabitha's shoulder because she saw a flash in the moonlight. Tabitha was wearing all three of the bracelets from the parure that Edilean had given Angus.

"Those are mine," Edilean said, nodding toward the bracelets.

Frowning in puzzlement, Tabitha touched the diamonds, then she looked at Edilean in disbelief. "These are real?"

When Edilean said nothing, Tabitha said, "Lord a' mercy," and took a few steps backward.

"You stole them from Angus and I want all of it back," Edilean said.

Tabitha was looking at the bracelets in wonder. "I thought they were pretty but I never thought they were . . . What? Diamonds?"

Edilean said nothing, just glared at Tabitha.

"You were going to *kill* me to get them?" Tabitha asked, her eyes wide. "You were gonna sneak up behind me and . . ." She put her hand up to her throat and looked at the man standing behind her.

"I'll take her into the woods and I'll make her sorry she bothered you," the man said.

Tabitha looked at Edilean. "All I have to do is say yes and you'll be dead—or wish you were—in about ten minutes." She looked at the man. "Take her and that one out to the road but don't hurt them. You understand me?"

The man grabbed Edilean's arm, but she wrenched it away. "I'm not leaving here until you give me back the parure."

"The what?" Tabitha asked.

"The set of jewels," Edilean said. "They belong to Angus."

"So why didn't *he* come and get them? Why'd he send *you* to do his dirty work for him?"

"He has no idea I'm here or that I know you stole the jewels."

"He doesn't know I took them," Tabitha said.

"How could he not?"

Tabitha gave a little smile. "He likes me. I saw it

in his eyes that first day on that rotten old ship. If you hadn't been around . . ." She gave a shrug. "They're mine now."

"No they're not!" Edilean yelled, as she launched herself onto Tabitha and knocked her to the ground.

"It's a girl fight," the man said under his breath, and the next minute he was yelling, "Fight! Fight!" and the few people who were still asleep came running.

"Get off of me!" Tabitha yelled as she tried to roll away from Edilean.

"If you don't give me those jewels back, I'll tear your hair out."

"Will you?" Tabitha said. "I'd like to see you try."

In the next second, Edilean gave such a fierce pull on Tabitha's hair that her head jerked back so hard her eyes watered.

Tabitha kicked out at Edilean's shin, but she missed when Edilean adroitly twisted her body to one side.

"She's got you now, Tabby," came a woman's voice.

Still looking as though she couldn't believe any of this was happening, Tabitha said, "If you don't stop this, I'm going to have to hurt you."

"You may try," Edilean said, "but I'm not leaving here until you give me the jewels. And if you won't give them to me then I'm going to *take* them."

"You can't—" Tabitha began but stopped when Edilean's fist hit her in the jaw. Stepping back, she put her hand to her face and moved her chin about, as though feeling if it was broken. In the next second, she jumped in the air and went after Edilean, who moved, so Tabitha landed on the ground. Everyone around the two women started laughing.

Edilean had known this was going to happen. She'd lived with women all her life, and she knew that no matter what class they were, when it came down to it, girls could fight as hard as males. She'd told Cuddy that what she wanted him to do was search wherever Tabitha was sleeping and get the jewels. She didn't think that winning a fight would make these outlaws turn over thousands of pounds' worth of diamonds to her. Her only hope was to create enough of a diversion so no one saw what Cuddy was doing.

Edilean glanced in Cuddy's direction, and when she saw that he was stirring, was sitting up and rubbing his sore head, she sighed in relief. Obviously, he hadn't been hurt too badly. All Edilean had to do was keep the entire crowd so occupied by her and Tabitha that they didn't notice what else was going on.

When she saw the man who'd grabbed her from behind glance in Cuddy's direction, she doubled up her fist and again hit Tabitha on the jaw. The man looked away from Cuddy.

Tabitha struck out at Edilean, but she moved to the left, then the right, and her fists missed.

"Where you'd learn to fight like this?" Tabitha asked, her fists up and moving from one side to the other.

"Girls' boarding school," Edilean said. "And so many men have been in love with me that they've taught me boxing and a bit of wrestling."

"In love with you?" Tabitha said. "Ha! They love your riches, that's all. Angus told me so."

"I don't believe you!" Edilean said as she struck out at Tabitha but missed the punch.

"You know where he told me? In bed. Nice big man, he is. I knew he wasn't married to you. He stood too far away from you. Ice Lady. That's what he calls you. And he *gave* me that jewelry."

Edilean didn't think—and that was her mistake. Tabitha's taunts made her so angry that when she leaped, she missed and hit the ground, her mouth filling with dirt. Before she could roll over, Tabitha was on top of her, and she outweighed Edilean by at least half a hundred pounds.

Tabitha grabbed Edilean's hair and pulled back hard, then dropped her so her face hit the ground again, but this time a stone hit her chin and she could taste blood in her mouth.

When Edilean turned over and the crowd saw the blood on her face, they started cheering, and money was exchanged as bets were placed.

Edilean was so dazed that when she got to her feet, she didn't see Tabitha's fist until it hit her in the jaw just below her left ear. Edilean moved backward, and as she did so she could see Cuddy searching through the belongings inside Tabitha's makeshift tent.

Edilean began to walk in a circle, each time moving farther away from Tabitha so she got her and the crowd away from the tent and Cuddy.

"Had enough?" Tabitha asked.

Tabitha was bigger, but Edilean was more agile. Edilean stuck out her booted foot, hooked it behind Tabitha's bare leg, and pulled. Tabitha hit the ground hard, jarring her teeth, and when she looked up at Edilean, she spit out blood.

"Have *you* had enough?" Edilean asked.

"Not nearly enough. Not from you or from Angus."

At the mention of the name, Edilean rammed her shoulder into Tabitha's midsection.

17

Angus was awakened by the sound of someone trying to kick the door to the barn down. "Always in a hurry," he muttered as he pulled on his trousers. He'd been up late the night before, getting two drunks up to their beds. Every time he'd close the doors to their rooms, they'd come out again and start punching each other. In the end he'd told them that if they did it again, *he* would start throwing punches. That had calmed them down enough that they went to their rooms and stayed there.

So now it was not quite dawn and someone was wanting in the barn. Angus's room was in the back, next to the tack room, away from the main tavern where the guests slept, and he liked that. It gave him some time off from the eternal demands of taking care of people and animals.

The pounding continued as he was buttoning his trousers. He was cursing under his breath when he heard the man outside say something that sounded like "Edilean." Angus paused for a moment, not believing his hearing, and told himself that was absurd. He'd told Edilean he was going to Williamsburg and that's where she thought he was.

There was another spate of pounding, and he heard a man's voice saying the word again. "Edilean! Edilean!"

Angus covered the floor in three steps as he reached the door and lifted the bar. In front of him was a young man in workmen's clothes—and in his arms was Edilean. She was asleep—or unconscious— and her beautiful face was bruised and swollen, her clothes torn and blood-spattered.

Angus slipped his arms under the man's and took Edilean from him. "What happened?" he asked as he carried her back to his small room.

"She fought a woman named Tabitha for this," Cuddy said as he pulled a great wad of diamond jewelry out of his pocket. "I hope it was worth it to you. It may have cost her her life." His voice was angry.

Angus glanced at the diamonds, not sure he understood anything as he bent down to put Edilean on the bed. "Get some hot water," he said. "And leave those here!"

"I don't have to—" Cuddy began, but with a look at Angus's face, he dropped the diamonds into his outstretched hand. "She said an earring and some bracelets are missing," he mumbled, then turned and ran out of the barn.

"Edilean," Angus said as he gently moved the hair off her face and tried to assess the damage. When she moaned, he saw that she was asleep. He smelled her breath and it looked as though she'd had some whiskey. Good!

Quickly, before the young man returned, Angus undressed her. He needed to see the extent of her injuries. Were any bones broken? If possible, he didn't want to have to call a doctor. He'd repaired many injuries in his lifetime and knew what to do.

Once she was nude, he couldn't help looking at her beautiful, perfect body, at the way her hips curved, her breasts rose. He remembered that she'd offered herself to him and that he'd turned her down. It was the most difficult thing he'd ever done in his life. Since that night, he'd thought of little else but her, and there wasn't a day that went by when he didn't think of going back to her and sweeping her into his arms.

He had to shake his head to clear it of those thoughts as he ran his hands over her smooth, perfect skin, trying to see if bones were broken. He could find none that were. She winced several times when his hands touched a sore place, but when he pressed harder, the bones didn't give.

She had bruises over most of her lovely body. They were just now turning blue, so it hadn't been long since she'd been injured. Her beautiful face, neck, and shoulders had the worst of the bruising. There was a small cut on her chin and a larger one on her shoulder, and both her forearms were scraped raw, but he didn't see anything that would need stitching or that would cause a scar.

"Edilean," he whispered. "What in the world happened to you?"

He glanced at the pieces of diamond jewelry on the table by the bed and wondered where they had come from. He knew they'd been in his pocket on the day he left the ship, and it wasn't until three days after they had all parted company that Angus realized the set was missing. He'd cursed his carelessness, but his mind had been on other things . . . meaning on Edilean. He'd been so despondent after they'd separated that he'd thought of nothing else. He missed her terribly. Several times he found himself turning to say something to her, or smiling at the thought of what she'd say if she were with him. Every time she wasn't there, he was freshly wounded.

He'd spent whole afternoons outside her town house, watching. He told himself he was protecting her, but every man who entered was like a stake through his heart. He knew she hosted endless tea parties for the young students who came down from Harvard College. He'd even seen her outside with them, laughing on the steps with four or five young men at a time.

Every day he had one of the waitresses in the bar check the newspaper; he expected to hear that Edilean had announced her engagement to one of them. He figured she'd marry some man who owned so much land that it was going to be named a state. And her husband-to-be would probably be so besotted with her that he'd name the state "Edilean."

Or maybe that was just Angus's wish. If he started a town, if she was with him, he'd name the place Edilean.

When Angus realized that the jewels had been stolen, he knew there was nothing he could do about it. For all he knew, Edilean had taken them back. He didn't think she would, but maybe she'd so much wanted him to stay in Boston with her that she'd made it impossible for Angus to leave.

Or maybe that was something he wanted to believe.

She stirred on the bed, groaning in pain.

"Ssssh, lass," he said. "I'm here now and I'll take care of you."

When he heard a man's footsteps coming toward the door, he covered Edilean's nude body with a blanket.

"I had to wait until the water got hot," Cuddy said from the doorway, and when he glanced at Edilean on the bed, his eyes widened. "You took her clothes off?" His anger at Angus and his concern for Edilean were evident in his tone.

"If I hear one more disrespectful word out of you, you will live to regret it," Angus said, his eyes flashing in threat.

"All right," Cuddy said as he plopped down heavily on a chair on the far side of the room. "It ain't none of my business, even if I did nearly get killed while helpin' her."

Angus dipped a cloth in the hot water and began

to gently wash Edilean's face. "I want to hear every word of what happened. Don't leave anything out."

Cuddy didn't like the way Angus was treating him, and he didn't like the way Miss Edilean had told him to take her to the Scotsman. Cuddy told her that Miss Harriet would do a far better job of patching her up than any man would, but Edilean had insisted. She'd said she'd walk if he wouldn't take her. Cuddy gave in when Edilean nearly fell from her horse. He got off his and got on behind her and five minutes later she'd fallen asleep against him. He'd been tempted to take her to Miss Harriet, but he didn't. He went miles out of the way to deliver her to some man who'd stripped her naked on a bed.

Cuddy didn't like the man, and his tone let him know it. Reluctantly, he told the story about Tabitha, but he didn't tell Angus how Edilean had sent him, Cuddy, out to look for Angus weeks before.

"So how did she know I was here?"

When Cuddy said nothing, Angus turned to look at him. "Did she send you to look for me?"

Cuddy nodded.

"And you told her in detail about where I was working and how I was living in the barn, didn't you?"

Cuddy gave a curt nod, and Angus relented. "Don't worry yourself, lad, she has a way of making men do things that they wouldn't normally do."

"She does that to me!" Cuddy said, and some of his anger left him. "I've run after her like I was her maid."

"So have I," Angus said as he stood up. "I don't think she's badly injured, just worn out. What did Tabitha look like after the fight?"

"Worse than Miss Edilean."

"Did she now?" Angus said, and there was pride in his voice. "She fought a big girl like Tabitha and won?"

"Yeah," Cuddy said, smiling. "I was in the tent most of the time, on my hands and knees searching through the woman's frillies, but I saw enough of the fight to know it was bloody. I can't believe the women didn't lose teeth and eyes."

Angus frowned. "That bad, was it?"

"Worse than you can imagine." Cuddy looked at Angus in question. "So why was she fighting for *you*? Your name's Harcourt, so are you related to her?"

"Her husband," Angus said without a thought. "More or less. You've had a rough night, so why don't you go inside and get some breakfast? If you want to sleep, tell Dolly I said to give you the best room."

"Her husband? But she has men courting her all day long. You never saw the number of horses I have to feed while they're inside trying to make her laugh. If you ask me, they want the money she has more than they want her. And I think that if they knew she could punch a face with a one-two jab, then come up under with her left"—he demonstrated—"I'm not sure they'd want her."

Angus couldn't help but smile at the boy's enthusiasm. "Go on," he said gently. "I'll take care of her.

You get something to eat and take a nap. You can go home this evening."

"But what about Miss Edilean? Miss Harriet will skin me alive if I go back without her."

"She'll go with you when you leave," Angus said. "She's just bruised and sore, nothing permanent. Now go and let her rest."

As Cuddy left the barn, he heard the door close behind him. Her husband, eh? No wonder Miss Edilean was so wary of those men who visited. She was already married to a tavern keeper, a man who spent his days serving beer. And no wonder she didn't show him off to the world. Chuckling, Cuddy went into the tavern and had a huge breakfast.

Edilean awoke with a start, and panic ran through her. She put her arms over her face in protection.

"There now, lass, you're safe with me," Angus said as he sat down on the bed by her.

She started to sit up, but she hurt too much. She looked about the room, noting the austerity of it. "Is this the tavern where you work?"

"It's the barn," he said. "I'm not worth enough for the owner to give up a bedroom above the tavern."

She knew he was opening a way for her to make a joke but she didn't. "Did Cuddy give you the jewelry?"

"Aye, he did."

"Could I see it?"

"No." He was smiling. "I know you've already seen what's missing."

"But I need to—"

When she started to sit up, he gently pushed her back down. "No, lass, what you need is rest. I hear that was one hell of a fight you had."

"It was nothing to what I did to Bessie Hightop when we were both fourteen. Her father is a duke, and she said I was the school freeloader, always looking for somebody to live off of."

"So you showed her, did you?"

"Actually, in the long run, I lost. Her father was told what happened and he made Bessie invite me to their house over Easter. I was very proud back then, so I went."

"And what happened?"

"Bessie's old grandfather, her mother's father, asked me to marry him."

Angus couldn't help laughing. "I wish I'd been there to hear you tell him what you thought of his proposal."

"When he suggested that I sit on his lap, I said his bony knees would hurt my backside."

"Oh, lass, but I've missed you so!"

Edilean didn't smile. "I've not missed you. After you threw me away like so much rubbish, the only thing I wanted to do was clear the obligation between us."

"Obligation?"

"That I owe you. You've certainly told me often

enough that if it weren't for me you'd now be at home in Scotland with your dear family."

"I also told you that you've given me an opportunity that I'd not have had without you."

"Yes, I did. When I gave you the parure, I was giving you a way to buy a farm and maybe later you could invite your family here to America. But that was taken from you. When Cuddy told me about your circumstances here, I knew that I was once again in your debt. You'd gone from being the laird of a clan to the stableboy."

"I don't think it was that bad," he said. "If things keep up the way they have been I could well own this place one day."

"Ha!" Edilean said as she grit her teeth against the pain and sat up. "If the owner has a third cousin thrice removed he'll leave the place to him rather than to you. When it comes to property, blood will always win."

"Edilean," Angus said, standing back and watching her. She had the blanket tucked under her arms and didn't seem to be the least concerned that she was nude under it. But his glance reminded her of the situation and of what had happened the last time they'd seen each other.

"Would you please hand me my clothes so I can get dressed and leave?"

The coldness in her voice made him cringe. When they'd been on the ship and she'd been angry at him, he'd laughed at her. To his mind, she'd been jealous of Tabitha, and if the truth were told, her anger had made him feel good. But this coldness of hers now was not something he liked.

"I thank you for——" she began.

"Stop it!" Angus said. "Right now, I want you to stop this! What the *hell* were you thinking that you rode into a camp full of criminals and got into a *fight*? Do you know how dangerous that was?"

"It was something I needed to do," Edilean said. "Would you please give me my clothes so I can leave?"

"No. You're not leaving until you've eaten and slept. I want to make sure you're all right."

"Oh, so now you're a doctor?"

"If you didn't think I could take care of you, why did you come *here*? Why didn't you go to your expensive house and let Harcourt's sister take care of you?"

He was glad when her eyes flashed fire. It was better than coldness. "Are you forgetting the reason I went to that band of outlaws in the first place?"

"To make me look like a fool?"

"I didn't have to work very hard to do that, did I?"

They glared at each other, neither speaking. After several minutes, Angus opened a cabinet, withdrew a clean shirt, and tossed it at her. "That's all you get for now. I want you to stay in that bed and rest." His voice was angry, but then he stopped and his eyes softened. "Edilean, whatever possessed you to do something like that?"

It was on the tip of her tongue to say "love," but she didn't. "I told you that I wanted to repay the debt

I owed you," she said as she slipped the big shirt over her head.

"That's it?"

"That's all of it, and we're even now. I no longer have to feel guilty that you left everyone you loved because of me. You can buy land and start a McTern village, and you can bring all your friends and relatives here to America. And once again you can be the laird of a clan. You can strut about and have them all look at you in adoration."

"Is that what you think I want?" he asked softly.

"I have no idea what you want," she said. "I'm not part of your clan."

He started to reply but instead he went to the door. "Now's not the time to argue this out. I want you to sleep, and I'll send word to Harcourt's sister that you're safe."

The moment he left the room, Edilean realized how very tired she was. At the moment she couldn't remember why she'd had Cuddy take her to Angus. She knew she should have returned to Harriet, to her own bed, but right now she was too tired to care where she was. She slid down in the bed and was asleep instantly.

Angus stood outside for a few minutes, his head back against the wall, his eyes closed. That he'd been so careless that he'd allowed the jewels to be stolen was humiliating enough, but that Edilean had found them and brought them back to him was almost more than he could stand. He'd been bested by a girl!

He looked back into the room and checked on her. As he thought, she was sound asleep. He pulled the cover higher over her and smoothed her hair out of her face.

He didn't know it was possible to love anyone as much as he loved her.

Since the moment he'd met her, she'd taken over his mind, his heart—his very life. He'd fought the feelings she awoke in him. In Scotland he'd fought hard against his desire to be with her, to look at her beautiful face, to just be near her. His anger that she'd come into his life and taken it over so completely had shown itself in ways that were out of character for him. He regretted that he'd sometimes reacted with violence—if dropping her into a horse trough could be considered violent.

No one had told him that love could produce feelings other than happiness. He'd thought that when a person fell in love he'd . . . He wasn't sure what he'd thought. That he'd hear angels singing?

But Edilean had produced every emotion in him—except at ten times their normal strength. When the rustlers stole a dozen sheep during the night the rage they produced in him was nothing compared to what he'd felt near Edilean. Anger, happiness, weakness, strength. He felt everything when she was near. She made him sure that he was the biggest, wisest, most honorable man who'd ever lived. Then in the next minute she made him feel lower than a worm.

Shaking his head, he touched her cheek, and she moved in her sleep. He couldn't describe what he'd felt when he saw that boy with an unconscious Edilean in his arms. Angus had thought he'd never see her again. He'd told himself that if he did hear she was to marry, he'd be glad for her. But just the sight of a boy touching her had sent him into feelings of murder. If Angus had been one of his ancestors he would have sliced the boy's head from his shoulders before even asking a question.

But all Angus's thoughts and feelings had turned to fear when he saw how battered she was, her beautiful face hidden under layers of dirt and blood.

Reluctantly, Angus left his bedroom to go into the tavern to work. He'd told Edilean a lie when he said he planned to buy the place. The truth was that he hated it. Serving beer and food all day, listening to endless complaints about everything from how hot the water was to how cold the food was, sickened him.

When he'd discovered the jewels were missing, he went into a rage that would have killed a lesser man, but on the night he slipped into her room, he believed he'd hidden everything from Edilean. He would have died before he let her see what a fool he'd been to have let them be stolen. The worst thing was that he couldn't figure out where and when. He'd spent days retracing his steps to look for them—to look for whoever had stolen them—but he came up empty. He could ask no one anything. Who was going to admit to having even seen the jewels?

Of course he'd thought of the women prisoners on the ship, but he'd naively thought that . . . Well, that they wouldn't steal from *him*. Or maybe he just didn't want Edilean to be right about Tabitha. He'd liked believing in Tabitha's innocence and Edilean's jealousy.

But Edilean had been right, and she'd figured out what Angus couldn't—and she'd done something about it.

Reluctantly, he went into the tavern. As always, there was so much work to be done that it was sundown before he realized it. Suddenly, it hit him what a fool he was. He was in the tavern and Edilean was in his room.

"What're you smilin' about?" the barmaid, Dolly, asked as she filled three pewter mugs of beer from the barrel behind the bar.

"Love," he said, and broke into a bigger grin. He looked across the bar at the tired travelers in the room, then he put his hands on Dolly's sizable waist and gave her a resounding kiss on the cheek. "I won't be working anymore today. In fact, I may never work in here again."

"The boss'll have your hide!"

"If he can find me, maybe he will."

In the next minute Angus was back in his room.

When he opened the door, Edilean was just waking up. "I feel awful," she murmured. "Every muscle in my body hurts."

"Let me see," he said as he sat on the edge of the bed and pulled back the cover. He touched her shoulders through the shirt, his fingers gently massaging her.

"Angus . . ." she whispered.

"Yes, what is it?" he asked, his face full of concern.

"If I don't go to the privy I'm going to explode."

He withdrew his hands, laughing. "Always practical, aren't you?"

"I'm well past practical. You have to leave so I can dress."

"Does that mean petticoats, corset, stockings, all of it? And of course I'll have to help you with the corset."

"I got a new one that laces up the front, but it would still take too long. I'll never make it," she said.

In a swift gesture, he picked her up, blanket and all. "Hide your face and no one will see what I'm carrying."

"Except that my feet are sticking out," she said.

"And such adorable feet."

Her head was under the blanket, and all she could see was his face. "Where are you taking me?"

"I'm carrying you into the bushes, what do you think? Or would you rather share our four-holer?"

"Bushes," she said. "Angus, what's going on? Has . . ." She hesitated. "Has something changed?" She knew she was pushing him, trying to make him say what she so wanted to hear, that he'd at last realized he loved her and wanted to spend his life with her.

"No, nothing's changed," he said. "It's the same as it was." He was smiling. He knew what she wanted him to say, but not yet. He'd told her the truth. Nothing had changed. He still loved her just as he did before they parted.

Edilean had no reply to his words, and a minute later, when he set her down, she found herself in high meadow grass, with trees shading them.

"I'll leave you here," he said. "Follow the path to me and I'll take you back."

It took her only minutes to do her business, then she stood and looked around her. The sun was going down, and the light across the field was beautiful. The brilliant colors of wildflowers were sprinkled among the grasses.

Instead of taking the path back to Angus, she made her way through the field to a big oak tree. The area under it was trampled down, and it reminded her of a place where she'd gone to be alone when she was a child. She'd grown up in the house her father's family had owned for four generations. As her father was rarely there, she'd spent her early life with governesses and nannies, and the oak tree had been where she escaped them. Smiling, she remembered that in her trunk, which was back in Scotland, she had a bagful of acorns from that tree. She planned to keep her girlhood vow and plant an acorn from that tree wherever she settled.

"It's beautiful here, isn't it?" Angus said softly from beside her.

"Yes."

"I often come here to get away from the tavern."

"Then you don't love the place?" she asked, laughter in her voice.

"I hate it." He didn't look at her as he put out his hand and took her small one. "Edilean," he said.

She turned, her eyes looking up at him in the soft light. No words needed to pass between them as he slipped his arms about her and put his mouth on hers.

They were alone under a tree, sweet-smelling grass beneath them, and the woman in his arms wore nothing but a long shirt.

Her mouth opened under his. He could feel her inexperience, but he could also feel her eagerness to learn—and it was an irresistible combination.

As he pulled her into his arms, he kissed her neck. "If I begin, I won't be able to stop."

"No one asked you to," she said, making him smile.

He put his arms under her legs, and lowered her to the ground as he lay beside her. "You must tell me if I hurt you," he said as he touched a bruise on her shoulder and she winced.

He pushed the shirt aside and kissed the bruise. "Better?"

"Much," she whispered. "But I have other places that need healing. My ribs were badly injured."

He put his hand on her leg, and inched up under the loose shirt. "Any bruises here?"

Her eyes were closed and her head tipped to one side as he kissed her neck. He could feel that she was cautious and holding back. With regret, he remembered when she'd been open to him, her eyes full of love and desire. This time, he'd go slow with her. And afterward . . . He couldn't allow himself to think about that, but somewhere in his mind was the thought that if she wanted him and he knew he wanted her, then why not? Love wasn't something that could be based on logic and practicality.

"What of this?" he whispered. "Does this ache? What about here?"

He put his hand up her thigh, to the center of her, and he felt her intake of breath.

In the next second, he'd pulled the shirt over her head, and she was nude before him. He wanted to look at her with eyes of love and lust, not as he had before when searching her beautiful body for injuries. In the gathering darkness the bruises looked almost silver.

"I will kiss every one of them," he whispered as his lips moved lower to her breast, then lower still.

It took a while but he began to feel her reluctance leave her and he felt her growing passion. He took his time, kissing her past the point where he was in agony with wanting her, but he knew he had to go slowly.

When she was moaning, her hands in his hair, he

moved onto her, afraid he'd crush her tiny form, but she pulled him to her, her legs clutching him.

When he entered her, she started to cry out, but he put his mouth to hers and she quietened. Minutes later, they both came to ecstasy.

18

IWANT TO HEAR all of it," Angus said. "Don't leave out even one gesture." They were in his bedroom, Edilean's head on his chest, and it was nearly dawn. They'd made love most of the night, twice under the tree, and when it grew dark, they'd moved indoors.

"You mean you want to hear about the hair pulling and the kicking and the biting?"

"Biting?!"

"No, no biting," Edilean said as she ran her hand over Angus's bare chest. "I don't think Tabitha wanted the fight, but then, she didn't know the jewels were real."

"And you believed her?"

Edilean raised up on one elbow. "Don't you dare talk to me about believing Tabitha! I did *not* believe what she said about you and her."

"What did she say?" he asked, and Edilean told him of Tabitha's words about having slept with Angus and what he'd said about Edilean.

"You didn't believe her?" Angus asked softly.

"No. I've always known she's a liar. *You* are the one who believed every word she said."

"I did not!" When Edilean kept staring at him, he said, "Perhaps I did. She seemed like a sweet girl."

"She's a liar and a thief," Edilean said.

He pushed her head back down to his shoulder. "You've made it clear what you think of her, but how did you guess that *she* was the one who'd taken the jewels?"

"Multiplication."

"What?"

"I multiplied your male intelligence by the size of her bosom and I never doubted who'd stolen the jewels."

"My male—?" Angus said, then, careful of her bruises, he lifted her upward. "I shall repay you for that!"

"And how will you punish me?"

"With kisses," he said, and proceeded to carry out the sentence.

But Edilean drew away and pushed the cover off him. When he started to pull it back, she put her hand over his. She wanted to *see* him. She wanted to look at the body she'd seen so often but that was always hidden under clothes.

He seemed to understand and he lay back on the pillow, his dark eyes watching her. She put her hand on his shoulder and pulled, wanting him to turn over. She could concentrate better if he wasn't looking at her.

His back was broad, with deep indentations from

muscle under smooth skin that held not an ounce of fat. She ran her hands from his shoulders to his slim waist—and when she felt the ridges, she gasped. The room was dim, so she stretched across him to reach the lamp. As she did so, her breasts rested on the back of his arm.

"Do you mean to torture me?" he asked.

She turned up the lamp, and looked at his bare back. The ridges she'd felt were scars, and there were several large ones. She ran her hand over one that went from under his arm to his spine. "What's this from?"

"A bullet."

When she said nothing more, just glared at him, he gave a one-sided grin. "I was sixteen and not so good at concealment and—"

"By 'concealment' do you mean sneaking around in the grass and spying on people drawing pictures?"

"Aye, that," he said. "I followed some rustlers, I got too close, they saw me, and shot me."

Bending, she kissed the long scar. "Who took care of you?"

"Kenna, my sister."

When she felt him hesitate, she lifted her head. "You're thinking of her new baby and wondering what she had, aren't you?"

"Aye, lass," he said. "Do you know me so well?"

"More than you think." When he started to turn over, she pushed him back down and touched another scar, what looked like a burn on the back of his arm.

"Fell into the fire when I was three."

"And these?" There were four jagged lumps on the right side of his waist.

"Shamus pushed me off a cliff and I landed on rocks."

"Ah, Shamus. And to think that had circumstances been different, now *he* would be here with me."

Angus laughed at that, and she could feel his body move against hers. She pushed the sheet down and ran her hands over the curve of his buttocks, then down to his heavily muscled thighs.

"Lass!" he said, his voice husky. "You will unman me."

"You mean no other woman has *looked* at you?"

"Not like this." He started to turn over, but she put her hand on his back and kept him in place.

"I'm not done with you yet." She felt another scar on his left thigh. "And this one?"

"Dragged by a horse over a broken piece of iron. I nearly lost my leg with that one."

"And you were?"

"Ten."

"I'm glad you came to me whole."

"Whole and growing," he murmured. "Edilean! I can take little more of this."

She moved down to his feet. There were several little scars around his ankles, but none that looked as though they'd threatened his life. She sat down at his feet and looked at the long, glorious, nude form of him before her. How strange it all was, she thought. She'd gone through her life being warned by nannies and teachers to keep her body covered at all times, but here she was, totally naked and staring at this magnificent man who had on not a stitch.

Slowly, she slid her body up his, feeling her breasts on every inch of him, kissing his warm, dark skin all the way up. When she reached his neck, he turned over to pull her on top of him. "Wait!" she said, "I want to see the front of you."

"How about if you look while sitting up?"

"Sitting—?" she began, but then he lifted her and sat her down on top of the part of him that was eagerly awaiting her. "I see," she said. "Sitting. What do I do now?"

"Anything you want to," he said in a way that made her smile—and feel powerful.

"Is it like riding a horse? Shall I try posting?" She went to her knees and began to move up and down, slowly and rhythmically. She'd spent a great deal of her life on a horse, and her thighs were strong.

"How about a gallop?" she said.

Angus pushed her down onto the bed, never breaking contact. "How about if your horse takes command and runs away with you?" he said as he thrust into her.

"Yes" was all she said.

An hour later, Edilean was asleep, her nude body half on his, half on the bed, and Angus wanted to stay with her forever, but he could hear people stirring about and he knew he must get up. If he didn't, within minutes someone would be pounding on his door, wanting to know where things were and why wasn't he handling whatever problem had come up.

This will be my last day, he thought as he eased himself out of the bed, careful not to disturb Edilean. He'd let her sleep some more, then he'd come back to the room and they'd . . . He wasn't sure what they'd do, but he knew that they'd do it together.

As he dressed, he watched her, looked at her beautiful, bruised face, at the way she twitched her nose while she slept, the way her small body showed under the covers.

I hope she's with child, he thought, and paused as he pulled on a shoe. Yes. With child. A little girl who looked just like her. They'd name her Catherine after his grandmother. Catherine Edilean. Angus smiled. What would the last name be? Since he was a wanted man, they couldn't use McTern, but then he didn't want to continue using the Harcourt name either. When she woke up, he'd have to talk to Edilean about it, and together they'd choose a new name.

When he was dressed, he tiptoed out of the room and went into the tavern.

Dolly glanced up at him. "Thought you'd quit. Or maybe you just want to because of the filly you have in your room."

Angus smiled. He was used to living where no secrets were kept. "Just another one," he said. "Nothing special."

"That's not what I heard." She nodded toward

the young man who'd brought Edilean to him the day before. He was sitting at a table with half a dozen other men, and he was telling a story that obviously fascinated them.

Angus turned away so Dolly wouldn't see his frown. "And what has he been telling people?"

"That she can fight as good as a man."

"What else?"

"There's more?"

Angus wanted to ask her if the bigmouthed young man had told who Edilean was, if he'd told where she lived.

Dolly stepped closer to him. "He hasn't told who your little lady is, if that's what you're worried about. In fact, the boy's made it seem that she's one of those transported criminals."

He looked at her sharply.

"I saw the two of you," she said, her eyes crinkling as she smiled. "I was young once. She's no criminal, and he's a good boy, that one." Turning away, she went out from behind the bar to serve breakfast to the men.

Angus drew a tankard of beer for himself and drank it in one gulp. He hadn't had any sleep during the night as Edilean had been . . . Smiling, he remembered the night, the kisses, the sounds, the positions. She had embarrassed and surprised him when she'd studied the back of him, but he'd loved it. It looked like her curiosity about the world extended to more than countries and manners. All in all, it had been a night of such pure joy that he thought that if he were to die now, he would regret nothing.

It was when he put his tankard down that he saw the handbill on the wall. It was the same one that had been posted in Scotland, and it was the picture that Edilean had drawn of him when his hair was wild and his face covered with whiskers.

For a moment Angus stood still, paralyzed, unable to move as he stared at the picture hung on a nail in the wall. The handbill hadn't been there yesterday.

When Dolly came back to the bar, he was still standing there. She got drinks and put them on a tray, but Angus still didn't move. When Dolly started out with her full tray, he caught her arm.

"Where did this come from?" he whispered, unable to make his voice work properly.

"A man brought it here last night. I thought it looked a bit like you." She was teasing him.

"Did you tell him that?" Angus asked.

Dolly took only a second to see what was on his face. "No. I told him nothing. I didn't like him. He's a beautiful man, but he knows it. He treated me like I was his slave."

"Where is he now?" Angus asked, swallowing hard.

"Asleep, I reckon. Go," she said in the next breath. "Do what you need to do. I'll hold him off as long as I can. A man like him won't like soup poured on his clothes, but I'll do it."

"Is he alone?"

"No. He has two thugs with him. Frightening-looking men. Angus . . ." Her face was full of fear and concern for him. "You can't stand up to all of them. You *must* go!"

For the second time in two days, Angus kissed Dolly's cheek, then he swiftly left the tavern. When he got to his room, he stopped outside the door. His instinct was to wake Edilean and tell her that James was there, that he'd come to America with his handbill and the warrant for Angus's arrest, and that he hadn't come alone.

Angus had always known it was a possibility that James would come to America to seek him out. You couldn't humiliate a man like James Harcourt and not expect retribution. But still, seeing the handbill had shocked him. If James had only come the day before! If he'd only come before Edilean and Angus had spent the night together, things would now be different. Angus could slip away, and no one would be hurt.

But now he was going to have to leave, and there would be a great deal of pain. Angus knew that he couldn't stay with Edilean. He couldn't even tell her that he was leaving. She would never agree that Angus had to get away and leave her behind. She'd want to go with him.

For a moment he rubbed his eyes to clear them. Above all else, he couldn't let Edilean know the truth. He couldn't go to her and say, "I love you but I have to leave you behind to protect you." She'd never agree to their parting, but that's what was going to have to happen. They'd have to separate forever.

It was as though he could see in a crystal ball and he knew the future. James would hunt Angus down wherever he went—and if Angus had a wife and children, he'd still find him. And then what? If James didn't have Angus killed outright, he would enjoy seeing Angus taken to jail. Imprisoned. If he couldn't be prosecuted in America, it was for sure that James Harcourt would find a time when Angus wasn't alert and he'd kidnap him and take him back to Scotland. There he'd be tried, convicted, and sentenced to death or maybe he'd receive "just" a lifetime to rot away in a stinking prison.

Then what would happen to Edilean? To their children? To the home they'd wanted to build?

Angus knew what Edilean would do. She'd fight for him. Just as she'd fought for him with the jewels, she'd fight in the courts. She'd fight James Harcourt; she'd fight the world to keep Angus out of prison. But she'd not win. Angus had run away with a girl who was still under the supervision of her guardian. The fact that he'd later married her would make him look worse rather than better. It would seem that he'd used her when she was but a girl and against her guardian's wishes.

And of course there was the gold. When Angus and Edilean ran off, legally, that gold was under the care of her uncle. Angus had "stolen" it from him.

No, there was no way that a court would listen to

his side or understand the truth. They'd never believe Angus's preposterous story, and he'd be condemned for life.

Could he take Edilean with him? Is that what he wanted for her? To spend her life in hiding so he wouldn't be captured? Then if he were taken, would she be condemned to daily trips to prison to see him? Or would she have to stand by and see him hanged?

He stood outside his bedroom, knowing that Edilean was in there, still asleep, and he was going to have to leave her. Again. Yet again, he was going to have to slip away from her and let her think that he . . . What? Didn't love her? Is it possible that she could believe that of him?

He had to *make* her believe that he cared nothing for her, he thought. He had to do all that he could to make her believe that he was the biggest cad in the world. The worst villain. That he'd had what he wanted from her and that was the end of it.

Part of him was sure that no matter what he said, she'd know he loved her—and she'd forgive him. She'd thought the worst of him after the night in her bedroom, but she'd forgiven him. He almost smiled when he remembered how she'd been so cool to him at first. But it had taken little to melt her.

Love was like that, he thought. Cold one moment, fiery the next.

But never in his life had he had to do anything close to what must be done now—and he knew this was unforgivable. Slowly, he opened the door to his room and slipped inside. In her sleep she'd pushed the cover half off of her. He started to replace it, but instead he sat down on the side of the bed and looked at her, at her small body on the bed, her breasts rising and falling as she slept. It had been his plan to ask her to marry him today. As she lay in his arms, he'd thought about the service and that afterward they'd go together to Virginia to start a life there. He imagined building the house they'd created while on the ship. He had the drawings with him, and they were something he treasured.

But that was all gone now. He'd not been cautious enough, hadn't taken the anger of James Harcourt seriously. It had all seemed so long ago and far away that he'd not put himself in the place of the other man. They had thwarted the long, carefully laid plans of a man who was without conscience or morals. Did they think he was going to sit back and take it?

Angus stroked Edilean's hair. He knew she was safe from Harcourt. There was nothing he could do to her. She was past eighteen now, and by her father's will, no longer under her uncle's care, and the gold was hers. If she married—Angus nearly choked on the thought—her husband could protect her from any claims that Harcourt made up. It would be easy to prove that he'd married the earl's daughter when he was supposed to be engaged to Edilean.

Angus's only worry was Harcourt's sister, Harriet. Would she take Edilean's side or her brother's?

But he knew the answer to that. Edilean had the money. It was a cruel fact of life, but a true one. From what Edilean had told him of Harriet, she was a sensible woman, and she despised her lazy, conniving brother.

Angus picked up Edilean's small hand, kissed each finger, and the palm. He held her hand to his face. "Don't hate me too much," he whispered, but he knew that he'd have to make her hate him. If he didn't, she'd follow him.

He got up and began to throw his clothes into a canvas bag. He hesitated over the diamonds, which were still on the table by the bed, but not to take them would seem disdainful of what she'd done for him. He took the necklace and the other pieces— they were too gaudy for Edilean to wear—but left the single earring.

After another look at her beautiful face and before he got to the point where he'd never be able to go, he left the room, closing the door behind him. Sitting outside was the young man who'd brought her the day before, and he jumped up when he saw Angus.

He looked at Angus as though he didn't know whether to call him "sir" or to smirk about what must have happened during the night. Behind him the two horses were saddled and ready.

"I didn't know if she'd be wanting to leave this morning," Cuddy said, and his anger of the day before was gone. "I can go back into Boston if she wants me to."

"She can do whatever she wants." Angus gave the boy a leer, as though they were men together and knew about the world. "I got what I wanted from her, if you know what I mean."

He saw the way the boy's spine stiffened, and Angus knew he'd rightly guessed that he was half in love with Edilean.

"Here," Angus said, tossing the boy a coin. "Take her home now. Wake her up and get her back to"— Angus waved his hand—"to wherever her sort comes from. Do you understand me? Take her *now*!"

"Yes . . ." Cuddy said. He was looking at Angus as though he wanted to kill him. "I'll take her away from here. I'll take care of her."

"You do that." Angus threw his pack over the better of the two horses.

"That's Miss Edilean's horse," the young man yelled. "You can't take that!"

Angus looked down at the boy from the saddle. "This is the least of what I've taken from her," he said with a smirk that was unmistakable.

"If I had a gun I'd kill you," Cuddy said under his breath.

"And save the devil from work?" Angus did just what Edilean had done and made the horse step backward to leave the stableyard. "Tell her from me that it was *most* enjoyable."

Cuddy watched the horse and rider leave the barn, then he said the foulest words he knew. He didn't want to wake up Miss Edilean, but he also wanted to get her out of there. It would be better if she got as far away from this place as soon as possible.

He took a few deep breaths, then knocked on the bedroom door.

19

Y OU DON'T FOOL me," Harriet said as she looked at Edilean across the breakfast table. "Something has deeply upset you."

"Talk about the pot calling the kettle black," she said, glaring at Harriet.

Edilean had been back from her night spent with Angus for three whole weeks now. And everything had changed. For her, being cast aside yet again had hurt so much that she was almost unable to feel it. The first time Angus left her, she took her rage out on some furniture and clothes, but this time her anger was so much deeper that she was unable to deal with it. It was as though a red-hot coal had been stabbed into her chest and was growing with each day. Things that had once been pleasurable were no longer. The men who called, with flowers and candy in their hands, didn't receive smiles. Instead, Edilean glared at them. She didn't act coy and flirt and make them feel that they were the smartest and wisest men on earth. Instead, she corrected their grammar and their poetry recitations, then told them they needed to finish school. The men crept out of her house with their faces red, muttering that they were needed elsewhere. They didn't return.

The first time Edilean repulsed an eligible man, she expected Harriet to give her a scolding, but she didn't—which was odd. Since they'd met, Harriet's main occupation had seemed to be to get Edilean married, but since Angus, since the night with the fight with Tabitha, it was as though Harriet had changed.

After her night with Angus, Edilean returned to the house in Boston, and she thought she'd do what she did before and disappear into her room and cry. But she didn't. She hadn't shed even one tear since then.

Edilean had expected that Harriet would lecture her about her wounds and her bloody clothes, but she didn't. Instead, Harriet had ordered hot water to be carried upstairs for a bath and she'd put out clean clothes for Edilean. But she hadn't asked a question about where she'd been or what she'd done. Instead, Harriet seemed to have her mind on something else, and she jumped at every sound.

After about the twentieth time that Harriet was startled by some everyday sound, Edilean said, "Do you think I'm going to hit you?"

"Why would I think you'd harm me?" Harriet asked.

"Because that's where I got all these bruises. From a fight."

Harriet seemed to come to the present enough to

look at her in curiosity. "Did you? And who did you fight?"

"Tabitha," Edilean said. "She—"

"I don't believe I know her," Harriet said quickly, but she was distracted again. "Was that a knock on the door?"

"I didn't hear it," Edilean said. "If it's a man, tell him he can go to hell."

Even the use of that word didn't make a dent in Harriet's distraction. She ran out of the room and Edilean heard her open the front door, but no one was there.

For weeks now, Harriet had been nervous and high-strung, so unlike her usual calm demeanor.

This morning was particularly bad for Edilean. She'd not allowed herself to say it out loud, but she'd hoped that she was with child. It was, of course, wrong to bring a child into the world out of wedlock, but that didn't keep her from hoping. When her time of the month came that morning, she knew that she and Angus were truly over. Done with. Forever. She didn't know what she'd done wrong, but she was sure that he didn't want her—and now she'd never have anything from him.

She looked at Harriet with cool eyes. "If you must know," she said as she buttered a roll, "I was thinking about Tabitha."

"Tabitha?" Harriet asked, then jumped half out of her seat when the maid dropped something in the parlor.

The fact that Harriet didn't remember the many stories that Edilean had told her about Tabitha was another sign that her mind wasn't on the present. "When are you going to tell me what's made you like this?" Edilean asked.

"It's nothing. Go on with your story. What about this Tabitha? Maybe we could have her for tea."

"With or without her leg irons?" Edilean asked, but Harriet didn't hear her because the maid dropped something else.

"I can't stand this!" Harriet said as she ran out of the room.

"No noise allowed," Edilean said under her breath, and pushed her plate away. Sometimes she thought of the difference between herself now and as she'd been before her uncle took her from school. While it was true that she'd had to be nice to a few people she didn't care for in order to get the best invitations, she'd had a feeling that she was worth the finest that life had to offer. Edilean Talbot had been absolutely *sure* that she was better than and above women such as Tabitha. And Margaret. That woman had asked Edilean for a job once they got to America, but Edilean hadn't even considered the idea.

In the last weeks she'd thought more and more about the fight with Tabitha. At the time, Edilean had felt justified about it. But now she wondered what happened to Tabitha afterward. Edilean vividly remembered the branding scar that Tabitha had shown her. Never in Edilean's life had she had to deal with something like that. Yes, her uncle had tried to make her marry a despicable man, and yes . . .

Edilean knew that there were a lot of "yes" answers to questions in her life. But in the end, she'd won. True, men had hurt her, but she'd ended up with a nice home and a fat bank account. Now when she went to the bank, the president came out and addressed her with exaggerated courtesy.

But what would happen to Tabitha? she wondered. After she lost the jewels, what was left for her? What had happened to Margaret and the other women on the ship? In fact, what happened to most of the women sent to America as prisoners? Did many of the men who bought their contracts brand them?

"Oh, no!" Harriet said. She'd come back into the room, sat down, and picked up the newspaper, but Edilean hadn't even noticed.

"What is it?" Edilean asked. "The cost of chicken go up again?"

"Worse," Harriet said. "Mr. Sylvester died."

"Before I could marry him?" Edilean asked. "What a shame."

"Before you could humiliate him so he wished he were in his grave," Harriet shot back. "Mr. Sylvester is the man who grows most of what you eat."

"Oh," Edilean said, uninterested. She had no idea what she was going to do with her day. If she painted one more picture of a flower bouquet she thought she might be sick.

"His poor wife. They have seven children, and the oldest is only ten."

"Making that many children probably killed him," Edilean said.

"You're in a worse mood than usual this morning. But then, you usually are in a bad way, aren't you? Are you sure you don't want to tell me about it?"

"I will when you tell me why you jump at every noise that's made in this house."

Harriet looked across the table at her for a moment, then went back to her newspaper. "I wonder what will happen to them now? I can't see Mrs. Sylvester tending to the farm when she has that many young children. Besides, she didn't strike me as being interested in growing the best apples."

Edilean couldn't contain how boring she thought this conversation was. "What's the difference? An apple is an apple."

"You wouldn't think that if you went to the market with me."

"I think I can find something better to do."

"What? Stay in this house all day and feel sorry for yourself? Draw more pictures of roses? You think I'm bad with my problems, but you're worse. You are— Oh!" Harriet cut off her tirade because there was a shout in the street, then what sounded like carriages hitting each other.

"Will you *please* stop jumping?!" Edilean shouted as she stood up from the table. "I'll go to the market with you. I'll look at all the apples. I'll do whatever you want if you'll just stop *jumping*!"

Harriet threw her napkin on the table and stood up. "I'll stop being startled when you stop retreating from the world every time that renegade of a man does something awful to you! When are you going to stop letting some man who has proven that he *does not want you* rule your every thought and action? When are you going to *grow up* and think about something other than your own pleasure in life? You didn't get what you want out of life. Neither did any of us! But *we* don't have your money and your exalted education so *we* can't sit around and paint butterflies while other people wait on us."

With that she left the room, her heels echoing on the wooden floors as she went upstairs to her bedroom and slammed the door.

Edilean sat back down in stunned silence, looking at the space where Harriet had been.

When Edilean turned around, she saw three maids standing in the doorway, looking at her. They scurried away when she saw them, but she'd seen their eyes. They'd heard every word Harriet had shouted at her, and their expressions said they agreed with her.

Did they hate her? Edilean wondered. She left the running of the household to Harriet, so she took little notice of the maids. The truth was that she didn't even know the names of two of them.

Edilean well knew that every word Harriet had said was true. Since the day she'd met Angus McTern, he'd dominated her every thought and deed. On the ship, it had been the worst. If it was good between her and Angus, she was happy. If it was bad, she was miserable. Happiness, sadness, all her emotions were controlled by a man who, as Harriet said, *did not want her.* She'd have to remember those words. But the truth was that she was sure she'd go to her grave remembering them. What would be on her gravestone? she wondered. HERE LIES EDILEAN TALBOT, WHO SPENT HER LIFE IN MISERY BECAUSE ANGUS MCTERN DIDN'T WANT HER.

All in all, Edilean thought, True Love was better to read about than to experience. In real life, love hurt more than it made a person feel good.

The problem was what to do about it all. How did one change one's self? In England, no one had questioned her validity. She was a wealthy young woman, nice to look at, and that was everything she needed to be. No one expected her to do anything except to marry well. But her father's will had changed that. He'd given her rights over her own money and her own life.

The problem was that in this new country people seemed to expect everyone to pull his or her own weight. Through the church in Boston, she'd met American women from wealthy families who worked harder than the maids. They made their own jam, dug their own potatoes, and an hour later delivered a nine-pound child. It was what she'd feared ending up with in Scotland.

Just the thought of all that made Edilean want to get on a ship and go back to England. She could buy herself a nice house and . . . She didn't know what was to happen after that. Sit there and wait for suitors to come to her?

When she heard Harriet in the hallway, Edilean got up and went to her. Harriet was angrily tying the ribbons on her bonnet.

"Would you mind if I went with you?" Edilean asked meekly.

"You do what you want to, you always do," Harriet said as she picked up a big market basket, and opened the front door.

Edilean grabbed her bonnet, but she didn't need to hurry because Harriet paused on the doorstep and looked around, as though she expected someone to leap out of the bushes. Edilean didn't ask who or what she was looking for because she knew Harriet wouldn't tell her.

Harriet hurried down the streets so fast that Edilean had to run to keep up with her. She held her bonnet on with her hand, the ribbons trailing out behind her. Four gentlemen doffed their hats at her, but she didn't have time for them.

Edilean had never been to a street market, but she'd been to many of Boston's better shops when she was buying what they needed for the house. To her mind, the decoration of a house was something that a "lady" did, but except for overseeing the kitchen garden, food wasn't her concern. She might go over the menu with the cook, but "ladies" didn't go to the fish market and haggle. All her life, she'd left that task to other people.

Harriet turned a corner, and Edilean stopped, her eyes open in wonder at the loud chaos before her. There seemed to be a hundred wagons, all of them laden with produce, meat, and homemade goods that had been brought to town to sell on market day.

"It's wonderful," she said under her breath.

Harriet turned to look at her, anger still on her face, but when she saw Edilean's expression, she softened. "Stay close to me and don't buy anything. These merchants will bargain you into the poorhouse."

Edilean nodded as she looked at the people and carts lining the street. She started to take a step forward, but Harriet pulled her back. She'd almost stepped into a pile of horse manure.

"What can I sell a pretty lady like you?" asked a man with most of his teeth black.

"Nothing!" Harriet said as she pulled Edilean forward. "He's a dreadful man who'd sell his own mother if he thought he could get a good price."

"Do you know all of these vendors?"

"Most of them," Harriet said. "You have to learn who you can trust."

"And you trusted Mr. Sylvester?"

"Completely. Oh! Look! His wife has the cart here. Come and see what she's brought."

They went to a large cart where the produce was displayed in a haphazard way that Edilean didn't think was very appealing, but Harriet didn't seem to notice as she began to paw through the vegetables. Edilean stood back and looked at the place. It was extremely busy, with what looked to be hundreds of people rushing about. Most of the women carried big baskets like Harriet's, and they were fighting crowds and arguing with sellers at the top of their lungs.

For all that it was exciting, there was also an air of frustration about the place, as though the men were enjoying themselves, but the women just wanted to get it all done and over with.

Behind the wagon was a young woman with a belly swollen with child and a toddler on her hip. She was gently crying into a handkerchief while three women hovered around her, looks of sympathy on their faces.

"Is that the widow?" Edilean asked Harriet.

"Yes. She's much younger than her husband was. She certainly looks young to have seven children, doesn't she?"

"Very young," Edilean agreed.

"Poor thing. I wonder what she'll do now."

"Sell the farm, make thousands, and marry someone else," Edilean said quickly.

"You seem sure of yourself," Harriet said as she picked up a plum and inspected it.

"Is it good enough for our table?" There was amusement in Edilean's voice.

"Why don't you go look around and see what the others have to offer?" Harriet said impatiently. "But just look; don't buy."

As Edilean took her up on the suggestion and began to walk around, she saw what Harriet meant. Several of the carts held produce that didn't look fit to buy. It had been thrown into the wagon, so it was bruised, which meant it would rot in a day or two.

When she got to the end of the long row, there was a woman with her back to her who looked familiar. When she turned, Edilean saw that it was Tabitha, and in spite of herself, she almost felt that she was seeing an old friend. Edilean knew so few people in America, and here was one of them.

She wasn't sure if Tabitha saw her, but when she moved away, Edilean followed. She turned a corner, then stopped, for Tabitha had disappeared.

In the next second, Tabitha slipped out from beside a building and confronted Edilean. "What do *you* want?" Tabitha asked in anger. "You didn't get enough of hurting me the last time? You came back to do more?" As she spoke, she was looking Edilean in her silk dress up and down with contempt.

"What happened to you after our confrontation?" Edilean asked, noting that Tabitha was filthy. On the ship she'd had enough pride in herself that she'd kept her hair neat and her clothes clean, but now she looked like she'd given up.

"What do you care?"

"I don't," Edilean said as she started to turn away.

"I could kill you for what you done to me," Tabitha called out after her.

"Whatever do you mean?" Edilean asked, looking back at her. "You're the thief, not me."

"How was I to know your lover had diamonds? I thought they were just glass. They were in his pocket like so much rubbish, and when I brushed up against him, I just slipped them out. Who carries diamonds about in his pocket?"

Edilean wondered the same thing but didn't say so. "And I took them from you and gave them back to him. Is that why you're so angry and so . . ." She looked her up and down.

"Dirty?"

Edilean gave a little shrug.

"They . . . the people in the camp took the bracelets, then threw me out on my own because of what you did to me. They said I was worthless to not know what I'd taken—and to let a lady like you beat me in a fight. But you was fightin' for your life. I wasn't."

"True," Edilean said coolly. "But I did beat you." She knew that, logically, she owed this woman nothing, but still, she couldn't seem to make herself leave. "Where are you living now?"

Tabitha's face hardened. "Anywhere I can. With whatever man will have me for the night."

A month ago, Edilean wouldn't have fully understood what Tabitha meant, but she did now. To think of doing *that* with a man you didn't love! It almost made her sick at her stomach. And Edilean well remembered that Tabitha had loudly declared she was no whore. She'd been branded by a man rather than bed him. But because of what Edilean had done to Tabitha, the woman was now walking the streets. "I have to go," Edilean said. "Someone is waiting for me."

"People always wait for rich women like you," Tabitha said with a sneer.

Edilean's temper rose to make her face red. "You may think you've had it easy, but I've been betrayed as often as you have!"

"So you didn't get the man?" Tabitha smiled. "At least I've heard something good today."

Edilean couldn't help it as her hands made into fists and she had an urge to punch Tabitha. They were glaring at each other like two dogs about to fight when Edilean said, "Why did you leave your father's farm?"

For a moment Tabitha looked startled, but then she straightened her shoulders. "He wasn't my father but my stepfather, and he married my mother to get at her daughters. After three years of it I ran away. What does that matter to you?"

Edilean took a step closer to her. "What kind of farm was it?"

"What does that mean?"

Edilean stared at her.

"It was a farm with cows and pigs and corn. What other kind of farm is there?"

"What if I bought a farm and gave you a job?"

"You? Buy a farm?" Tabitha asked, her lips curled into a sneer.

Edilean turned and started back down the street.

"Wait!" Tabitha called out.

Edilean stopped walking but she didn't turn around.

"Who else would be on the farm? I can't do it all by myself. There's a lot of work on a farm."

Edilean turned back around. "I haven't thought about this, so I don't know the details, but some man died a few days ago, and I think his farm is going to be for sale."

"And you thought you'd ask *me* to run it?"

"Why not? Or would you rather keep on making your living stealing and doing vulgar things with men?"

"I'd rather—" Tabitha started to make a sarcastic remark but thought better of it. "Will you get men to run the place? I have trouble with men."

"We all do," Edilean said with a sigh. "I was happy until I met James, then my uncle. And Angus . . ." She waved her hand. "That's over with. Harriet—she's the woman I live with—thinks I'm useless. In fact, nearly everyone I've met in the last year thinks I'm useless. I'd like to prove them wrong."

"You can't run a farm with just women."

"Why not?" Edilean asked.

"Because men have to . . . They have to lift heavy things."

"We'll get some big horses. I rode on a wagon pulled by Clydesdales, and they could have hauled mountains." As she spoke, what had been just a flippant thought was forming in her mind in a solid way. Why couldn't women run a farm business? They'd be known for having the best fruit at the market. It wouldn't be bruised and they'd display it beautifully. Edilean had a vision of green pears on yellow, watered silk.

She looked Tabitha up and down and remembered what she'd looked like when she was clean—and a picture began taking shape in her head. "Bound Girl," she said.

"What?"

"I'll form a business. 'Bound Girl.' That's what I'll name the company."

"Company?"

"Yes," Edilean said, then narrowed her eyes at Tabitha. "I know you're a liar and that you love to tell people long, sad stories about your life, but I'll tell you now that if you lie to *me* and if you ever so much as steal a hairpin from me, I'll throw you out. No second chances. No amount of begging and pleading will make me forgive you, and you'll be out on your own. Do you understand me?"

"Yeah," Tabitha said insolently.

"I'm serious and I want you to be too. Do we have an agreement?"

Tabitha thought about what Edilean was saying, and she took the smirk off her face. "You get me off the streets and I won't steal from you or lie to you. I won't say the same about what I'll do to others, but I'll stay away from you."

"You steal from men and you'll find yourself in

prison if not hanged, but that's up to you," Edilean said. "Now, come along. I have to tell Harriet."

Ten minutes later, she'd made her way through the crowd to Harriet, who was haggling with a man about the price of beans. "He's a thief," she said when she saw Edilean. "And look at these things. They have bugs on them."

"Take 'em or not, it don't matter to me," the man by the wagon said.

Muttering to herself, Harriet put them in her basket with the other produce she'd bought, and glanced at Edilean. "Why do you have that look on your face?" She leaned closer to her. "And why is that dreadful woman following you?"

"This is Tabitha."

"The one you . . ." Harriet looked back at Tabitha with eyes of wonder. "She looks like a lady of the evening."

"She is, and it's my fault," Edilean said as she took Harriet's arm and pulled her to one side where they wouldn't be heard. "I'm going to buy Mr. Sylvester's farm."

"Are you?" Harriet's face showed new amusement. "And what will you do with it? Plant roses?"

"That's a good idea. I can see white roses with dark red plums."

Harriet put her hand to Edilean's forehead. "You've had too much sun."

"I've had too much of everything and not enough of anything."

"When we get home I'm going to give you some laudanum and you can sleep."

"You and your brother and that blasted laudanum!" Edilean said.

"What about my brother?" Harriet asked stiffly.

"Nothing about your brother! Harriet! Will you stop acting as though you're my mother and *listen* to me? I'm going to buy a farm, and you and I are going to run it. You're going to handle the money, because you're so good at pinching every penny until it screams, and I'm going to handle . . ." Edilean wasn't sure what she was going to do, but she'd never been more sure in her life that she was going to do *this*.

"You can't buy a farm. You know nothing about farming," Harriet said. "You can't—"

"This morning you were complaining that I'd never done anything in my life, and now all you can say is that I can't do what I want to. No!" Edilean said when Harriet started to defend herself. "You stay here with Tabitha while I go talk to Mr. Sylvester's widow."

"You cannot think to leave me here with that . . . that woman!"

"Yes, I can," Edilean said as she pried Harriet's fingers off her arm. "And you'll be perfectly safe because believe me when I tell you that I know from experience that she's not very good in a fight."

Harriet looked as though she was going to faint.

Edilean turned to Tabitha. "Don't do anything to scare her or I'll not let you in on this."

Tabitha nodded but she looked at Harriet with a wicked gleam in her eye.

"Do buck up, Harriet," Edilean said. "After you give her a bath and clean clothes, you'll see that she's fairly presentable."

"Me?" Harriet said. "*I* am to bathe her? Are you mad?"

"Probably," Edilean said over her shoulder as she hurried toward the Sylvester wagon. "I am probably totally insane."

Part Two

THE AMERICAN FRONTIER
1770
FOUR YEARS LATER

20

"Harcourt," Colonel Wellman said, "I want you to find my daughter's . . . I hate to say it, her fiancé. The damned fool got himself kidnapped by the Indians."

"Which ones?" Angus asked.

"Which ones what?" the colonel snapped.

"Which tribe of Indians?"

"How the hell would *I* know? The savages are your job, not mine. All I know is that the idiot boy has disappeared, and my daughter is crying herself to sleep every night. Tell me, Harcourt, do *you* understand women?"

"Not in the least," Angus said honestly.

"I offered my daughter a *man*, but she'd rather have a worthless boy like Matthew Aldredge. When I heard that the coach he was on had been attacked, I was tempted to tell her the boy was dead. But she was there when I heard, so she knew the truth."

Angus didn't reply to what the colonel was saying. He'd learned early on that it was better to never give his opinion to anyone in the army, and especially not to an arrogant blowhard like Colonel Wellman. But since Angus wasn't in the army, Wellman felt he could talk to him freely. This consisted of hours of Angus having to listen to Wellman's lectures on everything from food to horse care to how everyone should run his own life.

Wellman's only weakness was his pretty young daughter, Betsy. According to him, she was virtuous, demure, and needed constant protection. The truth was that she was a self-centered little hussy who used her father's rank to threaten any man who tried to say no to her. Twice she'd come on to Angus. The first time he was polite, but the second time he said he'd take her to the captain and tell him the truth. After that, she left him alone.

The men who took her up on her offers lived in fear of being found out by her father. In the three years that Angus had been at the fort, Betsy had tearfully accused two young men of having made inappropriate advances to her. The truth was that she'd made the men's lives hell. At first, they'd loved the insatiable desires of the girl, but when she began to make them late for drills, when she would crawl into the barracks window at 3 A.M. and cry that he didn't love her anymore, the men tried to break it off. The girl then told her father a pack of lies, and the young men were sent off on some dangerous mission. Neither of them had returned alive.

But that was all before Captain Austin came to

the fort. He was short, stocky, ugly, and mean, and he didn't believe in mercy or leniency. He was fresh from England, descended from generations of soldiers, and to him there was only one way to do things: *his* way. But after Austin caught Betsy slipping about the post in the wee hours of the night, he put a stop to it. He told her father that his daughter was so beautiful he feared that she'd have her virtue taken by one of the Americans. Iron bars were put over her bedroom window. When Betsy started making eyes at a handsome young soldier newly arrived from North Carolina, Austin saw to it that the man was transferred.

The whole escapade greatly amused both the soldiers and the Watchers, as the four men who served as guides for the fort were called.

But it was a shock to all of them when Colonel Wellman told someone that he wanted his daughter to *marry* Captain Austin. As for Betsy, she told anyone who'd stand still that she'd rather marry the devil.

Now, Angus was hearing that young Betsy had an English fiancé. Angus's first thought was "poor man."

"He's worthless!" Colonel Wellman said. "Utterly without value. He's the youngest son of a rich man, but he'll receive nothing. Not a dime. And, he plans to become a clergyman. Can you imagine *my* daughter as the wife of a minister?"

Angus thought it was better not to answer that question. As always, Wellman had on his full uniform, red jacket and all. It was joked that the uniform was his skin. "Like a tattoo" was the consensus.

As for Angus, he was wearing the gear of a frontiersman. It was all deerskin, light, supple, and it protected him from the elements, as he spent most of his time out of doors. His job as a Watcher was to see that the borders were respected. The greedy American settlers weren't to encroach on the territory the government said belonged to the Indians, and the Indians weren't to destroy the property or the lives of the settlers. And too, there were a few angry Frenchmen still hanging around. The French and Indian War had ended eight years before, but there were still Frenchmen who believed that the land west of the Allegheny Mountains belonged to them.

"You want me to find her fiancé?" Angus asked.

"Yes. No. She wants him, but I don't. Why would a spunky girl like my Betsy want an effeminate, worthless, cowardly—?" He waved his hand. "Captain Austin said he'd been taken west of here, so find the boy. Or, better yet, bring back his body. Take some men and go get whatever you can find that's left of him. Men like him don't survive long out here."

"Mac, Connor, and Welsch," Angus said quickly. Most of the soldiers were English, but Mac was from the Highlands of Scotland, while Connor and Welsch had been born in America. Mac—Alexander McDowell—at thirty-six, was the oldest enlisted man. He'd been promoted for valor many times, but he'd been demoted for insolence an equal number of times. Right now he was down to corporal, and from the way Austin had been eyeing him, he'd soon be a private. T. C. Connor and Naphtali Welsch were young, new, and handsome. And they were already being targeted by Betsy, which meant that, without help, their lives wouldn't last long.

At the names, Wellman gave Angus a sharp look. "Sure you don't want to take some more experienced men than those last two?"

"Sure of it," Angus said but didn't explain further.

Wellman gave Angus a hard look, as though trying to figure out what was in his mind, but then he turned away. Angus wasn't a soldier and he wasn't English so, to Wellman's mind, there was no possibility of understanding him.

Angus waited patiently for the man to say he was dismissed. He well knew that the colonel was a stickler for obeying orders, and Angus did the best he could to stay out of trouble. Most of the time, taking orders stuck in his throat, but he didn't want to cause anyone to look into his background and find out about an Angus McTern who was wanted for kidnapping and theft.

"What are you waiting for?" Wellman said, as though Angus were standing around from idleness.

Angus grit his teeth and turned away before the man could see the anger that flashed across his face. He knew he'd have to put up with this man and this job for another year or two, then George Mercer, a representative of the Ohio Company, would return from England with a grant from the king, and Angus would be one of the men who was given a thousand acres in the new territory. All he had to do was keep his mouth shut and obey the rules the English made and he'd be set for life. It wasn't what he truly wanted—nothing without Edilean was—but it was the best he could do under the circumstances.

He left the colonel's office to step into the warm spring sunshine and saw that Mac, with young Connor and Welsch, was waiting for him. Angus looked into the shadows near the barracks and saw Captain Austin give a little smile before he disappeared inside the building. The man had known what the colonel was giving Angus to do, and he knew who Angus would choose to go with him. Damn him! Angus thought. He hated being known. If Jackknife Austin knew that much about Angus, then he probably knew he was hiding from someone.

"You want us?" Mac asked. Everyone complained that Mac's accent was so thick that they couldn't understand him, but to Angus's ear it sounded good. It reminded him of the cool hills of Scotland, and of his family. He'd never asked, but Angus had an idea that Mac also had a lot of secrets.

"I'll tell you everything on the way there," Angus said to Mac.

Welsch and Connor were so new at being soldiers that they looked to Mac to tell them what to do. He gestured with his head that they were to get their horses and ride out.

An hour later, the four of them were heading deep into the forest of what was basically uncharted land. All of it had been traveled by people for centuries, but little of it had been mapped. To Angus and Mac, used to the wild hills of Scotland, it was glorious country, but Connor and Welsch kept looking about them apprehensively.

"What's Wellman up to now?" Mac asked as he glanced back at the young men close behind them. They looked as though they expected a war party of Indians to jump out at any moment, or maybe a grizzly bear would attack. They'd all heard the trappers who came to the fort to sell their furs tell exciting stories about their encounters with wild animals and wilder people.

Angus dropped the English accent he used when around the soldiers and easily lapsed into his native Scots. "Betsy."

Mac groaned. "What is it now? She get some boy with child?"

Angus laughed. "If it could be done, she'd do it. No, it seems that she's engaged to a clergyman."

"May the saints save us!" Mac said. "Her married to a churchman! The Lord will send down a bolt of lightning."

"I'm more concerned that Austin will use his knife on him." Austin's nickname of "Jackknife" had preceded him as some of the soldiers had served under him in the French and Indian War, or the Seven Years War, as the English called it. The soldiers had seen what Austin could do with a knife to the bodies of the prisoners.

"I don't envy the man being engaged to someone Jackknife wants."

"Me either," Angus said, and told Mac about the kidnapping of her fiancé. "If he's still alive, I want to warn him of what to expect."

"About Austin or Betsy?"

"Either. Both," Angus said. "But if he's in love with her, whatever I say won't make a difference."

"Know that from experience, do you?" Mac asked. He was teasing, but when Angus didn't answer, he looked at him and saw that a curtain had come down over his face. Everyone knew that Angus Harcourt didn't gossip with the other men, didn't tell about his past, not even where he'd grown up. Mac knew that Harcourt wasn't his name, but no amount of hinting had made Angus reveal anything private about himself.

Angus nodded toward the young men behind them. "Austin knew I'd choose those two because Betsy's been eyeing them."

"And they've been looking at her." Mac turned in his saddle to look at the two men. T. C. Connor was tall, broad-shouldered, and handsome. He was a quiet man, watchful of everything that went on around him, and mostly kept to himself.

Naphtali Welsch wasn't as handsome, but with his red hair and flashing blue eyes, he made everyone want to be near him. He laughed and sang rowdy songs and made the men laugh no matter what Jackknife Austin had done to them. One day the men were nursing their blistered feet after Austin had taken them on a twenty-five-mile march. They were cursing the bad food, the heat, and talking about deserting, but "Naps," as he was called, started a game of seeing who could come up with the worst punishment for Austin. In the end, it had been T.C. who won when he made up an elaborate story that involved a plant that was found only in the far reaches of the new country. It ate people. When he finished spinning his yarn, their sore feet were forgotten and their moods had improved.

After that, the newcomers had become quite popular, Naps for his humor and T.C. for his stories—when he could be persuaded to tell one. They were rare and always involved plants of such magnificence that they left the men speechless.

"And he knew you'd choose me," Mac said. "Now, I wonder why?" He was being facetious.

"Maybe because he hates you?"

"Aye, that he does," Mac said with amusement. "I know more about the army than he does, and I get more respect from the men."

"And you can throw a knife better than he can," Angus added. "He doesn't like anyone to best him at anything."

"Including that little flirt that he's decided he wants."

"She's more than a flirt," Angus said.

Mac shook his head. "I don't know why she hasn't come up with child."

"If she did, her father would kill the man."

"Make him marry her, then kill him," Mac said.

"Do either of you know where we're going?" Naps asked from behind them.

"Kids!" Mac muttered, then said over his shoulder, "We'll let you know when we get there. Until then, keep your yap shut!"

"Did you understand what he said?" Naps asked T.C.

"My guess is that he told you to be quiet and wait to find out where you're supposed to die."

"You're a gloomy one."

"I'd like to come out here by myself and take some cuttings from these plants."

Naps groaned. "Please! No more plants. You have the things everywhere. What are you planning to do with them?"

T.C. shrugged. "I don't know. Open a museum maybe. I'd like to learn to paint so I could record them on paper. The dried specimens lose a lot as the color disappears."

"Don't you want something besides *plants* in your bed? Something warm and feisty like that little Betsy Wellman."

"I think that Miss Wellman is part of the reason you and I have been sent on this mission, whatever it is."

"Betsy? But what's she got to do with anything? You know, she and I have been talking about marriage. It would be nice to marry a colonel's daughter."

T.C. pulled a few leaves off a bush they passed. "Do you think that the colonel is going to let his daughter marry the son of a farmer from the north of England?"

"Are you jealous?"

"Since Miss Wellman has also talked to me about marriage, I can't very well be jealous, now can I?"

"You!" Naps said, and his usually happy face changed. "Look here! Betsy Wellman is *my* girl, not yours! And if you—"

"Shut up, the both of you," Mac growled at them. "Betsy Wellman talks about marriage to every good-looking young soldier. The only thing she wants to marry is what's in your trousers."

When Mac turned back around, Naps whispered, "What did he say?"

"That it was a beautiful day and he loved hearing us argue."

Naps blinked a few times at T.C., then laughed. "You're all right. You're a bit too bookish for a girl like Betsy, but you'll do. You have a girl back home?"

"Did have; don't now," T.C. said, and his tone told that he wasn't going to say any more on the subject.

"Heaven help me, but they're fighting over the tramp," Mac said to Angus. "I think that when we stop for the night you should tell them the truth."

"Me?" Angus asked. "What makes you think I'm qualified to tell anyone about women?"

"All right, I'll tell you what to say and you tell them. They can understand you."

Angus gave a bit of a smile. "That makes more sense." For a while they rode in silence and Angus thought about what he knew of Austin and how he'd had the men waiting for him. Austin knew that Angus would take the men Betsy Wellman was after and that would get them out of her grasp for a few days.

"So we're to find this preacher Betsy Wellman wants to marry and take him back to her? Austin won't like *that*!" Mac said.

As soon as he heard the words, Angus knew what Austin was doing. "We're going the wrong way," he said as he turned his horse around. "We have to go to the payroll wagon."

Mac followed Angus, but he didn't understand what was going on. "Payroll wagon? But I thought Indians had kidnapped the boy."

"That's what Wellman thinks. But how did the boy get from the east of us to the west? Why didn't we hear of it?"

"Maybe one of Connor's plants carried him," Mac shouted as Angus rode ahead of them, but he wasn't listening. He was riding hard toward a trail that he knew would take them to the far side of the fort. Once a month the heavily guarded payroll wagon came in, and it was time for it. If Betsy's fiancé was to arrive it would make sense that he'd come in with the payroll. If the boy had been taken, it was from that wagon. Angus wasn't sure, but he felt that he'd been sent on a wild goose chase—and it wasn't hard to guess who had sent him and why.

He led the men hard. There were places where the trail was so narrow their horses could hardly move, but Angus didn't slow down. He didn't know what Austin had planned, but Angus was sure that he wasn't going to allow someone else to marry the woman he wanted.

Angus glanced back now and then and saw that Mac was easily keeping up with him, but the two young soldiers were hanging on for dear life. They weren't used to riding and certainly not accustomed to trails that were used mostly by animals.

An hour after sundown, he took pity on the boys and called a halt. Mac shook his head in disgust as the young men tumbled out of their saddles, sore and stiff and tired. Muttering that the young ones were weaklings, Mac gathered firewood while Angus slipped into the bushes and returned with three rabbits, which Mac put on spits over the fire.

"I'll never be able to walk again," Naps said. His red hair gleamed in the firelight.

"Good!" Angus said in an accent they could understand. "Maybe it'll keep you away from Betsy Wellman."

"Another jealous man," Naps said, grimacing as he tried to sit down.

Angus looked at T.C., who was quiet, but his face showed that he was in just as much pain. "What about you? You think Betsy is the love of your life?"

"I like a woman who can read," T.C. said as he held his hands out to the fire.

"Not all of us can spend our lives in a schoolroom," Angus said in his thickest burr, his teeth held together.

"What he means," Mac said slowly, so the young men could understand him, "is that if you want to stay alive, you'll stay away from the colonel's daughter."

"But—" Naps began.

"Austin will have you killed," Mac said.

"Like in the Bible," T.C. said. They all looked at him, as though they hoped he'd tell one of his stories. But T.C. just shrugged. "King David wanted Bathsheba, so he sent her husband to the front of the war, where he was killed."

When he said no more, the others were disappointed, and Angus looked at the young man hard. He'd been told that the reason Thomas Canon "T. C." Connor had joined the army was because he'd been in love with a young woman in Williamsburg, but her father had married her off to a rich old man. T.C. had been roaming the new country since then, collecting plant specimens wherever he went. Angus didn't know if the story was true or just gossip—and T.C. answered no question about his past.

"I think we need to get some rest," Angus said. "I'll take the first watch, then you." He nodded at T.C. "Naps, then Mac, you take the last watch. At first light we'll leave."

"Could you tell us where we're going?" Naps asked.

Angus hesitated, but then relented. "I think that

Austin has arranged for Miss Wellman's fiancé to be killed."

Naps didn't seem to hear anything but "fiancé." "She's engaged to someone else?"

Angus shook his head at the young man and gave Mac a glance to say that the boy would never learn. "Turn in, all of you. I'll wake you when your time to watch comes." He glared at Naps. "And let me tell you that your life won't be worth much if you fall asleep on watch."

Naps looked out into the darkness and shivered. "You don't have to worry about me. This place scares me so much that I won't be able to sleep at all." Ten minutes later, he was snoring so loudly that Mac kicked him.

The next morning, before the sun was fully up, the four men rode out and Angus set a hard pace for them.

"Can this man take care of himself?" Mac asked when they stopped to rest the horses.

"No," Angus said. "Wellman called him 'effeminate.' "

"What does that mean?" Naps asked.

"Like a girl," T.C. answered.

"Then Betsy won't have any trouble choosing the right man," Naps said, yet again turning everything back around to her.

Angus started to say something about the girl but didn't. "Let's go. I know where it's most likely that the payroll wagon was ambushed."

Minutes later, they were riding again, and when Angus saw smoke, he kicked his tired horse forward. "We may be too late," he said over his shoulder.

When they were at the top of a ridge, Angus held up his hand for them to halt, and he slid off his horse to crouch down among the trees. Behind him, Mac made hand gestures to the young soldiers that they were to get down and be silent. Mac went to squat next to Angus.

Below them was what was left of the payroll wagon. It had been burned, and near it were the bodies of two soldiers.

"Where are the other guards?" Mac whispered.

"I'm not sure, but it's my guess that Austin ordered the wagon to have only two guards."

"An open invitation to thieves," Mac said.

"Thieves and murder."

"Do you think the preacher's body is on the other side?"

"I don't see it," Angus said, "but I'm sure it's nearby, and I'd lay money on it that he's been scalped. Austin would want people to believe that the Indians did it."

Mac didn't let his face show his shock at what Angus was saying. "Something like this could cause a war. The payroll is from the government. Do you think Austin would risk that just for a common girl like Betsy?"

"I think he likes to win whatever he wants and he'll use whatever methods he can," Angus said. "I'll take Welsch and go that way, you take Connor and come in from the south. Be careful and make as little noise as possible. The killers have probably taken the money and run, but maybe they're still around. Take no chances."

Mac nodded, then went back to tell the men, who were standing behind them rubbing their sore legs.

Angus went down the hill quietly, concealing his body in the bushes that grew along the way. Twice, Welsch skidded on the loose gravel, and both times Angus scowled at him.

When they reached the bottom of the hill, Angus motioned for Welsch to stay there and wait, and he looked relieved. Angus stealthily made his way around the burned wagon, glancing quickly at the two men on the ground to see if they were dead. His guess was that they'd been there for at least a day and a half, and he hoped he was wrong about the boy. Maybe the robbers took the payroll, killed the guards, and kidnapped the boy. If that was so then they were in the wrong place. By now the boy—if he was still alive—was many miles to the west, just as Wellman had said.

Angus hid behind some trees and looked about him. If the men had been dead for over a day, then the wagon had only recently been set on fire. That meant that someone had been there since the murders.

When he saw or heard no one, Angus stepped out of hiding and began to look around the wagon. There were faint footprints leading south, where he knew there was a river.

Quietly, his moccasins making no sound, Angus

went back to Welsch, who was still sitting under the trees and waiting. "No one's here but I don't trust this place," he said softly. "Get the others and I'll meet you over there. See that big oak tree?"

"I don't know an oak from a daisy," Welsch said.

"Ask Connor. Go there and wait for me, and stay out of sight."

"Gladly," Welsch said as he stood up on his stiff legs.

It was thirty minutes before Angus met the other men in the shade of the oak tree.

Mac handed him a hardtack biscuit. "See anything?"

"Someone got away. There were four men who attacked the wagon, and they were all white. Indians walk lighter. There's a bloody place where a wounded man lay for a while and it's possible they thought he was dead."

"Maybe he dragged himself off into the bushes."

"I think so. You two ready to go?" Angus asked Welsch and Connor.

They nodded and minutes later the four of them were on horseback again, with Angus in the front. He was leaning over the saddle so far the other men didn't see why he wasn't unseated. He was looking at the ground, following the trail the wounded man had left behind.

"He's going to the river," Angus told them, and put his finger to his lips for them to remain silent. He dismounted, took his horse's reins, and began to walk over the rocky path. In the distance, they could hear the water rushing.

In the next minute, Angus stepped out of the bushes, and what he saw so astounded him that he just stood there and stared. Curious, the other three moved to stand beside him.

Sitting on a big rock beside a small river was a tall blond young man. His face and shoulders were hideously covered with blood and he looked to be sewing his scalp back together.

Angus tied his horse to a bush and went to the man. "Need any help with that?"

"No. I'm fine," he said, glancing at the other men who were close behind Angus. "I meant to go on and try to get to the fort, but my head wouldn't stop bleeding and the blood got in my eyes so bad I couldn't see."

With every stitch the young man made, the others winced. His fingers were long and moved easily as he held the ridges of his scalp together and sewed.

"Have you done that often, lad?" Mac asked.

"Not to myself," the man said with a bit of a grin, but since his face was so bloody he looked more horrible than pleasant.

"So what happened?" Angus asked as he sat down across from the young man. "And who are you?"

"Matthew Aldredge." He held out his hand to shake, but it was covered with blood. "Sorry. I'll clean up when this is done."

"I could—" Angus began.

"No!" Matthew said. "Really. I'd rather do it myself. Did you see the wagon?"

"Yes," T.C. said. "And the dead bodies."

"Poor men," Matthew said. "They were killed right away."

"Who did it?" Angus asked.

Matthew made a couple of stitches in his head, then put his hands down to rest them. The needle and thread dangled by his right eye, making him even more grotesque-looking. "I assume I was supposed to think they were Indians, but unless they've started speaking French, the men were in disguise. I take it the wagon I was on usually carries gold?"

"There wasn't any on it?" Angus asked.

"None that the murderers could find," Matthew said as he got up and went to the river. Bending, he washed his hands in the cool water. "They were angry and they killed all of us."

At that, T.C. and Naps looked at him with wide eyes.

"You mean that they shot you in the head and thought you were dead," Angus said.

"Yes. That's it exactly. I don't know how long I lay there with my head split open, but it was most of a day. The only thing I can think of to explain why I didn't bleed to death is that my blood seems to coagulate rapidly."

"They shot all three of you, then set the wagon on fire?" Mac asked.

"Actually, I was the one who set the wagon on

fire. I figured a rescue party was looking for me so I thought I'd send out a signal."

"You took a big chance," Angus said.

Matthew sat down and again started sewing his head. "This is easier to do on a cow than on myself."

The four men gave him a weak smile. He really was quite hideous-looking. How could anyone lose that much blood and still be alive?

"Are you a doctor?" Naps asked.

"No, just a farmer."

"And you're here to marry Betsy," Naps said, anger in his voice.

"Actually, I came here to tell her that I won't marry her. I thought that was a lot kinder than writing her a letter."

"But she's expecting to get married," Naps said, sounding like he was ready to fight for Betsy's honor.

"I know," Matthew said. "It was the oddest thing. When I was with her, she was all I could think about, but after she left, I could barely remember her. We corresponded and . . . Well, when you read letters written by someone and when you're not distracted by a pretty face, you see things that you didn't see before."

"Like that she's as dumb as a fence post?" Mac said.

"Exactly!" Matthew answered.

"What did he say?" Naps whispered to T.C.

"That he's not good enough for a girl like Betsy," T.C. answered quickly.

"Anyway," Matthew said, "when I woke up, the sun was much lower in the sky, so I knew it'd been hours since we were attacked. I'd seen that one of the horses eluded capture, so I hoped to find him, but I'm afraid that I lost consciousness. That was yesterday. Today, I managed to set the wagon on fire, then I came here to the river."

"You don't know where the men who robbed you went, do you?" Angus asked.

"My French isn't very good, but does the phrase 'three pretty daughters' mean anything to you?"

"McNalty," Angus and Mac said in unison.

Angus looked at Matthew. "Can you ride?"

"Of course," Matthew said. "If you'll give me a few minutes, I'll wash this blood off."

"We can't take the time," Angus said.

"Besides, I like it," Mac said, grinning at the young man. "I bet that under there, you're a pretty boy."

Matthew grinned, showing bloodstained teeth. "Ugly as mud."

As Mac mounted his horse, he looked at the other men. "In fact, I'd say that, except for me, the best-looking men at the fort are right here."

Angus paused for a moment with his foot in the stirrup, then glanced at Mac. "And you're the man Austin hates the most."

"Who's Austin?" Matt asked as he got on the horse behind T.C.

"Think of the worst man you've ever met," T.C.

said. "Now triple it and you haven't come close to Austin."

Angus wasn't sure what was going on, but he knew that it was bad. And with every second he was more sure that Austin was behind it. The fact that *he*, Angus, had been sent to find the fiancé seemed to be part of the plot.

If Angus had been alone, he would have headed east and gone back to civilization, the army be damned, but he had three soldiers and a man who looked more dead than alive with him, so he couldn't leave. He thought maybe the whole thing about the "three pretty daughters" was part of the trap, but he couldn't be sure. He hated having to leave the two dead soldiers who'd inadvertently become part of Austin's treachery unburied, but they needed to get to the McNalty cabin as quickly as possible.

"Where the hell are you taking us?" Mac asked as he tried to keep up with Angus.

"A shortcut," Angus said over his shoulder, and looked back at the men behind him. He was surprised but pleased to see that Connor and Aldredge had traded places and the blood-smeared young man was now holding the reins to the horse, while Connor held on for dear life. Angus saw at once that Matthew Aldredge knew a great deal about horses.

"Like a girl, is he?" Angus said to Mac as he nodded toward the young man as he led his horse across a stream full of slippery, moss-covered rocks. Poor Welsch was scared to death.

"I'll switch them," Mac said, reading Angus's thoughts. "You go on, we'll catch up with you."

"I'll leave a trail," Angus said, and in the next moment he was gone.

Mac had Connor and Welsch trade places so Naps could have a break. After he mounted, Naps threw his arms around Aldredge's waist, put his head against his back, and said, "You're second only to Betsy," which made them all laugh.

Mac led them quick and hard as he tried to catch up with Angus. He knew where the McNalty cabin was, but he also knew that Angus was a great deal more familiar with the country than he was.

He tried to follow the trail that Angus left, but he was having trouble seeing the broken branches. The bushes all looked alike to him—but not to T.C.

"There!" T.C. called ahead. "On that *Kalmia*."

Mac gave him a look that could have set his hair on fire.

"That shrub on your right," T.C. said meekly.

Mac motioned for him to come forward, and T.C., alone on a horse that he could barely ride, was made the leader. It was easy for him to see what was wrong with a plant and where Angus had left a trail. And he surprised even himself when he so quickly adjusted to his new role of authority. When Naps, still holding on to Matt, reached out to touch a plant, T.C. ordered him to stop. "That's poisonous!" he said. "Don't touch anything unless I tell you to."

Naps looked surprised, as it seemed that in an instant T.C. had gone from being his equal to his commander.

By sundown they'd traveled over fifteen miles, and Mac knew they were close to the McNalty cabin, but he wasn't going anywhere without Angus. Besides, there was a swift-moving river nearby, and he didn't want to cross that in the dark. "We'll camp here and wait."

"But what about the McNalty family?" T.C. asked, but Mac had had enough of the young man's being the leader. It took only one look before T.C. was silently removing the saddle from his horse and helping to set up camp.

They had just unloaded the horses when Angus appeared out of the darkness.

"What did you see?" Mac asked him.

Angus was looking at Matt. His face was covered in blood that had dried to a dark brown and he looked scary. "You have any soap?"

"Sure," Mac said with a half grin to emphasize his sarcasm. "What you want it scented with? Roses?"

Angus looked at T.C. "Can you find something that he can clean himself with?"

T.C. couldn't conceal his pride in being asked to help. Quietly, he left the camp to go into the darkness.

Angus sat down beside Mac. "I went to their cabin. I didn't go inside or let them know I was there, but I watched. I didn't see anyone, but I did see a lot of footprints around the place. Something isn't right, but I don't know what it is." He lowered his voice, and nodded toward Matt. "To tell you the truth, I'm afraid to deliver him to the fort. He can tell Wellman's daughter that he doesn't want her, but I don't trust Austin not to decide he wants to hurt the boy anyway."

Mac was just starting a fire but he put it out. "I think we should have a cold camp tonight. And to-morrow——"

"I'm going to take Aldredge back east. I don't think he's safe here. You take the soldiers back to the fort."

"And let Austin have them?"

"I leave it to you to make them understand that if they want to live, they'll have to stay away from Betsy Wellman."

"And how will they understand me?" Mac asked, only half joking.

"Make them understand you. I'm going up there to sleep." Angus looked up at a hill well above them. "I wish this were over. I'd rather——"

"I know," Mac said, "fight the Campbells."

Smiling, Angus stood up and slipped away into the darkness.

A few minutes later, T.C. returned with big leaves filled with an almost white clay still wet from where he'd dug it up at the side of a stream. His pockets were filled with long green leaves. "Put this clay all over your face, and when it's dry, we'll go down to the stream to wash it off."

"Are those plants poisonous?" Naps asked, a bit jealous that T.C. was no longer as useless as he felt.

"They'll help heal your wounds," T.C. told Matt as he handed him the clay. They had only moonlight to see by, but the clay almost glowed, and T.C. made sure that Matt covered all his blood-encrusted skin. When he was done, T.C. led him down the hill to the stream to help him wash it off. When he was clean, T.C. twisted the comfrey leaves and gently applied them to the deep cut on Matt's head. Together, they went back up the hill to where Mac and Naps were waiting for them. After arranging the order of the watch, Mac settled down to sleep.

About an hour before dawn, Angus woke him, his finger to his lips to be quiet. T.C. was standing to one side, a rifle over his shoulder. Angus made gestures to tell Mac to pack and get out of there, then he woke the other two. Matt awoke easily, but Angus had to put his hand over Naps's mouth to keep him silent. Within minutes, they had their horses saddled and were ready to leave the camp.

As Angus put his foot in the stirrup, the first shot rang out, and it was followed by a volley of gunfire that echoed through the woods.

Before the sounds cleared, Naps had fallen. Angus grabbed the young man before he hit the ground, but he couldn't keep the frightened horse from running away.

Shots began to come at lightning speed. Angus pulled Naps to safety behind some trees while Mac tried to get the horses. Only Angus's horse remained steadfast amid the whizzing bullets.

"Down!" Angus shouted to T.C. and Matt. "Get down on the ground and stay there."

Angus's only thought was that he had to get the men under his care to safety. He glanced down at Naps. Blood was seeping out of his shoulder and his eyes were closed, but Angus didn't think the injury was life threatening. "Don't move a muscle," he said to the boy.

Naps didn't open his eyes, just grimaced against the pain and nodded.

Crouching and running at the same time, Angus made his way to Mac, who was standing behind a tree, his rifle ready to shoot.

"You see anyone?" Angus asked over the gunfire.

"Not a person, but the shots are coming from three places."

Angus was glad that Mac had kept calm enough that he hadn't run into the open firing. Three of the horses had run away, and that meant they were low on ammunition. If this was to be a long battle, they'd need all that they had.

"Good man," Angus said as he put his hand on Mac's shoulder. "I know this area, so give me a minute with the boys, then we'll get out of here."

Mac didn't answer but raised his rifle, took careful aim and fired. In the distance there was a cry. Mac had shot one of them—but that made the bullets come at them faster.

Still crouching, Angus went through the bushes to where T.C. and Matt were hiding behind a rock. "Are you all right?"

"Fine," T.C. said as he fired a shot.

"No new injuries," Matt said as he reloaded.

With the growing light, Angus could at last see Matthew Aldredge's clean face. He was indeed a handsome young man, with blue eyes and a strong jaw. Angus could see the huge cut in his scalp and thought about how Matt had sewn it together by himself. He's a much better man than Betsy Wellman deserves, he thought.

Angus looked at T.C. "Do you know what a cardinal sounds like?"

"Yes."

"When I give the whistle, I want you two to come immediately. Do you understand me? Stop shooting and come to me."

Both young men nodded, then Angus made his way back to where Naps lay on the ground, looking up at him. "I'm going to take you to a place that's safer than here. Can you walk?"

"Sure," Naps said, which made Angus frown. He recognized false bravery when he heard it. Naps might have several injuries but he'd rather die than let the others know he was badly wounded.

Angus looked down at him and saw a dark spot on his trousers. When he touched it, Naps gave a muffled cry of pain. It looked as though the boy had been shot in at least two places. "I'm going to carry you."

"I can walk," Naps said. "Just tell me where to go and I'll get there."

"Shut up," Angus said, "and don't give me any

trouble." Bending, he lifted Naps and slung him over his shoulder, then started walking north. It wasn't easy to move quickly with the sturdy young man weighing him down, but Angus did it. He'd camped in that area a few times and knew that nearby was a small cave. It was up a steep hill and difficult to get to, but it had once sheltered him from a ferocious storm.

As Angus climbed, he tried to plan what he was going to do. If he could get all the men into the cave, they would be protected on three sides. Based on the number of gunshots he was hearing behind him, there were at least four gunmen. When he heard a sound to his left, he stopped and listened, but it was an animal, so he kept moving.

The struggle to get up the hill with Naps's body across his shoulder gave Angus something to think about other than that he'd been an idiot. It hadn't taken him long to figure out that Captain Austin was behind the whole thing, but Angus still hadn't taken the necessary precautions. He'd been so concerned that Austin would harm the McNalty family that Angus hadn't looked after the men under his care. Austin might not know the countryside very well, but with the traders coming into the fort often, he'd had access to men who did. Several of the French traders were ruthless and still bitter that they'd lost the American territory to the English.

If the men who'd dressed as Indians and killed the soldiers on the pay wagon were trappers, then they knew the countryside even better than Angus did. Some of them had lived there most of their lives. They would know the trails that Angus would use to get to the McNalty cabin. And if they knew he was going there, that meant they knew that Aldredge wasn't dead. It was Angus's guess that when they'd all sat there, watching Matt sew his head back together, they'd been watched. Had it been soldiers in the woods around them, Angus would have heard them, but trappers? No. They were as good in the forests as Angus was.

By the time Angus reached the cave, he wondered if they'd ever get out alive. There was water trickling down the back of the cave wall, but they had no food and little ammunition, and, worse, they had a wounded man. How would they escape from men who could walk across dry leaves and not make a sound? How would they elude men whose clothes matched the forest? Many times, Angus had stood ten feet from Wellman's soldiers and they'd not seen him, so he knew what true frontiersmen could do.

When Angus reached the cave, he put Naps down gently, but the boy still groaned in pain. The right half of his body was covered in blood from the two wounds.

"I have to go get the others," Angus said, wondering if he'd ever again see the young man alive. He well remembered that when he'd used the cave there was a stack of dry firewood in the corner. It was an unwritten rule of woodsmen that they replace what they'd used. At least they could have a fire.

"Damnation!" Angus muttered as he started down the hill. That no one shot at him let him know exactly what was going on. The men shooting at them knew one of them was wounded and they knew where Angus was taking him. But the cave was their only choice at the moment. With Welsch being wounded and with Connor, both of them hardly being able to stay on a horse, it would be impossible to get them all out alive. No, what Angus had to do was get them all into the cave, then he'd have to leave them under Mac's protection while he, Angus, went for help.

T.C., Matt, and Mac were where he'd left them, but the younger men were out of ammunition.

"They shoot like they have a keg of powder," Mac grumbled.

"We need to get the men up that hill. There's a cave up there, and I put Welsch in it."

"How bad is he?"

"I don't know, but if I were to guess, I'd say he's losing too much blood to make it."

Mac nodded toward T.C. and Matt. "Put those two on him. Sewing and plants. They're good at those."

Nodding in agreement, Angus turned toward the hill, Mac behind him. When he silently passed the young men, he gave the distinctive whistle of the red cardinal, and T.C. told Matt they had to go.

It took nearly an hour to get to the cave because they had to wait behind trees when the gunfire got too heavy. They watched Angus, waiting for him to tell them what to do. He'd stand and fire while Connor ran, then he'd reload and let Aldredge go. Mac was always last and always reluctant to leave Angus holding the gunmen off.

When they finally reached the cave, Matt immediately went to Naps. He used the knife he wore at his waist to cut away Naps's clothes so he could look at the wounds. After he'd examined him, he went to the others standing in the center of the cave.

"The bullets have to be removed," Matt said. "They're lead, and if they stay in there very long they'll poison him. Even as it is, I'm not sure . . ." He trailed off, glancing back at Naps, who was lying on the cold floor and trying to breathe through the pain.

"Then do it," Angus said. "Get the bullets out and wrap him up as best you can. I'm going to try to find the horses and get us out of here."

"Me?" Matt began, but one look from Angus stopped him. "Yes, sir," he said. "I'll do what I can."

Angus looked at T.C., who was studying something that was growing from the wall of the cave. "Help him. Do whatever needs to be done."

Angus moved close to the mouth of the cave, where he could see out but not be seen; Mac was right beside him.

"You know what's going on, don't you, lad?"

"I think Austin's hired some trappers and I think they mean to kill us."

"All over a girl as worthless as Betsy Wellman."

"There are women you fight for and women who

don't deserve it," Angus said under his breath, but Mac heard him.

"Sounds like you wish you'd done more fighting."

"There are some things that a man can't fight." Angus moved away from the wall and went to where Matt was hovering over Naps. His eyes asked whether the boy was going to be all right, but Matt shrugged that he didn't know.

"I'm going down," Angus said. He looked at the four men and hated leaving them. Mac knew how to take care of himself, but the others were young and inexperienced. "My horse will come when I call and I'll ride for the fort. It's not that far away, and I'll bring help back."

T.C. and Matt nodded at this, and Naps gave a faint smile, as though he now knew that he'd be saved, but Mac looked at Angus with serious eyes. Mac was going to be left alone with three neophytes, little ammunition, and heaven only knew how many men surrounding them.

"It's the only way," Angus said. "None of you would make it through them."

"Aye, lad, I know," Mac said softly, and his eyes said that he knew that when Angus returned—if he did—they wouldn't be alive.

"I have to go now," Angus said. "I can't wait until dark."

"I know," Mac said. "Go on, then. Tell the colonel hello for us. And if you see Austin you might hit him for me."

Angus put his hand on Mac's shoulder. "If anything happens to you or the lads, I'll kill him."

"Fair enough," Mac said, then, after one more glance at the three young men, Angus slipped out of the cave and into the sunlight.

He stayed behind trees and rocks and moved as silently as he could, but he still felt that he was being watched. Whoever was shooting at them had allowed them to get into the cave, but he doubted if they were going to let Angus get to his horse and ride to the fort.

It was slow progress going down the hill. Angus would take two steps then wait. It's what he'd learned how to do when he was a boy, moving about the heather on his belly, looking for any sign of the rustlers.

When he got within fifty feet of where they'd camped the night before, he gave the low whistle that he'd trained his horse to come to, but the animal didn't show up. He wasn't sure but he thought he heard a laugh in the distance. If the men were trappers and lived their lives alone in the woods, then they knew a bird whistle from a man's.

As Angus walked along the edge of the riverbank, he tried to calculate how long it would take him to run the distance to the fort. Three days, he thought, but if he could get a horse from one of the trappers . . .

Slowly, stealthily, he made his way toward where the gunmen were hiding. He thought he was nearly there when he heard the unmistakable whiz of an arrow. Ducking, he swerved and missed the arrow, but his foot slipped on the wet grass and he lost his balance. He grabbed at a tree but couldn't reach it. In the next second he felt himself falling down the cliff and heading for the river. As he tried to curl himself into a ball, his hands covering his head in protection, he knew he was going to die because he was sure he heard bagpipes.

Angus hit the water hard, but he came up to the surface quickly, and for a moment the current carried him. As he passed a tall rock, he grabbed it and held on. With water in his face, he looked at the bank, trying to see if a gunman was standing there. Or a man with a bow. Instead, he thought he saw Shamus—and he was smiling at him in delight.

Angus shook his head to clear it, then looked back at the bank, but who or what he'd seen was gone. There were just trees and grasses.

Angus looked at the rushing water and thought about how to get himself out. He knew of a place to cross the river, but it was nearly a mile upstream. He needed to get back to the nearest bank and try to find his horse.

He moved from rock to rock, using his arms and legs to hold himself against the current. When he again thought he heard bagpipes, he was sure that when he went under he must have hit his head. When he got to the bank he was weak from the exertion, but he didn't stop. He still had to climb up the embankment.

He grabbed a tree root and hauled himself up,

using the roots as a rope. When he got to the top, a hand appeared before his face. Angus was so startled that he almost fell backward, but the hand stayed where it was and a familiar voice said, "Give me your hand, lad, and I'll help you up."

Angus looked up to see his uncle Malcolm lying on his belly, his hand extended. He wore a set of bagpipes on his back.

All Angus could do was stand there, his feet on the side of the steep, muddy bank, his hands holding on to a tree root, and stare, his mouth open in astonishment. "Am I dead?" he at last said.

In a sweet tone, Malcolm said, "Aye, you are, lad, and I'm here to welcome you into Heaven. Take my hand so we can go meet the Lord."

Angus's eyes were wide but then he heard a guffaw that he'd heard since he was a child. Turning, he saw Shamus standing there, laughing at him in a derogatory way.

Angus looked back at Malcolm. "Now I know you're lying. Shamus will *never* be allowed into Heaven." Taking Malcolm's hand, he hauled himself upward. When he was again standing, dripping wet, he still could do nothing but stare at Malcolm and Shamus. "What . . . ?" he began. "How . . . ?"

"We came to visit you," Malcolm said.

"And we ended up saving your life!" Shamus said, smirking. "If it hadn't been for us, you'd be dead now. Why couldn't you get away from them? There were only six of them."

"And it took the both of you to get rid of them?" Angus asked, still in shock at seeing them.

"Naw," Malcolm said. "I went after you, and Tam went up to the cave where you hid those others. Shamus dealt with the Frenchmen. A Scot's worth more than a dozen Frenchmen."

Shamus was looking at Angus with a half grin that said it was clear to see who the superior man was.

"Tam is here?" Angus asked.

"Aye. Seeing to the others," Malcolm said. "Do you give us no greeting?"

"Malcolm, I . . ." Angus began, but then stopped. "I don't know how . . ."

"Ah, lad," Malcolm said, embarrassed. "I didna mean to make you weep. A drink of good whiskey will do to thank me."

"I'll buy you a bottle," Angus said as he put his arm around Malcolm's broad shoulders and held on. All that had happened since he'd last seen the man went through his head in a series of visions. It seemed so long ago, and he'd been such an innocent back then. He remembered trying to save Edilean from a forced marriage and how he'd ended up on a ship with her and heading to another country. And he'd fallen in love with her so hard that every day without her was an ache inside him. He saw her face every hour of every day, longed for her, wondered where she was and what she was doing.

"Lad!" Malcolm said. "We thought you'd be glad to see us."

"I am," Angus said, but his voice caught in his throat, and he could say no more.

"Where's the girl?" Shamus asked.

"What girl?"

"The one you ran off with. The one you stole the gold from."

"I did not—" Angus began but Malcolm cut him off.

"Could you boys wait a while before fighting? I think we need to get to the others, and Tam wants to see you."

"Aye, Tam," Angus said, grinning, his arm still so tight around Malcolm's strong shoulders that he was causing the man pain, but Malcolm didn't complain. "You got them *all*?" Angus asked, looking at Shamus as though he doubted that he really could take down six men.

"Hmph!" Shamus snorted. "Didn't take me but a minute. They were standing in plain sight. Anyone could have seen them."

Angus couldn't help grinning at Shamus's arrogance. He looked at Malcolm. "So what do you think of this new country?"

"Too hot," Malcolm said. "Give me the coolness of Scotland. And their whiskey is bad."

"And they think we're English," Shamus said, as though that was the final insult.

"With your accent?" Angus said happily. "Can they understand you?"

"Not many can," Shamus said, and for a moment his eyes told Angus that he was glad to see him.

"Up there," Angus said, nodding toward the path to the cave. Shamus went up, but Angus stood where he was, with his arm firmly around Malcolm's shoulders.

"You must let me go, lad," Malcolm said gently. "I'm not a ghost and I'm here to stay."

"Ghost," Angus said, smiling. "You didn't come here in a coffin full of sawdust, did you?"

"No," Malcolm said slowly, "but why would you ask that? Is that how *you* sneaked into this country?"

"No," Angus said, his smile widening. "I came here as an English gentleman."

"I want to hear every word of this story," Malcolm said.

"I'll be glad to tell it to you."

21

"No, no, no, no!" Angus said, his words echoing off the cave walls. "I will *not* do it. I refuse. And that's the last time I'm saying it."

Last night, a fire had made the cave almost homelike. Mac had taken Angus's horse and was on his way back to the fort to get help, while T.C., Matt, and Naps had stayed with Angus. Thanks to Matt's surgery and the plants that T.C. had found, Naps was resting comfortably, passing drowsily in and out of consciousness from the brew that T.C. had given him.

Tam, Shamus, Malcolm, and Angus sat around the fire and talked in the Scottish burr that the other men couldn't quite make out.

They'd spent hours exchanging stories. Angus made them all laugh uproariously with his account of how he got rooked into helping Edilean escape her uncle's treacherous plan. The first time he said her name, his breath caught and he didn't know if he could go on, but the second time was easier. By the time he was well into his story, he was smiling and remembering it all fondly.

He started telling the men about James Harcourt's wife's ugliness and how she'd tried to get him to stay in bed with her, but Malcolm cut him off by sending a burning branch flying. When they got it cleaned up, Malcolm asked about James, so Angus told of hitting James on the head with a candlestick. "And Edilean shaved me," he said in an almost dreamy voice.

"She shaved your beard off?" Shamus said. "I knew there was something different about you."

Throughout the story, Shamus kept shaking his head and muttering, "A wagonload of gold. The trunks were full of gold." He sounded as though he couldn't believe what he was hearing—and what he'd lost.

Angus told of dressing in James's clothes and boarding the ship. For a few moments he was silent as he let himself remember the time with Edilean on the ship. He thought of tying her corset, of teasing her, of making her laugh. He could see it all so clearly that it was almost as though he could touch her.

"Angus!" Tam said, bringing him back to where he was.

Angus smiled, even though he hardly recognized him. Tam had grown until he was as tall as Angus. He was no longer the boy who trailed after his bigger, older cousin. In the four years that they'd been separated, Tam had become a man, and Angus regretted that he'd not been there to see him grow and change. But then, Angus wondered if his going was the reason that Tam had grown up so quickly. With Angus gone, Tam was now the one to inherit . . . What? Angus thought. There was nothing left of the McTern clan to inherit but the responsibility.

"I've entertained you enough," Angus said at last. "You didn't come all the way across the ocean just to hear my stories. What have you come for?"

"We—" Shamus began, but when Malcolm gave him a hard look he closed his mouth.

"Kenna thanks you for the silk dress you sent her," Tam said.

"And how is she?" Angus tried to keep his voice steady as he thought about the sister who'd once been so close to him. "How many children does she have now?"

"Six," Malcolm said. "She liked that the dress you sent her had . . ." He didn't quite know what to say.

"An expandable front," Angus said.

"Ah, so that's what she meant," Malcolm said, then sipped his coffee and was silent.

"What are the lot of you up to?" Angus asked suspiciously. "How did you even find me?"

"That was easy enough," Shamus said. "What with your picture everywhere, there were a lot of people with information about you."

Angus grimaced.

"That's true," Malcolm said slowly. "But it's also true that we wanted to see you." He glanced at the leather clothes Angus had on. "This country suits you."

"When you can stay alive," Shamus said.

"Out with it!" Angus said loudly, making the men on the far side of the cave jump. Even Naps stirred in his sleep.

"Miss Edilean's uncle died," Tam said.

"Did he?" Angus said and couldn't help a bit of a smile. It was one less person who was after him.

"And he left all his property to Miss Edilean."

"Good," Angus said, looking from one to the other of them, but they were silent. "You want to buy the place from her, don't you?"

"For a peppercorn a year," Malcolm said quickly. "I think she'd agree to that."

"She don't need the money," Shamus said, "not with all those slave girls of hers."

"Slaves?" Angus said. "I can't imagine that Edilean would own a slave."

"That's not what he meant," Malcolm said, glaring at Shamus to keep his mouth shut. "Miss Edilean has . . . Well, it's . . ." He looked at Tam for help.

"She started a business in Boston called 'Bound Girl.'"

Angus looked at him in astonishment. "Are you saying that she opened a . . . a house of . . . ?"

"Did this new country put your mind in the gutter?" Malcolm snapped. "Miss Edilean is a *lady*. Mind what you say about her, boy!"

"Or you'll turn me over your knee?" Angus asked, smiling at the familiarity of it all.

Tam leaned forward. "She sells the best and the most vegetables and fruit in Boston. She has a company that she owns and runs with the help of women who used to be indentured servants."

"I like her handbill," Shamus said, grinning.

"What's he talking about?" Angus asked.

"Well," Tam said slowly, "Miss Edilean does have a rather, uh, enticing sign for her business."

"A girl," Shamus said, "big and healthy, with her sleeves rolled up. Good muscles on her, and she's got—" He made a gesture to show a large bosom. "Damn handsome woman!"

They all looked at Shamus for a moment, then turned back to Angus. "Is this true? Edilean runs a business?"

"From what we were told, she has over a hundred employees, all women, and she owns half a dozen farms," Malcolm said. "How long has it been since you've seen her?"

"Four years, three months, and twenty-two days," Angus said quickly, then looked embarrassed. "I think. It's just a guess."

"You always were good at guessing," Malcolm said but lowered his head to hide his smile.

"So Edilean started a business," Angus said in wonder. "And it's doing well?"

"Very well," Malcolm said. "She earns a lot of money, and she's used it to set up a couple of houses for women without husbands, widows and such. She helps a lot of women."

"There were nine bound women on the ship when we came over," Angus said, staring at the fire, remembering. "But Edilean didn't like them. She hired one of them to do some sewing for her, but I could tell that she had no intention of keeping her on after the voyage. Funny how you think you know someone but don't. I can't imagine Edilean running a business and certainly not hiring women like them."

When his head came up, he was smiling. "She got into a fight—a bloody fistfight—with one of the prisoners named Tabitha. Edilean—"

"Big girl? Pretty?" Tam asked.

"Yes," Angus said. "You didn't meet her, did you?"

"If she's the Tabitha we heard about, she's Miss Edilean's farm manager," Tam said. "She runs all the farms and she doesn't take any guff off anyone."

Angus's mouth dropped open. "Edilean and Tabitha work *together*?"

"What did they fight about?" Shamus asked, his eyes alight at the thought.

"Diamonds," Angus said, and looked back at Malcolm and Tam. "Edilean and Tabitha together. What a world this is! Tell me, is Edilean still living with Harriet Harcourt?"

"Oh, yes," Tam said. "Harriet takes care of the money for all of the business."

Angus narrowed his eyes at them. "How long have you three been in this country?"

"A while," Malcolm said.

"Over three months," Shamus said. "It took some time to find you. It wasn't hard, mind you, but it took time. Did you know that we could turn you in for a thousand pounds?"

When Angus started to say something, Tam interrupted. "Don't worry, James Harcourt is taken care of. His sister Harriet pays him to stay away from Miss Edilean."

"She does what?"

"Pays him to stay away," Shamus said loudly, as though Angus were deaf. "Gives him a remittance. It's common enough."

"Are you telling me that the lot of you have spent three months snooping into Edilean's private affairs?"

Malcolm looked at Tam who looked at Shamus, then they all looked back at Angus. "Yes," Malcolm said. "That's just what we've been doing."

"And what does Edilean know of this?"

"Nothing," Tam said. "We were careful to stay out of her sight. And that wasn't easy, as she runs around in her little carriage constantly. I remember one morning I was walking down the street and there she was. I was sure she'd recognize me, but she was having it out with some man about some fruit—she doesn't like for it to be bruised—so she didn't see me."

The story was so like Edilean that it caused a pain in Angus's chest. "Has she—? I mean, are there . . . ?"

"Men?" Shamus asked, then when the others glared at him, he threw up his hands. "What's the problem with all of you? I think you should get on with it and *tell* him."

"Tell me what?" Angus asked.

"We worked with a lawyer," Malcolm said, and turned to Tam. "You tell him."

"We thought that since Miss Edilean is so rich, what with the gold and the business, we might persuade her to give the McTern estate back to us. We don't think she wants it. It means nothing to her."

"You told me that, and I said that you won't have any trouble. Edilean has a very generous nature. I'm sure she'll give you the rotting old place even without the peppercorn. Don't tell me you're afraid to ask her."

"It's not that . . ." Tam said, looking at Malcolm.

Angus turned to Shamus. "Would you tell me what they can't seem to get out?"

Shamus opened his mouth to speak, but Malcolm blurted out the truth. "You're wanted for kidnapping her, so she has to swear before a judge that she ran off with you of her own free will. Once you're cleared, she can give the place to you because you're the laird, then you can give it to Tam, as he's next in line."

"I see," Angus said. He sat still for a moment, then got up and walked to the back of the cave. Naps was asleep, but T.C. and Matt looked wide awake as they listened to what the Scotsmen were saying. Angus didn't know how much they could understand, but from the looks on their faces, they were getting the gist of what was going on. Angus thought of the words *kidnapping* and *wanted* that were being bandied about.

He looked back at Malcolm. "You're saying that

you want *me* to go to Edilean and ask her to tell a judge that I didn't kidnap her, and that she went with me of her own free will."

"Exactly," Malcolm said brightly. "She could give the place directly to Tam, but he's not the laird. It has to go down the line, all in proper order."

"And the problem with that is that I'm thought to be a criminal."

"Lawler was the only one who had any right to want you dead," Tam said.

"That's because it was his niece and his gold that you stole," Shamus said.

"I didn't—" Angus began, but then stopped. "I'm sorry, but I can't do what you want."

"Why not?" Tam asked, his face showing his anger. "You want to keep being the laird even though you live *here*?"

"Of course not!" Angus said, but he thought about Tam's words. To give up his birthright? Could he do that? He'd spent most of his life trying to give honor back to the name that his grandfather had almost destroyed, so could he just walk away from it?

"He won't do it," Tam said to Malcolm. "I told you he wouldn't."

"Do you want to go back to Scotland?" Malcolm asked softly, looking at Angus. "Is that what you want, lad?"

Angus glanced at them and knew he couldn't say what was in his mind. They were so fresh off the boat from the old country that they still smelled of heather, but Angus had been in America for years, and he liked the feeling that a man could do or be anything. Right now, if he waited long enough, he'd get a thousand acres. The land would be his own, and he could do with it whatever he wanted. In Scotland, nothing had belonged to him, and what he did was always overseen by others. Even now, if he were given charge of the McTern lands, he'd still be expected to look out for hundreds of people. No, he didn't want to go back. "No," he said at last. "I want to stay here."

Tam's face lost its angry look and he seemed a bit ashamed of the way he'd nearly attacked his cousin.

"So then you will go back with us to see Miss Edilean," Malcolm said, smiling in relief.

"Sorry," Angus said, "but I can't do that."

"Why not?" Tam asked. "You don't like her?"

Angus gave a little guffaw at that absurdity. "She doesn't like *me*," he said.

"You had a spat," Malcolm said. "That's understandable. Is that why you're here and she's there?"

"Are you two married or not?" Shamus asked. "And why are you called Harcourt?"

"It's a long story," Angus said.

"I got time," Shamus said, "and I like a good lie if it's well told."

"It's all true and I'm telling you that I can*not* go to Edilean and ask anything of her. She . . . Well, the truth is that she hates me."

"From what the captain of the *Mary Elizabeth* told us, that's not true," Tam said.

"He said you two were together every minute." The familiar smirk was back on Shamus's face. "Did you—" He made a vulgar gesture.

Angus got to his feet, his fists clenched, but before Shamus could get up, Malcolm called them down. "Sit!" he ordered Angus. "And you stay where you are." He ran his hand over his face. "You two have been fighting since you were born."

"You jealous, old man?" Shamus said, still with his fists clenched and ready to take on Angus.

"Old man," Malcolm said under his breath, then raised his head. "I'm young enough to deal with you two." He looked at Angus. "You *have* to go to Miss Edilean and ask her to do this."

"You're not understanding the problem," Angus said. "I'm more than willing to ask her, but if I went to her, she'd say no just to get me back."

"For what?" Tam and Shamus said in unison.

"Nothing that I plan to talk about."

Malcolm took a deep breath. "We all have our problems with women, but they can be made up."

"Have the papers drawn up and I'll sign whatever you want," Angus said.

"No. We were told that a judge must *see* you with Miss Edilean to make sure that you're both telling the truth."

"That won't work," Angus said firmly. "Edilean will tell them to arrest me."

"Maybe if you tell us what happened, we can do something about it," Malcolm said, his voice full of exaggerated patience. All of them, even the two men sitting against the far wall, looked at Angus.

Angus thought about how he'd made love to Edilean, then left her there. He remembered the horrible things he'd said to her servant—which, no doubt, he'd told Edilean. Yes, Angus had had a reason for everything he did, but still, the result was not something that a woman would forgive.

"No," Angus said. "I'm not telling anyone anything. You're going to have to figure out a different way to get what you want. I'll sign whatever you need, but I am *not* going to confront Edilean and ask her to do this."

That was last night, and this morning they were still after him. At least Tam and Malcolm were. Shamus stood in the background, looking at Angus with an expression that said he thought Angus was a coward who couldn't even stand up to a girl.

"No," Angus repeated. "I will *not* do this and you can stop asking me."

After the sun had been up for a couple of hours, Mac returned with a wagon and half a dozen soldiers. Angus stepped away from the Scotsmen to talk to him.

"I didn't tell them anything at the fort," Mac said. "I didn't figure anyone would believe me if I said we thought Austin had done all this. The colonel was angry that Aldredge was still alive. When I told him that the boy was coming here to break up with Betsy, the old man got even more angry. It's my advice that Aldredge go back east."

"I agree," Angus said.

Mac was looking at the Scotsmen who were standing at the mouth of the cave and watching the soldiers carry Naps down to the wagon. Thanks to Matt and T.C., Naps was much better this morning.

Mac lowered his voice. "If I were you, I wouldn't return to the fort either. Austin didn't say much but his face was beet red. He's very angry that you didn't let us get killed."

Angus's heart plummeted. If he left the employ of the army, when Mercer returned from England with his petition signed by the king, Angus would no longer be on the list to get a thousand acres of land.

"Where'd *they* come from?" Mac asked, nodding toward the three Scotsmen standing apart from the others.

"Home," Angus said. "Scotland."

Mac raised an eyebrow. "As if I didn't know that. Mind if I talk to them? I'd like to be around someone who can understand me."

Angus shrugged, glad to have some time alone to think. For a moment he considered cursing all the women of the world. His life had been fine until women entered it. First there was Edilean, who he'd tried to help and ended by getting himself wanted for kidnapping and theft. Then there'd been Tabitha, who'd made Edilean so jealous that it caused a rift between them. And now, here was little Betsy Wellman, who might cause him to lose his future.

Angus was allowed about five minutes' peace before Malcolm came to him.

"Good lad, that one," he said, nodding toward Mac. "He talks like an American, but I can't hold that against him. He told me that if you go back to the fort some man might see to it that you get killed."

"I can take care of myself," Angus snapped.

"Seems to me that the only thing that interests you is yourself," Malcolm said, and went back to the others.

For a moment Angus thought about grabbing his rifle and heading out. He'd become a trader who lived on what he took from the woodlands. He'd sleep on the ground. He'd spend his time alone, never seeing anyone but the animals. He'd—

He knew what he was going to do. He was going to go to Edilean and get that straightened out. Maybe by now, after four long years, she had forgiven him at least somewhat. Maybe she'd found out, or figured out, why he'd done what he had. It was possible that she'd seen that the handbills were again being distributed, so she'd know why Angus had had to leave her.

And maybe if he sent word back to Colonel Wellman that he was going into the wilderness to look for the killer of the soldiers, that would hold his place open so he'd still get his land. Maybe—

He looked across the opening of the cave and Malcolm was watching him, a question on his face. Angus gave a small, quick nod, and Malcolm's eyes softened.

Angus thought of Edilean's wrath when she saw him again, and murmured, "May the Lord have mercy on me."

22

ANGUS KNEW HE'D never been so nervous in his life. He fidgeted at the cravat around his neck and wondered if he'd tied it properly. Maybe he'd ask Edilean for her help with the neckcloth. But then, maybe she'd tighten it and strangle him.

Beside him in the coach sat Tam, with Shamus and Malcolm across from them. They all seemed to be a bit in awe of Angus in his gentleman's clothes. They were from James Harcourt and had been stored in a trunk in the back of the tavern where Angus used to work.

Dolly was glad to see him and wanted him to stay. "It's been horrible since you left. We can't keep the place goin'."

"I can't stay," Angus said in the English accent he used with her. Behind him, Malcolm, Tam, and Shamus stood back and watched.

When Angus emerged from the back room wearing Harcourt's clothes, they'd stood there and stared at him.

"You look English," Malcolm said, shock in his voice.

"Sounds it too," Shamus said. "If we have a war, which side will you be on?"

"The only war is going to come when Edilean sees me again."

Tam looked down at his own clothes, which were rough to begin with and were now dusty and frayed. "She won't like *us*."

Angus shook his head. "Her quarrel is with me. You'll be all right. Shall we go and get this over with?"

"Yes, we shall," Shamus said in his version of an imitation of Angus's accent, but it came out sounding like a foreign dialect—and it made the four of them laugh.

"Come on, lad," Malcolm said. "It can't be as bad as you think it will be. My guess is that by now she's forgotten all about whatever it was that made her angry in the first place."

"Perhaps," Angus said, but he didn't think that was true.

They piled into a hired carriage and went to the town house where Edilean lived with Harriet Harcourt. At the last moment, Angus felt his knees weaken, but Shamus delighted in pushing him out of the carriage so hard that Angus almost hit the ground. He recovered himself, but his nerves were such that he didn't even reprimand Shamus.

The three Scotsmen surrounded Angus so he couldn't escape, and they moved forward up the steps to the front door. As Malcolm pulled the cord for the bell, he put his hand on the small of Angus's back to steady him.

A pretty maid answered the door.

"We're here to see Miss Edilean," Malcolm said, but she just stared at him in consternation.

"Miss Edilean," Angus said in his English accent.

"Is she expecting you?" the young woman asked, blocking the double doorway.

"We have some fruit to sell her," Shamus said, then louder. "Fruit, girl! Apples."

"Ah, yes, fruit. Won't you come in and I'll get her."

She led them into a large, sunlit room with a marble fireplace in one wall. Before it were two high-backed chairs on one side and a settee covered in yellow silk on the other. On the floor was a large carpet with wildflowers woven into the border. It was a truly beautiful room, and the three Scotsmen stood in the doorway staring at it but not entering.

"Come on," Angus said impatiently. "She won't want to meet us in the hallway."

Shamus and Malcolm sat down on the settee and looked about them nervously, while Tam and Angus took the chairs.

"You've changed," Tam said, looking across a little table at Angus.

"Fancy clothes don't change who a man is inside," Angus said.

"Then maybe you were like this before you got the clothes."

"Like what?" Angus asked, frowning.

"Like this room. Like this house. You fit in here." Tam raised his hand. "And it isn't just the clothes and that way you can talk. It's something else."

Angus wasn't sure what Tam meant, but he didn't think that now was the time to ask him more, for he heard Edilean's voice in the hallway.

"You didn't ask them who they were?" they heard Edilean say.

"No, ma'am, I forgot."

"From now on, Lissie, don't let people into my house unless you know them. Oh, heavens! Don't look like I'm going to beat you! Go to the kitchen and let Harriet talk to you."

As they heard the girl's footsteps retreat, they looked toward the doorway in expectation.

As for Angus, he sank back against the chair, letting the high sides of it hide him from the doorway. He hadn't been prepared for what the sound of her voice would do to him. It was all he could do to keep from running to her and gathering her in his arms. He didn't realize how very much he'd *missed* her! Just plain, old-fashioned *missed* her. Her humor, her no-nonsense approach to life, her strong likes and dislikes. He remembered how she'd won the battle that he was going to America with her. And she'd been right. If he'd stayed in Scotland he was sure that by now he'd be in prison.

"And how may I help you on this—?"

He heard Edilean's voice but couldn't see her for

the wing on the chair, but he knew she'd stopped when she saw Malcolm, Shamus, and Tam.

"Oh!" she said, and there was delight in her voice. "Oh, how lovely! I never thought I'd ever see you again. I—"

She broke off when she saw Angus in the far chair.

Slowly, he bent forward and looked at her. She was as beautiful as ever, maybe more so. She had on a long linen smock over her dress, and her hair was disarranged so that wispy tendrils hung about her face. He wanted to hold her, kiss her.

"You!" Edilean said, then she turned and ran from the room.

With a groan, Angus started to get out of the chair.

"Sit!" Malcolm said. "You said you'd do this and you're going to."

"She hates me."

"I didn't hear that in her voice," Malcolm said. "Did you, Tam?"

He was starry-eyed, looking as young as he had when Angus last saw him in Scotland. "She's prettier than I remembered. How could you do anything to hurt her?" Tam glared at Angus.

"I didn't hurt her on purpose!" Angus said. "I hurt her to save her from something worse."

"And what would that be?" Tam asked, his voice hostile.

Before Angus could answer, they heard the scurry of feet in the hallway.

"She's coming back," Tam said and he sat up straighter.

It wasn't Edilean who entered the room, but three serving girls carrying huge trays. They set one on a table in the center of the room, then pulled two other tables beside it and put the other trays on them. It was a lavish tea, with huge blue and white china pots full of steaming hot tea, and dishes covered with little sandwiches, scones, cookies, and cakes with colored icing.

As soon as the girls had set the trays down, they left the room, shutting the doors behind them.

Malcolm was the first to recover his astonishment. "Don't look like she's mad at you at all. Come on, lads, let's have something to eat." He picked up a teapot and filled four cups.

Shamus and Tam eagerly took plates and began to fill them, but Angus held back.

Tam ate three little tea sandwiches in rapid succession, then turned to look at Angus in admiration. "Whatever you did to her, it couldn't have been too bad. Look at this food."

Angus was still frowning, but part of him was beginning to relax. Maybe Edilean had seen the handbills. Maybe she'd realized why Angus left. Perhaps she even thought more of him for having given up so much to protect her.

Malcolm held out a cup of tea to Angus. "Come on, lad, drink it while it's hot."

Angus reached for the cup but halted when he heard a thud outside the parlor door. It sounded as though something heavy had been dropped on the floor.

"Unless I miss my guess," Malcolm said, "that was a piece of baggage. Looks like this time she doesn't mean to let you leave alone."

Angus took the cup of tea and downed it in one gulp as two more thuds came.

"She's certainly planning something," Tam said, now looking at Angus as though he were the epitome of manhood. "What did you do to make her . . . well, to want you."

"I ain't so sure it's baggage," Shamus said, his mouth full. "These cakes are good."

"It's all good," Malcolm said as he settled back, cup in hand, a full plate on his lap. "I can see why you'd want to stay here, lad. She sets a good table."

Angus put the teacup down and went to stand in front of the fireplace. Another thump came. "I don't like this. I want to know what she's doing." He took a step toward the door, but both of the doors flew open, and there stood Edilean—with a rifle in her hands. Two women stood behind her, and on the floor was an arsenal of firearms. The only thing missing was a cannon.

Angus's mouth dropped open in surprise, but he'd had too many years of dodging bullets to stand still when a rifle was aimed at him. "Get down!" he yelled while he dove for cover behind a chair. Tam hit the floor, but Malcolm and Shamus sat where they were, not hesitating in their eating.

The bullet missed Angus by inches, hitting the

chair and sending stuffing flying. "Edilean!" he said from behind the chair. "We can talk about this."

"I never plan to speak to you again," she said as she hoisted a second long, heavy rifle and fired it at him. The bullet tore through the chair arm. He moved his legs a second before he would have been hit.

Angus peeked around the destroyed chair. Edilean was standing in the doorway, and the two young women flanking her glowed with good health—and humor. As one loaded the rifle Edilean had just fired, the other one handed her a pistol. Both girls looked very happy, as though they'd wanted to do this all their lives.

"Edilean, please," Angus said. As he spoke, he motioned to Tam, who was hiding behind the other chair, to make a run for the window. It was closed, but nearby there was a heavy silver candlestick on a tall cabinet. Angus pantomimed that Tam should use that to break the window and get out.

Edilean cocked a pistol, aimed, and fired directly at Angus, but he rolled away and the shot went into the floor, tearing a hole in the pretty rug. In the next second, Tam threw the candlestick at the window, it broke and he started out. But there were two young women standing outside, and they were holding loaded pistols aimed at him. He paused with his foot on the windowsill.

"I'm not the one you want," Tam said.

One of the girls cocked her pistol. "We can't be sure of that, now can we?"

"But I don't even look like him!" Tam said.

"We were told that he's big and beautiful," the second girl said, raising her pistol toward Tam's head.

"Well, I guess there is a similarity between us," Tam said, smiling, and he started out the window. But the first girl pulled the trigger, missing Tam by little more than an inch.

He went back in and crouched on the floor by Angus, who gave him a look of disgust.

"Ever hear of clan loyalty?" Angus asked.

Tam shrugged. "This is your personal fight."

Angus grimaced as he looked around the chair and saw Edilean aiming another pistol at him. "For God's sake, Malcolm. Help us in this."

"Ain't my way to interfere in love," Malcolm said as he licked jam from his fingers.

"*This* is love?" Angus rolled away from another near-miss shot. "Then give me hate."

Malcolm said, "I do indeed like these biscuits."

Shamus looked at Edilean standing in the doorway, holding a rifle longer than she was, and at the two young women beside her, pistols in their hands. "I think I like everything about this country."

Angus said, "Edilean, if you'd just give me a moment to explain I could clear this up. It really is just a misunderstanding." As he spoke, he half rolled, half ran to the other side of the room and crouched down behind the settee. He figured she wouldn't shoot at him if Malcolm was between them.

"Malcolm," Edilean said as she took another

pistol, "would you please move to the left?" She shot through the settee, but the bullet went through Malcolm's shirt, grazing his upper arm. "Oh, I am so sorry," Edilean said. "I meant my left, not yours."

Malcolm glanced at the wound, and continued eating. "That's all right, lass, it's a common enough mistake."

"Did I hurt you?" Edilean asked.

"No, not at all," Malcolm said. "These little raspberry tarts sure are good."

Angus, behind the settee, rolled his eyes, then stood up and said firmly, "Edilean, this is ridiculous! You're going to hurt someone."

She took a pistol from one of the women. "I mean to *kill* you," she said, her jaw clenched. She looked at Malcolm and said sweetly, "Harriet made those. I'll have her give you some."

"Edilean," Angus said, "if you kill me they'll *hang* you."

She gave him a cold look. "Not after I tell them what you did to me." She looked back at Shamus. "It's good to see you again. Have you been well?"

"Well enough," Shamus said. "Was that really gold in the back of that wagon I was supposed to drive for you?"

Edilean blinked at him. She'd been away from Scotland so long that she didn't understand what he'd said.

Angus, still standing behind the settee, which now had a huge hole in the center of it, translated.

"Yes, it was gold," Edilean said.

"Damn!" Shamus said.

"He said—" Angus began.

"I could understand *that*!" Edilean said angrily. "You have *always* thought that I'm incompetent and worthless."

"I've never thought any such thing!" Angus said. "If you'll stop this lunacy and give me time to explain, I could tell you—"

"Edilean," said a woman who came to the doorway, "whatever are you doing?"

"Tabitha?" Angus asked. "Is that you?"

Edilean looked from one to the other, at the way Angus's face was breaking into a smile, and she fired again.

Angus just had time to dive under the settee, his head between Shamus's and Malcolm's feet.

In the next second a woman came running from the back of the house and Angus recognized her as Harriet Harcourt.

"Edilean!" Harriet said. "Have you lost your mind?"

"Hand me a loaded pistol," Edilean said to the woman behind Harriet.

Harriet pushed the girl's hand away. "This is absurd! You can't shoot at people and you can*not* destroy the furniture again!"

Angus backed out from under the settee and stood up, his face showing his relief. "That's just what I've been telling her."

Harriet looked at Angus and her face turned to anger. "You! Give me that pistol!" She snatched the pistol from the girl and fired at Angus, who went back down under the settee.

Tam, still on the other side of the room, hiding behind a chair, said, "What the hell did you *do* to these women?"

"I'd rather not talk about it," Angus said from under the couch.

It was Malcolm who stopped it all. Suddenly, he stood up and was staring at Harriet.

Shamus looked up at him. "What's wrong with you? If you don't sit down, you'll make all this stop."

Edilean looked from Malcolm to Harriet, then back again. "Harriet," she said softly, "why don't you take Malcolm into the kitchen, patch up his wound, and get him some more of those little tarts you made?"

Harriet and Malcolm just stood there, staring at each other.

Edilean turned to Tabitha, who was watching everything with a wide grin on her face. "Would you please help those two into the kitchen?"

Angus nodded across the room to Tam, who pushed the chair over. In the confusion of the noise, Angus quickly slipped out of the room and put himself between Edilean and the weapons, but he didn't touch her. "Are you over your hissy fit now?"

Edilean's face showed her rage; her fists were clenched at her sides. "If I had a knife I'd cut your throat. I want you to get out of my house and never return."

"Tam has something he wants to say to you."

"Tam may stay. In fact, all the rest of you may spend the night. But you"—she glared at Angus—"*you* must go."

"Edilean, I know you hate me and maybe you have a right to, but—"

"Maybe?" she said, her voice nearly a screech.

"All right, you *do* have every right to hate me, but please listen to what they have to say. And please know that I'll do anything to help them."

Before she could say anything else, he took the few steps toward the door. Tabitha was looking at him in amusement, while Harriet's eyes blazed hatred. Angus bent toward Harriet and said softly, "How is your brother? Living well?"

In a second, Harriet's face went from anger to fear, and she glanced at Edilean, as though terrified that she'd heard him.

Angus left the house, the door was slammed behind him, and he hurried down the stairs. There was a crowd of people outside, all of them having heard the shots.

"What's going on in there?" a man asked.

"Gun cleaning," Angus said as he made his way through them. He hitched a ride on a milk wagon and went back to the tavern where he'd once worked. He knew that Malcolm would want to know where he was staying, so it would be better to be somewhere known. Besides, Dolly kept her ears open and she'd know as much as anyone, and Angus wanted some information.

When Malcolm had told him that Harriet was paying her brother James to stay away from Edilean, Angus had been so concerned about having to confront Edilean that he'd not thought about it much. But now it was taking over his mind. He'd only mentioned the matter to Harriet as an afterthought. He hadn't liked the way she'd been looking at Malcolm. What was the woman after by throwing herself at his uncle?

But when Angus had mentioned James, Harriet's anger had changed to fear. So, he thought, Edilean didn't know anything about the payments going to Harcourt. If Harriet was taking care of Edilean's money as Tam had said she was, did that mean she was embezzling from Edilean?

If Edilean knew nothing about Harriet's treachery, then how did Malcolm know? When it came to that, exactly what had they been doing in America for three whole months? And who had paid their passage across the ocean, and their room and board once they got here?

Angus knew that there was a great deal more to why Malcolm, Tam, and Shamus were in this country than just signing some papers—and Angus meant to find out what they weren't telling him.

23

HARRIET WAS MOVING quickly around the dining room, putting out the best china, polishing the silver with her apron, checking the glasses for smudges.

Edilean was sitting at the end of the table, reading the newspaper, and finishing her tea. "Harriet, will you please stop fidgeting? I've seen where those men live, and I can assure you that they don't know Wedgwood from Limoges. They'd be happy if you dumped all the food on a slab of bread."

"There is such a thing as lineage, and even though the men have no money, their bloodline still tells."

"Bloodline? Whatever are you talking about?"

"Tam is to be the laird of the McTern clan," Harriet said. "Didn't you know that? When Angus relinquishes the title, it will belong to young Tam."

"And if anything happens to Tam, it goes to Malcolm," Edilean said softly. "Are you thinking of being the laird's wife?"

"Don't be ridiculous," Harriet said as she turned

away, but not before Edilean saw the blush that rose in her cheeks.

"I hope a bloodline doesn't mean as much to you as it does to your brother."

"Why would you mention him?" Harriet said, turning back to look at Edilean. "Have you heard anything from him?"

"No," Edilean said. "I merely mentioned him because your love of bloodline reminded me that he chose an earl's daughter over me. Are you interested in Malcolm because of his ancestry?"

"Interested in him? I have no idea what you mean," Harriet said haughtily.

"You—" Edilean began but stopped herself. Harriet was so mad about Malcolm that they caused giggles wherever they went. All the girls who worked for Edilean's company saw it and tittered behind their hands. Harriet was what one thought of when an old maid was mentioned. She had a look about her of someone who had dried up inside. But since she'd met Malcolm three weeks before, she'd begun to blossom. She was like a plant that hadn't been watered in forty years, but at the first drops of rain it was coming back to life.

Harriet had always been stern with the girls who worked for them, but they'd found that under her harsh-seeming ways she had a good heart. In public she might berate one of them for not keeping a good account of her expenses, but they knew that in private she often slipped them a pound or two when one was in desperate need.

And it was Miss Harriet who met the ships and bought the contracts of the young women who arrived in America. Some were frightened, some looking forward to adventure, but some were hardened criminals looking out for what they could get. Miss Harriet had a good eye as to which ones to employ and which to leave to their own fates. She took care of the women, arranging where they were to live and often overseeing their health. Sometimes the conditions on board the ships were so bad that they arrived barely alive. Harriet saw to it that they were given good food and a clean room. When they were well, they went to work on the farms.

Because of her kindness to them, they were happy for her to have found Malcolm. They loved to see her nearly skipping with happiness, and they smiled when they saw Malcolm pick a flower and hand it to her.

As for Edilean, she'd only returned last night. After that day when she'd thrown Angus out of her house, she and Malcolm had spent hours together, and he told her about her uncle dying and their plan of making Tam the laird. Edilean had readily agreed to return the property her uncle had stolen from them, but she felt sick at the idea of appearing before a judge and saying nice things about Angus. She'd have to say that she willingly ran off with him, that he'd treated her well, and that he'd never used any force on her. Malcolm said she'd probably be asked to embellish the story so it sounded as though Angus had done her a good deed, that he was the best of men, and deserved to be released from an unfair accusation.

It all made sense, but Edilean still hated the idea of spending any time with Angus. They'd have to rehearse their story before going to the judge to make sure they said the same things, so that meant hours together.

After Malcolm finished telling what they wanted of her, Edilean mumbled that she needed time to think about it all. But she couldn't bear thinking about it. That evening, she tossed a few clothes into a case, called for the big green carriage with the crest on the door and Cuddy as her driver, and headed south to the colony of Connecticut. She'd heard of a farm for sale there that had acres in fruit, and she wanted to look at it. Originally, she'd decided that it was too far away from Boston to be of interest to her, but after seeing Angus, after trying to kill him, she wanted to get away.

Harriet, who so loved overseeing every aspect of Edilean's life, hadn't protested her leaving. Harriet had, in an instant, turned all her motherly affections to Malcolm. She hovered over him in the kitchen and had four girls running up and down the stairs as she had a room prepared for him.

Harriet's quick desertion of Edilean was yet another blow to her on a day that reeked with them. In fact, Harriet hardly noticed when Edilean left.

When Edilean returned yesterday, she saw that her house had become "theirs." Malcolm and Harriet were a couple in everything but legality and bedding. There was new furniture in the parlor, new linens on the beds—and Harriet was sleeping in Edilean's room. She'd given Malcolm her room with the excuse that she had no idea when or even if Edilean was going to return.

"Why wouldn't I return to my own house?" Edilean snapped. "Where else was I going to live?"

"Now, girls," Malcolm said, "we can solve this all if the lads and I move out."

"No!" Harriet half screamed, and glared at Edilean.

"No, of course you can't leave," Edilean said and had to bite her tongue from making a sarcastic reply about guests who stayed for three whole weeks.

At dinner she felt like the outsider as Tam, Shamus, Malcolm, and Harriet had become great friends and talked as though they'd known one another all their lives. Harriet played the hostess with perfection.

Edilean sat at the end of the table and watched it all with feelings of jealousy, but also with a sense of being an unneeded and unwanted visitor. She had become the one who didn't belong in her own house.

The truth was that she'd felt more at home in the three weeks she'd spent in Connecticut. Right away, she'd seen that the farm was a place she wanted to buy. It had been well kept, and the fruit was going to be abundant. The man who owned it had died unexpectedly and left behind a wife and two young daughters. Edilean made an excuse by saying she wanted to stay with the woman while she readied herself to leave the farm, but the truth was that Edilean wanted to do anything rather than return to the house where she'd last seen Angus. She still hadn't recovered from the violence of her emotions when she first saw him. Every moment they'd spent together, both private and public, had run through her mind. But the prominent memory was of how he'd just walked away from her. Left her there in his bed. He didn't even stay long enough to tell her to her face that he'd had what he wanted from her and was done with her. No, he'd told that to Cuddy.

It had taken nearly two days to get Cuddy to tell the full truth of what Angus had said, but she'd done it. Calmly, the young man had said, "Would you like me to kill him for you?" Edilean had been tempted to say yes, but she didn't. But as a result of Cuddy's loyalty he was one of only three men she'd kept in her employ when she started Bound Girl. The other two men were too old to discharge.

After Angus had so coldly left her, Edilean had borne her heartache without a tear, and she'd never told Harriet what had happened. To compensate, Edilean had started Bound Girl and buried herself in as much work as she could humanly manage.

It had all gone well until she walked into her own parlor and there he was. He sat there looking at her as though he'd just seen her last week and now he wanted to put his arms around her. And then what? Take her to bed, have a night of ecstasy, then leave her for another four years? Is that what he thought of her?

Just as had happened before, Edilean's mind left her. She ran from the room and told the girls who were in the back loading boxes of fruit that she needed them. She knew that they were so grateful to her for saving them that they'd do anything she wanted. If she'd told them to take the guns and shoot Angus, they would have done it and damn the consequences!

But Edilean had wanted the pleasure of seeing him suffer. She wanted to see him lying dead at her feet—or that's what she told herself.

After it was over, after the weapons had been taken from her, she couldn't bear to stay in that house. She didn't want to see any of them. She didn't want to see the three Scotsmen, who reminded her of Angus, didn't want to see Harriet simpering over Malcolm. She didn't even want to see the girls, who reminded her of the company she'd started because of what Angus had done to her.

When she got into the carriage she wasn't sure where she was going. It wasn't until she was an hour away that she remembered the handbill Harriet had shown her about the farm for sale in Connecticut. It took days to get there, but when she'd arrived, the widow, Abigail Prentiss, had welcomed her, and by the next evening they'd formed a friendship. Abigail was her age, and she'd been born in England into the same class. They even knew some of the same people.

When she was just seventeen, Abby had fallen in love with an older man who owned a farm in America. Her family protested that she couldn't go that far away, but Abby had made up her mind. They married three months after they met, and Abby was expecting a baby a week later. Now, with two daughters, aged four and three, to support, she didn't know how she was going to do it alone.

"I can help you with that," Edilean said, and gave a great sigh.

From there it went to Abigail listening to Edilean's problems; she told her about Angus. While it was true that Abby had been in love with John Prentiss when she married him, she admitted to Edilean that it had not been a match made in Heaven.

"I think I wanted to get away from my mother as much as I wanted anything else, and there was John, such a very nice man, who owned a big farm in America, and I saw a way to leave my mother. He was a lovely man."

"But not one you'd want to kill if he betrayed you."

Abby laughed. "I don't think I could feel that way about any man."

"Good," Edilean said. "It's awful. I can't decide if I love him or hate him."

"Aren't they the same thing?"

They were in her orchard, many of the trees were in bloom, and the bees were buzzing all around them. Her little girls, blonde and beautiful, were chasing butterflies. Edilean knew that she envied Abby. She'd had a "correct" life, marrying a man, then having children. Edilean felt that her own life had been topsy-turvy, everything always backward to what it should be. She'd had no parents to speak of and no marriage—but she'd had a wedding night.

"What will you do now?" Abby asked.

"Go back to Boston and . . ." She gave another sigh. "I guess I'll run Bound Girl, although I think Tabitha and Harriet could manage quite well without me. I was needed to make them believe they could start such a company, but now they do all the work. I . . ." She trailed off. While it was true that she worked all day long and ran everything, it seemed that lately her heart wasn't in it. She was to turn twenty-two this year, and she wasn't married or even being courted by a man. There were still many men trying for her hand, but they seemed to get older every year. A woman who was extremely successful in a business was not something a younger man wanted to take on. Whereas they loved the idea of marrying a rich heiress, a woman who was taking over the produce market through intelligence and shrewd decisions was not their idea of a good wife.

"I don't know what I'm going to do," Edilean said, and she had a vision of herself looking like Harriet, of being forty-plus, with no husband, no family. If she owned all the orchards in all thirteen colonies she'd still be alone. "What about you?" Edilean asked. "After I buy your farm, where will you go?"

"Williamsburg," Abby said firmly. "I went there once with John and I loved the place. It's a city, but it has the atmosphere of an English village. And Virginia is beautiful."

"With a lot of eligible bachelors?" Edilean asked, and they looked at each other and laughed.

Edilean meant to stay in Connecticut for only a few days, but she ended up staying at Abby's farm for three weeks. She left because she feared that Bound Girl might need her. If Harriet was still enamored of Malcolm she wouldn't be paying attention to the business, and if Tabitha wasn't constantly supervised, who knew what she'd do? Reluctantly, Edilean left the farm and her new friend, and went back to Boston.

But no one paid much attention to her arrival. There were no crises that only she could handle. In just a few weeks, her household had changed so much that she felt she didn't know it. Harriet's every sentence seemed to start with, "Malcolm says—"

As for Tabitha, she'd taken the opportunity to buy some new wagons and have the company's Bound Girl symbol painted on them. Edilean thought they were hideously garish and said so. "But they sell more" was Tabitha's reply.

Now, Edilean was watching Harriet dither about as she set the table as though the king were coming when it was just Malcolm, Tam, and Shamus. As far as Edilean knew, Shamus still ate all his food with a spoon.

She left the table, unable to sit there and— She hated to think that she was such a shallow person, but it was difficult not to feel jealous and envious of the happiness that everyone in her household seemed to have found.

She went to the big warehouse where the produce from the farms came in. Usually, she was so busy that she could think of nothing else, but today she was distracted. She kept remembering Abigail and her beautiful young daughters.

When Tabitha said something to Edilean, she just stared at her.

"You comin' down with somethin'?" Tabitha asked her.

"Yes. No," Edilean said as she looked at two young women who were bent over boxes of cherries and saw that they were watching her and laughing. No doubt all of Boston knew about her shooting at some man. And they could easily guess why.

Edilean grabbed her skirts and fled the warehouse. All in all, she thought, it would have been better to have killed Angus and now be sitting in a jail cell.

She wandered about Boston for a while, looking at what the stores had to offer, and listening to men complain about England. Edilean didn't understand what the problem was. If the men thought King George was bad, they should read the history books and look at past kings. What did the Americans think they were going to do? Start a new country without a king? Really! Sometimes she didn't understand Americans at all.

It was dusk by the time she got back to the house, and she hadn't eaten all day. She asked to have a tray taken to her room. She ate little of the food, then undressed down to her chemise and went to bed. She fell asleep instantly.

She was awakened by a shot and angry shouts coming from downstairs. "Now what?" Edilean muttered as she slipped her arms into a dressing gown and went out her door. She had to wait her turn to go down the stairs as the three men and Harriet were ahead of her.

When Edilean got to the parlor, the others were blocking her view. They were standing there and staring, transfixed into immobility by whatever they were seeing. "Would you mind!" she said angrily as she pushed through them. When she got to the front, she also stood still and stared. Two candles were lit in the room, and her good silver candlesticks were sticking out of a bag on the floor. Beside the bag was the body of James Harcourt, and he had a bullet hole smack in the middle of his forehead. He was staring sightlessly at the ceiling.

Over him stood a large woman with her back to them, but they could see the pistol in her hand. "That's what you get for stealing my life from me," the woman said. "You bastard. I hope you're already in Hell. I wish you were alive so I could kill you again."

The woman drew back her foot and proceeded to kick James's inert body. Suddenly, in a fury, she began to kick him over and over, her feet moving so fast they were a whirl of motion. "I hate you! Do you hear me? I hate you. Hate you!"

Shamus pushed past the others, went to the woman, and grabbed her arm, but she fought him off. She turned her anger onto Shamus and began to hit him with her fists and kick at his shins with her hard-soled shoes.

"There now," Shamus said, pulling her close so her arms were pinned between his body and hers. She was a large, strong woman, and Shamus was the only one who could have held her still. When he got her arms to stop pounding him, he pushed her head down to his shoulder and turned her face to the others, who were still standing in the doorway.

It took all Edilean's self-discipline to keep from gasping, for the woman was extraordinarily ugly. Her nose was huge and curved down so it overshadowed her sharp chin.

Harriet said, "Prudence."

Edilean didn't know the name, but she knew who had the most reason to kill James Harcourt, and she'd heard about his wife's unfortunate looks. "James's wife," she said.

Edilean came out of her lackluster mood. "Harriet!" she said sharply, then had to repeat herself. "Harriet! Listen to me! I want you to get her upstairs and give her some of that laudanum your brother loves . . . loved so much. Are you listening to me?" When Harriet didn't respond, just kept staring at her brother's body on the floor, Edilean looked at Malcolm for help.

"It's over," he said softly, and took Harriet into his arms. "It's all over now. He won't be bothering you anymore."

"When has James bothered her?" Edilean asked.

"He's been blackmailing Harriet for years."

"You knew?" Harriet asked as she raised her head from his shoulder to look at him.

"Yes, we knew, and we've been waiting for him to return. Come now, and we'll get you back to bed. Shamus! Take Miss Prudence upstairs. We'll put the women in the same bed and give them that . . ." He looked at Edilean.

"Laudanum," she said, blinking at him. Blackmail. She couldn't help wondering how Harriet had paid the blackmail. James wouldn't be cheap.

"What you're thinking is right," Malcolm said, glaring at her, anger in his voice. "It was your company's money that paid the blackmail, but Harriet was protecting *you*. If you plan to try to put her in prison, I tell you now that you'll have to go through *me* first." With that, he helped Harriet up the stairs; Shamus with Prudence was right behind him.

Edilean was left standing in the parlor door, with James's dead body on the floor not ten feet from her. But she was in much more shock from what Malcolm had just said than she was at James's death. What had she done to make him or anyone else think that she'd prosecute Harriet? Harriet had taken care of her for years. Harriet had—

Edilean refused to think any more about what had been said to her. Right now, the most important question was what to do about the dead man lying in her parlor. She slowly walked into the room and looked down at him. The light was dim, but she could see that James wasn't nearly as handsome as he used to be. Or was it that she had become used to American men, who spent their lives out of doors and worked hard in their lives? By comparison, James looked pale and weak.

Whatever it was, she wondered what she'd ever seen in him.

"Miss Edilean?"

She turned to see Malcolm standing in the doorway, and she couldn't help her cold expression when she looked at him. "Is Harriet all right?"

"Much better, thank you," Malcolm said, his voice contrite. "I said some things to you that were uncalled for. It was in the heat of the moment, and I want to apologize. I know that Harriet has been nearly driven insane by that . . . that man." He sneered at James's body sprawled on the floor.

"I understand," Edilean said, but she was lying. She was hurt that he could even think she would prosecute Harriet. "I would never do anything bad to her."

"I know that, but she worries so."

"But now she has you to take care of her." Edilean raised her hand when he started to speak. "I think that all this can be hashed out later. Right now we need to do something about this man's body."

"You mean to call the sheriff?"

"So he can give Prudence a medal?"

Malcolm blinked a couple of times, then smiled. "That's the way we all feel, but I wondered, since you once . . ." He shrugged.

"Loved him? Maybe I did. But I was a schoolgirl and he was beautiful. I can be forgiven that idiocy, can't I?"

"I think you should be forgiven everything."

"Now that that's settled, what do we do with him? My floor is going to be ruined."

Malcolm laughed. "Between shots fired into it and now blood on it, I think you might have to have this floor replaced. Unless there are more men in your life and we should expect cannon fire at any moment."

Edilean laughed too, and plopped down onto a chair. "What *are* we going to do with this body?"

"You have to ask Angus."

Edilean thought he was making a joke. "So he can dress it up as an Indian and blame them for this? I tell you that these Americans blame the poor Indians for everything. Only last week—" She broke off when she looked at Malcolm's face. He wasn't joking.

"All right," she said at last. "Go get him. And while you're gone, I'll pack and get out of here. I may move to that farm in Connecticut permanently."

"No," Malcolm said, moving to stand on the other side of James's body. "*You* have to go get him."

"Me? Did you forget that I'm the one who tried to kill him in this very room just three weeks ago? If you can't go, send Tam. Angus adores his young cousin."

"Angus is, well . . . He's a bit angry at us right now and won't speak to us."

"What did you do to him? No, on second thought, don't tell me."

"We didn't tell him all of the truth about why we came to America."

"There's more than about my uncle dying?"

"It was Miss Prudence who paid our way here, and she hired us to find her husband."

Edilean stared at him for a moment. "I don't know the law that well, but I think you three could be considered an accessory to murder."

Malcolm shrugged.

"So Angus is angry at your participation in this? Since when did he become a champion of James Harcourt?"

Malcolm glanced at the window. "You know, lass, I don't mean to rush you on this, but I think you should go right away. It's hours before daylight, but we may need all that time of darkness. I don't think that in the morning the maid will keep quiet at the sight of a dead body on the floor of the parlor."

"Would that be the maid who was transported for grave robbing, or the one who was sentenced because she used a whip on her stepfather?"

Malcolm shook his head at her. "Oh, lass, if only I were younger. But you must go get Angus. He knows this country but we don't. He'll know what to do and how to hide a dead man. We'd go, but he said he'd have nothing to do with us until we tell him the whole truth, but we swore to Miss Prudence that we wouldn't."

"And Angus has a soft spot for her."

"Please tell me that's a jest," Malcolm said seriously. "Shamus is quite taken with the woman and she with him. If Angus also wants her it will cause great problems. They'll—"

"How do I know what he wants?" Edilean half shouted, then glanced at the ceiling when she heard what sounded like a muffled cry.

"I must go!" Malcolm said. "And so must you. Angus is at the tavern where he used to work." He rushed from the room.

"Of course he is," Edilean said. "Where else would he be? In that same room, asleep in that same bed." She wanted to run upstairs and tell the men that she could *not* do this. She would do anything but go see Angus, but then she looked down at the body on her floor and thought about poor Prudence being hanged for shooting someone who so very much deserved killing, and Edilean headed for the doorway. But she turned back and gave James's rib cage a good swift kick. "That's from me," she said, and left the room.

24

"Angus!" Edilean said as she stared down at him in bed. He was lying on *that* bed, the one that held so many memories for her, and he was smiling. She had no doubt that he was dreaming something good. And why not? He got everything he ever wanted, didn't he? In the four years that she'd heard nothing from him he must had bedded a hundred women. Maybe a thousand.

She resisted the urge to turn around and leave the room, but Tam was waiting outside the barn, and she figured he'd send her back in. Malcolm had been shocked when Edilean said she'd go to Angus alone.

"Brigands!" he said under his breath.

"We don't have them in America," Edilean said, her eyes wide in innocence.

Malcolm had looked at her in shock, but Tam laughed. "She has no intention of going to Angus."

Edilean gave him a sharp look because that was exactly her plan.

"I'll go with you and protect you," Tam said,

"even though this new country has no idea what crime is."

When he said he'd meet her in back of the house with the horses saddled, she'd reluctantly agreed. She went upstairs to dress, and on impulse, she went into Tam's room and opened the chest at the foot of his bed. At nineteen, he was a foot taller than she was, but he was very slim, so his clothes might come close to fitting her. If she was going to have to sneak through the night, she couldn't do it wearing thirty-five yards of silk.

Everyone was in the bedroom with Prudence and Harriet, so no one saw Edilean hurry past wearing a large white shirt, a vest that was big enough to hide her breasts, knee britches, and white stockings. She had on her own work shoes, which were plain black leather with big silver buckles. She'd tied her hair at the nape of her neck and let it hang down her back.

When she got outside where Tam was impatiently waiting for her, his eyes widened at the sight of her, but she gave him a look that dared him to say anything. But when she swung up into the saddle by herself, he said, "Good boy!" and rode out of the courtyard ahead of her.

It took them over an hour to get to the tavern where Angus lived, and they found that the barn that held his room was bolted from the inside. It was Edilean who told Tam that he had to hoist her up to the second floor so she could climb into the loft. He managed to stand on his horse and lift Edilean up until she caught the rope that hung down from the pulley over the loft door. She was sure there was a great deal more touching of her backside than was quite necessary, but she said nothing to Tam.

She grabbed the rope, and managed to shinny up it to reach the bottom of the open door. She had to swing forward on the rope, and below her, she heard Tam's quick intake of breath, but she made it inside, landing on the wooden floor and rolling almost to the ladder down to the floor below. "You're not worth this," she muttered as she dusted herself off.

When she stuck her leg out to shake off the hay, she rather liked not having on a corset and not being encumbered with a full, long skirt. With a glance about to make sure no one was looking, she did a bit of a dance on the wooden floor, lifting her knees up to almost her waist.

"Edilean!" came Tam's loud whisper from outside. "Whatever are you doing? I can hear you jumping!"

With a grimace, she stopped dancing and thought about the days when Tam was so enamored of her that he'd stared at her in fascination. Now he told her to hurry up.

Sighing, she turned and went down the ladder to the ground floor and tiptoed to Ángus's door. When all the horses moved to the front of their stalls to look at her, she was tempted to stay with them, and she'd tell Tam that Angus wasn't there. She'd say that he was probably with another woman. Maybe she'd tell him that—

The memory of James Harcourt lying on her parlor floor brought her back to reality. Angus's door was closed and she thought about knocking, but she was afraid someone might hear. They hadn't heard the many noises she and Angus had made on the night they'd made love in that room, but maybe he'd arranged that.

She tried the latch, it opened, she went inside, and a moment later she was looking down at his sleeping face. Quickly, she lit a candle, and the fact that she knew where it and the flint were made her more angry.

"Angus!" she said. "You have to wake up!" When he didn't stir, she went closer to him—and he reached out one of his long arms and pulled her on top of him. Before she could stop him, he tried to kiss her, but she pushed away. "I don't have time for this!" she said into his ear. "There's a dead body in my front parlor."

"It's probably mine," he said, his eyes closed, "because I'm in Heaven now."

She pushed at him harder, but his arms still held her on top of him. "Will you stop it! I'm serious. James Harcourt is in my house and he's dead."

Angus opened his eyes and looked at her. "Harcourt?"

"Oh, so you *can* hear me."

"I heard you leaping about upstairs. Edilean, it's one thing to shoot at me while, of course, being careful to miss, but it's something altogether different to actually kill someone."

"You idiot!" she said as she gave a major push that got her off of him so she was standing by the bed. "*I* didn't kill him."

He rose up on his elbows. "But you seem to enjoy shooting at people. All right," he said at her look. "Who did kill him?"

Edilean put her hands on her hips. "What do you mean, that I was careful to miss you? I tried to hit you but you kept leaping around. You're worse than our goats!"

"Goats?" Angus ran his hand over his face. "Edilean, what in the world are you talking about?"

"I'm trying to make you listen to me. It's never happened before, but I'm still trying. James Harcourt is dead, and he's bleeding on my parlor floor. We have to get rid of the body and Malcolm sent me to get you. He said that you know how to do every underhanded, lying, sneaking, illegal thing there is, so you'd know what to do to keep Prudence from being hanged."

After staring at her in silence for a few seconds, Angus threw back the blanket, got out of bed, and began to dress. "Prudence? Is she one of your slave girls?"

"They're bound girls, not slaves. But no, she's not in my employment. You should know who she is, as you tussled with her in bed."

Angus groaned as he pulled on his breeches. "Not your jealousy again!"

"Jealousy?!" Edilean's fists clenched at her sides. "I

have *never* been jealous of you, no matter how many women you've had."

"Oh? Then why did you hire Tabitha if not to keep her away from me?"

"Why you vain, arrogant—" She started to kick his shin, but he moved back.

Angus smiled. "You won't catch me like that again."

Edilean put her hands over her face as though she were crying. "Oh, Angus, I'm so very frightened. James was . . . It was awful." The minute Angus stepped near her, she kicked him in the shin, and he yelped in pain.

"I'm tempted to turn you over my knee for that."

"Try it," she said.

"It would be too easy." For a moment they glared at each other. "Who is Prudence?!" he said at last.

"James's wife."

"His wife?" Angus looked puzzled for a moment, then understood. "Oh, yes, his wife."

Edilean gave him a cold little smile. "So you do remember her. I remember that you wouldn't let me see her, but you let me believe she was so beautiful that you envied James."

"I did not!"

She glared at him.

Angus tried to suppress a smile. "Perhaps I did. Would you like to kick my other shin? It's not bleeding."

"You're not going to get 'round me, Angus . . . What is your name now?"

"Harcourt." He shrugged. "It was easier than thinking up a new name. Shall we go? Or do you want to stay here and argue some more?"

"I don't want to do anything with you."

Angus opened the door to his room and let Edilean leave ahead of him. In the close quarters of the room he'd not been able to see her clearly. "What in the world are you wearing?" he asked, his voice showing his shock.

"Tam's clothes."

"Ah," Angus said coldly. "Tam. Is he still staying with you?"

"As if you don't know everything there is to know about my life," Edilean said as Angus lifted the latch on the barn door. Tam was just outside, mounted, and holding the reins to Edilean's horse.

Angus looked at Tam. "If I do this, I want to be told everything."

"We made a vow to Miss Prudence, but I think it's gone past that now."

Edilean put her foot up to the stirrup of her horse, but Angus picked her up by the waist and set her aside. "What do you—?" she began but cut off when Angus swung up into the saddle, and offered his hand down to her. "I'd rather ride with Tam," she said.

Angus started to get off the horse.

Edilean muttered a curse word under her breath, and put her hand up to his, and he pulled her onto the saddle in front of him. It wasn't two seconds after they started moving that he began talking to her, his mouth close to her ear.

"I left you that morning because James showed up at the tavern. He hung up handbills of me. I didn't want you to love a man who was to be executed."

"Is that supposed to make me forgive you?" Edilean was trying to sit up straight and stay away from his big, warm body. She had on only a cotton shirt and a vest, and it was cold out.

"I did think that if you knew my reason for leaving you that night you might feel more kindly toward me."

His breath was warm against her face, and she well remembered the sweet smell of it. "I'm to feel good that you decided my entire future in a second? Without asking me what *I* wanted to do? You had your way with me, then you left me there to rot! Tabitha walked the streets, and she was *never* treated so badly."

Angus leaned away from her, his back stiff. "You told her about me?"

"Oh, yes."

"You told Tabitha, one of your bound girls, about you and me?" His voice showed his disbelief.

Smiling, Edilean said, "Every word. And for your information, Tabitha and I have become good friends. I have to bail her out of jail now and then, and I've had to dock her more than a year's wages to repay the people she steals from, but when you overlook that quirk about her, she can be pleasurable company. She knows everything about snaky men."

"Snaky? Oh. As in snakes."

"Lying, cheating—"

Angus sighed. "I get the idea. So tell me what happened about James—if you can drag yourself away from reciting all my faults, that is."

"It will be difficult, but then I've had years and years and years to think on your faults."

"That would be six, but I was away only four."

"Six what?" she asked.

"Years. One 'years' plus another 'years' plus—" He stopped when she twisted in the saddle to look at him. "Sorry. You were about to tell me about Harcourt and his wife. I don't know anything about them together."

"Except that she killed him."

"Yes, I do know that, but *why* did she kill him?"

Edilean turned to give him a look.

"Oh, right. I see your point. He deserved it. I'm afraid I have to agree with her. Where is she now?"

"With Shamus."

"With . . . ?" Angus's face showed his horror. "You left that frightened woman with *Shamus*?"

"After Prudence shot James she began to kick him, and Shamus was the only one big enough to hold her. But then I guess you know all about the size and shape of her, being as you spent so much time in bed with her."

"And lived to tell of it," Angus said under his breath.

"What?"

"Nothing. I'm just trying to think how I'm going to dispose of a body in a town the size of Boston. Where did she shoot him?"

"I told you. In my parlor."

"No! Where on his body?"

"In his head. Dead center. A perfect shot."

"I'm glad *she* wasn't shooting at me," Angus mumbled.

"Does that mean you think she's a better shot than I am?"

"No, dear, I'd never think that. Edilean, why did you leave that poor, distraught woman with a ruffian like Shamus?"

"You know, as far as I can tell, you're the only person who thinks Shamus is bad. So what happened? Did he thrash you when you were children?"

She was too close to the truth, and as they were approaching the house, he didn't answer her.

25

THE FIRST THING they heard when they opened the door was laughter. Under the circumstances, it was an incongruous sound, and Angus looked at Edilean in question.

She shrugged. "I think it's love. It seems to be everywhere around me, not for me, but around me. Surrounding me. Like a disease that I can't catch."

Angus rolled his eyes, and went to the room where just three weeks before Edilean had come close to shooting him. When she started toward the kitchen where the laughter was coming from, he grabbed her hand.

"I don't want to see . . . him again."

"If you want my help, you have to stay with me."

"And why is that?"

"Because if James Harcourt is dead, then I plan to do my best to get you to forgive me for every bad thing I've ever done to you."

His words nearly took her breath away, but she would have died before she told him that. "I'll never forgive you," she said.

Angus smiled. "Funny how your words say one thing but your eyes another." He pulled her into the sitting room.

Lying on the floor was indeed James Harcourt, and he had a bullet wound in his forehead. Under his head was a big, green wax-covered canvas.

"Harriet must have done that," Edilean said, smiling fondly. "I complained about my floor, so she protected it."

"I think you should have a little respect for the dead," Angus said, looking down at the man.

"Not for him. I guess you knew that James was blackmailing Harriet."

"I was told only recently, and I can assure you that I wasn't told much." Angus bent down to look at the body. "I tried to find out—" He was interrupted by a loud burst of laughter from the kitchen. "Who's in there?"

"I'm not sure, but I assume it's Malcolm and Harriet, and Shamus and Prudence."

For a moment, Angus's mouth opened and closed. "They've paired off like that?"

"Why not?" Edilean said. "It's a normal thing to do. In fact, I just met a young widow who I think would be a perfect match for Tam. She's a few years older than he is, but I think they'll like each other. I'm going to invite her here. I know Tam's going back to Scotland to be the laird, but maybe she'll want to go with him."

"And live in that old keep? Without glass windows? Will she want to have to look after over two hundred people who are of the McTern clan?"

"I don't know," Edilean said. "That sounds more like something Harriet would like to do. She mothers all the bound girls. She—" Her eyes widened.

Angus gave a smile, for he'd read her mind. "You say that Malcolm likes Harriet?"

"You were there when they met, so you saw how they looked at each other."

"You mean the day you were shooting at me? I beg your pardon for being otherwise occupied and not realizing Harriet's glares at my uncle were a love interest."

She ignored his complaint. "Harriet and Malcolm are inseparable. She'd follow him if he said he was going to set up house on the moon."

"I think that describes the McTern keep rather well."

He stood up again and looked down at James. "First, we have to get rid of this body and make sure that Mrs. Harcourt isn't charged with murder. After that's done, we can plan other things."

"Like sending Malcolm and Harriet back to Scotland and keeping Tam here?"

"Our minds work exactly alike," Angus said, smiling at her, love in his eyes.

"Our minds are nothing alike," she said. "And now that I think about it, it's a very bad idea. Malcolm and Harriet are too old to have children, so who would inherit?"

They looked at each other and said, "Kenna," in unison.

"It's good to see that the two of you have made up," Malcolm said from the door.

Edilean glanced at Angus as though to ask how much Malcolm had heard.

"We can make up anything," Angus said, "but I can't forgive *you*. This has come about because you didn't tell me the whole of why the lot of you were in this country. If you'd told me, I could have stopped this before it happened."

"And how would you have done that?" Malcolm asked, unperturbed. He had a large pewter mug of beer in his hand, and he looked as though he'd drunk several of them.

"By getting Mrs. Harcourt out of the country, that's how," Angus said.

"But she didn't want to leave until she'd done what she came here to do."

"Are you saying that you helped her kill him?"

Malcolm shrugged. "She didn't plan on doing that, but if she had, I could see why. You should get her to tell you the whole story. You and Miss Edilean left Scotland and had a laugh at having stopped Harcourt's treachery, but you left poor Miss Prudence to bear the brunt of his rage. He didn't like being crossed. Now, lad, what are you going to do with that body to get rid of it?"

"Hack it into pieces and take it out bit by bit."

Edilean gasped, her hands to her throat, but Malcolm laughed. "I'll get my saw."

"Tell Tam to get the large carriage ready." He looked at Edilean. "Do you still have the heavy trunks that the gold was transported in?"

She nodded. "They're in the attic."

"Then have Shamus get one of them down here." He looked at Malcolm. "Is Prudence fit to travel and to talk? Or have you made her so drunk that she's incoherent?"

Glancing toward the kitchen, Malcolm lowered his voice. "You don't know her, do you, lad? She can outdrink Shamus."

Angus lifted his eyebrows so high they nearly disappeared in his hair.

"I guess now you wish you'd married *her*," Edilean muttered as she started to follow Malcolm out of the room.

But Angus caught her arm and pulled her close to him as his mouth came down on hers and he kissed her with all the pent-up emotion and longing that he'd felt for the last four years. When he stopped, her feet were off the floor and she was completely in his arms.

"I want to get something straight between us," he said. "I've been in love with you for what seems to be my entire life. From the first moment I saw you I've not been able to stay away from you. In Glasgow I couldn't bear to leave you.

"Edilean," he whispered, his lips on her neck. "I'm sorry that I left you after our one night together, but I had to. There were demands for my arrest. If I'd remained with you, I would have been caught, then what would you have done?"

"Stayed by your side," she whispered, her arms around his neck, her eyes closed at his kisses.

"Exactly," he said. "You would have watched while I was dragged away to prison—or to the gallows. Then you would have—"

"Could you two do this later?" Tam asked from the doorway.

"You're just angry because you have no woman of your own," Angus said, his eyes still on Edilean's.

"If I did have one, I'd want to protect her from the sun rising and being caught with a dead man on her floor."

Angus gave one more kiss to Edilean and set her down. "Go!" he said to her. "Get Shamus to bring that trunk down." He looked at Tam, who was frowning. "Is the carriage ready?"

"It has been ready for about an hour," Tam said, exaggerating.

"Good, then get the women into it."

"I don't think—" Tam began, but Angus cut him off.

"As far as I know, I'm still the laird and I didn't ask what you think. Get all the women into the carriage and do it quickly."

Tam hesitated for only a second before hurrying back to the kitchen.

When Angus was alone in the room, he looked down at the body of James Harcourt on the floor.

With his death and that of Edilean's uncle, the fear that Angus had lived under for so long was gone. There would be no one else who would testify that Angus had stolen the gold—and Edilean.

It seemed to Angus that most of his life he'd been on the run and in hiding. It wasn't true, but it certainly felt so. Now he was free, and he and Edilean could at last be together—if she'd have him, that is. At that thought, he smiled. Her mind might still be angry at him, but he'd just proved that her body wasn't.

It took forty-five minutes to get James into the trunk and the heavy box on the back of the carriage. Malcolm and Shamus rode on the top front, guiding the four horses, with Tam on the back, and Angus inside with Edilean beside him, Harriet and Prudence across from him. When Angus had told Malcolm the name and address of where they were going, Malcolm smiled. "The lad whose life you saved?" he asked.

"Yes," Angus answered. "Matthew Aldredge. He's in Boston now and going to school here."

"To become a doctor?" Malcolm asked.

Angus nodded. "He'll know what to do with a dead body." Angus got inside the carriage beside Edilean.

There'd been a brief scrimmage inside the carriage when Harriet said that it was impossible for Edilean to go out in public wearing the clothes of a man. "Your . . . your limbs are exposed!" she said.

"Yes, they are." Edilean extended a leg and looked at it in the breeches that were much too big. "But they feel wonderful. I'm thinking of cutting my hair and dressing as a boy all the time."

"You're much too pretty," Prudence said. "It won't work." The solemnity of her voice brought them all back to the present.

"Edilean can stay in the carriage so no one will see her," Angus said as they pulled out of the courtyard between the house and the carriage shed. He settled back against the seat, looked at Prudence in the dim light, and said, "I want to hear every word of your story."

She began by apologizing to Angus for her behavior on the night she first met him. "I was unhappy about my marriage and I thought you were one of James's many creditors."

Angus shrugged in dismissal and ignored the look Edilean was giving him. This would be something else he'd have to explain, he thought with a grimace.

He still wasn't used to the look of Prudence. She was a large, mannish-looking woman, with big hands and wide shoulders. The only thing feminine about her was her thick auburn hair.

Harriet reached out and squeezed Prudence's big hand, and Angus realized that they were sisters-in-law, and it looked as though they were friends as well. "I think I should start," Harriet said as she looked at Edilean. "Remember about four years ago when you returned from your meeting with Tabitha?"

"Meeting?" Edilean asked. "You mean when I fought her nearly to the death, then spent the night—." She glanced at Angus. "I do believe that I remember that night. After that you were so nervous you jumped at every sound."

"That's because James had shown up the day before with papers saying you were his wife."

"His what?" Edilean asked. "I never married him!"

"I know, but he had marriage papers with *your* name on them. He told me that he was going to a lawyer to make a case that you and he were married in England, but you'd used his name and his gold to run off with your lover to America."

"He couldn't have got away with it," Edilean said.

"He also had a sworn statement from the captain of the ship you two sailed on that you traveled as Mr. and Mrs. Harcourt. You still used the name Harcourt."

"But—" Edilean began.

"He had your uncle's backing," Prudence said. "I didn't see it, but I was told that there was a letter from your uncle certifying that you were the wife of James Harcourt."

Edilean fell back against the cushioned seat. She couldn't comprehend such outright lies.

Angus took her hand in his and held it. "And what about you?" he asked Prudence. "What happened to you after that night you and I, uh . . . met?"

"I went back to my father's house, and I'm glad to say that he was happy to see me. Without me there, the few servants we had were running the place, and my father couldn't even get a decent meal out of them. I put it all back in order and we never spoke of my husband or what happened."

Angus looked at Harriet. "And you paid James off."

"It was the only thing I could think to do."

"Why didn't you tell *me*?" Edilean asked. "I could have handled James."

"You were so unhappy about whatever had happened that night." Harriet cut her eyes at Angus. "I couldn't bear to add to your misery. And you were overwhelmed with the business you were just starting. I couldn't put more burdens onto you."

"So you paid him off instead," Edilean said. "How did you do it?"

Angus squeezed Edilean's hand, but she didn't stop looking at Harriet.

"I made a few adjustments in the accounting books. It wasn't so difficult to do."

"How much did you give him?" Edilean asked. "Whatever it was, it wouldn't be enough for James, since he thought he was entitled to *all* of it."

"We can talk about numbers later," Angus said as he looked at Prudence. "What I want to know is how you got back into this and how my family became involved."

"James killed me," Prudence said.

Both Angus and Edilean stared at her.

Harriet's eyes filled with tears as she held Prudence's hand with both of hers. "It was all my fault."

She looked at Edilean. "You're right about the money. James kept wanting more and more. I . . . *you* paid the rent on a town house in New York and you bought him clothes. You paid his liquor bills. You—"

"For how long?" Edilean asked.

"Until I couldn't stand it anymore. Three years."

"I don't even want to think about how much it totaled," Edilean said. "Is James the reason our profits were down in the third year of the business?"

"Yes," Harriet said as tears began to roll down her cheeks. "Edilean, I'm so sorry. You trusted me completely, but I betrayed that trust. I—"

"You saved her," Angus said impatiently. "How did James—?" He looked at Prudence and softened his voice. "How did he 'kill' you? And why? If you were in England, what harm did you do him?"

"When I stopped paying James," Harriet said, "as you can imagine, he went wild with anger. We had a terrible fight and he swore that he would get me back. He said he was going to go to Edilean's uncle and get him to help. Remember that Edilean was still under her uncle's guardianship when she ran off with you."

"Did he go?" Angus asked.

"Yes," Prudence said. "I don't know the full details of that meeting, but I think Lawler laughed at him."

"That sounds like the man," Angus said.

"What I do know," Prudence said, looking at Edilean, "is that your uncle told James that there was nothing he could do because he was married to *me*."

"Show them," Harriet said, looking at Prudence.

After a slight hesitation, she untied the scarf at her bodice and pulled it away. Edilean gasped at the sight of the scar on her throat. It was deep and red and seemed to encircle her entire neck.

"I had just been to the home farm that day," Prudence said, "as we had a new calf born during the night. I was walking back and two men on horseback came thundering along the road. I stepped to the side, out of their way, but they came so close that I fell backward onto the verge. When I heard one of them dismount, I shouted at him to watch where he was going."

Harriet held Prudence's hand tighter.

"The man was large, bigger even than my Shamus."

At the endearment, Angus tightened his grip on Edilean's hand but gave no outward sign that he'd heard.

"He . . . He . . ." Prudence stopped talking and turned her head away.

"The man put a knotted garrote around her neck and proceeded to strangle her," Harriet said. "He twisted and pulled until Pru passed out and he thought she was dead." Harriet took a breath. "While my brother sat on his horse and watched."

Edilean gasped. "I'm so sorry," she said to Prudence. "This is all my fault. I was fascinated with James because he wasn't like the others. He was the only man who didn't pursue me. If I hadn't—"

"I'm not going to let you blame yourself," Harriet said. "Even as a child, my brother was horribly spoiled. Our mother used him against our father." She waved her hand. "It doesn't matter now."

"You recovered," Angus said to Prudence.

"I did, but only by accident. I'd forgotten the cake the farmer's wife had baked for my father, and she came hurrying down the road in her little pony trap, trying to catch me. I think she's why James and his hired killer didn't stay to make sure I was dead. They must have heard her because by the time she saw me lying by the road, they were gone." She took a breath. "For three months afterward I could drink only liquids. Everything had to be mashed up for me, and it was nearly a year before I had full use of my voice."

Harriet looked at Angus. "The strain of it all caused her father's heart to give out."

"After he died," Prudence said, "I had to sell everything to pay off the debts. The house, the home farm, all of it was sold. It's where my family had lived for four hundred years, but it's gone now."

"So you came to America to find James," Angus said.

"No. First, I went to your uncle," she said to Edilean.

"But why? You couldn't have thought that he'd help you. He wasn't a man who believed in justice."

When Prudence didn't answer the question, Angus asked, "How did you know of him?"

"That day," Prudence said, shaking her head. "That day when everything changed." She glanced at Angus with a look that almost made him smile, but Edilean was watching him intently, so he didn't. Prudence meant the day when Angus and Edilean had foiled James in his attempt to escape to America with the gold. "I slept all that day and only woke when James came into the room. He was staggering about from the drug, but he was lucid enough to be in a rage. He had on only his underclothes." Prudence put her hand to her mouth, as though to stifle a giggle. "The only clothes he had were what he had on; the rest of them were on the ship—and on you."

Prudence looked at Angus's waistcoat. "I believe that one was James's favorite."

"Was it?" Edilean said. "I like it the best too. But then, I always did like James's taste."

"He charged everything to you," Prudence said.

"I know, I saw the bills. But I didn't have to pay them," she said, smiling.

"What did he do after he found out the ship had sailed?" Angus asked.

"Went insane with rage. He'd planned it all so carefully."

"He told you about what he'd done?" Angus asked.

"Not straight out, not as though he was talking to me." Prudence tightened her mouth so that what lips she had couldn't be seen, and her pointed chin almost came up to touch the tip of her nose. "He raged about how he'd married something like me to get the gold of the beautiful one, but that you"——she glanced at Angus——"you stole everything. James said I was——"

"I think we can all guess what James said," Edilean said loudly. "Did you leave him that day?"

"Yes," Prudence said. "I took the public coach to my father's house, and I didn't see or hear from James again until three years later when I was being strangled—and he was sitting on a horse looking down at me and smiling."

"But when you healed, you went to see Lawler," Angus said.

"I wanted to know if he knew where *you* were," she said to Edilean.

"Me?" she asked and moved back in the carriage. She may have been able to fight off Tabitha, but Edilean knew that if this woman attacked her, she wouldn't win.

Angus gave Edilean's hand a reassuring squeeze. "It's my guess that you were looking for something that Edilean had."

"Yes," Prudence said, looking hard into Angus's eyes.

Edilean said nothing, but she sat up straighter in the carriage. The parure. That's what Prudence was after. But that was long gone. Angus had taken it with him on the night he'd left Edilean.

"What you want is safely in a bank vault here in Boston," Angus said.

"What?" Edilean said. "I gave those to *you*. Are you telling me that after all I went through to get those back from Tabitha's thieving hands that you put them in a bank and didn't sell them?"

"They were never mine," Angus said. "How could I take such things?"

"Would you mind telling me what you're talking about?" Harriet asked.

"The whole set is safe?" Prudence asked, and when Angus nodded, she started crying loudly. "It hasn't been sold? Didn't go to James to pay his gambling debts? You still have it?"

From above them, Shamus looked through the window to the inside of the carriage and glared directly at Angus. "You make her cry and I'll tear you into pieces."

"It's all right, Shamus, dear heart," Prudence said, sniffing, and blowing her nose loudly into the handkerchief that Harriet handed her. "It's fine. I'll tell you everything later."

After another look of warning at Angus, Shamus sat back up on the driver's seat.

Angus reached between the two women and slid the window shut. Prudence grabbed his hand. "You are a good man."

"Sometimes," Edilean murmured.

"I would really like to be told what everyone is talking about," Harriet said, so Edilean told her.

"A parure? An entire set of jewelry?"

"Diamonds," Edilean said.

Prudence nodded. "My father told me about them just before he died. I didn't know he still had them, and neither did the bank. He told me that he'd kept them for his daughter's wedding and that's what they were for." She blew her nose again. "He could have sold them and paid off a lot of debts but he didn't. He saved them for me and had them secretly placed in my trunk. He didn't let me see them before the wedding, for fear that James would steal them. He rightly guessed that James would never look inside my trunk. We didn't have a marriage of intimacy."

"When we get this done, I'll give you the entire set," Angus said. "An earring is missing, and some bracelets but—"

"I have all the pieces," Edilean said, and they all looked at her. "My footman found them after the man who stole the diamonds from Tabitha sold them."

"And why did you want the rest of the set?" Angus asked. "I'd think that if you hated me, you'd want nothing to do with any of it."

Edilean kept her eyes on Prudence and didn't answer him. "I guess you met Malcolm when you went to my uncle."

"Yes," Prudence said, and her face softened. "And it was there that I met Shamus. He knew a great deal about you, about where you'd gone, and who you went with, and about the wagon full of trunks of gold. Oh!" she said.

"What is it?" Harriet asked.

"The trunks of gold. James talked of little else when he found out that you'd sailed without him and now . . . Now . . ."

"He's inside one of the trunks," Angus said, and whispered, "Be careful what you wish for."

"You got Malcolm, Shamus, and Tam to help you," Edilean said.

"Yes," Prudence answered. "I had some money from the sale of my family's estate, so I paid our way to America."

"So you were on the ship with Shamus?" Edilean asked.

"I was," Prudence said, and her entire face took on a glow.

"How lovely," Edilean said.

"How strange," Angus muttered, then moved his leg away from Edilean before she could kick him.

"He's such a kind man, but he's been ill treated all his life. Shamus wants to start over, where people don't judge him by what his father did."

"Like loosening the cinch on a girl's saddle?" Angus muttered.

"He would *never* do such a thing! He's a kind, thoughtful man." Prudence gave Angus a look that let him know what Shamus had told her of *him*.

Angus glanced at Edilean as though for sympathy, but she'd always liked Shamus. Angus moved aside the leather curtain over the window and glanced outside. "We're almost there." He looked back at Prudence. "I want you to tell me how you came to shoot James."

Everyone in the coach was quiet, their eyes fixed on Prudence.

"I didn't mean to," she began. "I was . . . Shamus and I were . . ."

"In Cuddy's room over the carriage house," Harriet said impatiently. "We all know that, and, by the way, I think you paid Cuddy much too much for the use of his room." Harriet looked at Edilean. "Ever since he helped you that night when you and—" She broke off for a moment. "Anyway, I think Cuthbert takes too much liberty on himself."

"Did he embezzle half the year's profits?" Edilean shot back at her.

"I did that because—" Harriet began but Angus cut her off.

"You two can settle this later. I make it a rule to never argue when there's a dead body in the same carriage with me. Now, Mrs. Harcourt, you were saying?"

"Please don't call me that," Prudence said. "I can't bear the name. I will be glad to take Shamus's name of Frazier. We—"

Angus gave her a hard look.

"Yes, right, back to the shooting. I looked out and saw a light in the kitchen of the house, and I thought it was Harriet and that something was wrong, so I went inside. But when I got there, the light had moved to the parlor. There was James, filling a bag with the silver candlesticks. I guess I made a sound because he turned around and he had a pistol in his hand.

"He said, 'But you're dead.'

"I tried to think quickly and I said, 'Yes, I am and I've come to take you to the grave with me.'

"He said, 'Like hell you will,' and he aimed the pistol at me. I leaped, we tussled, the gun went off, and he fell to the floor. Dead. I believe I screamed."

For a moment the others were silent as they looked at her. Each of them knew that her story was a fabrication, but no one said anything. A wrestling match with a pistol does not leave one person with a bullet hole squarely in the middle of his forehead. In his midsection perhaps, but not in his head. Besides, they all knew that the pistol Prudence had used belonged to Cuddy.

Harriet and Edilean looked at Angus to see what he would say.

"It's as I thought," he said. "It was self-defense."

"Yes, clearly," Harriet said, and looked at Edilean, who said, "It couldn't be anything else."

No one looked at the other for fear their doubts would show.

Angus was glad when the carriage halted. "We're here. I think it would be better if I went in and talked to the young man alone. He and I know each other, but not all that well, and I'm afraid this might be a shock for him. I'll sort it out, then we can all go home. All right?"

The three women nodded and sat there while Angus got out of the coach. When they were alone, Edilean looked at the others and said, "Who's going to get out first?" Since by the time she finished the sentence, she was half outside, it was a rhetorical question. Prudence, by sheer size, was second, and Harriet came last, smoothing her hair and trying her best to look as though she were on a mission that was nothing like what they were actually doing.

Harriet glared at Edilean in her masculine clothing and started to speak, but Edilean gave her a look that made her close her mouth.

The three women went into the house of Matthew Aldredge, the three Scotsmen behind them.

26

Two weeks, Edilean thought. Two entire, whole weeks since she'd seen Angus. After that night when they'd gone to Matthew Aldredge's house, and after what happened to poor James's body, Angus said he wouldn't be returning to the house with them.

It wasn't until that moment that Edilean realized she'd been looking forward to the coming fight they'd have. Angus would tell her how sorry he was for having left her, she'd tell him that she'd never forgive him, then— And then they'd end up with him on his knees begging her to marry him. She would, of course, finally say yes, but she'd take her time, and she planned to make him suffer.

Edilean had even imagined how she'd work with Harriet and Prudence to plan their triple wedding in the largest church in Boston. They'd all get married together, but afterward, they'd separate to go on their bridal tours. Edilean felt dizzy with the romance of it all.

But as with everything with Angus, nothing went

as she'd planned. Angus stayed behind with Matthew while the others went back to Edilean's house. For two days she'd smiled, anticipating that Angus would come to the front door with his arms full of roses and apologies on his lips. While the other couples around her snuggled and cooed at each other, Edilean kept smiling as she imagined what would happen when she next saw Angus. Would he have a ring for her?

But the days went by, and he didn't show up. On the fifth day, Shamus volunteered to go find him. "And I'll tell him what I think of him for treating you this way, Miss."

"Oh, Shamus," Prudence said, her voice full of love. "You'd hurt him."

"It's what I mean to do," Shamus said in a voice that was deeper than normal.

Edilean could almost see Angus rolling his eyes and telling Shamus that he was ready to take him on anytime, anywhere. But Angus wasn't there, and no one knew where he was.

Just as she knew they would, the others had paired off permanently. Malcolm asked Harriet to marry him and go back to Scotland to live. She hadn't hesitated in saying yes, and at the end of the summer they were to be wed. Since then, they'd not stopped talking about all the things they were going to do in their new, old country. Malcolm told her in detail about every person of the McTern clan, so Harriet felt as though she already knew them. Edilean heard Harriet going over the names of the children.

"And Kenna has six children, five boys and one girl. Her daughter's name is . . . No! Don't tell me, I'll remember."

Edilean couldn't bear to hear such happiness.

As for Shamus and Prudence, they seemed to care about only one thing, and that was the physical part of their lives. After one afternoon when she and Harriet and Malcolm had returned to the house to hear some enthusiastic pounding from upstairs, Malcolm gave Shamus a piece of his mind, and their wedding was also to be at the end of the summer.

There was one unexpected development, though. To Edilean's horror, Tam started making eyes at Tabitha—and Edilean let Tabitha know what she thought of the situation. "He's a boy!" she half yelled at Tabitha. "Just a boy and you're—"

Tabitha was unperturbed by Edilean's anger. "I'm what can teach him all he needs to know." She looked Edilean up and down. "So did he leave you again?"

"No!" Edilean shouted. "He did not 'leave' me. Angus—" She broke off because she had no idea where Angus was or what he was doing. The day after they'd gone to Matthew Aldredge's house, Malcolm had insisted that Edilean sit with him in the parlor so he could talk to her at length about Angus's fine qualities.

"Lass," Malcolm said, "he'd never do to you what you think he has. When he left you before, he did it for your own good." Malcolm went on to tell Edilean in detail what Angus had done after James again put up the handbills for Angus's arrest. Years later, it had taken Malcolm, Shamus, and Tam a lot of time to find Angus. They'd told him that it'd been easy to find him, but it hadn't been. It was as though Angus had disappeared off the face of the earth, and they began to think that James Harcourt had found him and had him killed.

For weeks the three Scotsmen went from city to city, searching for him. The problem was that they had no picture of Angus without his beard, and they had no idea what name he was using.

It was Shamus, drinking in a tavern in Charleston, who heard about a man named Angus Harcourt who worked with the army in the far west. "Slips around in the dark like he can see in it as well as in sunlight," the former soldier said.

"What's he look like?" Shamus asked.

"Big man."

"As big as me?" Shamus shot at him.

"I've seen mountains smaller than you," the man said, making Shamus smile. "No, Angus is a big man but he's also pretty."

"Pretty?" Shamus asked in disbelief. "You mean like a girl?"

"No, more like a . . ." The man waved his hand. "The girls like him, but I heard he's been havin' trouble with the fort commander's daughter."

"Ah." Shamus gave a half smile. "Think he'll marry her?"

The man laughed. "Not if Captain Austin has

anything to do with it, he won't. He's a nasty piece of work. Downright scary."

"So where is this Angus Harcourt?" Shamus asked.

"I can't tell you but I could draw a map."

"So," Edilean said to Malcolm, "Angus was at some fort with another woman."

"No, lass," Malcolm said, frustrated. "He was *not* with her. As far as we could find, he's not been with a woman since he left you."

"I don't believe that. I think he's had hundreds, thousands of women. I think—"

"He left you because he had to!" Malcolm said loudly. "Canna you see that the man is daft about you and always has been? Why do you think we laughed so hard that first time he saw you? We all knew he'd been struck by a bolt of lightning. And when he threw you in the horse trough! Ah, now, that was proof that—"

"That he hated me," Edilean said gloomily.

"It showed he was fightin' what he felt for you," Malcolm said as he reached out and took her hands in his, and lowered his voice. "In a way, Angus had been the laird since his father died. It was *my* father who cheated the McTerns out of what was theirs, but the lairdship goes down through the oldest sons. Our clan is an old one, and they looked to the eldest son of the eldest son even though he was just a boy."

"I understand," she said. "Like the divinity of kings."

"I guess so. But even as a boy, Angus tried to make

up to all of us for what his grandfather did. Angus had no life of his own until he saw you, none at all."

Standing up, Edilean looked down at Malcolm, her face cold. "I'm sick unto death of hearing about how wonderful Angus McTern is. Sick of it! Do you hear me? If he's so in love with me, where is he? Why isn't he *here*? Why aren't I planning my wedding as Harriet and Prudence are? Why isn't some man sneaking kisses with me when he thinks no one is looking? Why—?" She couldn't say any more but turned and ran up the stairs to her room.

"I don't know," Malcolm whispered as he sat alone in the room. Surely Angus couldn't have run off again, he thought. Surely the lad couldn't have abandoned Edilean. It wasn't possible.

It was when Shamus gave her a look of pity that Edilean changed her mind about Angus and began to defend him. Every time she entered a room, the engaged couples would break apart and look guilty.

"That's it!" Edilean said at dinner one night as she stood up and threw her napkin down. "Maybe none of *you* believe in him, but *I* do! I don't know what Angus is doing, but I know that when he's finished, he'll come for me."

The others' faces didn't change. Harriet tried to look as though she believed Edilean, but the others looked at her with sympathy.

"I'm sure he will," Tam said, but there was no enthusiasm in his voice.

After that night, Edilean decided to quit waiting and to go about her business. The first thing she took care of was Tam and Tabitha. Knowing that Tam had a kind heart, she asked if he'd please help her with a task that she couldn't handle by herself. What she needed was for him to journey all the way down to Williamsburg to get Mrs. Abigail Prentiss to sign the final papers that transferred her farm to the Bound Girl company. Edilean held her breath as she handed the papers to Tam because she was staking everything on her belief that he couldn't read. She gave him a sheaf of documents that dealt with a farm she'd bought three years before. "Oh! And take this," she said, handing him a bolt of yellow silk. "Abby said she'd make it into a dress for me. She's an excellent dressmaker." Edilean didn't know if Abby could sew or not. "You won't come back without the dress, will you? Even if you have to wait for her to finish it?"

Tam looked about for a reason to get out of the long trip. "Maybe your coachman, Cuddy, would be better at this."

"Than you?" Edilean asked, batting her lashes. "How can you say that? I couldn't trust *him* with these papers, now could I? But if you think that you can't do it . . ."

"No," Tam said with a sigh, "I'll do it. But maybe she could send the dress later."

"Perhaps," Edilean said, "but she's a recent widow and she might like someone to talk to. If you're going to be the laird of the clan, then perhaps you should get some practice in comforting widows."

Tam straightened his shoulders a bit and took the leather portfolio she handed him. "It might be good for me to see more of this new country."

"I think that's a splendid idea," Edilean said.

The next day after Tam left, she told Tabitha, who laughed and shrugged. "Maybe I'll get Harriet to take me back to Scotland with her and I'll get a man there."

"Isn't there a law saying you can never return to England?"

Tabitha shrugged. "I guess I'll have her send me a man then. By the way, how often have you seen *your* man in the last five years?"

In the past, Tabitha's innuendos had made Edilean angry, but not now. "It takes a man time to recover from a night with *me*," she said, and turned and left. Tabitha's laughter echoed behind her.

By the fourth week of Angus's absence, the others seemed to have accepted that he was never returning. Even Malcolm had lost his faith that Angus was going to come back to them.

One day Edilean overheard him talking to Harriet and saying that he was disappointed in Angus, that he'd misjudged the boy. It was all Edilean could do to keep from giving him a piece of her mind, but she didn't. They'd see, she thought. If Angus was alive, he was going to come back to her.

It was at the end of the sixth week, while Edilean was at the market inspecting the produce stands that had made her company so prosperous, that a closed carriage stopped near her. It was an ordinary carriage, black, worn along the footings, obviously hired, but when she moved, it moved. When she stopped, it stopped. The fifth time it halted, she knew Angus was inside the carriage.

"Excuse me," she said to one of the three women who worked for her and who was overseeing the big produce cart. "Would you tell Harriet that I might not be home for dinner but not to worry about me?"

"Of course," the young woman said. She'd been transported for stealing a silver bowl from the earl who owned the house where she'd worked since she was nine. That the man had been raping her since she was thirteen meant nothing to the court.

As Edilean started walking toward the carriage, the girl called out, "Where shall I tell her you've gone?"

"To paradise," Edilean said over her shoulder just as the door opened. It was dark inside, but she could see Angus, and he was wearing the tartan he'd had on the first time she saw him.

He leaned forward just enough that his hand was at the door. She took it, stepped into the carriage, and shut the door behind her, and they started moving. She took the seat across from him and stared at him, almost afraid to speak for fear that he'd disappear and it would all be a dream.

"I guess you thought I'd left you again," he said at last, looking at her in the dim light, his eyes devouring her.

"I did for the first two weeks, but not after that."

Her heart was beating hard in her throat and her fingertips seemed to vibrate with wanting to touch him. Was his skin as warm as she remembered?

Angus gave a little smile. "You knew that I'd come back for you?"

"Certainly."

His smile broadened. "You trusted me?"

"As far as I can throw you," she said.

Angus laughed, and for a moment their eyes locked, and in the next second, she propelled herself into his arms. His mouth took hers and kissed her with longing and hunger. "I missed you," he said, his lips on her neck. "I thought of you every second of every day."

"I never thought of you once," she said, her eyes closed, her neck arched. When his mouth moved down her neck to her shoulders, she leaned farther back, letting his strong arms hold her. He pulled the neck kerchief away with his teeth, and moved downward to her breast.

"Where are you taking me?" she asked.

"Do you care?" His hand was moving up her skirt.

"No, I don't," she said, her hands moving over his body. "Angus! You have on nothing beneath your skirt."

"Kilt. Move your hand to the side. No, the other side."

"Oh," she said as she put her hand around the part of him that showed how much he wanted her.

With a groan, Angus put his head back against the seat. "You are better than I remembered."

Abruptly, the coach halted and there was a knocking on the roof. "Sir!" a man's voice said. "We have arrived."

"Kill him for me," Angus whispered.

When Edilean felt the movement of the carriage that meant the driver was getting down, she removed her hand from under Angus's garment, sat up, and picked her scarf off the seat. "He's going to open the door."

"Let me die now," Angus said, his eyes still closed.

She pulled his kilt down so the bottom half of him was covered and smoothed her hair. When the driver opened the door, they were sitting on opposite sides of the carriage and looking quite proper.

Edilean looked outside and saw that they were at Boston Harbor. "Why have you taken me here?" she asked Angus. "I think we should go home and—"

She broke off and stared ahead of her. There in the harbor was the *Mary Elizabeth*, the ship she and Angus had traveled to America on. She looked back at him. "What . . . ? How . . . ?"

Angus recovered himself enough to breathe again. "I had some business to do and I happened to hear that Captain Inges was making a trip back to Glasgow, so I thought we might go with him."

"Back to Scotland?" she asked. "Oh. To see your clan." It looked as though he'd changed his mind about remaining as the laird. She had a vision of the derelict old keep and all the people who looked up to Angus—and how she'd be the lady of the castle.

Would she ever see America again? This new country was where she'd shown everyone, including herself, that she was *worth* something.

"No, you don't see," Angus said as he got out of the carriage and helped her down. "You don't see at all. I need to go back home to pass the clan on to Tam. We have to do it legally."

He held out his arm to her, and she took it. Angus, in his old-fashioned kilt with his knees bare, was causing a bit of a stir. Both men and women were staring at him, but it was the women whose eyes sparkled.

When he led her toward the ship, Edilean pulled back. "Did everyone else know about this? You told them and not me? Is everything packed and on board?"

Angus halted. "If by 'them' you mean Malcolm and Tam and——"

"And Harriet and Prudence and Shamus."

"Yes, the entire lot of them. Might as well have the whole clan here. The answer is no, I didn't tell any of them anything. They know nothing."

"Which is exactly as much as I know." Edilean put her heels down firmly on the ground and looked at him. "I want to know what's going on. Where have you been?"

Angus looked as though he was contemplating picking her up and carrying her up the gangplank to the ship, but then seemed to think better of it. "If you must know—not that I wasn't going to tell you, just not here in public—I went back to the fort."

"But that's—"

"A long way away," Angus said. "I gave up sleep and food, but I did it. I sold my shares in the Ohio Company to Captain Austin."

"Oh, yes, the man who's in love with a girl you wanted."

Angus gave her a look.

"Sorry," she said. "I'm only repeating what I was told."

"I do wish you'd stop listening to gossip."

"When you stop running off and leaving me to deal with it alone, I will."

Angus gave a smile, took her by the shoulders, and looked as though he was going to kiss her, but then he glanced at the people around them and didn't. "I promise that I'll tell you everything when we're on board, but in private."

"Angus," Edilean said, "you really can't expect me to board a ship sailing for Scotland without any preparation. I need clothes and books and gifts. I can't visit your family empty-handed. And did you forget about my business? Who can run it without me? I know you think I'm worthless, but I have many people to look after, and they—"

"Captain Inges said that this time we couldn't travel with him unless we were properly married, so he's waiting with his Bible to perform the ceremony."

She blinked at him.

"At last I've said something that you can make no reply to," Angus said in wonder. "Now, do you want to go on board and get married, or do you want to go back to that house of yours and gloat to those people who think I've abandoned you and sign papers for that business of yours?"

For a moment all Edilean could do was open and close her mouth a few times. At last she said, "You have a ring?"

"Solid gold." Reaching out, he touched her blonde hair. "Not that I need any gold, for this is worth more than all the gold in the world."

She leaned her cheek against his hand for a moment, then she grabbed her skirt, lifted it, and began to run up the gangplank. "Come on!" she called to him. "Do you think I have all day?"

Chuckling, Angus ran up the gangplank after her.

Epilogue

THEY WERE IN bed in the captain's cabin, nude beneath the sheet, and Edilean was still staring at her left hand.

"You're going to wear it out just from looking at it," Angus said, yawning.

"You're the one who's worn out."

"I'll show you who's tired," he said, but then he gave another jaw-cracking yawn and lay back down, with Edilean's head on his shoulder. Moonlight shone into the cabin, and the water was lulling him to sleep.

"Why this?" Edilean asked. "Why not stay in Boston and be married there?"

"And share you with all the others?" he said.

"Are you saying that I've been . . . That I have . . . ?"

He kissed her bare shoulder. "Been unfaithful to me? Nay, lass, I'm not. I talked to people in Boston and there's been no hint of any man with you."

"What does that mean, that you 'talked' to people? Did you ask about me?"

"I dinna have to, did I? All of Boston talks of the beautiful Miss Edilean who runs a business with all those women. You've done something that no one believed could be done."

"I did, didn't I?" she said, snuggling against him. "But what does that have to do with this?" She waved her hand at the ship.

"With the way you take care of people, I figured you'd want to get married in the biggest church and you'd want to walk down the aisle with Harriet and Prudence beside you. Then I'd have to share my wedding day with Shamus."

"You did all this just to get away from Shamus?"

"Nay," Angus said tiredly. "I did it all to get you to myself. I don't want to share you at the wedding or afterward or ever again. I've had all I can take of being separated from you."

For a while, Edilean was content to lie against him, and she could feel him drifting off to sleep. She hadn't heard the full story of what he'd done after the night James had been killed, but she would. She thought how they'd have a lifetime together to tell each other everything. For now they were going to have at least three weeks, and if the weather was bad they could be on the ship for longer. When they arrived in Glasgow, they'd go back to the old keep where she'd first met him and . . . She smiled as she thought of the Scots laughing and saying that they'd known on that first day that their beloved Angus had fallen in love and how they'd been glad of it.

Edilean glanced at Angus, asleep now, and she ran her hand over his bare chest. Hers and hers alone. Forever, she thought.

And it's a good thing they were married, because she had yet to tell him that she'd received a letter from Abigail Prentiss saying that Tam wanted to stay in Williamsburg and not return to Scotland. When Angus made over the lairdship to someone, it would be to Malcolm, not young Tam.

"Stop thinking so much and go to sleep," Angus said.

"I can't help it," Edilean said. "So much has happened, so much has—" She could feel Angus's body move, as though he were laughing. "What?"

"James," he said.

"All of you thought it was very funny, but *I* didn't."

Angus looked at her.

"Well, after the first few minutes, I didn't."

Angus kept looking at her.

"All right, I laughed harder than anyone else did, but I shouldn't have. I wonder what happened to him?"

"Matt said his body would probably be sold to the college to use for dissection."

"How awful!" Edilean said as she thought back to that night. Angus hadn't liked it very much when all three women rushed into Matthew Aldredge's little house right behind him.

When the eyes of all the women widened at the

sight of the beautiful Matt, Angus glanced down at Edilean and said with his mouth half closed, "Don't even think of marrying him off to someone."

"I have no idea what you mean," she said haughtily, and shook hands with Matt.

Malcolm and Tam came inside a few minutes later and greeted Matt, and the men started talking in quiet tones about what to do with the body of James Harcourt. Their voices were so low that the women had to strain to hear them. Edilean was the only one who noticed that Shamus slipped into the room. Once again, as big as he was, he was able to move about unnoticed. He went to the window so he could watch the carriage. Matt was just a poor student, and his little house wasn't in the best of neighborhoods.

She didn't want to join the crowd that was discussing the gruesome task of disposing of James's body, so she went to stand by Shamus.

For a few moments they stood there in silence, then quietly, Shamus said, "It was me that cut the cinch."

"I know," Edilean said without looking at him.

"And I wouldn't have brought back your money."

She knew that it was difficult for him to make this apology and she wanted to make it easy for him. "Prudence won't let you get out of line again."

"Aye, that she won't," he said, laughter in his voice. "She's like you and thinks I'm . . ."

"An honorable man."

"She does and I will be, but . . ."

When he trailed off, she looked at him.

"But not to Angus," he said softly.

Edilean almost giggled. "But not to Angus." She started to say more, but when she saw a shock of surprise on his face, she looked out the window.

Beside the expensive green carriage was an old wagon with three men on it. They were moving slowly so they made no sound, and they motioned to each other in gestures.

"We—" Edilean said, meaning to go get Angus, but Shamus quickly put his finger to his lips for her to be silent.

She was puzzled, but when he pointed out the window, she looked. The men on the wagon were thieves, and they were stealing the big trunk from the back of the carriage.

Standing beside Shamus, Edilean watched in fascination as the men labored with the big trunk as they slid it onto the wagon bed. When it was securely on the wagon, two men jumped onto the seat and took off, while the third one started for the carriage, meaning to steal it and the horses. But Shamus moved with snakelike speed and was out the door in seconds.

The thief was alone, and when he saw the bulk of Shamus, he ran into the darkness.

Edilean was behind Shamus, and for a moment they just stood there in silence. The street was dark, with no one around. It hit them both at the same time that their huge problem of what to do with James's body was now solved.

Shamus looked down at Edilean, gave a little

smile, and she smiled back at him, and in the next minute they were laughing. Edilean started laughing so hard that she couldn't stand up and would have fallen if Shamus hadn't caught her. She held on to him and he held on to her and they supported each other as they howled with laughter.

The others came rushing outside, fighting to wedge through the doorway.

"What in the world—?" Angus began as he snatched Edilean away from Shamus.

"Honey bear?" Prudence said sweetly but with an undertone of anger. "What have you been doing out here with Edilean?"

Shamus was laughing too hard to answer. He pointed at Edilean, grabbed his legs just above his knees, and kept on laughing—as did she.

"Shamus!" Prudence said in a voice that caused sleeping birds to fly off the roof. Four dogs began howling and a rooster thought it was dawn breaking and began to crow. "I demand that you tell me what's going on."

"I think we've been robbed," Malcolm said from the back of the carriage.

Matt said, "We've had a lot of robberies around here. Nasty place. What did they steal?"

Harriet put her hand to her mouth. "They didn't take the . . . the . . . ?"

Edilean started laughing harder. "They did. They took James."

"Oh," Prudence said, eyes wide. "They took the trunk?"

"Bloody hell," Tam said, speaking for the first time. "Where do you think they took it?"

"To the devil," Malcolm said, looked at Harriet, and they began laughing too. Harriet kept her handkerchief over her mouth and pretended that she wasn't happily relieved—after all, he had been her brother—but it was so good to know that no one was going to prison and no one would be hanged that she couldn't control herself. They weren't going to be caught disposing of the body or in having anything to do with the dead man.

They all looked at one another, and the words in their eyes were that it was really and truly *over*.

But after that night, Angus disappeared without a word to anyone, and for the first week afterward, they all feared that someone would come to question them about James. At the very least, they expected someone to tell them that Harriet's brother's body had been found. But as the days passed and nothing happened, they stopped worrying about it.

And now, Edilean and Angus were married, they were in each other's arms, and they were on their way back to Scotland to take care of the legal matters of giving the clan's lands back to the McTerns.

"I'm glad it all happened," Edilean said sleepily. "If I hadn't had such a greedy uncle I would have married James and—"

"And been broke within a year," Angus said. "He would have spent you dry."

"When we get back to America, what are we going to do?"

"Run your Bound Girls," Angus said. "I look forward to telling all those women what to do every day."

"You?" she asked, rising up on her elbow. "Since when do *you* run *my* company?"

"If you don't want me to, we could always go to Williamsburg and build a town."

"What are you talking about?"

"I traded Captain Austin my land for his."

"I don't understand."

Angus pushed a strand of hair behind her ear. "You're looking at the owner of a thousand acres of land just outside Williamsburg. I'm going to build us a house, and lay out some streets. I thought maybe some of the clan might like to return to Edilean with us."

"Edilean?"

"That's what I've named the town."

She lay back against his arm. "A town named for me. Do you think I might plant an oak tree in the center of it?"

"Do what you want with it. It's your town." He moved to put a bare leg over hers.

"I thought you were exhausted."

"I was, but I'm not anymore."

Smiling, Edilean put her lips up to be kissed.

Turn the page for a preview of Jude Deveraux's
newest novel in the Edilean Series

Scarlet Nights

From Atria Books

1

Fort Lauderdale, Florida

I think we've found her," Captain Erickson said.
His voice was forced, showing that he was working
hard to control his jubilation.

They were sitting at a picnic table at the Hugh
Taylor Birch State Park, just off A1A in Fort Lauder-
dale. It was a September morning, and South Florida
was beginning to cool off. By next month the weather
would be divine.

"I guess you mean Mitzi," Mike Newland said, for
just yesterday the captain had given him a thick file on
the family. Mizelli Vandlo was a woman several police
departments, including the fraud squad of Fort Lau-
derdale, plus the Secret Service—for financial crimes—
and the FBI—for violence—had been searching for for
years. As far as anyone knew, the only photo of her had
been taken in 1973, when she was sixteen and about to
marry a fifty-one-year-old man. Even then, she was no
beauty and her face was easily remembered for its large
nose and lipless mouth.

When the captain didn't answer, Mike knew that a Big Job was coming and he worked to keep his temper from rising to the surface. He'd just finished an undercover case that had taken three years and for a while there had been contracts out on his life.

Although Mike had never worked on the Vandlo case, he'd heard that a few years ago there had been major arrests in the family, all of it happening on one day, but in several cities. But Mitzi, her son Stefan, and some other family members had somehow been tipped off and had quietly slipped away. Until recently, no one had known where they went.

Mike poured green tea from a thermos into a cup and offered it to the captain.

"No thanks," the captain said, shaking his head. "I'll stick with this." He held up a can of something that was full of additives and caffeine.

"So where is she?" Mike asked, his voice even more raspy than usual. He often had to answer questions about his voice, and his standard half-lie was that it was caused by a childhood accident. Sometimes he even elaborated and made up stories about tricycles or car wrecks, whatever appealed to him that day. No matter what the story, Mike's voice was as intimidating as his body was when he went into action.

"Ever hear of . . . ?" As the captain fumbled in his shirt pocket for a piece of paper, Mike could tell that he was excited about something other than finding Mitzi. After all, this was at least the sixth time they'd heard she'd been found. "Ah, here it is." The captain's eyes were dancing about. "Let's see if I can pronounce the name of this place."

"Czechoslovakia no longer exists," Mike said, deadpan.

"No, no, this town is in the U.S. Somewhere up north."

"Jacksonville is 'up north.'"

"Found it," the captain said. "Eddy something. Eddy . . . Lean."

"Eddy Lean is a person's name, not a place."

"Maybe I'm saying it wrong. Say it faster."

A muscle worked in Mike's jaw. He didn't like whatever game the captain was trying to play. "Eddy-lean. Never heard of it. So where—?" Halting, Mike took in a breath. "Ed-uh-lean," he said softly, his voice so low the captain could hardly hear him. "Edilean."

"That's it." The captain put the paper back into his pocket. "Ever hear of the place?"

Mike's hands began to shake so much he couldn't lift his cup. He willed them to be still while he tried to relax his face so his panic wouldn't show. He'd told only one man about Edilean and that had been a long time ago. If that man was involved, there was danger. "I'm sure you've found out that my sister lives there," Mike said quietly.

The captain's face lost its smile. He'd meant to tease Mike, but he didn't like seeing such raw emotion in one of the men under his command. "So I was told, but this case has nothing to do with her. And before you ask, no one but me and the attorney general know about her being there."

Mike worked on controlling his heart rate. Many

times before he'd been in situations where he'd had to make people believe he was who he wasn't, so he'd learned to keep calm at all costs. But in those times, it had been his own life in danger. If there was something going on in tiny Edilean, Virginia, then the life of the only person who mattered to him, his sister Tess, was in jeopardy.

"Mike!" the captain said loudly, then lowered his voice. "Come back to earth. No one knows about you or your hometown or your sister, and she's perfectly safe." He hesitated. "I take it you two are close?"

Mike gave a one-shoulder shrug. Experience had taught him to reveal as little about himself as possible.

"Okay, so don't tell me anything. But you do know the place, right?"

"Never been there in my life." Mike forced a grin. He was back to being himself and was glad to see the frown that ran across the captain's face. Mike liked to be the one in charge of a situation. "You want to tell me what this is about? I can't imagine that anything bad has happened in little Edilean." Not since 1941, he thought as about a hundred images ran through his mind—and not one of them was good. While it was true that he'd never actually been to Edilean, the town and its inhabitants had ruled his childhood. He couldn't help it as he put his hand to his throat and remembered *that* day and his angry, hate-filled grandmother.

"Nothing has happened, at least not yet," the captain said, "but we do know that Stefan is there."

"In Edilean? What's he after?"

"We don't know, but he's about to marry some hometown girl." The captain took a drink of his cola.

"Poor thing. She grew up in a place that sells tractors, then Stefan comes along with his big-city razzle-dazzle and sweeps her off her feet. She never had a chance."

Mike bent his head to hide a smile. The captain was a native of South Florida where there were stores on every corner. He felt sorry for anyone who'd ever had to shovel snow.

"Her name's Susie. Or something with an S." He picked up a file folder from beside him on the bench. "It's Sara—"

"Shaw," Mike said. "She's to marry Greg Anders. Although I take it Greg Anders is actually Mitzi's son, Stefan?"

"You sure know a lot about the place for someone who's never been there." The captain paused, giving Mike room to explain himself, but he said nothing. "Yeah, he's Stefan, and we have reason to believe that Mitzi is also living in that town."

"And no one would pay attention to a middle-aged woman."

"Right." The captain slid the folder across the table to Mike. "We don't know what's going on or why two major criminals are there, so we need someone to find out. Since you have a connection to the place, you're the winner."

"And here I'd never considered myself a lucky man." When Mike opened the folder, he saw that the first page was from the Decatur, Illinois, police department. He looked at the captain questioningly.

"It's all in there about how Stefan was found. An off-duty cop was on vacation in Richmond, Virginia, with his wife, and he saw Stefan and the girl in a dress shop. The cop found out where they lived. As for you, a guy you worked with a long time ago knew about Edilean and your sister." When Mike frowned at that, the captain couldn't help grinning. Mike's secrecy—or "privacy" as he called it—could be maddening. Everybody in the fraud squad would go out for a few beers and afterward the captain would know whose wife had walked out, who was getting it on with a "badge bunny," and who was having trouble with a case. But not Mike. He'd talk as much as the other guys as he told about his training sessions, his food, and even about his car. It seemed like he'd told a lot about himself, but the next day the captain would realize that he'd learned absolutely nothing personal about Mike.

When the Assistant U.S. Attorney General for the Southern District of Florida called and said they thought one of the most notorious criminals in the U.S. might be in Edilean, Virginia, and that Mike Newland's sister lived there, the captain nearly choked on his coffee. He would have put money on it that Mike didn't have a relative in the world. In fact, the captain wasn't sure Mike had ever had a girlfriend outside a case. He never brought one to the squad functions, and as far as the captain knew, Mike had never invited anyone to his apartment—which changed every six months. But then, Mike was the best undercover cop they'd ever had. After every assignment, he'd had to hide until all of the people he'd exposed were in prison.

Mike closed the folder. "When do I go and what do I do?"

"We want you to save her."

"Mitzi?" Mike asked in genuine horror. "So she can stand trial?"

"No, not her. The girl. Of course we want you to find Mitzi, but we also want you to save this Sara Shaw. Once the Vandlos get whatever it is they want from her, no one will ever see her again." He paused. "Mike?"

Mike looked at the captain.

"If your sister really is there and if they find out about you . . ."

"Don't worry," Mike said. "Right now Tess is in Europe on her honeymoon. I'll tell her to keep her new husband out of town until this is solved one way or the other."

The captain opened another folder and withdrew an 8 x 10 glossy of a woman with dark hair and eyes. She was stunningly beautiful. She was standing on a street corner waiting for the light to change, and a slight wind had blown her clothes close to her body. She had a figure that made a man draw in his breath. "Does your sister really look like this?"

Mike barely glanced at the photo. "Only on her worst days."

The captain blinked a few times. "Okay." He put a picture of Sara Shaw on the table. The young woman had an oval face, light hair, and was wearing a white dress that made her look as sweet as Mike's sister looked, well, tempting. "She's not Vandlo's usual type."

Mike picked up the photo and studied it. He wasn't about to tell the captain that he knew quite a bit about Sara Shaw. She was one of his sister's two best friends, which said a lot, since Tess's sharp tongue didn't win over many people. But from their first meeting Sara had seen past Tess's biting words and extraordinary looks to the person beneath.

"Do you know her?"

"Never met Miss Shaw, but I've heard some about her." He put the picture down. "So no one has any idea what the Vandlos want in Edilean?"

"There's been a lot of research both from a distance and locally, but everybody who tried drew a blank. Whatever it is, Miss Shaw seems to be at the center of it. Is she rich but no one knows about it? Is she about to inherit millions?"

"Not that I've heard. She just opened a shop with . . ." His sister kept him up-to-date on the gossip in Edilean but it wasn't easy to remember it all. Now it seemed that every word she'd told him was of vital importance. "With her fiancé, Greg Anders. Tess hates the man, says he snubs everyone who isn't buying something from him. But Tess does all of Sara's accounting so she's made sure Sara hasn't been put into debt by him."

"That sounds like a Vandlo." The captain hesitated. "Your sister manages people's finances?" His tone said that he couldn't believe a woman who looked like Tess could also have a brain.

Mike had no intention of answering that. He well knew the captain's curiosity about his private life and he wasn't going to reveal anything. "So you want me to catch these criminals, but I'm also to get the lovely Miss Shaw away from Stefan Vandlo? Is my assignment to follow and watch? Or am I to do more than that?"

"You have to do whatever you must to keep her

alive. We think Stefan will murder Sara the minute he gets what he wants from her—and what he seems to want most is marriage."

"My hunch is that since the dresses in the shop are expensive, Sara must get into a lot of rich houses. Maybe the Vandlos want to see what's in them."

"That's what we thought, too, but as her boyfriend, Vandlo already has access to the houses and no robberies have been reported. It's bigger than that and no one has a clue what it is." The captain tapped the folder. "After you read what's in here, I think you'll see that this scam of theirs is much more than just stealing a few necklaces. It's got to be if both mother and son are there." He lowered his voice. "We think Stefan divorced his wife of nineteen years just so his marriage to Miss Shaw will be legal—which means he'll inherit whatever she owns after she dies in some so-called 'accident.'" He looked at Mike expectantly. "You're sure you have no idea what's connected to Miss Shaw that's so valuable that two of the most evil conners in the world have prepared so well for this?"

"None whatever," Mike said honestly. "The McDowells are rich and Luke Adams lives there, but—"

"The author of the Thomas Canon books? I've read every one of them! Hey! Maybe you can get me an autographed copy."

"Sure. I'll be a tourist who's lost his way."

The captain became serious again. "Too distant. You're going to have to use your connections to your sister, to the town, anything you can find, to get close enough to this girl to talk her out of marrying Stefan.

We do *not* want it set up that he can inherit what is hers. And you have to do this right away because the wedding is in three weeks."

Mike looked at him in disbelief. "What am I supposed to do? Seduce her?"

"No one would ask you to do this if we didn't think you could. And, besides, I seem to remember that you've succeeded with several women. There was that girl in Lake Worth. What was her name?"

"Tracy, and she got ten to twenty. This one is a *good* girl. How do I deal with her?"

"I don't know. Treat her like a lady. Cook for her. Pull out her chair. Girls like her fall for gentlemen. I'm sure that's how Vandlo got her. And before you ask, no, you can't kidnap her and you can't shoot Stefan. This young woman, Sara Shaw, has to stay there to help you find out what those two want." The captain grinned in a malicious way. "We've arranged for Stefan to be away for the whole time before the wedding. We gave him some family troubles that he can't ignore."

"Such as?"

"Even though he divorced his wife, we know he's still attached to her, so we arrested her on a DUI charge—which was easy. She's done a lot of drinking since Stefan left her, so we just picked her up one night, and now she's facing jail. We let her call him in the wee hours, and just as we'd hoped, he came immediately. If he gives us any trouble, we'll lock him up until he cools off." The captain smiled. "I wonder what he told his fiancée to explain why he went running off to his ex-wife?"

Mike was closing his thermos, his mind still on

how to accomplish this mission. "I doubt if a liar like Vandlo had told her about his ex-wife."

"Eventually, you'll have to tell Miss Shaw the truth, so that should be a point in your favor. Whatever you do, you just have to do it *fast*," the captain said. "And never forget that this young woman would be the fourth one to disappear after she got attached to Stefan Vandlo. He used a fake name and took those girls for everything they had. Then the girls 'disappeared' and the boyfriend, Vandlo, couldn't be found."

"Yeah, I read that," Mike said. "And if it weren't for some vague eyewitness reports, we wouldn't know who he was."

"Right, because Stefan left nothing behind, not so much as a fingerprint. And you know the rule: no evidence; no conviction. Personally, I'd like to arrest the man right now, but the higher ups want an undercover operation so we can get the mother. We take away her son and she'd just start using her nieces and nephews. She's the brains so we have to get *her* out of action. Permanently."

Mike looked at his watch. "I just need to stop by my apartment to get some things, then I can leave—"

"Uh, Mike," the captain said in a tone of apology, "it looks like you haven't seen the news in the last couple of hours. There's something else you need to know."

"What happened?"

The captain took the last documents from the bench and handed them to him. "I'm really sorry about this."

When Mike opened the folder, he saw a computer printout of a news story. *Apartment Burned,* the headline read. *Cigarettes to Blame, Say the Authorities.*

Mike's anger flared as he looked at the photo. It was his six-story apartment building and flames were coming out of the corner of the fourth floor—*his* apartment.

He put the papers with the others before he looked up at the captain. "Who did it?"

"The Feds say it must have been . . . Let me check. I don't want to misquote anyone." His voice was sarcastic as he flipped a paper over. " 'A fortuitous accident' is what they called it. Lucky for them, that is." The captain's eyes were sympathetic. "I'm sorry about this, Mike, but they want you to go there clean. Your story is that your apartment burned down, so you decided to take a much-needed vacation from police work. It makes sense that you'd stay at your sister's apartment since it's empty. It's supposed to be a coincidence that her place is on the same property as Miss Shaw's. We— they—want you to lie as little as possible. Oh, yeah, I nearly forgot." He reached into his pocket, pulled out a new BlackBerry, and handed it to Mike. "Stefan cut his teeth on pickpocketing so when you do meet with him he'll take your phone. We don't want him to find any numbers on it that would give you away. While you're in Edilean you're to contact us *only* through your sister. Will that be all right with her?"

"Sure," Mike said, and renewed his vow to tell Tess to stay away. The case must be really serious if they'd burned down his apartment. He'd never tell anyone, but Tess had been sending him baked goods from her friend Sara Shaw for years now, and it was Mike's opinion that anyone who could bake like she could deserved to be saved.

When Mike was silent, the captain said, "Sorry about your clothes." They all knew Mike was a "dresser." "What did you lose?"

"Nothing important. Tess keeps whatever means anything to me in a storage bin in—" He hesitated. "In Edilean."

"My advice is that you don't visit it." The captain wanted to lighten the mood. "Again, too bad about the apartment. I was going to volunteer to look after your goldfish."

Mike snorted as he stood up. He didn't have goldfish or a dog or even a permanent home. He'd lived in furnished, rented apartments since he left his grandparents' home at seventeen.

Mike glanced at the roadway that wound through the park. He'd take a run—he needed it—then go. "I'll leave in two hours," he said. "I should be in Edilean about ten hours after that—if I use the siren now and then, that is."

The captain smiled. "I knew you'd do it."

"Want to go for a run with me?"

The captain grimaced. "I leave that torture to you. Mike?"

"Yeah?"

"Be careful, will you? Stefan has a bit of a conscience—or at least a fear of reprisals—but his mother . . ."

"Yeah, I know. Could you put together more info for me on mother and son?"

"How about if you jog over to my car right now and I give you three boxes full of material?"

Mike gave one of his rare laughs, making the captain look at him in question.

"You have something in mind, don't you?"

"I was thinking of how to introduce myself to Miss Shaw and I remembered a story my sister told me about a very old tunnel. It just happens to open right into the floor of my sister's bedroom. All I have to do is move Miss Shaw in there."

The captain waited, but Mike didn't elaborate. "You've only got three weeks. Think you can entice Miss Shaw away from a big-city charmer like Stefan in that time?"

Mike gave a sigh. "Usually, I'd say yes, but now . . ." He shrugged. "In my experience, the only way to get a woman is to find out what she wants, then give it to her. It's just that I have no idea what a woman like Sara Shaw could possibly want." He looked at the captain. "So where are these boxes of info? I need to get out of here." Mike followed him to his car.

Ramsey McDowell was sound asleep when he heard Bonnie Tyler's *Holding Out for a Hero* blasting from his wife's cell phone. Groaning, he put the pillow over his head and tried to shut out the noise—and shut out his feelings. It was her brother calling her, a man Rams had never met, a man more elusive than a ghost, more secretive than a spy. But even though he'd never *seen* the man, Rams had heard more about him than he cared to. According to his bride, her brother was the smartest, most industrious, most heroic and, of course, the best looking man on the planet.

"She's succeeded in making you jealous, hasn't she?" his cousin Luke had said, laughing. "Don't worry, old man, a few days—or years—in a gym and you might live up to his reputation."

Jealous or not, Ramsey knew that his wife halted everything—meals, arguments, even sex—if her phone emitted that outrageous song.

"He is *not* a hero," Ramsey said the first time Tess had jumped off of him to run to her phone. "He's just a policeman."

"Detective," Tess said over her shoulder. She was nude and the sight of her beautiful body running was enough to make him forgive her. But that had been weeks ago and he was tired of the daily calls.

Tess said, "He usually only calls me once a week but he's off now so we can talk all we want."

"All we want" turned out to be *every day* and with the way the man caught them in the midst of every "activity," Rams thought a camera had been set on them. Even now, on their honeymoon, he still called her.

"Mike!" Tess said as she picked up her phone. Her voice was breathless and a bit frightened. "Is something wrong?"

Rams looked at the clock. On European time, it was the wee hours of the morning. Why couldn't the man get a girlfriend like normal people did?

"All right," Tess said softly into the phone as she sat back down on the bed. "Of course I'll do it."

Rams moved the pillow off his head and looked at her with curiosity. He'd never heard her use that tone before.

"Mike, you'll be careful, won't you? No, I mean it. *Really* careful."

Rams sat up in bed and watched her more closely. There was enough light in the room that he could see tears in her eyes. "What's wrong?"

She held up her hand for him to stop talking. "I understand completely. Luke will do whatever I ask him to."

"Luke will do what?" Ramsey asked.

Tess looked at her husband. "Would you please be quiet? This is important."

Angrily, Rams flung back the covers, pulled on his trousers that were hanging over a chair, and opened the curtain to look at the mountains outside. Behind him, Tess kept talking.

"Yes, I think it's in good condition, and besides me, only Luke knows about it. I'm sure he didn't tell Joce. He was afraid she'd want to explore it and he's always thought it was too dangerous." Pausing, Tess smiled. "Not yet, but Rams is working on it with enthusiasm and endurance. Yeah, the first one will be named Michael."

In an instant, Ramsey's anger left him and he stretched out on the bed beside his wife. He didn't like the way she'd told intimacies about them to her brother, but he did like that she'd said she planned to have children. They'd not talked about having kids, but he now realized he hadn't done so in fear that she'd say she didn't want any. Tess was a woman of very strong opinions. But once he was over his first pleasure of hearing that she did want children, Ramsey began to imagine a dozen of them, all with a name in some form of Michael: Michaela, Michalia, Mickey, Michelle—

"What an extraordinary call," Tess said as she clicked off her phone.

"I draw the line at Mickey. No mice."

Tess gave him a look of disgust. "Are you going to start on your jealousy again?"

"I'm not—" Rams began but stopped himself. "So why did your brother feel he had to call you in the middle of the night? Or is he playing James Bond in a country where it's now teatime?"

"He just arrived in Edilean."

Rams looked at her. "Your brother is in *our* hometown and you aren't packed yet?"

"No, and I'm not going to. He wants us to go on an extended honeymoon—and stay away from home."

"Not that I object, but why does he want us to do that?"

"It seems that my big brother has been sent to Edilean on a case."

"But he—" Ramsey swallowed. Tess's brother went undercover for big cases. Huge cases. He dealt in crimes that had international repercussions. He infiltrated gangs that were at war with each other—he'd been shot repeatedly.

Rams got off the bed and went to the closet.

"What are you doing?"

"I'm going home; you're staying here. If your brother's been sent to Edilean, then something is very wrong."

"If you go, I'll follow you and that will put my brother in danger. And Mike said that if I'm there *I* might become a target. Is that what you want?"

Turning, Ramsey looked at her. She wore no makeup or clothing, and she was so beautiful he could hardly stand upright. He still couldn't believe that when he'd asked her to marry him just four weeks ago, she'd said yes. Three weeks later they'd been married in a private ceremony with only a dozen guests. It was how they'd both wanted it. In fact, Tess had said, "If you think I'm going to make a fool of myself by wearing a hundred yards of white silk and having a bunch of women around me in pink dresses, then you've asked the wrong woman to marry you. Spend the money on a rock. I want a ring big enough to dance on." He'd happily done just what she asked. And he'd added a pair of diamond earrings—all of which she was wearing now. Just the diamonds, her skin, and hair.

"What's going on in Edilean?" Rams asked. "Who is in danger?"

"You know Mike can't tell me anything. His cases are top secret. If anyone found out, lives could be lost."

Ramsey gave her a piercing look. As far as he could tell, her brother didn't keep secrets from her.

Tess sighed. "Sara."

Ramsey took a deep breath. "My cousin Sara? Sweet, dear Sara? It's that bastard she wants to marry, isn't it?"

"Yes," Tess said simply. "He's not who he says he is."

"Now there's news! I've disliked him from the moment I first saw him."

"All of us have felt the same way, but he's helped Sara to recover, and their customers love him. Mike wants us to do some things."

"Mike wants *us* . . . ?" Ramsey grimaced. "If he

asked *us* for help then he meant for you to tell me about Sara, didn't he?"

Tess smiled. "Do you think I'd tell you anything Mike didn't want me to?"

Ramsey started to, yet again, tell her what he thought of her elusive, secretive brother, but he didn't. "Okay. I'll bite. What does he want us to do?"

"First," Tess said as she lowered her voice and slid down in the bed, "he wants nieces and nephews. He says he's sick of having no kids to buy Christmas presents for."

"Did he now?" Rams said as he slipped off his trousers and slid under the covers. "And what else did your very intelligent brother ask for?"

"To figure out what Sara owns that a thief would want. It seems that Greg is a big-time crook and Sara has something he's gone to a lot of trouble to get." When Rams started to move away, Tess pulled his face down to hers. "And you're to take me to Venice."

"For how long?" he murmured.

"Until Mike says we can return."

Ramsey didn't like the autocratic way his brother-in-law was making decrees, but he would do whatever he must to keep his beloved wife safe. Abruptly, he pulled away from kissing her neck. "What kind of gifts does your brother give to kids?"

"C-4." When Ramsey gave her a look of horror, she laughed. "I don't know. Why don't we wait and see?"